大学英语水平测试系列 **710分**

大学英语五级水平测试试题集

（710分版）

College English Practice Tests (Band 5)

主编　胡金环　王　伟

编者　白淑霞　王　博

　　　王晓燕　杨剑波

　　　于建凯

U0132913

上海外语教育出版社

外教社 SHANGHAI FOREIGN LANGUAGE EDUCATION PRESS

图书在版编目(CIP)数据

大学英语五级水平测试试题集(710分版)/胡金环,王伟主编.
—上海:上海外语教育出版社,2008
(大学英语水平测试系列710分)
ISBN　978-7-5446-0728-5

Ⅰ.大…　Ⅱ.①胡…②王…　Ⅲ.英语—高等学校—水平考试—习题
Ⅳ.H319.6

中国版本图书馆 CIP 数据核字(2008)第 039059 号

出版发行:**上海外语教育出版社**
　　　　　　(上海外国语大学内)　邮编:**200083**
电　　话: 021-65425300 (总机)
电子邮箱: bookinfo@sflep.com.cn
网　　址: http://www.sflep.com.cn　http://www.sflep.com

责任编辑: 杭　海

印　　刷: 上海外语教育出版社印刷厂
经　　销: 新华书店上海发行所
开　　本: 787×1092　1/16　印张21　字数 506 千字
版　　次: 2008 年 12 月第 1 版　2008 年 12 月第 1 次印刷
印　　数: 3 500 册

书　　号: ISBN 978-7-5446-0728-5 / G·0347
定　　价: 39.00 元

前　言

本书共收录了 10 套大学英语五级水平测试题,覆盖了新大纲的六大题型:写作、快速阅读、听力理解(短对话、长对话、短文理解及复合式听写)、仔细阅读理解(篇章阅读理解、篇章词汇理解或简短问答)、完形填空或改错、翻译。所有试题采用全真题的形式编排。每套试题均附有答案、简单的解题说明、作文范文。最后附有听力部分的录音材料。

对于即将参加六级考试的同学来说,本试题集起着承上启下的作用。测试题的题型、格式、记分方法等均与六级真题相同,而内容较六级试题容易。在选材上,注重材料的实效性、现实性、知识性等,并注重题材的广泛性与多样性,文章大都摘自英美报刊、杂志等。

每套测试题包含的题型如下:

第一部分:写作(Writing)。共 15 分,考试时间为 30 分钟。写作部分测试学生用英语进行书面表达的能力,要求思想表达准确、意义连贯、无严重语法错误。体裁包括议论文、说明文、应用文等。

第二部分:快速阅读理解(Reading Comprehension〔Skimming and Scanning〕)。共 10 分,10 个小题,每题 1 分。时间为 15 分钟。快速阅读部分采用一篇 1 000 字左右的文章,要求学生运用略读和查读的技能从篇章中获取信息,常用的题型有是非判断、句子填空等。

第三部分:听力理解(Listening Comprehension)。共 35 分,35 个小题,每题 1 分,其中听力对话占 15 分,听力短文占 20 分;时间为 35 分钟。听力对话部分包括短对话和长对话的听力理解;听力短文部分包括短文理解和短文听写,短文理解的题型为选择题。听力素材选用对话、讲座、广播电视节目等真实材料。

第四部分:仔细阅读理解(Reading Comprehension〔Reading in Depth〕)。共 25 分,时间是 25 分钟。要求学生阅读 3 篇短文,其中两篇题型为多项选择题,每篇长度为 300－350 词;另一篇题型为选词填空或简答题。仔细阅读部分除测试篇章阅读理解外,还测试篇章语境中的词汇理解。

第五部分:完形填空(Cloze)或改错(Error Correction)。共 10 分,时间是 15 分钟。完形填空测试学生各个层面上的语言理解能力和运用能力;改错测试学生的词汇、语法和上下文理解的综合能力。

第六部分:翻译(Translation)。共 5 分,每小题 1 分,时间是 5 分钟。翻译部分是汉译英测试,共 5 个句子,一句一题。句中的一部分内容已用英语给出,要求学生根据全句意思将汉语部分译成英语。翻译必须符合英语语法结构和表达习惯,用词准确。

本书在编写过程中，由于时间仓促，疏漏和错误之处在所难免，敬请广大学生和英语教育界同仁批评指正。在编写过程中参阅了大量国内外相关资料，采用了一些很有价值的文章，在此我们向有关机构、作者和资料提供者一并致以诚挚的谢意。

编　者
2008 年 7 月

CONTENTS

PART ONE

PRACTICE TESTS

PRACTICE TEST 1

Part I   Writing

(30 minutes)

注意：此部分试题在答题卡1上。

Part II   Reading Comprehension (Skimming and Scanning)

(15 minutes)

Directions: *In this part, you will have 15 minutes to go over the passage quickly and answer the questions on **Answer Sheet 1**.*

For questions 1 – 7, mark

Y (for YES)   *if the statement agrees with the information given in the passage;*

N (for NO)   *if the statement contradicts the information given in the passage;*

NG (for NOT GIVEN)   *if the information is not given in the passage.*

For questions 8 – 10, complete the sentences with the information given in the passage.

Oral English Proficiency Evaluation

All pilots shall meet the language proficiency requirements when they fly internationally.

Why is it important to initiate evaluation of language proficiency rapidly?

While the formal evaluation of language proficiency is only required as of 5 March 2008, there are good reasons to start formal evaluation of language proficiency much earlier:

  a. for recruitment purposes: It is likely that most air traffic service providers and airlines will want their new recruits to meet the language proficiency requirements as a prerequisite for recruitment;

  b. for benchmarking purposes: The establishment of the training program required to bring existing staff to the appropriate level would require an accurate assessment of the level of language proficiency of existing staff; and

c. to be prepared for the 5 March 2008 deadline.

What should be the scope and depth of the evaluation?

The scope of the evaluation is the "speaking and listening ability" which is specified in Annex 1 for pilots and air traffic controllers. The depth of the evaluation is defined by the Holistic Descriptors and the Standards for Operational Level 4.

Holistic Descriptors

Proficient speakers shall:

a. communicate effectively in voice-only (telephone/radiotelephone) and in face-to-face situations;

b. communicate on common, concrete and work-related topics with accuracy and clarity;

c. use appropriate communicative strategies to exchange messages and to recognize and resolve misunderstandings (e.g. to check, confirm, or clarify information) in a general or work-related context;

d. handle successfully and with relative ease any linguistic challenges presented by a complication or unexpected turn of events that occurs within the context of a routine work situation or communicative task with which they are otherwise familiar; and

e. use a dialect or accent which is intelligible to the aeronautical community.

For more information, please refer to the Appendix of Annex 1.

ICAO Rating Scale for Operational Level 4

A speaker is proficient to Operational Level 4 if the ratings for the following criteria are high:

Pronunciation:

(Assumes a dialect and/or accent intelligible to the aeronautical community.)

Pronunciation, stress, rhythm, and intonation are influenced by the first language or regional variation but only sometimes interfere with ease of understanding.

Structure:

(Relevant grammatical structures and sentence patterns are determined by language functions appropriate to the task.)

Basic grammatical structures and sentences patterns are used creatively and are usually well controlled. Errors may occur, particularly in unusual or unexpected circumstances, but rarely interfere with meaning.

Vocabulary:

Vocabulary range and accuracy are usually sufficient to communicate effectively on common, concrete, and work-related topics. Can often paraphrase successfully when lacking vocabulary in unusual or unexpected circumstances.

Fluency:

Produces stretches of language at an appropriate tempo. There may be occasional loss of fluency on transition from rehearsed or formulaic speech to spontaneous inter-action, but this does not prevent effective communication. Can make limited use of discourse makers or connectors. Fillers are not distracting.

Comprehension:

Comprehension is mostly accurate on common, concrete, and work-related topics when the accent or variety used is sufficiently intelligible for an international commu-nity of users. When the speaker is confronted with a linguistic or situational complica-tion or an unexpected turn of events, comprehension may be slower or require clarifi-cation strategies.

Interactions:

Responses are usually immediate, appropriate, and informative. Initiates and maintains exchanges even when dealing with an unexpected turn of events. Deals ade-quately with apparent misunderstandings by checking, confirming, or clarifying.

For information on the complete ICAO language proficiency rating scale, please refer to the Attachment to Annex 1.

Do native speakers need to be evaluated and how?

Native speakers need to be evaluated. However, in this case, it is possible to use a process similar to that which is routinely used today to ensure that applicants do not have a speech impediment that would affect their capacity to operate safely. This as-sessment can also be extended to non-native language assessment at the highest or ex-pert level. This is because native speakers can easily identify other speakers with native and/or expert language proficiency through fluent and natural use of the language. Similarly, completely inadequate proficiency is also relatively easy to identify.

In practice, language proficiency assessment for native and/or expert speakers can consist of an interview with a representative from the Licensing Authority such as a flight examiner. If a problem is noticed (speech impediment or inappropriately strong regional accent) during such an interview, the applicant should be referred to a spe-cialist for follow-through.

What is the best evaluation method?

In any large-scale testing situation, it is accepted that the best practice is to permit a number of test/assessment options. For non-native language assessment, formal evaluation can currently include any of the following:

a. an official test score on commercially available language tests (or other language tests available);

b. a test score on an internally developed language test;

c. an assessment provided by an outside language-testing expert (available through many universities or commercial testing agencies); or

d. an assessment provided by an in-house language-testing expert.

The format of the formal assessment will be determined by the State, but the *Manual on the Implementation of the ICAO Language Proficiency Requirements — Doc 9835-AN 1453* provides specific suggestions on how States can assess the suitability and reliability of testing solutions that would be proposed by the industry.

Are there any tests already available?

Efforts to develop appropriate and commercially available aviation-specific testing instruments are underway and aviation-specific test options are already available and more will become available in the near future.

Most of the commercially available English knowledge tests such as TOEFL are not appropriate for the purpose of testing English competency for pilots and air traffic controllers. The main reason is that those tests have not been designed for testing the "speaking and listening ability" required by Annex 1. Some oral proficiency tests are available but they are generally designed for a context (e.g. business) that is not that of civil aviation and are therefore not fully satisfactory.

Generally speaking, the evaluation of the speaking and/or listening skills requires face-to-face contact between tester and test-taker, or semi-direct contact, through recorded speaking prompts and recorded responses that are analyzed later by the tester. Other testing methods and in particular those using only the computerized versions are not appropriate.

注意：此部分试题请在**答题卡** 1 上作答；8－10 题在**答题卡** 1 上。

1. Most air traffic service providers and airlines will want their new recruit to be proficient in language, but the existing staffs are not required to undertake any training program of language proficiency.

2. The language proficiency evaluation covers the "speaking and listening ability."

3. Proficient speakers shall communicate accurately and clearly in face-to-face

situations only.

4. Proficient speakers are not allowed to make errors of grammatical structure in communication in any case.

5. When lacking vocabulary in unusual situations, a proficient speaker can express his idea with familiar words without interfering with meaning.

6. Native speakers will take fewer procedures in evaluation than non-native speakers.

7. For non-native language evaluation, the air traffic service providers and airlines can determine the format of the formal assessment.

Part III   Listening Comprehension   (35 minutes)

Section A

Directions: *In this section, you will hear 8 short conversations and 2 long conversations. At the end of each conversation, one or more questions will be asked about what was said. Both the conversation and the questions will be spoken only once. After each question there will be a pause. During the pause, you must read the four choices marked A), B), C) and D), and decide which is the best answer. Then mark the corresponding letter on **Answer Sheet 2** with a single line through the centre.*

注意：此部分试题请在**答题卡**2上作答。

11. A) It's less expensive.   C) Buses are not safe.
    B) It is the only thing available.   D) Buses are too crowded.

12. A) He'd like the machine-translated texts revised.
    B) He is in need of some machine translation software.
    C) He does not think machine translation software is of much help.
    D) He does not think the woman's translation is up to standard.

13. A) 8.   C) 6.
    B) 4.   D) 5.

14. A) The government can strengthen the marriage bond by formulating appropriate policies.
    B) Divorce rates can be reduced with government intervention.
    C) Change of social attitude can influence marriage and divorce.
    D) The climate of a country affects both marriage and divorce.

15. A) He is a dentist.   C) He's a surgeon.

B) He's a physician.   D) He's a chemist.

16. A) She spends too much money.   C) She should get a job.
    B) She works in a factory.   D) She likes to argue.

17. A) The man does not eat chicken.
    B) The woman has some dietary restrictions.
    C) The man wants to change the menu.
    D) The woman is responsible for food arrangements.

18. A) A play.   C) A lecture.
    B) A TV program.   D) A film.

Questions 19 to 22 are based on the conversation you have just heard.

19. A) Friendship.   C) Cultural ignorance.
    B) Conflicts in the world.   D) Education.

20. A) China.   C) Korea.
    B) Japan.   D) Germany.

21. A) By using a compass.   C) By the oases.
    B) By the sun and stars.   D) By instinct.

22. A) Because she thinks cheese is too sweet.
    B) Because she thinks cheese is greasy.
    C) Because her mother doesn't like cheese.
    D) Because she doesn't like the smell of cheese.

Questions 23 to 25 are based on the conversation you have just heard.

23. A) Boss and secretary.   C) Husband and wife.
    B) Customer and waitress.   D) Lawyer and client.

24. A) On the carpet.   C) In his pocket.
    B) In the dustbin.   D) On the table.

25. A) He thinks housework doesn't matter.
    B) He thinks housework is very important.
    C) He thinks housework is boring.
    D) He thinks housework is interesting.

Section B

Directions: *In this section, you will hear 3 short passages. At the end of each passage, you will hear some questions. Both the passage and the questions will be spoken only once. After you hear a question, you must choose the best answer from the four choices marked A), B), C) and D). Then mark the corresponding letter on Answer Sheet 2 with a single line through the centre.*

注意：此部分试题请在**答题卡 2** 上作答。

Passage One

Questions 26 to 29 are based on the passage you have just heard.

26. A) By asking native speakers for explanations.
    B) By reading good books in the foreign language.
    C) By comparing their speech with that of native speakers.
    D) By speaking without regard to native speakers.

27. A) They will not learn very much about foreign culture.
    B) They will not learn about the history of the foreign language.
    C) They will not have to worry about making mistakes.
    D) They will not take advantage of available language models.

28. A) Because communication is the primary goal of language learning.
    B) Because native speakers like foreign students who try to learn their language.
    C) Because native speakers will ignore their mistakes.
    D) Because everyone makes mistakes when trying to communicate in a strange language.

29. A) Mistakes are not important in the process of learning a language.
    B) Making mistakes can help learners discover the rules of the language.
    C) Learners are very afraid of making mistakes.
    D) Native speakers often do not tell foreign language learners about their mistakes.

Passage Two

Questions 30 to 32 are based on the passage you have just heard.

30. A) Avoid their former ones.
    B) Accept their new ones.

C) Forget being shut in certain stalls.

D) Go directly for the one they were released from.

31. A) Cows have a better memory than sheep.

B) Cows can remember what happened in the past.

C) Cows are happy when seeing a familiar face.

D) Cows are different from sheep in developing a partnership with people.

32. A) Animals can feel pain or joy as humans do.

B) Animals have all the feeling that humans have.

C) Animals can do the same thing that happened in the past.

D) Animals have their own subjective experience.

Passage Three

Questions 33 to 35 are based on the passage you have just heard.

33. A) Because they like the taste of tar in cigarettes.

B) Because smoking makes them feel relaxed.

C) Because smoking means cancer to them.

D) Because smoking reduces the risk to their health.

34. A) Being busy.

B) Taking a break.

C) Certain social custom.

D) Comfort to a person feeling tense.

35. A) Many people don't know it is the tar that causes cancer.

B) Health experts try to persuade people to give up smoking entirely.

C) The manufactures try to keep selling cigarettes in the future.

D) People will not give up smoking easily with cigarettes less dangerous.

Section C

Directions: *In this section, you will hear a passage three times. When the passage is read for the first time, you should listen carefully for its general idea. When the passage is read for the second time, you are required to fill in the blanks numbered from 36 to 43 with the exact words you have just heard. For blanks numbered from 44 to 46 you are required to fill in the missing information. For these blanks, you can either use the exact words you have just heard or write down the main points in your own words. Finally, when the passage is read for the third time, you should check what* *you have written.*

注意：此部分试题在**答题卡2**上；请在**答题卡2**上作答。

Part IV   Reading Comprehension (Reading in Depth)
(25 minutes)

Section A

Directions: *In this section, there is a passage with ten blanks. You are required to select one word for each blank from a list of choices given in a word bank following the passage. Read the passage through carefully before making your choices. Each choice in the bank is identified by a letter. Please mark the corresponding letter for each item on Answer Sheet 2 with a single line through the centre.* <u>*You may not use any of the words in the bank more than once.*</u>

Questions 47 to 56 are based on the following passage.

As civilization proceeds in the direction of technology, it passes the point of supplying all the basic __47__ of life — food, shelter, clothes, and warmth. Then we are faced with a choice between using technology to provide and fulfill needs which have hitherto been __48__ as unnecessary or, on the other hand, using technology to reduce the number of hours of work which a man must do in order to __49__ a given standard of living. In other words, we either raise our standard of living above that necessary for comfort and happiness or we leave it at this level and work shorter hours. I shall take it as axiomatic that mankind has, by that time, chosen the __50__ alternative. Men will be working shorter hours in their paid employment. It follows that the housewife will also expect to be able to have more __51__ in her life without __52__ her standard of living. It also follows that human domestic servants will have completely __53__ to exist. Yet the great majority of the housewives will wish to be relieved completely from the routine operations of the home such as scrubbing the floors or the bath or the cooker, washing the clothes or washing up, dusting or sweeping, or making beds.

By far the most logical step to __54__ the housewife of routine, is to provide a robot slave which can be trained to the requirements of a particular home and can be programmed to carry out half a dozen or more standard operations (for example, scrubbing, sweeping and dusting, washing up, laying tables, making beds), when so switched by the housewife. It will be a machine having no more __55__ than a car, but having a memory for instructions and a limited degree of instructed or built-in adaptability according to the positions in which it finds various types of objects. It will operate other more __56__ machines, for example, the vacuum cleaner, or clothes-washing machine.

注意：此部分试题请在**答题卡**2上作答。

A) articles	I) former
B) looked	J) emotions
C) earn	K) essentials
D) lessening	L) specialized
E) ceased	M) regarded
F) leisure	N) lowering
G) cling	O) relieve
H) latter	

Section B

Directions: *There are 2 passages in this section. Each passage is followed by some questions or unfinished statements. For each of them there are four choices marked A), B), C) and D). You should decide on the best choice and mark the corresponding letter on **Answer Sheet 2** with a single line through the centre.*

Passage One

Questions 57 to 61 are based on the following passage.

There are two main hypotheses when it comes to explaining the emergence of modern humans. The "Out of Africa" theory holds that homo sapiens burst onto the scene as a new species around 150,000 to 200,000 years ago in Africa and subsequently replaced archaic humans such as the Neanderthals. The other model, known as multiregional evolution or regional continuity, posits far more ancient and diverse roots for our kind. Proponents of this view believe that homo sapiens arose in Africa some 2 million years ago and evolved as a single species spread across the Old World, with populations in different regions linked through genetic and cultural exchange.

Of these two models, "Out of Africa," which was originally developed based on fossil evidence, and supported by much genetic research, has been favored by the majority of evolution scholars. The vast majority of these genetic studies have focused on

DNA from living populations, and although some small progress has been made in recovering DNA from Neanderthal that appears to support multi-regionalism, the chance of recovering nuclear DNA from early human fossils is quite slim at present. Fossils thus remain very much a part of the human origins debate.

Another means of gathering theoretical evidence is through bones. Examinations of early modern human skulls from Central Europe and Australia dated to between 20,000 and 30,000 years old have suggested that both groups apparently exhibit traits seen in their Middle Eastern and African predecessors. But the early modern specimens from Central Europe also display Neanderthal traits, and the early modern Australians showed affinities to archaic Homo from Indonesia. Meanwhile, the debate among palaeoanthropologists continues, as supporters of the two hypotheses challenge the evidence and conclusions of each other.

注意：此部分试题请在**答题卡** 2 上作答。

57. What is the main idea of this passage?
    A) Fossils remain very much a part of the human origins debate.
    B) The passage primarily discusses evidence that supports the "Out of Africa" theory.
    C) The passage primarily discusses two hypotheses and some evidence on the human origins debate.
    D) The passage mainly tells about the difficulties in obtaining agreement among theorists on the human origins debate.

58. All the following are true EXCEPT that _____.
    A) the "Out of Africa" model has had more support from scholars
    B) the multi-regional model goes back further in history
    C) three methods of gathering evidence are mentioned in the passage
    D) DNA studies offer one of the best ways in the future to provide clear evidence

59. It can be inferred from the passage that _____.
    A) there is little likelihood that the debate will die down
    B) the debate will interest historians to take part in
    C) the debate is likely to be less important in the future
    D) there is likely to be an end to the debate in the near future

60. Which of the following is NOT true about the two hypotheses?
    A) One hypothesis dates the emergence of homo sapiens much earlier than the other.
    B) Both hypotheses cite Africa as an originating location.

C) Genetic studies have supported both hypotheses.

D) Both hypotheses regard Neanderthals as the predecessors of modern humans.

61. According to the passage, the multi-regional evolution model posits far more diverse roots for our kind because _____.

A) this has been supported by fossil evidence

B) populations in different regions were linked through genetic and cultural exchange

C) evidence from examinations of early modern human skulls has come from a number of different parts of the world

D) DNA from Neanderthal appears to support multi-regionalism

Passage Two

Questions 62 to 66 are based on the following passage.

Some people say that the study of liberal arts is a useless luxury we can not afford in hard times. Students, they argue, who do not develop salable skills will find it difficult to land a job upon graduation. But there is a problem in speaking of "salable skills." What skills are salable? Right now, skills for making automobiles are not highly salable, but they have been for decades and might be again. Skills in teaching are not now as salable as they were during the past 20 years, and the population charts indicate they may not be soon again. Home construction skills are another example of varying salability, as the job market *fluctuates*. What's more, if one wants to build a curriculum exclusively on what is salable, one will have to make the courses very short and change them very often, in order to keep up with the rapid changes in the job market. But will not the effort be in vain? In very few things can we be sure of future salability, and in a society where people are free to study what they want, and work where they want, and invest as they want, there is no way to keep supply and demand in labor in perfect accord.

A school that devotes itself totally to salable skills, especially in a time of high unemployment, sending young men and women into the world armed with only a narrow range of skills, is also sending lambs into the lion's den. If those people gain nothing more from their studies than supposedly salable skills, and can't make the sale because of changes in the job market, they have been cheated. But if those skills were more than salable, if study gave them a better understanding of the world around them and greater adaptability in a changing world, they have not been cheated. They will find some kind of job soon enough. Flexibility, an ability to change and learn new things, is a valuable skill. People who have learned how to learn can learn outside of school.

That is where most of us have learned to do what we do, not in school. Learning to learn is one of the highest liberal skills.

注意：此部分试题请在**答题卡 2**上作答。

62. We can infer from the passage that the author is in favor of _____.
    A) a flexible curriculum that changes with the times
    B) a liberal education
    C) keeping a balance between the supply and demand in the labor market
    D) teaching practical skills that can be sold in the current job market

63. The word "fluctuate" in the first paragraph most probably means _____.
    A) following a set pattern　　　C) changing in an irregular way
    B) remaining steady　　　D) becoming worse and worse

64. According to the author, in developing a curriculum schools should _____.
    A) consider what skills are salable
    B) focus on the ability to adapt to changes
    C) take the current job market into consideration
    D) predict the salability of skills in the future job market

65. According to the author, which of the following is more likely to get a job in times of high unemployment?
    A) A car repairman.
    B) A person with the ability to learn by himself.
    C) A person with quite a few salable skills.
    D) A construction worker.

66. We can learn from the passage that _____.
    A) many students feel cheated by the educational system
    B) schools that teach practical skills fare better during hard times
    C) liberal arts education is being challenged now
    D) extracurricular activities are more important than classroom learning

Part V Cloze
(15 minutes)

Directions: *There are 20 blanks in the following passage. For each blank there are four choices marked A), B), C) and D) on the right side of the paper. You should choose the ONE that best fits into the passage. Then mark the corresponding letter on Answer*

Sheet 2 with a single line through the centre.

注意：此部分试题请在**答题卡 2** 上作答。

There are more than forty universities in Britain — nearly twice as many as in 1960. During the 1960s eight completely new ones were founded，and ten other new ones were created ___67___ converting old colleges of technology into universities. In the same period the ___68___ of students more than doubled ，from 70,000 to ___69___ than 200,000. By 1973 about 10% of men aged from eighteen ___70___ twenty-one were in universities and about 5% of women.

All the universities are private institutions. Each has its ___71___ governing councils，___72___ some local businessmen and local politicians as ___73___ as a few academics（大学教师）. The state began to give grants to them fifty years ___74___ ，and by 1970 each university derived nearly all its ___75___ from state grants. Students have to ___76___ fees and living costs，but every student may receive from the local authority of the place ___77___ he lives a personal grant which is enough to pay his full costs，including lodging and ___78___ unless his parents are ___79___ .

67. A) with   C) at
    B) by   D) into
68. A) amount   C) lot
    B) quantity   D) number
69. A) more   C) less
    B) much   D) fewer
70. A) with   C) from
    B) to   D) beyond
71. A) self   C) own
    B) kind   D) personal
72. A) making   C) including
    B) consisting D) taking
73. A) good   C) little
    B) long   D) well
74. A) ago   C) after
    B) before   D) ever
75. A) suggestions C) profits
    B) grades   D) funds
76. A) make   C) change
    B) pay   D) delay
77. A) what   C) where
    B) which   D) how
78. A) living   C) food
    B) drinking   D) shelter
79. A) poor   C) kindhearted
    B) generous   D) rich

Most __80__ take jobs in the summer __81__ about six weeks, but they do not normally do outside __82__ during the academic year.

The Department of Education takes __83__ for the payment which covers the whole expenditure of the __84__, but it does not exercise direct control. It can have an important influence __85__ new developments through its power to distribute funds, but it takes the advice of the University Grants Committee, a body which is mainly __86__ of academics.

80. A) professors   C) politicians
    B) students   D) businessmen
81. A) at   C) with
    B) since   D) for
82. A) travel   C) experiment
    B) work   D) study
83. A) responsibility C) duty
    B) advice   D) pleasure
84. A) government   C) universities
    B) school   D) committees
85. A) at   C) on
    B) to   D) from
86. A) consisted   C) made
    B) composed   D) taken

Part VI Translation   (5 minutes)

Directions: *Complete the sentences on* **Answer Sheet 2** *by translating into English the Chinese given in brackets.*

注意：此部分试题请在**答题卡** 2 上作答。

87. _____ (尽管我的祖母不识字), she had a good stock of myths and legends.

88. Despite his wealth, Sam Walton still drove around in _____ (一辆福特牌旧汽车).

89. In the eyes of some businessmen, consumers' health _____ (不如利润重要).

90. The new president _____ (要求我们大学内所有的老师和学生) conduct themselves with honesty and never tell lies.

91. According to the manager, what he wants is _____ (一个简单而有效的销售方案).

Part VI Translation

(5 minutes)

Directions: Complete the sentences on Answer Sheet 2 by translating into English the Chinese given in brackets.

答题卡 1 (Answer Sheet 1)

学校:

姓名:

划线要求

| | 准 | 考 | 证 | 号 | |

[0]	[0]	[0]	[0]	[0]	[0]	[0]	[0]	[0]	[0]	[0]	[0]	[0]	[0]	[0]
[1]	[1]	[1]	[1]	[1]	[1]	[1]	[1]	[1]	[1]	[1]	[1]	[1]	[1]	[1]
[2]	[2]	[2]	[2]	[2]	[2]	[2]	[2]	[2]	[2]	[2]	[2]	[2]	[2]	[2]
[3]	[3]	[3]	[3]	[3]	[3]	[3]	[3]	[3]	[3]	[3]	[3]	[3]	[3]	[3]
[4]	[4]	[4]	[4]	[4]	[4]	[4]	[4]	[4]	[4]	[4]	[4]	[4]	[4]	[4]
[5]	[5]	[5]	[5]	[5]	[5]	[5]	[5]	[5]	[5]	[5]	[5]	[5]	[5]	[5]
[6]	[6]	[6]	[6]	[6]	[6]	[6]	[6]	[6]	[6]	[6]	[6]	[6]	[6]	[6]
[7]	[7]	[7]	[7]	[7]	[7]	[7]	[7]	[7]	[7]	[7]	[7]	[7]	[7]	[7]
[8]	[8]	[8]	[8]	[8]	[8]	[8]	[8]	[8]	[8]	[8]	[8]	[8]	[8]	[8]
[9]	[9]	[9]	[9]	[9]	[9]	[9]	[9]	[9]	[9]	[9]	[9]	[9]	[9]	[9]

Part I   **Writing**   **(30 minutes)**

Directions: *For this part, you are allowed 30 minutes to write a composition on the topic Examination-Oriented or Quality-Oriented Education. You should write at least 120 words following the outline given below in Chinese:*

1. 目前的情况：应试教育
2. 正在发生的改变：素质教育
3. 我对这一改变的看法

Examination-Oriented or Quality-Oriented Education

答题卡 1 (Answer Sheet 1)

....
....
....
....
....
....
....
....
....
....
....
....
....
....
....
....
....
....

Part II   Reading Comprehension (Skimming and Scanning)   (15 minutes)

1. [Y] [N] [NG]   2. [Y] [N] [NG]   3. [Y] [N] [NG]   4. [Y] [N] [NG]
5. [Y] [N] [NG]   6. [Y] [N] [NG]   7. [Y] [N] [NG]

8. Most of the commercially available English knowledge tests are _____
   for proficiency testing for pilots and air traffic controllers.

9. Some existing oral proficiency tests are not satisfactory because they are generally designed for _____ not related to civil aviation.

10. It is inappropriate to adopt other testing methods especially those using only _____
    _____.

答题卡 2 (Answer Sheet 2)

学校:	准 考 证 号														

姓名:

学校:

姓名:

划线要求

准 考 证 号

[0] [0] [0] [0] [0] [0] [0] [0] [0] [0] [0] [0] [0] [0] [0]
[1] [1] [1] [1] [1] [1] [1] [1] [1] [1] [1] [1] [1] [1] [1]
[2] [2] [2] [2] [2] [2] [2] [2] [2] [2] [2] [2] [2] [2] [2]
[3] [3] [3] [3] [3] [3] [3] [3] [3] [3] [3] [3] [3] [3] [3]
[4] [4] [4] [4] [4] [4] [4] [4] [4] [4] [4] [4] [4] [4] [4]
[5] [5] [5] [5] [5] [5] [5] [5] [5] [5] [5] [5] [5] [5] [5]
[6] [6] [6] [6] [6] [6] [6] [6] [6] [6] [6] [6] [6] [6] [6]
[7] [7] [7] [7] [7] [7] [7] [7] [7] [7] [7] [7] [7] [7] [7]
[8] [8] [8] [8] [8] [8] [8] [8] [8] [8] [8] [8] [8] [8] [8]
[9] [9] [9] [9] [9] [9] [9] [9] [9] [9] [9] [9] [9] [9] [9]

Part III Section A   Section B

11. [A] [B] [C] [D] 16. [A] [B] [C] [D] 21. [A] [B] [C] [D] 26. [A] [B] [C] [D] 31. [A] [B] [C] [D]
12. [A] [B] [C] [D] 17. [A] [B] [C] [D] 22. [A] [B] [C] [D] 27. [A] [B] [C] [D] 32. [A] [B] [C] [D]
13. [A] [B] [C] [D] 18. [A] [B] [C] [D] 23. [A] [B] [C] [D] 28. [A] [B] [C] [D] 33. [A] [B] [C] [D]
14. [A] [B] [C] [D] 19. [A] [B] [C] [D] 24. [A] [B] [C] [D] 29. [A] [B] [C] [D] 34. [A] [B] [C] [D]
15. [A] [B] [C] [D] 20. [A] [B] [C] [D] 25. [A] [B] [C] [D] 30. [A] [B] [C] [D] 35. [A] [B] [C] [D]

Part III Section C

Scientists say they have (36) _____ evidence that jogging is good for people. This latest European research (37) _____ headline-making stories about people who die of a heart attack while running on the (38) _____. Danish researchers (39) _____ that those who jog regularly are far less likely to die prematurely than those who do not. Their work, (40) _____ in last Saturday's issue of the *British Medical* (41) _____, sifted through data from a Copenhagen heart study. The study covered more than 4,500 men (42) _____ 20 to 79 with no history of cardiac problems. The group was followed from mid-1970s until November 1998. It is found that (43) _____ joggers were nearly two and a half times less likely to die prematurely than non-joggers. (44) _____ _____, including smoking, drinking, diabetes, education and household income to try to explain this big difference in mortality. (45) _____ _____. (46) _____.

答题卡 2 (Answer Sheet 2)

Part IV   Section A

47. [A][B][C][D][E][F][G][H][I][J][K][L][M][N][O]
48. [A][B][C][D][E][F][G][H][I][J][K][L][M][N][O]
49. [A][B][C][D][E][F][G][H][I][J][K][L][M][N][O]
50. [A][B][C][D][E][F][G][H][I][J][K][L][M][N][O]
51. [A][B][C][D][E][F][G][H][I][J][K][L][M][N][O]
52. [A][B][C][D][E][F][G][H][I][J][K][L][M][N][O]
53. [A][B][C][D][E][F][G][H][I][J][K][L][M][N][O]
54. [A][B][C][D][E][F][G][H][I][J][K][L][M][N][O]
55. [A][B][C][D][E][F][G][H][I][J][K][L][M][N][O]
56. [A][B][C][D][E][F][G][H][I][J][K][L][M][N][O]

Section B

57. [A] [B] [C] [D]
58. [A] [B] [C] [D]
59. [A] [B] [C] [D]
60. [A] [B] [C] [D]
61. [A] [B] [C] [D]
62. [A] [B] [C] [D]
63. [A] [B] [C] [D]
64. [A] [B] [C] [D]
65. [A] [B] [C] [D]
66. [A] [B] [C] [D]

Part V   **Cloze**   **(15 minutes)**

67. [A] [B] [C] [D]   72. [A] [B] [C] [D]   77. [A] [B] [C] [D]   82. [A] [B] [C] [D]
68. [A] [B] [C] [D]   73. [A] [B] [C] [D]   78. [A] [B] [C] [D]   83. [A] [B] [C] [D]
69. [A] [B] [C] [D]   74. [A] [B] [C] [D]   79. [A] [B] [C] [D]   84. [A] [B] [C] [D]
70. [A] [B] [C] [D]   75. [A] [B] [C] [D]   80. [A] [B] [C] [D]   85. [A] [B] [C] [D]
71. [A] [B] [C] [D]   76. [A] [B] [C] [D]   81. [A] [B] [C] [D]   86. [A] [B] [C] [D]

Part VI   **Translation**   **(5 minutes)**

87. _____

88. _____

89. _____

90. _____

91. _____

PRACTICE TEST 2

Part I Writing   (30 minutes)

注意：此部分试题在答题卡 1 上。

Part II Reading Comprehension (Skimming and Scanning)
                                                                      (15 minutes)

Directions: *In this part, you will have 15 minutes to go over the passage quickly and answer the questions on **Answer Sheet 1**.*

For questions 1 – 7, mark

Y *(for YES)*   *if the statement agrees with the information given in the passage;*

N *(for NO)*   *if the statement contradicts the information given in the passage;*

NG *(for NOT GIVEN)*   *if the information is not given in the passage.*

For questions 8 – 10, complete the sentences with the information given in the passage.

Why DIY?

The reasons why people engage in DIY (Do It Yourself) have always been numerous and complex. For some, DIY has provided a rare opportunity for creativity and self expression. For others it has been an unwelcome necessity, driven purely by economic considerations. Then there has been a group which feels that a building can never be a home unless it has been altered and modified to reflect a change of occupancy. A final group has traditionally taken the line that if you want a job done well, you must do it yourself.

The same four basic species of DIYers exist today, although these various motives may now overlap very substantially. The perfectionist in search of the good job done well is often also driven by a desire for creativity. There are also two new categories of motive — the pursuit of DIY as a leisure activity and DIY as a form of occupational therapy. These, again, overlap with other reasons.

DIY as necessity

There is a significant number of young homemakers (38% of our informants) for whom there is no option but DIY. Their new home, whether bought on a mortgage which consumes a major slice of their income, or rented at similarly challenging rates, will often require essential refurbishment and even structural repair.

Some of these people are reluctant first-time DIYers. They would much prefer to hire professionals, but can't afford to do so. The majority, however, welcome the opportunity that need has forced upon them to get involved for the first time in the real business of creating a home — with all of its unfamiliar physical labour and the learning from scratch of new techniques. In time, many will migrate to one of the other categories of DIYer, continuing to exercise their new found talents and enthusiasm when no longer forced by financial constraints to do so.

DIY as territorial marking

Even those who have bought a brand new "starter home," the type which increasingly proliferates around the edges of our towns and cities, will feel compelled to add personal touches of a less dramatic kind to disguise its otherwise bland and expressionless nature. Putting a "personal stamp on the place" was one of the most frequently reported motives for DIY, with 72% of sample seeing this as being a very important aspect.

DIY as self-expression

Many young people today are frustrated artists — their latent creative talents just waiting for the chance to reveal themselves. There are also those seeking opportunities for a sense of achievement and personal fulfillment. DIY provided just such opportunities for the overwhelming majority of our informants (84%). They spoke at length of their sense of pride after completing their very first DIY task, and about how this experience gave them the drive to tackle more ambitious projects.

This sense of creative achievement comes both from the choices made by the first-time DIYer — the selection of colours, textures and components to apply to the "canvas" of the home — and from the application of specific skills and techniques. The manufacturers of DIY materials clearly understand this and now provide a wide range of "arty" products to fuel creative urges. At the same time, they make the materials themselves much easier to use — the DIY equivalent of painting by numbers. Special paint effects, which once required the specialist knowledge and training of the true professional, can now be achieved straight out of the can with a simple brush. While ragging, dragging and distressing may be considered passé in the colour supplements, a new generation of home decorators takes pride in new-found talents.

DIY as perfection-seeking

A large proportion of first-time DIYers (63%) distrust builders and decorators. They feel that most are "cowboys" and that even the more reputable ones are very unlikely to have the same loving attention to detail and care as the DIYer. Some had previously suffered from the alleged bodges of small builders, while others were proud of the fact that no tradesman of this kind had ever set foot in their home.

Within this group there were those who were content for builders to perform basic or structural work, and to undertake tasks such as plastering which are beyond the competence of most DIYers, particularly the younger novices in our sample. The finishing work, however, was something these people kept for themselves — the final "perfecting" of what otherwise would be just a mediocre result.

This drive for perfection was also evident among the "strippers" in this group. The idea of putting wallpaper over existing paper, or even paint on the top of preceding coats, was anathema. Everything needed to be taken back to the bare plaster or the naked wood before any new decoration could be applied. Some informants recognised that this search for perfection could sometimes go too far: "It's an obsession for me really. There's always something I'm working on. I'm never happy with anything."

The problem perfectionists face is that progress can be very slow. One young female partner of such a perfectionist said: "My boyfriend spent so long decorating the bedroom that I had to hire someone to do the living room." The living room was finished first. When perfectionists are obliged, by nagging or circumstance, to speed things up, other problems can result: "The only time I rushed a job was when we had friends coming for the weekend. I was so unhappy with it that I painted it again after they had gone."

DIY as leisure activity

For a significant minority of first-timers (28%), DIY is seen as a novel and entertaining pastime. It is not really work, but something akin to entertainment, shared by both partners and even the children in the case of young families. "It's just great fun" enthused one of our sample.

The idea that DIYing is akin to a trip to the lions of Longleat may seem strange. But for these informants home-making was sufficiently different from, and infinitely preferable to, the dull routines of weekday work to constitute a weekend break. The results of such activity were rewarding, but probably less so than engaging in the activity itself.

DIY as therapy

"It's therapeutic, isn't it? I'm always in my own little world when I'm doing DIY — it's great." So said a young man of 27 in our sample. "For me it's occupational therapy," said another informant. For them and others it was their way of getting rid of stress after a long day at work — a way of switching off and using the repetitive nature of many DIY tasks as a way of relaxing. Others hinted at a similar process, where DIY was almost an end in itself, rather than just a means of achieving a better home. In this sense they were similar to those who saw DIY as a form of leisure, but it was the psychological effects which were emphasized by 18% of our sample.

While people in this group might sound like sad anoraks, lacking the basic social skills to get a life outside of the home, they were quite the opposite. DIY provided a transitional stage between work and play — something which allowed them to unwind and rid themselves of tensions, becoming more sociable in the process.

注意：此部分试题请在**答题卡** 1 上作答；8 – 10 题在**答题卡** 1 上。

1. All the DIYers enjoy DIY very much.
2. DIY needs physical labor and techniques.
3. Those who regard DIY as necessity will no longer engage in it once their new house is done.
4. One motive for DIY is to characterize their house.
5. DIY can help young people to gain confidence.
6. The manufacturers of DIY materials instruct DIYers to do their work.
7. DIYers will make the finishing work an extraordinary one by themselves.

Part III Listening Comprehension　　　　　(35 minutes)

Section A

Directions: *In this section, you will hear 8 short conversations and 2 long conversations. At the end of each conversation, one or more questions will be asked about what was said. Both the conversation and the questions will be spoken only once. After each question there will be a pause. During the pause, you must read the four choices marked A), B), C) and D), and decide which is the best answer. Then mark the corresponding letter on **Answer Sheet 2** with a single line through the centre.*

注意：此部分试题请在**答题卡** 2 上作答。

11. A) Because there is something wrong with the shower.

    B) Because there is something wrong with the bathtub.

    C) Because the woman did not work efficiently.

    D) Because there is something wrong with the water tap.

12. A) Because of our brains.

    B) Because of the complex world.

    C) Because of our genes and the experiences we have had.

    D) Because no one is perfect.

13. A) Yes, she will.   C) No, she won't.

    B) Well, maybe not.   D) None of the above.

14. A) Gas station.   C) Lost and found department.

    B) Police station.   D) Bar.

15. A) If the woman is a senior.

    B) If the woman uses the Internet.

    C) If the woman has read the advertisement carefully.

    D) If the woman will attend graduate school.

16. A) Make more copies of the letter.

    B) Find out when the new job begins.

    C) Refer to a new edition.

    D) Get a more recent reference letter.

17. A) In a train.   C) In a bus.

    B) In a plane.   D) In a shop.

18. A) Satisfied with their price.

    B) Displeased with the quality.

    C) Dissatisfied with their technology.

    D) Happy with the modern mass-production techniques.

Questions 19 to 22 are based on the conversation you have just heard.

19. A) At Kathy's school.   C) At Mrs. Strong's home.

    B) In the police station.   D) On the phone.

20. A) Kathy's teacher.   C) The police.

    B) Kathy's friend.   D) Mrs. Strong's neighbor.

21. A) A whole day.   C) The whole morning.

    B) The whole afternoon. D) A whole night.

22. A) Red.   C) Blue.
    B) Brown.   D) Yellow.

Questions 23 to 25 are based on the conversation you have just heard.

23. A) In Great Britain.   C) In the United States.
    B) In Australia.   D) In Germany.

24. A) Music.   C) Art.
    B) Computer science.   D) English.

25. A) Classmates.   C) Teacher and student.
    B) Manager and secretary.   D) Father and daughter.

Section B

Directions: *In this section, you will hear 3 short passages. At the end of each passage, you will hear some questions. Both the passage and the questions will be spoken only once. After you hear a question, you must choose the best answer from the four choices marked A), B), C) and D). Then mark the corresponding letter on* **Answer Sheet 2** *with a single line through the centre.*

注意：此部分试题请在**答题卡 2** 上作答。

Passage One

Questions 26 to 29 are based on the passage you have just heard.

26. A) Touring.   C) On vacation.
    B) Traveling for business.   D) Writing.

27. A) Commercial, transient and vacation hotels.
    B) Transient, vacation and resort hotels.
    C) Transient, resort and residential hotels.
    D) Vacation, resort and residential hotels.

28. A) About 13,000.   C) About 300,000.
    B) About 30,000.   D) About 3,000.

29. A) It is a small single room.
    B) It is meant for the use of one person.
    C) It is meant for the use of two people.

D) It is meant for the use of a group of persons traveling together.

Passage Two

Questions 30 to 32 are based on the passage you have just heard.

30. A) Researchers were not sure whether sleep habits had an effect on a person's weight.
    B) Researchers found out the exact reasons why females were more likely to gain weight.
    C) Researchers found that women who slept less time every night was easier to gain weight.
    D) Researchers didn't think that lack of sleep was the main cause to gain weight.

31. A) The best way to make females fatter.
    B) Study links lack of sleep to weight gain in females.
    C) How did 68,183 middle-aged women lose weight?
    D) Lack of sleep, males get fatter than females.

32. A) They eat more.
    B) They feel tired.
    C) They don't often exercise.
    D) They control their appetite.

Passage Three

Questions 33 to 35 are based on the passage you have just heard.

33. A) The speed of a man-made satellite.
    B) The pull of the earth.
    C) The speed of the moon.
    D) The pull of the moon.

34. A) Because they travel at a certain speed.
    B) Because they are very light in weight.
    C) Because the earth's gravity keeps them from going straight off into space.
    D) Both A) and C).

35. A) It will go straight off into space.
    B) It will fall to the earth.
    C) It will circle the earth forever.
    D) Both A) and C).

Section C

Directions: *In this section, you will hear a passage three times. When the passage is read for the first time, you should listen carefully for its general idea. When the passage is read for the second time, you are required to fill in the blanks numbered from 36 to 43 with the exact words you have just heard. For blanks numbered from 44 to 46 you are required to fill in the missing information. For these blanks, you can either use the exact words you have just heard or write down the main points in your own words. Finally, when the passage is read for the third time, you should check what you have written.*

注意：此部分试题在**答题卡**2上；请在**答题卡**2上作答。

Part IV　Reading Comprehension (Reading in Depth)

(25 minutes)

Section A

Directions: *In this section，there is a passage with ten blanks. You are required to select one word for each blank from a list of choices given in a word bank following the passage. Read the passage through carefully before making your choices. Each choice in the bank is identified by a letter. Please mark the corresponding letter for each item on Answer Sheet 2 with a single line through the centre.* **You may not use any of the words in the bank more than once.**

　　If I were a boy again, I would practice __47__ oftener, and never give up a thing because it was hard or __48__. If we want light, we must __49__ darkness.

　　If I were a boy again, I would school myself into a good habit of attention; I would let nothing come between me and the subject in hand. I would remember that a good skater never tries to skate two directions at once.

　　If I were to live my life over again, I would pay more attention to the __50__ of the memory. I would __51__ that faculty by every possible means, and on every possible __52__. It takes a little hard work at first to remember things __53__, but memory soon helps itself, and gives very little troubles.

　　If I were a boy again, I would cultivate courage. "Nothing is so mild and gentle as courage, nothing so cruel and pitiless as cowardice," says a wise author.

　　If I were a boy again, I would look on the cheerful side. Life is very much like a mirror: if you smile upon it, it smiles back upon you; but if you __54__ and look doubtful on it，you will get a similar look in return.

If I were a boy again，I would ___55___ of myself more courtesy towards my companions and friends，and indeed towards other strangers as well.

Finally，instead of trying hard to be happy，as if that were the sole purpose of life，I would，if I were a boy again，try ___56___ harder to make others happy.

注意：此部分试题请在**答题卡** 2 上作答。

A) dominant	I) accurately
B) necessarily	J) inconvenient
C) conquer	K) still
D) demand	L) cultivation
E) strengthen	M) more
F) invaluable	N) occasion
G) frown	O) explicit
H) perseverance	

Section B

Directions: *There are 2 passages in this section. Each passage is followed by some questions or unfinished statements. For each of them there are four choices marked A), B), C) and D). You should decide on the best choice and mark the corresponding letter on **Answer Sheet 2** with a single line through the centre.*

Passage One

Questions 57 to 61 are based on the following passage.

A number of factors related to the voice reveal the personality of the speaker. The first is the broad area of communication，which includes passing on information by use of language，communicating with a group or an individual，and specialized communication through performance. A person conveys thoughts and ideas through choice of words，by a tone of voice that is pleasant or unpleasant，gentle or harsh，by the rhythm that is inherent within the language itself，and by speech rhythms that are flowing and regular or uneven and hesitant，and finally，by the pitch and melody of the utterance. When one speaks before a group，his tone may indicate unsureness or fright，confidence or calm. At interpersonal levels，his tone may reflect ideas and feelings over and above the words chosen，or may belie it. Here the speaker's tone can consciously or unconsciously reflect intuitive sympathy or antipathy, lack of concern or interest, fatigue, anxiety, enthusiasm or excitement, all of which are usually discernible by the acute listener. Public performance is a manner of communication that is highly specialized with its own techniques for obtaining effects by voice and/or gesture. The motivation derived from the text, and in the case of singing, the music, in combination with the performer's skills, personality, and ability to create empathy will determine the success of artistic, political or pedagogic communication.

Second, the voice gives psychological clues to a person's self-image, perception of others, and emotional health. Self-image can be indicated by a tone of voice that is confident, shy, aggressive, outgoing, or high-spirited, to name only a few personality traits. Also the sound may give a clue to the façade or mask of that person, for example, a shy person hiding behind an overconfident front. How a speaker perceives the listener's receptiveness, interest, or sympathy in any given conversation can drastically alter the tone of presentation, by encouraging or discouraging the speaker. Emotional health is evidenced in the voice by free and melodic sounds of the happy, by constricted and harsh sound of the angry, and by dull and lethargic qualities of the depressed.

注意：此部分试题请在**答题卡 2** 上作答。

57. What does the passage mainly tell us?
    A) Communication styles.
    B) The connection between voice and personality.
    C) The production of speech.
    D) The function of the voice in performance.

58. By saying "At interpersonal levels, his tone may reflect ideas and feelings over and above the words chosen," the author means that _____.
    A) a high tone of voice reflects an emotional communication
    B) feelings are more difficult to express than ideas
    C) the tone of voice can carry information beyond the meaning of words
    D) feelings are expressed with different words rather than ideas

59. Why does the author mention "artistic, political or pedagogic communication" at the end of the first paragraph?
    A) To contrast them to singing.
    B) To introduce the idea of specialization of performance.
    C) As examples of public performance.
    D) As examples of basic styles of communication.

60. What kind of people can be well aware of the feeling reflected by the speaker's

tone?

A) A skillful singer.   C) A trained actor.

B) A good listener.   D) A specialized psychologist.

61. How is emotional health indicated in communication?

A) By the speaker's ability to perceive the listener's interest.

B) By the speaker's talent of controlling his tone of presentation.

C) By the free and melodic sounds of the speaker.

D) By a tone of voice that is confident.

Passage Two

Questions 62 to 66 are based on the following passage.

The San Andreas Fault is a fracture at the congruence of two major plates of the earth's crust, one of which supports most of the North American continent, and the other of which underlies the coast of California and the ocean floor of the Pacific. The fault originates about six hundred miles from the Gulf of California and runs north in an irregular line along the west coast to San Francisco, where it continues north for about two hundred more miles before angling into the ocean. In places, the trace of the fault is marked by a trench, or, in geological terms, a rift, and small ponds called sag ponds that dot the landscape. Its western side always moves north in relation to its eastern side. The total net slip along the San Andreas Fault and the length of time it has been active are matters of conjecture, but it has been estimated that, during the past fifteen million years, coastal California along the San Andreas Fault has moved about 190 miles in a northwesterly direction with respect to North American. Although the movement along the fault averages only a few inches a year, it is intermittent and variable. Some segments of the fault do not move at all for long periods of time, building up tremendous pressure that must be released. For this reason, tremors are not unusual along the San Andreas Fault, and some of them are classified as major earthquakes.

It is worth noting that the San Andreas Fault passes uncomfortably close to several major metropolitan areas, including Los Angeles and San Francisco. In addition, the San Andreas Fault has created smaller fault systems, many of which underlie the smaller towns and cities along the Californian Coast. For this reason, Californians have long anticipated the recurrence of what they refer to as the "Big One," a destructive earthquake that would measure near 8 on the Richter scale, similar in intensity to those that occurred in 1857 and 1906. The effects of such a quake would wreak devastating effects in the life and property in the region. Unfortunately, as pressure continues to build along the fault, the likelihood of such an earthquake increases substantially.

注意：此部分试题请在**答题卡** 2 上作答。

62. What is the main topic of the passage?
    A) The tremors and earthquakes along the San Andreas Fault.
    B) Different kinds of faults.
    C) The introduction of the San Andreas Fault.
    D) The location of the San Andreas Fault.

63. Which of the following statements is true?
    A) The San Andreas Fault keeps active all the year round.
    B) There will be a destructive earthquake along the San Andreas Fault in the near future.
    C) People are quite sure of the exact length of the San Andreas Fault.
    D) Along the San Andreas Fault lie many important cities.

64. Along the San Andreas Fault, tremors are _____.
    A) very unpredictable   C) small and insignificant
    B) rare, but disastrous   D) frequent events

65. Where does the fault lie?
    A) South of the Gulf of California.   C) West of the Gulf of California.
    B) North of the Gulf of California.   D) East of the Gulf of California.

66. How does the author give the definition of the San Andreas Fault?
    A) Intense pressure built up between segments.
    B) Occasional tremors and earthquakes.
    C) A plate that underlies the North American continent.
    D) A crack in the earth's crust between two plates.

Part V   Cloze   (15 minutes)

Directions: *There are 20 blanks in the following passage. For each blank there are four choices marked A), B), C) and D) on the right side of the paper. You should choose the ONE that best fits into the passage. Then mark the corresponding letter on* **Answer Sheet** *2 with a single line through the centre.*

注意：此部分试题请在**答题卡 2**上作答。

Time "talks" in the American culture and, for that matter, in many other cultures. __67__ it says is crucial in our relations with others. Some societies __68__ seriously their promises to meet deadlines and keep appointments, and they __69__ penalties for being late or not completing a task in the __70__ time. In the United States, being late repeatedly for class in schools may lead to __71__. Late papers may __72__ as much as a 10 percent reduction in the grade, or even a failing grade.

Perhaps the most __73__ dimension in culture is the use of time. Each culture has its own concept of time. In Germanic cultures punctuality is a __74__ of respect and politeness; being late is rude. Germans believe people should be exactly __75__ time, neither too early nor too late. To the Indonesian, time is an endless pool; why be __76__ or hurry? All cultures __77__ their own time system for granted and believe other cultures operate with the __78__ time frame. __79__, misunderstandings are __80__. To function in a foreign country, we must know its time system.

__81__ Edward Hall the principal difference between cultures is whether they are monochromic or polychromic. In monochromic cultures (United States, Northern Europe) people do things one by one. They follow schedules be-

67. A) That   C) Which
    B) What   D) Whether
68. A) keep   C) take
    B) make   D) follow
69. A) impose   C) sponsor
    B) pay   D) issue
70. A) needed   C) necessary
    B) required   D) essential
71. A) suspension C) suspended
    B) suspend   D) suspense
72. A) result in C) add to
    B) result form D) result
73. A) critical   C) basic
    B) serious   D) elementary
74. A) symbol   C) remark
    B) significance D) sign
75. A) in   C) on
    B) at   D) against
76. A) pressured C) depressed
    B) urged   D) spurred
77. A) take   C) do
    B) make   D) accept
78. A) opposite   C) equal
    B) different D) same
79. A) Thus   C) Furthermore
    B) Moreover   D) Additionally
80. A) available C) inaccessible
    B) inevitable D) impossible
81. A) To   C) As for
    B) As to   D) With

cause time can be squandered or saved. __82__ is essential, and one __83__ is late has __84__ a grave offense. In polychromic cultures (Southern Europe, Latin America, Middle East) the people do many things at once, and relationship come __85__ schedules. A business appointment scheduled or a specific time may be delayed several hours __86__ the latecomer look after a family matter or a business crisis.	82. A) Responsibility C) Promptness
	     B) Hurry D) Frankness
	83. A) who C) whose
	     B) which D) what
	84. A) made C) done
	     B) committed D) taken
	85. A) before C) between
	     B) after D) into
	86. A) if C) when
	     B) while D) since

Part VI   Translation   (5 minutes)

Directions: *Complete the sentences on **Answer Sheet 2** by translating into English the Chinese given in brackets.*

注意：此部分试题请在**答题卡** 2 上作答。

87. Obviously, our company couldn't have developed into such a large modern venture _____ （如果没有技术上的革新和发明）.

88. The World Bank _____ （敦促中国改革养老保险制度） to overcome the social and economic pressure expected to result from the rising life expectancy rate.

89. If you do have financial difficulties, you can _____ （申请学生贷款）.

90. When _____ （客观题和主观题并用）, however, a fairly clear picture of the students' knowledge can usually be obtained.

91. The rise of volcanic activity will _____ （给地球气候带来灾难性影响）, and millions could die from respiratory ailments as ash and greenhouse gases fill the air.

答题卡 1 (Answer Sheet 1)

学校:
姓名:
划线要求

准　　考　　证　　号

[0]	[0]	[0]	[0]	[0]	[0]	[0]	[0]	[0]	[0]	[0]	[0]	[0]	[0]	[0]
[1]	[1]	[1]	[1]	[1]	[1]	[1]	[1]	[1]	[1]	[1]	[1]	[1]	[1]	[1]
[2]	[2]	[2]	[2]	[2]	[2]	[2]	[2]	[2]	[2]	[2]	[2]	[2]	[2]	[2]
[3]	[3]	[3]	[3]	[3]	[3]	[3]	[3]	[3]	[3]	[3]	[3]	[3]	[3]	[3]
[4]	[4]	[4]	[4]	[4]	[4]	[4]	[4]	[4]	[4]	[4]	[4]	[4]	[4]	[4]
[5]	[5]	[5]	[5]	[5]	[5]	[5]	[5]	[5]	[5]	[5]	[5]	[5]	[5]	[5]
[6]	[6]	[6]	[6]	[6]	[6]	[6]	[6]	[6]	[6]	[6]	[6]	[6]	[6]	[6]
[7]	[7]	[7]	[7]	[7]	[7]	[7]	[7]	[7]	[7]	[7]	[7]	[7]	[7]	[7]
[8]	[8]	[8]	[8]	[8]	[8]	[8]	[8]	[8]	[8]	[8]	[8]	[8]	[8]	[8]
[9]	[9]	[9]	[9]	[9]	[9]	[9]	[9]	[9]	[9]	[9]	[9]	[9]	[9]	[9]

Part I　　　　　　　　　　　**Writing**　　　　　　　　**(30 minutes)**

Directions: *For this part, you are allowed 30 minutes to write a composition on the topic* **The Problems of the Only Child in a Family.** *You should write at least 120 words following the outline given below in Chinese:*

1. 存在的问题
2. 导致问题的原因
3. 解决问题的办法

The Problems of the Only Child in a Family

答题卡 1 (Answer Sheet 1)

Part II Reading Comprehension (Skimming and Scanning) (15 minutes)

1. [Y] [N] [NG]   2. [Y] [N] [NG]   3. [Y] [N] [NG]   4. [Y] [N] [NG]
5. [Y] [N] [NG]   6. [Y] [N] [NG]   7. [Y] [N] [NG]

8. DIY is similar to _____.

9. For DIYers, housework is preferable to _____.

10. DIY as therapy can help people _____.

答题卡 2 (Answer Sheet 2)

Part III Section A   Section B

11. [A] [B] [C] [D]　16. [A] [B] [C] [D]　21. [A] [B] [C] [D]　26. [A] [B] [C] [D]　31. [A] [B] [C] [D]
12. [A] [B] [C] [D]　17. [A] [B] [C] [D]　22. [A] [B] [C] [D]　27. [A] [B] [C] [D]　32. [A] [B] [C] [D]
13. [A] [B] [C] [D]　18. [A] [B] [C] [D]　23. [A] [B] [C] [D]　28. [A] [B] [C] [D]　33. [A] [B] [C] [D]
14. [A] [B] [C] [D]　19. [A] [B] [C] [D]　24. [A] [B] [C] [D]　29. [A] [B] [C] [D]　34. [A] [B] [C] [D]
15. [A] [B] [C] [D]　20. [A] [B] [C] [D]　25. [A] [B] [C] [D]　30. [A] [B] [C] [D]　35. [A] [B] [C] [D]

Part III Section C

Most of the waiters, waitresses, and cooks in restaurants are not employed on a full-time (36) _____. If they were full-time employees, they would (37) _____ at least the (38) _____ wage plus benefits such as the cost of health, dental, life (39) _____ and a saving plan for (40) _____. But for the many who are part-time employees and (41) _____ no additional benefits, (42) _____ helps defray the additional costs that the part-time employee faces for the outside (43) _____ of such benefits. (44) _____.

Usually the amount of tip ranges from 10% to 15% of the consumption. (45) _____, not when you are paying the bill. (46) _____

_____. If this is the case, the menu will read "includes tax and gratuity."

答题卡 2 (Answer Sheet 2)

Part IV   Section A   **Section B**

47. [A][B][C][D][E][F][G][H][I][J][K][L][M][N][O]   57. [A] [B] [C] [D]
48. [A][B][C][D][E][F][G][H][I][J][K][L][M][N][O]   58. [A] [B] [C] [D]
49. [A][B][C][D][E][F][G][H][I][J][K][L][M][N][O]   59. [A] [B] [C] [D]
50. [A][B][C][D][E][F][G][H][I][J][K][L][M][N][O]   60. [A] [B] [C] [D]
51. [A][B][C][D][E][F][G][H][I][J][K][L][M][N][O]   61. [A] [B] [C] [D]
52. [A][B][C][D][E][F][G][H][I][J][K][L][M][N][O]   62. [A] [B] [C] [D]
53. [A][B][C][D][E][F][G][H][I][J][K][L][M][N][O]   63. [A] [B] [C] [D]
54. [A][B][C][D][E][F][G][H][I][J][K][L][M][N][O]   64. [A] [B] [C] [D]
55. [A][B][C][D][E][F][G][H][I][J][K][L][M][N][O]   65. [A] [B] [C] [D]
56. [A][B][C][D][E][F][G][H][I][J][K][L][M][N][O]   66. [A] [B] [C] [D]

Part V   **Cloze**   **(15 minutes)**

67. [A] [B] [C] [D]   72. [A] [B] [C] [D]   77. [A] [B] [C] [D]   82. [A] [B] [C] [D]
68. [A] [B] [C] [D]   73. [A] [B] [C] [D]   78. [A] [B] [C] [D]   83. [A] [B] [C] [D]
69. [A] [B] [C] [D]   74. [A] [B] [C] [D]   79. [A] [B] [C] [D]   84. [A] [B] [C] [D]
70. [A] [B] [C] [D]   75. [A] [B] [C] [D]   80. [A] [B] [C] [D]   85. [A] [B] [C] [D]
71. [A] [B] [C] [D]   76. [A] [B] [C] [D]   81. [A] [B] [C] [D]   86. [A] [B] [C] [D]

Part VI   **Translation**   **(5 minutes)**

87. _____

88. _____

89. _____

90. _____

91. _____

PRACTICE TEST 3

Part I   Writing   (30 minutes)

注意：此部分试题在**答题卡** 1 上。

Part II   Reading Comprehension (Skimming and Scanning)
(15 minutes)

Directions: *In this part, you will have 15 minutes to go over the passage quickly and answer the questions on **Answer Sheet 1**.*

For questions 1 – 7, mark

Y *(for YES)*   *if the statement agrees with the information given in the passage;*

N *(for NO)*   *if the statement contradicts the information given in the passage;*

NG *(for NOT GIVEN)*   *if the information is not given in the passage.*

For questions 8 – 10, complete the sentences with the information given in the passage.

GRE General Test Overview

What Is It?

The GRE General Test measures verbal reasoning, quantitative reasoning, critical thinking, and analytical writing skills that have been acquired over a long period of time and that are not related to any specific field of study.

Verbal Reasoning — The skills measured include the test taker's ability to

- analyze and evaluate written material and synthesize information obtained from it;
- analyze relationships among component parts of sentences;
- recognize relationships between words and concepts.

Quantitative Reasoning — The skills measured include the test taker's ability to

- understand basic concepts of arithmetic, algebra, geometry, and data analysis;

- reason quantitatively;
- solve problems in a quantitative setting.

Analytical Writing — The skills measured include the test taker's ability to

- articulate complex ideas clearly and effectively;
- examine claims and accompanying evidence;
- support ideas with relevant reasons and examples;
- sustain a well-focused, coherent discussion;
- control the elements of standard written English.

Who Takes It and Why?

Prospective graduate applicants take the General Test. GRE test scores are used by admissions or fellowship panels to supplement undergraduate records and other qualifications for graduate study. The scores provide common measures for comparing the qualifications of applicants and aid in evaluating grades and recommendations.

Where Do People Take It?

The General Test is offered year-round at computer-based test centers in the U.S., Canada, and many other countries. It is offered at paper-based test centers in areas of the world where computer-based testing is not available. See which format is available in your area.

Who Accepts It?

Any accredited graduate or professional school, or any department or division within a school, may require or recommend that its applicants take the General Test, a Subject Test, or both. If approved by the GRE Board, a non-accredited institution can also receive test takers' scores.

Computer-Based General Test Content and Structure

The computer-based General Test has three sections.

In addition, one unidentified pretest section may be included, and this section can appear in any position in the test after the analytical writing section. Questions in the pretest section are being tested for possible use in future tests, and answers will not count toward your scores.

An identified research section that is not scored may also be included, and this section would always appear in the final section of the test. Questions in the research section are included for the purpose of ETS research, and answers will not count toward your scores.

Total testing time is up to three hours, not including the research section. The directions at the beginning of each section specify the total number of questions in the section and the time allowed for the section.

The analytical writing section is always first. For the Issue task, two topics will be presented and you will choose one. The Argument task does not present a choice of topics; instead, one topic will be presented.

The verbal and quantitative sections may appear in any order, including an unidentified verbal or quantitative pretest section. Treat each section presented during your test as if it counts.

Typical Computer-Based GRE General Test

Section	Number of Questions	Time
Analytical Writing	1 Issue Task*	45 minutes
Analytical Writing	1 Argument Task*	30 minutes
Verbal	30	30 minutes
Quantitative	28	45 minutes
Pretest**	Varies	Varies
Research***	Varies	Varies

* For the Issue task, two essay topics are presented and you choose one. The Argument task does not present a choice of topics; instead one topic is presented.

** An unidentified verbal or quantitative pretest section may be included and may appear in any order after the analytical writing section. It is not counted as part of your score.

*** An identified research section that is not scored may be included, and it is always at the end of the test.

Paper-Based General Test Content and Structure

The paper-based GRE General Test contains five sections.

In addition, one unidentified pretest section may be included, and this section can appear in any position in the test after the analytical writing section. Questions in the pretest section are being tested for possible use in future tests, and answers will not count toward your scores.

Total testing time is up to $3\frac{3}{4}$ hours. The directions at the beginning of each section specify the total number of questions in the section and the time allowed for the section.

The analytical writing section is always first. For the Issue task, two topics will be presented and you will choose one. The Argument task does not present a choice of topics; instead one topic will be presented.

The verbal and quantitative sections may appear in any order, including an unidentified verbal or quantitative pretest section. Treat each section presented during your test as if it counts.

Typical Paper-Based General Test

Section	Number of Questions	Time
Analytical Writing	1 Issue Task*	45 minutes
Analytical Writing	1 Argument Task*	30 minutes
Verbal (2 sections)	38 per section	30 minutes per section
Quantitative (2 sections)	30 per section	30 minutes per section
Pretest**	Varies	30 minutes

* For the Issue task, two essay topics will be presented and you will choose one. The Argument task does not present a choice of topics; instead, one topic will be presented.

** An unidentified verbal or quantitative pretest section may be included and may appear in any order after the analytical writing section. It is not counted as part of your score.

Modified Versions of Verbal and Quantitative Questions

The test you take may include questions that are modified versions of published questions or of questions you have already seen on an earlier section of the test. Some modifications are substantial; others are less apparent.

Thus, even if a question appears to be similar to a question you have already seen, it may in fact be a different question and may also have a different correct answer. You can be assured of doing your best on the test you take by paying careful attention to the wording of each question as it appears in your test.

The GRE Program is currently investigating the feasibility of reusing questions that have been published in GRE practice materials. As part of that investigation, you may see questions from these materials on a test you take.

注意：此部分试题请在**答题卡** 1 上作答；8－10 题在**答题卡** 1 上。

1. This passage gives a general description of the GRE General Test.
2. The GRE General Test measures abilities and skills that are not related to any specific field of study.
3. College students must take GRE General Test before graduation.
4. The computer-based General Test is offered only in the U. S. and Canada.
5. Some schools may require or recommend that its applicants take both the GRE General Test and a GRE Subject Test.
6. Total testing time for computer-based General Test is up to three hours, including the research section.
7. Test fee for the computer-based General Test is higher than that for the paper-based GRE General Test.

Part III　Listening Comprehension　　(35 minutes)

Section A

Directions: *In this section, you will hear 8 short conversations and 2 long conversations. At the end of each conversation, one or more questions will be asked about what was said. Both the conversation and the questions will be spoken only once. After each question there will be a pause. During the pause, you must read the four choices marked A), B), C) and D), and decide which is the best answer. Then mark the corresponding letter on **Answer Sheet 2** with a single line through the centre.*

注意：此部分试题请在**答题卡 2** 上作答。

11. A) To the college in the corner.
    B) To the poetry class.
    C) To the coffee house near the college.
    D) To the man's house for coffee.

12. A) The cost of fixing the window.
    B) The difficulty of cleaning up the broken glass.
    C) The possible harm to the people involved.
    D) The type of punishment he will give Tommy.

13. A) Men are slaves of their habits，but women are not.
    B) Human beings' purposeful efforts may enable them to break old habits and build new ones.
    C) It is impossible for us to break old habits and form new ones.
    D) It is easy to break habits.

14. A) Electrician.　　　　　　　　　C) Physician.
    B) Teacher.　　　　　　　　　　D) Bus driver.

15. A) Because she does not like it.
    B) Because it does not fit her very well.
    C) Because it is too formal for the occasion.
    D) Because the man likes the other dress better.

16. A) Objective.　　　　　　　　　C) Hostile.
    B) Timid.　　　　　　　　　　　D) Sympathetic.

17. A) The daughter studied for a test.　C) The family stayed awake.

B) The daughter had a nightmare.   D) The house was on fire.

18. A) Talking with a woman in her room.
    B) Explaining something to the woman.
    C) Apologizing to the woman.
    D) Listening to the woman complaining.

Questions 19 to 22 are based on the conversation you have just heard.

19. A) She thinks it was very formal.
    B) She thinks it was very difficult.
    C) She thinks she failed in the interview.
    D) She thinks it turned out very well.

20. A) Questions about all kinds of energy sources.
    B) Questions about her qualifications.
    C) Questions about her personal life.
    D) Questions about her interest in the documentaries.

21. A) Energy.   C) Solar power.
    B) Wind power.   D) Coal.

22. A) Because she answered all the questions well.
    B) Because she has a degree.
    C) Because she had actually made some preparations about the documentaries'
       subjects before the interview and knew the purpose of making the documenta-
       ries.
    D) Because she is interested in making documentaries.

Questions 23 to 25 are based on the conversation you have just heard.

23. A) Taking part in an expedition to the Caribbean.
    B) Taking part in a cooking course.
    C) Teaching how to cook Indian food.
    D) Meeting new friends.

24. A) America.   C) Australia.
    B) England.   D) Mexico.

25. A) He is a sailor.   C) He is a cook.
    B) He is a teacher.   D) He has no fixed job.

Section B

Directions: *In this section, you will hear 3 short passages. At the end of each passage, you will hear some questions. Both the passage and the questions will be spoken only once. After you hear a question, you must choose the best answer from the four choices marked A), B), C) and D). Then mark the corresponding letter on Answer Sheet 2 with a single line through the centre.*

注意：此部分试题请在**答题卡 2** 上作答。

Passage One

Questions 26 to 29 are based on the passage you have just heard.

26. A) In 776 B.C.
    B) In 394 A.D.
    C) In 1924.
    D) In 1896.

27. A) Rome.
    B) Athens.
    C) Paris.
    D) Istanbul.

28. A) To test athletes.
    B) To organize world competition.
    C) To encourage better understanding.
    D) To satisfy youth's love for athletics.

29. A) Two.
    B) Six.
    C) Four.
    D) Nine.

Passage Two

Questions 30 to 32 are based on the passage you have just heard.

30. A) They use perfume and apple pies.
    B) They use regular showers.
    C) They use videos and toys.
    D) They use tasty pet foods.

31. A) Americans look on their pets as part of the family.
    B) Four Seasons Hotels buy food for pets from China.
    C) A mouse may be kept as a pet in America.
    D) American people like to talk about pets in their spare time.

32. A) Pets in America.
    B) How to Raise Pets.
    C) Pets — A High Cost.
    D) Wild Animal Protection in America.

Passage Three

Questions 33 to 35 are based on the passage you have just heard.

33. A) Automobiles have brought convenience to people.
    B) Automobiles have improved efficiency of factories.
    C) Automobiles have stimulated the development of many countries' industry.
    D) Automobiles have improved people's standard of living.

34. A) Air pollution.   C) Petroleum shortages.
    B) Traffic jams.   D) Boundary disputes.

35. A) Hateful.   C) Sarcastic.
    B) Neutral.   D) Negative.

Section C

Directions: *In this section, you will hear a passage three times. When the passage is read for the first time, you should listen carefully for its general idea. When the passage is read for the second time, you are required to fill in the blanks numbered from 36 to 43 with the exact words you have just heard. For blanks numbered from 44 to 46 you are required to fill in the missing information. For these blanks, you can either use the exact words you have just heard or write down the main points in your own words. Finally, when the passage is read for the third time, you should check what you have written.*

注意：此部分试题在**答题卡**2上；请在**答题卡**2上作答。

Part IV   Reading Comprehension (Reading in Depth)

(25 minutes)

Section A

Directions: *In this section, there is a passage with ten blanks. You are required to select one word for each blank from a list of choices given in a word bank following the passage. Read the passage through carefully before making your choices. Each choice in the bank is identified by a letter. Please mark the corresponding letter for each item on **Answer Sheet 2** with a single line through the centre. **You may not use any of the words in the bank more than once.***

The Chinese people, in their drinking of tea, place much significance on the act of "savoring." "Savoring tea" is not only a way to 47 good tea from mediocre tea, but also how people take 48 in their reverie and in tea-drinking itself. Snatching a bit of leisure from a busy schedule, making a kettle of strong tea, securing a serene space, and serving and drinking tea by yourself can help banish fatigue and frustration, improve your thinking ability and 49 you with enthusiasm. You may also imbibe it slowly in small sips to appreciate the subtle allure of tea-drinking, until your spirits 50 up and up into a sublime aesthetic realm. Buildings, gardens, ornaments and tea sets are the elements that form the ambience for savoring tea. A 51 , refreshing, comfortable and neat locale is certainly 52 for drinking tea. Chinese gardens are well known in the world and beautiful Chinese landscapes are too 53 to count. Teahouses tucked away in gardens and nestled beside the natural beauty of mountains and rivers are enchanting places of repose for people to rest and 54 themselves.

China is a country with a time-honored 55 and a land of ceremony and decorum. Whenever guests visit, it is necessary to make and serve tea to them. Before serving tea, you may ask them for their preferences as to what kind of tea they fancy and serve them the tea in the most appropriate teacups. In the course of serving tea, the host should take careful note of how much water is remaining in the cups and in the kettle. Usually, if the tea is made in a teacup, boiling water should be added after half of the cup has been consumed; and thus the cup is kept filled so that the tea retains the same bouquet and remains pleasantly warm throughout the entire course of tea-drinking. Snacks, sweets and other dishes may be served at tea time to 56 the fragrance of the tea and to allay one's hunger.

注意：此部分试题请在**答题卡** 2 上作答。

A) recreate	I) indignity
B) tranquil	J) inspire
C) stimulate	K) complement
D) desirable	L) delight
E) discern	M) monotonous
F) miraculous	N) soar
G) numerous	O) civilization
H) primarily	

Section B

Directions: *There are 2 passages in this section. Each passage is followed by some questions or unfinished statements. For each of them there are four choices marked A), B), C) and D). You should decide on the best choice and mark the corresponding letter on* **Answer Sheet 2** *with a single line through the centre.*

Passage One

Questions 57 to 61 are based on the following passage.

For laymen ethnology is probably the most interesting of the biological science for the very reason that it concerns animals in their normal activities and therefore, if we wish, we can assess the possible dangers and advantages in our own behavioral roots. Ethnology also is interesting methodologically because it combines in new ways very scrupulous field observations with experimentations in laboratories.

The field workers have had some handicaps in winning respect for themselves. For a long time they were considered as little better than amateur animal-watchers — certainly not scientists, since their facts were not gained by experimental procedures; they could not conform to the hard-and-fast rule that a problem set up and solved by one scientist must be tested by other scientists, under identical conditions and reaching identical results. Of course many situations in the lives of animals simply cannot be rehearsed and controlled in this way. The fall flocking of wild birds can't be, or the homing of animals over long distances, or even details of spontaneous family relationships. Since these never can be reproduced in a laboratory, are they then not worth knowing about?

The ethnologists who choose field work have got themselves out of this impasse by greatly refining the techniques of observing. At the start of a project all the animals to be studied are live-trapped, marked individually, and released. Motion pictures, often in color, provide permanent records of their subsequent activities. Recording of the animals' voices by electrical sound equipment is considered essential, and the most meticulous notes are kept of all that occurs. With this material other biologists, far from the scene, later can verify the reports. Moreover, two field observers often go out together, checking each other's observations right there in the field.

Ethnology, the word, is derived from the Greek *ethos*, meaning the characteristic traits or features which distinguish a group — any particular group of people or, in biology, a group of animals such as a species. Ethnologists have the intention of studying "the whole sequence of acts which constitute an animal's behavior." In abridged dictionaries ethnology is sometimes defined simply as "the objective study of animal behavior," and ethnologists do emphasize their wish to eliminate myths.

注意：此部分试题请在**答题卡2**上作答。

57. What's the meaning of the word "laymen" in the first sentence?
    A) People who are amateur biologists.
    B) People who love animals.
    C) People who are not trained as biologists.
    D) People who stand aside.

58. "The field workers have had some handicaps in winning respect for themselves." This sentence implies that _____.
    A) ethnologists who work in the field are handicapped
    B) ethnologists are looked down upon when they work in the field
    C) ethnologists meet with a lot of difficulties when doing field work
    D) ethnologists have problems in winning recognition as scientists

59. According to the explanation of the scientific rule of experiment in the passage, "hard-and-fast" means experiment procedures _____.
    A) must be carried out in a strict and quick way
    B) must be followed strictly to avoid false and loose results
    C) are difficult and quick to follow
    D) are hard and unreasonable for scientists to observe

60. What is ethnology according to the passage?
    A) An old Greek science.
    B) A science for amateurs.
    C) A pseudo-science.
    D) A new branch of biology.

61. The meaning of the underlined words in "details of spontaneous family relationships" can be expressed as _____.
    A) animals acting like a natural family
    B) natural family relationships
    C) animal family behavior that cannot be preplanned or controlled
    D) quickly occurring family relationships

Passage Two

Questions 62 to 66 are based on the following passage.

Can electricity cause cancer? In a society that literally runs on electric power, the very idea seems preposterous. But for more than a decade, a growing hand of scientists and journalists has pointed to studies that seem to link exposure to electromagnetic fields with increased risk of leukemia and other malignancies. The implications are unsettling, to say the least, since everyone comes into contact with such fields, which are generated by everything electrical, from power lines and antennas to personal computers and microwave ovens. Because evidence on the subject is inconclusive and often contradictory, it has been hard to decide whether concern about the health effects of electricity is legitimate.

Now the alarmists have gained some qualified support from the U. S. Environmental Protection Agency. In the executive summary of a new scientific review, released in draft from late last week, the EPA has put forward what amounts to the most serious government warning to date. The agency tentatively concludes that scientific evidence "suggests a causal link" between extremely low-frequency electromagnetic fields — those having very long wavelengths — and leukemia, lymphoma and brain cancer. While the report falls short of classifying ELF fields as probable carcinogens, it does identify the common 60-hertz magnetic field as "a possible, but not proven, cause of cancer in humans."

The report is no reason to panic — or even to lose sleep. If there is a cancer risk, it is a small one. The evidence is still so controversial that the draft stirred a great deal of debate within the Bush Administration, and the EPA released it over strong objections from the Pentagon and the White House.

At the heart of the debate is a simple and well understood physical phenomenon: when an electric current passes through a wire, it generates an electromagnetic field that exerts forces on surrounding objects. For many years, scientists dismissed any suggestion that such forces might be harmful, primarily because they are so extraordinarily weak.

Doubts about weak, so-called nonionizing radiation began to grow in 1979, when a study of cancer rates among Colorado schoolchildren found that those who lived near power lines had two to three times as great a chance of developing cancer. The link seemed so unlikely that when power companies paid to have the original study replicated, most scientists expected the results to be negative. In fact, the subsequent study supported the original findings, which have since been buttressed by reports showing increased cancer rates among electrical workers.

While many experts still express skepticism, there has been a definite shift of attitude in the scientific community about the possible health effects of electromagnetic fields, as a recent series in *Science* magazine made clear.

注意：此部分试题请在**答题卡**2 上作答。

62. "In a society that literally runs on electric power, the very idea seems preposterous." What does the sentence imply?
    A) Because people depend mostly on electricity, they cannot get cancer.
    B) The idea that electricity causes cancer seems absurd in a society that almost depends on electric power to develop.
    C) People get cancer easily in the society that runs mainly on electricity.
    D) It is believed that people are likely to get cancer in a society that runs mainly on electricity.

63. What is the author's attitude towards the conclusion of scientists that the exposure to electromagnetic fields might increase the risk of leukemia and other malignancies?
    A) They haven't got strong evidence.   C) The author agrees to the conclusion.
    B) It is believable.   D) Their conclusion is reasonable.

64. Which of the following statements is true?
    A) It has been proved that the common 60-hertz magnetic field is a cause of cancer in humans.
    B) People pay much attention to the recent EPA report.
    C) There is no controversy between the White House and EPA on such a point that some kinds of cancer are caused by electromagnetic fields.
    D) The consequent study could not prove the findings that those who lived near power lines were easier to develop cancer.

65. The meaning of the underlined words in "While the report falls short of classifying ELF fields as probable carcinogens" can be expressed as _____.
    A) is shown to be not true
    B) is not good enough
    C) fails to reach the standard that people expected or need
    D) does not have enough of work

66. Why did power companies pay to have the original study replicated?
    A) Because the power companies refused to accept the results of the study of cancer rates in 1979.
    B) Because the power companies wanted to know the health conditions of their workers.
    C) Because the power companies planned to increase their sales.
    D) Because the power companies were interested in this kind of study.

Part V   Cloze   (15 minutes)

Directions: *There are 20 blanks in the following passage. For each blank there are four choices marked A), B), C) and D) on the right side of the paper. You should choose the ONE that best fits into the passage. Then mark the corresponding letter on **Answer Sheet 2** with a single line through the centre.*

注意：此部分试题请在**答题卡**2 上作答。

My grandparents believed you were either honest or you weren't. There was no state in __67__. They had a simple motto __68__ on their living-room wall："Life is like a field of newly fallen snow；__69__ I choose to walk every step will __70__." They didn't have to talk about it — they demonstrated the motto by the __71__ they lived.

They understand instinctively that integrity means having a personal __72__ of morality and ethics that is not relative __73__ the situation at hand. Integrity is an inner standard for __74__ our behavior. Unfortunately, integrity is in short __75__ today — and getting scarcer. __76__ it is the real bottom line in every __77__ of society. And it is something we must demand of __78__. A good test for

67. A) middle   C) half
    B) between   D) center
68. A) hanging   C) hangs
    B) hanged   D) to hang
69. A) which   C) where
    B) what   D) and
70. A) show   C) reveal
    B) say   D) express
71. A) method   C) manner
    B) way   D) road
72. A) measure   C) self
    B) agreement   D) standard
73. A) to   C) in
    B) with   D) on
74. A) analyzing   C) judging
    B) commenting   D) criticizing
75. A) store   C) storage
    B) supply   D) use
76. A) But   C) Therefore
    B) Thus   D) So
77. A) realm   C) time
    B) place   D) area
78. A) ourselves   C) themselves
    B) myself   D) himself

this value is to look at __79__ I call the Integrity Triad（三元素）, which __80__ of three key principles：	79. A) that C) what B) which D) whether 80. A) makes up C) constitutes B) consists D) composes
Stand __81__ for your convictions in the face of personal pressure. When you know you are right，you can't __82__.	81. A) strong C) determined B) firm D) powerful 82. A) break down C) go down B) give in D) stick to
Always give others __83__ that is rightfully theirs. Don't be afraid of those who might have a better idea or who might even be smarter than you are.	83. A) trust C) success B) credit D) criticism
Be honest and open about who you really are. Be yourself. Don't __84__ in a personal	84. A) take C) relate B) commit D) engage
cover-up of areas that are __85__ in your life. When it's tough，do it tough.	85. A) pleasant C) unpleasant B) enjoyable D) good
Self-respect and a clear __86__ are powerful components of integrity and are the basis for enriching your relationship with others.	86. A) conscience C) realization B) conscious D) awareness

Part VI   Translation   (5 minutes)

Directions: *Complete the sentences on **Answer Sheet 2** by translating into English the Chinese given in brackets.*

注意：此部分试题请在**答题卡** 2 上作答。

87. The size of the furniture should be _____
（与房间的大小相称）.

88. Not until many years later _____
（整个事件的真相才为世人知晓）.

89. _____（不管你从哪个角度看），nuclear power will reduce the problem of an energy shortage.

90. Though we had put forward a proposal to reduce cost，the board members

_____（似乎没有认真考虑）.

91. He _____（多次死里逃生）during the war but stood
    loyal to his country even though he underwent many ordeals.

答题卡1 (Answer Sheet 1)

学校:
姓名:
划线要求	

准		考		证		号	

[0]	[0]	[0]	[0]	[0]	[0]	[0]	[0]	[0]	[0]	[0]	[0]	[0]	[0]	[0]
[1]	[1]	[1]	[1]	[1]	[1]	[1]	[1]	[1]	[1]	[1]	[1]	[1]	[1]	[1]
[2]	[2]	[2]	[2]	[2]	[2]	[2]	[2]	[2]	[2]	[2]	[2]	[2]	[2]	[2]
[3]	[3]	[3]	[3]	[3]	[3]	[3]	[3]	[3]	[3]	[3]	[3]	[3]	[3]	[3]
[4]	[4]	[4]	[4]	[4]	[4]	[4]	[4]	[4]	[4]	[4]	[4]	[4]	[4]	[4]
[5]	[5]	[5]	[5]	[5]	[5]	[5]	[5]	[5]	[5]	[5]	[5]	[5]	[5]	[5]
[6]	[6]	[6]	[6]	[6]	[6]	[6]	[6]	[6]	[6]	[6]	[6]	[6]	[6]	[6]
[7]	[7]	[7]	[7]	[7]	[7]	[7]	[7]	[7]	[7]	[7]	[7]	[7]	[7]	[7]
[8]	[8]	[8]	[8]	[8]	[8]	[8]	[8]	[8]	[8]	[8]	[8]	[8]	[8]	[8]
[9]	[9]	[9]	[9]	[9]	[9]	[9]	[9]	[9]	[9]	[9]	[9]	[9]	[9]	[9]

Part I　　　　　　　　　　**Writing**　　　　　　　　　**(30 minutes)**

Directions: *For this part, you are allowed 30 minutes to write a composition on the topic Keeping Healthy. You should write at least 120 words following the outline given below in Chinese:*

1. 健康的重要性
2. 保持健康的途径
3. 我的做法

Keeping Healthy

答题卡 1 (Answer Sheet 1)

Part II   Reading Comprehension (Skimming and Scanning)   (15 minutes)

1. [Y] [N] [NG]   2. [Y] [N] [NG]   3. [Y] [N] [NG]   4. [Y] [N] [NG]
5. [Y] [N] [NG]   6. [Y] [N] [NG]   7. [Y] [N] [NG]

8. _____ section can appear in any position in the test after the analytical writing section，and answers to the questions in this section will not count toward your scores.

9. Modified versions of verbal and quantitative questions may be included in the test you take；these modifications can be substantial or _____.

10. The GRE Program is presently investigating _____ that have been published in GRE practice materials.

答题卡 2 (Answer Sheet 2)

学校:		准　　考　　证　　号

学校:

姓名:

划线要求

[0]	[0]	[0]	[0]	[0]	[0]	[0]	[0]	[0]	[0]	[0]	[0]	[0]	[0]	[0]
[1]	[1]	[1]	[1]	[1]	[1]	[1]	[1]	[1]	[1]	[1]	[1]	[1]	[1]	[1]
[2]	[2]	[2]	[2]	[2]	[2]	[2]	[2]	[2]	[2]	[2]	[2]	[2]	[2]	[2]
[3]	[3]	[3]	[3]	[3]	[3]	[3]	[3]	[3]	[3]	[3]	[3]	[3]	[3]	[3]
[4]	[4]	[4]	[4]	[4]	[4]	[4]	[4]	[4]	[4]	[4]	[4]	[4]	[4]	[4]
[5]	[5]	[5]	[5]	[5]	[5]	[5]	[5]	[5]	[5]	[5]	[5]	[5]	[5]	[5]
[6]	[6]	[6]	[6]	[6]	[6]	[6]	[6]	[6]	[6]	[6]	[6]	[6]	[6]	[6]
[7]	[7]	[7]	[7]	[7]	[7]	[7]	[7]	[7]	[7]	[7]	[7]	[7]	[7]	[7]
[8]	[8]	[8]	[8]	[8]	[8]	[8]	[8]	[8]	[8]	[8]	[8]	[8]	[8]	[8]
[9]	[9]	[9]	[9]	[9]	[9]	[9]	[9]	[9]	[9]	[9]	[9]	[9]	[9]	[9]

Part III　Section A　　　　　　　　　　　Section B

11. [A] [B] [C] [D]　16. [A] [B] [C] [D]　21. [A] [B] [C] [D]　26. [A] [B] [C] [D]　31. [A] [B] [C] [D]

12. [A] [B] [C] [D]　17. [A] [B] [C] [D]　22. [A] [B] [C] [D]　27. [A] [B] [C] [D]　32. [A] [B] [C] [D]

13. [A] [B] [C] [D]　18. [A] [B] [C] [D]　23. [A] [B] [C] [D]　28. [A] [B] [C] [D]　33. [A] [B] [C] [D]

14. [A] [B] [C] [D]　19. [A] [B] [C] [D]　24. [A] [B] [C] [D]　29. [A] [B] [C] [D]　34. [A] [B] [C] [D]

15. [A] [B] [C] [D]　20. [A] [B] [C] [D]　25. [A] [B] [C] [D]　30. [A] [B] [C] [D]　35. [A] [B] [C] [D]

Part III　Section C

The new medical insurance system that will see gradual introduction this year will change the life and healthcare for China's 400 million (36) _____ residents.

Unlike now, employees of (37) _____ owned enterprises will no longer be (38) _____ under the new (39) _____. People who have enjoyed virtually free medical care working for government offices and state-owned businesses will have to learn to be (40) _____ when dealing with health problems. Employees of China's state-owned enterprises and institutions (41) _____ enjoyed free medical care with expenses (42) _____ by the government and state-owned enterprises. According to the new system, both the employers and the employees will share medical expenses.

Enterprises will contribute six percent of the entire (43) _____ salaries to medical care insurance. (44) _____.

(45) _____

_____.

(46) _____

_____.

答题卡 2 (Answer Sheet 2)

Part IV   Section A   **Section B**

47. [A][B][C][D][E][F][G][H][I][J][K][L][M][N][O]   57. [A] [B] [C] [D]
48. [A][B][C][D][E][F][G][H][I][J][K][L][M][N][O]   58. [A] [B] [C] [D]
49. [A][B][C][D][E][F][G][H][I][J][K][L][M][N][O]   59. [A] [B] [C] [D]
50. [A][B][C][D][E][F][G][H][I][J][K][L][M][N][O]   60. [A] [B] [C] [D]
51. [A][B][C][D][E][F][G][H][I][J][K][L][M][N][O]   61. [A] [B] [C] [D]
52. [A][B][C][D][E][F][G][H][I][J][K][L][M][N][O]   62. [A] [B] [C] [D]
53. [A][B][C][D][E][F][G][H][I][J][K][L][M][N][O]   63. [A] [B] [C] [D]
54. [A][B][C][D][E][F][G][H][I][J][K][L][M][N][O]   64. [A] [B] [C] [D]
55. [A][B][C][D][E][F][G][H][I][J][K][L][M][N][O]   65. [A] [B] [C] [D]
56. [A][B][C][D][E][F][G][H][I][J][K][L][M][N][O]   66. [A] [B] [C] [D]

Part V   **Cloze**   **(15 minutes)**

67. [A] [B] [C] [D]   72. [A] [B] [C] [D]   77. [A] [B] [C] [D]   82. [A] [B] [C] [D]
68. [A] [B] [C] [D]   73. [A] [B] [C] [D]   78. [A] [B] [C] [D]   83. [A] [B] [C] [D]
69. [A] [B] [C] [D]   74. [A] [B] [C] [D]   79. [A] [B] [C] [D]   84. [A] [B] [C] [D]
70. [A] [B] [C] [D]   75. [A] [B] [C] [D]   80. [A] [B] [C] [D]   85. [A] [B] [C] [D]
71. [A] [B] [C] [D]   76. [A] [B] [C] [D]   81. [A] [B] [C] [D]   86. [A] [B] [C] [D]

Part VI   **Translation**   **(5 minutes)**

87. _____

88. _____

89. _____

90. _____

91. _____

PRACTICE TEST 4

Part I　Writing　　　　　　　　　　　　　　　(30 minutes)

注意：此部分试题在**答题卡** 1 上。

Part II　Reading Comprehension (Skimming and Scanning)
(15 minutes)

Directions: *In this part, you will have 15 minutes to go over the passage quickly and answer the questions on* **Answer Sheet 1**.
　　For questions 1 – 7, mark
　　Y *(for YES)*　　　　　　*if the statement agrees with the information given in the passage;*
　　N *(for NO)*　　　　　　*if the statement contradicts the information given in the passage;*
　　NG *(for NOT GIVEN)*　　*if the information is not given in the passage.*
　　For questions 8 – 10, complete the sentences with the information given in the passage.

Film Festival Application Instructions

Eligibility（申请资格）

　　The 2007 Academy Film Festival Grants are directed to festivals occurring during the 2008 calendar year. Funding will be distributed in December 2007.

　　Grants are not offered to individual festivals in successive years.

　　Only festivals based in the United States that have held five festivals, and the latest in 2006, are eligible to apply.

　　Screening programs, be they weekly/monthly screening series or end-of-semester student screening programs, are not eligible to apply. Festivals that do not screen films in a theatrical setting are also not eligible to apply.

　　Eligible film festivals may apply for grants at three funding levels, depending on the cash budget of the festival.

- Festivals with cash budgets of less than $200,000 can apply for a grant of up to $10,000.
- Festivals with cash budgets from $200,000 to $600,000 can apply for a grant of up to $20,000.
- Festivals with cash budgets greater than $600,000 can apply for a grant of up to $30,000.

To maximize the distribution of funding to festivals, the Academy's Festival Grants Committee may approve grants for less than the amount requested. In recent years, this has been the case more often than not.

Guidelines and Instructions

Completed applications must be received at the Festival Grants office by June 29, 2007. Under no circumstances will extensions be granted.

Grant requests must target one or more concrete elements within the festival. Festivals may not request general support. Proposals should be specific and thorough in their description of the elements for which the request is made.

Film festivals are encouraged to submit proposals that make festival events more accessible to the general public, especially to underserved segments of the population; that give screening opportunities to minority and less visible filmmakers; and that bring the public into contact with films and filmmakers.

Grants may be used to support seminars, conferences or other educational events within a festival.

Grants may not be used to support any of the following: the screening of an individual new film; competitions or awards programs; the screening of works produced specifically for television or any other event or program that primarily involves work produced for television; parties, hospitality suites, tribute dinners or similar festival activities; the development, production or completion of motion pictures.

All proposals must be accompanied by four copies of the most recent festival program book.

All proposals must include proof of a festival's non-profit status.

While the festival elements described in the proposal carry the most weight, factors such as the focus of a festival and its geographical location may also be considered in making the final determinations. The manner in which the Academy will be acknowledged during the festival also is of some importance.

Festivals will receive notification of their status by November 2007.

Press releases concerning festival grants can be found at http://www.oscars.org/press.

Application Template (申请模式)

Your proposal should be completed and assembled according to the following template.

Note: Do not staple the pages. Do not insert title or section heading pages between the proposal segments.

(1) Application form

Fill out the form completely. The application form is a downloadable and fillable PDF document. Please make sure that it includes your current contact information as well as statistics from your most recent festival.

(2) Proposal — no longer than two pages.

Request statement — a single sentence describing the proposed project and the grant amount requested. (This statement should also appear on the application form.)

Proposal paragraphs — several paragraphs outlining the element(s) for which support is requested. They should provide as much detail as possible, as briefly as possible and should mention how the element(s) will affect the festival's current and projected audience. You may offer alternatives here to give the committee an opportunity to select from among several scenarios.

Mission Statement — one or more paragraphs broadly describing the goals of the festival as well as delineating how each proposed element supports those goals.

History of the festival — a brief description of the festival, including some past highlights (events, tributes, films, honored guests, etc.).

Description of the parent organization — a brief outline of the yearly activities of the festival's parent organization, if it is film-related. If you have already used your two page allotment, do not include this segment. If you have previously received an Academy Festival Grant, do not include this paragraph.

(3) Acknowledgments — no longer than a single page.

A list of the ways in which the festival will acknowledge the Academy's grant. As stated in the Guidelines and Instructions page, you might include here, as appropriate, mention of the Academy's support in the festival program's sponsorship pages and elsewhere; a full-page ad in the program; ability to screen the Academy trailer before selected screenings; verbal acknowledgment of the Academy at various events, etc.

(4) Income/expense statement — no longer than two pages.

This should include a broad financial overview of the most recent festival.

(5) Budget — no longer than two pages.

This should include a budget for the proposed element(s), a simple breakdown of anticipated costs and an overview of the entire projected festival budget.

(6) Proof of festival's non-profit status.

(7) Four copies of the most recent festival program — or other similar material.

Completed application packages should be sent to：

Gale Anne Hurd

Chair，Festival Grants Committee

Academy of Motion Picture Arts and Sciences

1313 North Vine Street

Hollywood，CA 90028 – 8107

Applications must be received by June 29, 2007. Under no circumstances will extensions be granted.

Packages may be mailed or sent via a delivery service such as FedEx or UPS.

For additional information，call (310) 247 – 3031 or e-mail grants@oscars.org.

注意：此部分试题请在**答题卡** 1 上作答；8 – 10 题在**答题卡** 1 上。

1. This passage instructs the reader how to apply for the 2007 Academy Film Festival Grants.

2. Film festivals based in Canada are also eligible to apply.

3. In recent years，the Academy's Festival Grants Committee often approves grants for less than the amount requested.

4. Applications after June 29, 2007 will not be granted.

5. Grants can be used to support the development，production or completion of motion pictures.

6. The festival elements described in the proposal are the most important factor in making the final determinations.

7. The application form can be downloaded at http://www.oscars.org.

Part III   Listening Comprehension   (35 minutes)

Section A

Directions: *In this section, you will hear 8 short conversations and 2 long conversations. At the end of each conversation, one or more questions will be asked about what was said. Both the conversation and the questions will be spoken only once. After each question there will be a pause. During the pause, you must read the four choices marked A), B), C) and D), and decide which is the best answer. Then mark the corresponding letter on **Answer Sheet 2** with a single line through the centre.*

注意：此部分试题请在**答题卡** 2 上作答。

11. A) Mary didn't call.

    B) Mary will call next time she comes to town.

    C) Mary called to say that she would come to town some time later.

    D) Mary hoped to come and see them some other time.

12. A) Outside an art gallery.　　C) In an exhibition.

    B) Outside a bookstore.　　D) In front of a library.

13. A) She was beside herself with joy.

    B) She cried because she didn't like the gift.

    C) She was sad because the gift was squeezed out of shape.

    D) She gave her son a present in return.

14. A) A new car.

    B) A car shown to and driven by customers.

    C) A used car for sale.

    D) An old car shown to customers.

15. A) They have two children already.

    B) Mrs. Taylor wishes to have children，but her husband doesn't.

    C) They will start a family as soon as they get married.

    D) They don't want children for the time being.

16. A) In New York.　　C) In Washington.

    B) In Boston.　　D) In Michigan.

17. A) Eat somewhere else.　　C) Wait in line.

    B) Go to the restaurant.　　D) Have a test.

18. A) The bus is usually late when it snows.

    B) The time on her schedule may no longer be correct.

    C) She isn't sure where her bus schedule is.

    D) She can't give the man a ride to work tomorrow.

Questions 19 to 22 are based on the conversation you have just heard.

19. A) They are just friends.　　C) They are husband and wife.

    B) They are going to get married.　　D) They are classmates.

20. A) She is a feminist.

    B) She is willing to be a housewife.

    C) She wants to depend on the man financially.

    D) She thinks women are more special than men.

21. A) To stand when they enter a room.
    B) To open car doors and front doors for them.
    C) To share the housework with them.
    D) To let them sit first and eat first.

22. A) He thinks the woman's opinion is old-fashioned.
    B) He doesn't want to marry the woman for her opinion.
    C) He agrees with her completely.
    D) He cannot understand her.

Questions 23 to 25 are based on the conversation you have just heard.

23. A) They are looking for an apartment to rent.
    B) They are looking for a job.
    C) They are selling apartments.
    D) They are discussing how to furnish an apartment.

24. A) Cheap one-bedroom apartment near a park.
    B) Cheap two-bedroom apartment on a quiet street.
    C) Cheap one-bedroom apartment on a noisy street.
    D) Cheap two-bedroom apartment without furniture.

25. A) $350.   C) $390.
    B) $400.   D) $415.

Section B

Directions: *In this section, you will hear 3 short passages. At the end of each passage, you will hear some questions. Both the passage and the questions will be spoken only once. After you hear a question, you must choose the best answer from the four choices marked A), B), C) and D). Then mark the corresponding letter on* **Answer Sheet 2** *with a single line through the centre.*

注意：此部分试题请在**答题卡 2** 上作答。

Passage One

Questions 26 to 29 are based on the passage you have just heard.

26. A) In Victorian times.   C) In 1979.
    B) In 1969.   D) It's not clear.

27. A) It was opened in the 20th century.

   B) It was built under the busy streets of London.

   C) A lot of workers worked for the Victoria Line.

   D) No one checks and collects the tickets on the platform.

28. A) To check the train.   C) To start the train.

   B) To stop the train.   D) To send signals.

29. A) The train will stop automatically if no signal is sent from the command spot.

   B) Most of the control work is done by computers but not by human beings.

   C) It's very safe to travel on the Victoria Line.

   D) Accidents occasionally happen on the Victoria Line.

Passage Two

Questions 30 to 32 are based on the passage you have just heard.

30. A) Because there was a draught and mustard seeds were difficult to get.

   B) Because the couple did not think much about the wise man's words.

   C) Because the searching for the ingredient took many months.

   D) Because all of the families had experienced loved ones' death.

31. A) We should always ask for others' help.

   B) It is possible to bring a dead person back to life.

   C) Death is natural and is part of our life cycle.

   D) Happiness is the best medicine for sorrow.

32. A) They began to live a normal life again.

   B) They were so disappointed that they killed themselves.

   C) They were so sad that they became seriously ill.

   D) They adopted a child from another family.

Passage Three

Questions 33 to 35 are based on the passage you have just heard.

33. A) To learn from the handicapped.   C) To help the handicapped learn.

   B) To teach people useful things.   D) To train gifted people.

34. A) To protect its students.

   B) To serve the community well.

   C) To offer help to the homeless.

D) To help its students become independent.

35. A) Most of it is done in nearby towns.
    B) Most of it is done in students' homes.
    C) Most of it is done in special schools.
    D) Most of it is done in the Bancroft Community.

Section C

Directions: *In this section, you will hear a passage three times. When the passage is read for the first time, you should listen carefully for its general idea. When the passage is read for the second time, you are required to fill in the blanks numbered from 36 to 43 with the exact words you have just heard. For blanks numbered from 44 to 46 you are required to fill in the missing information. For these blanks, you can either use the exact words you have just heard or write down the main points in your own words. Finally, when the passage is read for the third time, you should check what you have written.*

注意：此部分试题在**答题卡 2** 上；请在**答题卡 2** 上作答。

Part IV Reading Comprehension (Reading in Depth)

(25 minutes)

Section A

Directions: *In this section, there is a passage with ten blanks. You are required to select one word for each blank from a list of choices given in a word bank following the passage. Read the passage through carefully before making your choices. Each choice in the bank is identified by a letter. Please mark the corresponding letter for each item on Answer Sheet 2 with a single line through the centre. You may not use any of the words in the bank more than once.*

American agriculture, one of the great ___47___ in which the Americans take pride, has produced ___48___ foods and other ___49___ enough to feed the nation and bring in great sums of cash from world markets by exporting its surplus products of grain, cotton, peanut, soybean, tobacco, vegetable, fruit, livestock, poultry, egg, dairy and other animal ___50___.

Modernization of farming operations and ___51___ of advanced agricultural science are the secret of the miraculous achievement. During the past 35 years, ___52___ changes have taken place in farms, ranches, orchards, plantations, poultry farms, dairy farms throughout states: Arkansas, Illinois, Indiana, Kansas, Kentucky, Michigan, Minnesota, Mississippi, Missouri, Nebraska, Ohio, Tennessee, Texas, Wisconsin — the Middle West, the breadbasket of America. A great army of agricultural machines take all manipulations on farms, __53__ humans and horses — plowing land, sowing seeds, planting seedlings and saplings, spreading fertilizers, spraying pesticides, irrigating fields, harvesting crops, drying grains, picking tomatoes, collecting potatoes, milking cows, feeding chickens, watering livestock, hatching chickens, gathering eggs, cleaning pens, removing manure, washing cattle, etc. Besides, they prepare hybrid feed for cattle and chickens by __54__ computers to monitor the process and determine the proper ingredients. They control and adjust the temperature and moisture inside greenhouses using sensors and automatic devices. Veterinary service helps them to stamp out __55__ diseases that would otherwise lead to heavy losses of livestock and poultry. TV, telephones can help them to get information just in time to prevent disaster, to react to markets, and to __56__ professionals.

注意：此部分试题请在**答题卡**2上作答。

A) application	I) programming
B) reject	J) affluent
C) epidemic	K) progressing
D) revolutionary	L) necessities
E) enlist	M) achievements
F) replacing	N) physically
G) consult	O) products
H) worldwide	

Section B

Directions: *There are 2 passages in this section. Each passage is followed by some questions or unfinished statements. For each of them there are four choices marked A), B), C) and D). You should decide on the best choice and mark the corresponding letter on **Answer Sheet 2** with a single line through the centre.*

Passage One

Questions 57 to 61 are based on the following passage.

The e-mail facilitates communication, shrinks the world and saves the office secretary a huge amount of work. But the whole concept of e-mail is tragedy, for it is an ephemeral thing, a symbol of our short-termism and our disregard of history, transferring our records from the tangible to the intangible.

It's not that I'm a technophobe, but I recognize e-mail for what it is: a symbol of a civilization which is turning its back on measured thought and permanence, which lives in the instant thrill of the here-and-now-and-gone-forever; instant gratification in an age of information overload, no time to savor anything.

The National Library of Scotland, belatedly, is creating an archive of blogs, journals and e-mails written by leading Scots. Curators will harvest websites and inboxes for things of cultural significance, describing it as a "digital repository" containing what will come to be regarded as the manuscripts of the 21st century.

It all sounds very admirable: the e-mails of JK Rowling, Ian Rankin and Alasdair Gray captured for posterity. (JK's e-mails to her investment manager would be the best read of all. Except those are precisely the ones that will never be kept and never be seen.)

I hope I'm wrong, but it is easy to be skeptical about a) the archive's longevity and b) its ability to mine the important stuff. As any biographer knows, the best source of a person's soul are not the letters they keep for posterity, but those never intended to be seen again: the casual opinion, the throwaway jibe, the expression of intense, hidden love.

For e-mails, magnify that effect a zillion times. Treasure troves of informal letters from famous people still turn up, decades after they were written. E-mails will never do so. Text messages, another vital source of information, have even less chance of surviving.

Historians and biographers of the famous, I fear, face a very lean future in a digital age. But you don't have to be famous, or seek to research the famous, to feel a sense of loss, of a void opening up. We leave no footprints now.

Over a lifetime, most of us keep letters and cards from friends and family, a precious repository of love, wisdom and memories. I even inherited a letter written on a ship by a brave female cousin emigrating to Van Diemen's Land, as Tasmania was known, from Northern Ireland in 1783 — spidery ink on two sides of paper thinner than tissue that somehow traveled safely back around the globe.

But all this will go: the handwriting which gives its own separate clues to an age and an individual; the type of paper; the art of the envelope; the tear stains and the smell of long-forgotten experiences.

Oh, hit the delete key and stop being such a has-been.

注意：此部分试题请在**答题卡 2** 上作答。

57. What does the passage mainly tell us?
    A) The importance of people's e-mail inbox.
    B) The situation of the historians in the information age.
    C) Digital repository of some leading Scots.
    D) The negative effects of e-mail in a digital age.

58. What does the word "mine" mean in the sentence "its ability to mine the important stuff "?
    A) To dig holes in the ground in order to find and obtain coal，diamonds，etc.
    B) To delve into an abundant source to extract something of value.
    C) To find something unusual in the archive.
    D) To show the function of the archive.

59. What does "that effect" refer to in the sentence "For e-mails，magnify that effect a zillion times"?
    A) The archive's longevity.
    B) The archive's ability to mine the important stuff.
    C) E-mail — the best source of a person's soul.
    D) E-mail's inability to reproduce treasure troves.

60. Why does the author cite the letter written by a female cousin as an example?
    A) To show his admiration for her bravery.
    B) To express his gratitude to his cousin.
    C) To express his objection to e-mails.
    D) To voice his dissatisfaction with the present society.

61. What's the author's attitude towards e-mail in a digital age?
    A) It is the most important in our daily life.
    B) It can capture important stuff in the archive.
    C) People cannot live without an e-mail inbox in the information era.
    D) We should treasure the precious old forms of keeping our history，which cannot be done only through e-mail.

Passage Two

Questions 62 to 66 are based on the following passage.

Once thought to be the ultimate restorative，and hailed by writers from Shakespeare to John Lennon，sleep is becoming a dirty word for the British. More and more

Britons are abandoning its soothing influence for round-the-clock hedonism as they go clubbing, shop at supermarkets, watch videos, surf the Web, and clock in to work at all hours.

Scientists estimate the British people now take about two hours' less sleep each day than their grandparents, damaging wakefulness in a way that poses serious health risks.

Last week, the Government launched a major advertising campaign — "Don't Drive Tired"— aimed at sleep-deprived motorists, who are now reckoned to be responsible for more road deaths than drunken drivers. "More and more people opt for 24-hour jobs and lifestyles. Consider a broker in Tokyo or London. He/she may have to monitor share or commodity prices around the clock. A significant proportion of the British public now does some kind of shift work and has regularly disrupted sleep, with figures constantly rising," said sleep researcher Dr. John Shneerson.

This month, scientists will hold a conference in a bid to highlight ways to help people survive lifestyles in which they risk being starved of sleep — a condition that leads to loss of attention, inability to make complex decisions and a tendency to suffer mild paranoid delusions. Studies of astronauts and solo sailors are expected to play a major role in pinpointing solutions.

Research by Dr. Claudio Stampi, who worked with lone yachtswoman Ellen Mac-Arthur, has shown that it is possible to survive on just four hours' sleep a day.

"You can't take drugs out in the mid-ocean. You have to be alert, but refreshed. The answer turned out to be catnapping," Stampi said. "You don't try to take a single long rest." Just keep having naps — four or five a night, each between 20 and 80 minutes long.

"Ellen never had a single bout of sleep that was longer than two hours — and that worked because the first bit of sleep a person takes is the most recuperative. The trick is to try to maximize that."

注意：此部分试题请在**答题卡** 2 上作答。

62. What seems to be the cause of sleep loss among many Britons?
    A) They can do well with little sleep.
    B) They have to monitor share or commodity prices around the clock.
    C) They prefer to take several catnaps instead of major sleep episodes.
    D) Their lifestyles.

63. According to Dr. Claudio Stampi's research, _____.
    A) it is unnecessary to sleep long hours

B) it is better to have shorter sleep times

C) it is almost impossible to survive on just four hours' sleep a day

D) it is possible to sleep fewer hours by taking several naps at night, yet stay energetic

64. What does the word "restorative" mean in the first sentence?

A) It is a thing that makes one feel better, stronger.

B) It is a good thing to do.

C) It is a bad thing to people's health.

D) It brings negative effects to health.

65. What were Shakespeare and John Lenon's attitudes towards sleep?

A) They were against it.

B) They welcomed it.

C) They described it as being very bad.

D) They ignored it.

66. What is the main idea of the passage?

A) What scientists have discovered about taking naps.

B) People in the UK are losing a lot of sleep.

C) The acute loss of sleep among UK people due to their lifestyles, and scientists' efforts to pinpoint solutions to the problem.

D) The negative effects brought about by sleep loss.

Part V Cloze

(15 minutes)

Directions: *There are 20 blanks in the following passage. For each blank there are four choices marked A), B), C) and D) on the right side of the paper. You should choose the ONE that best fits into the passage. Then mark the corresponding letter on Answer Sheet 2 with a single line through the centre.*

注意：此部分试题请在答题卡 2 上作答。

Japan is getting tough about recycling — and not in the paper and plastic kind of way. Starting in 2001, the country will require that all electronic goods — TVs, VCRs, stereos, and more — be recycled. But recycling won't be

__67__ consumers; __68__ , the devices will be sent to the original manufacturer for

proper __69__ .

The new law __70__ a few challenges to manufacturers, who are now rushing to set up collection networks and perfecting techniques to disassemble and recycle older products. __71__ an eye toward the future, they are also

__72__ easily recycled materials into new products. Plastics, a major component of most electronics products, pose a particular __73__ because they degrade __74__ age,

losing strength and flexibility __75__ reprocessed. NEC Corp. overcomes this problem by creating a plastic sandwich, __76__ the filling is 100 percent recycled plastic and the outer layers a mixture of 14 percent recycled material. The resulting plastic has sufficient strength and toughness for use as a casing for desktop PCs. The company, in __77__ with plastic resin（树脂）maker Sumitomo Dow, has also developed a new plastic, which engineers claim __78__ its mechanical properties through repeated recycling. NEC uses the plastic, __79__ is also flame-retardant（防火

的）, in battery cases for notebook PCs. __80__ , Matsushita Electric, maker of the Panasonic brand, is refraining from plastic __81__ magnesium（镁）. Magnesium, says the company,

67. A) put to   C) left to
    B) given to   D) left for
68. A) however   C) yet
    B) instead   D) still
69. A) disposition   C) displacement
    B) discharge   D) disposal
70. A) poses   C) takes
    B) introduces   D) puts

71. A) With   C) In
    B) By   D) Through
72. A) combining   C) connecting
    B) integrating   D) synchronizing
73. A) shortage   C) opposition
    B) question   D) obstacle
74. A) as   C) through
    B) with   D) throughout
75. A) even if   C) despite
    B) now that   D) if only
76. A) in which   C) in that
    B) for which   D) for that

77. A) intercourse   C) corporation
    B) cooperation   D) participation

78. A) retains   C) conserves
    B) maintains   D) reserves
79. A) that   C) what
    B) this   D) which
80. A) Meanwhile   C) Likewise
    B) Nevertheless   D) therefore
81. A) in favor of   C) in the light of
    B) in terms of   D) in relation to

is ideal __82__ recycling because it retains its	82.	A) of	C) to
		B) for	D) at
original strength __83__ repeated reprocessing. Matsushita has developed molding techniques to form magnesium into the case for a 21-inch TV. __84__ , the magnesium case and energy-saving features make the TV about twice as expensive as an ordinary model. The company hopes, __85__ , that increased use of magnesium will eventually __86__ down prices.	83.	A) in	C) for
		B) at	D) through
	84.	A) Unfortunately	C) Accidentally
		B) Misfortunately	D) Incidentally
	85.	A) additionally	C) moreover
		B) however	D) furthermore
	86.	A) count	C) take
		B) bring	D) pull

Part VI   Translation   (5 minutes)

Directions: *Complete the sentences on **Answer Sheet 2** by translating into English the Chinese given in brackets.*

注意：此部分试题请在**答题卡**2上作答。

87. Operating a vehicle while intoxicated is a serious offence，but few cases _____ _____（能成为报纸头条新闻）unless they involve serious injury.

88. The competition _____（本身并不重要）. What counts is your participation.

89. Looking at him，it's hard to imagine he once _____（前途无量）as a smart young New York book editor.

90. _____（我们的生活费用确实有很大增长），but the quality of our life has improved significantly because our wages have doubled over the same period.

91. _____（从顾客那里得到的反馈信息）who have tried the new soap is very positive.

答题卡 1 (Answer Sheet 1)

学校:
姓名:
划线要求

准		考		证			号							
[0]	[0]	[0]	[0]	[0]	[0]	[0]	[0]	[0]	[0]	[0]	[0]	[0]	[0]	[0]
[1]	[1]	[1]	[1]	[1]	[1]	[1]	[1]	[1]	[1]	[1]	[1]	[1]	[1]	[1]
[2]	[2]	[2]	[2]	[2]	[2]	[2]	[2]	[2]	[2]	[2]	[2]	[2]	[2]	[2]
[3]	[3]	[3]	[3]	[3]	[3]	[3]	[3]	[3]	[3]	[3]	[3]	[3]	[3]	[3]
[4]	[4]	[4]	[4]	[4]	[4]	[4]	[4]	[4]	[4]	[4]	[4]	[4]	[4]	[4]
[5]	[5]	[5]	[5]	[5]	[5]	[5]	[5]	[5]	[5]	[5]	[5]	[5]	[5]	[5]
[6]	[6]	[6]	[6]	[6]	[6]	[6]	[6]	[6]	[6]	[6]	[6]	[6]	[6]	[6]
[7]	[7]	[7]	[7]	[7]	[7]	[7]	[7]	[7]	[7]	[7]	[7]	[7]	[7]	[7]
[8]	[8]	[8]	[8]	[8]	[8]	[8]	[8]	[8]	[8]	[8]	[8]	[8]	[8]	[8]
[9]	[9]	[9]	[9]	[9]	[9]	[9]	[9]	[9]	[9]	[9]	[9]	[9]	[9]	[9]

Part I   Writing   (30 minutes)

Directions: *For this part, you are allowed 30 minutes to write a composition on the topic* ***The Advantages and Disadvantages of Computers.*** *You should write at least **120** words following the outline given below in Chinese:*

1. 应用电脑的好处
2. 应用电脑的负面影响
3. 结论

The Advantages and Disadvantages of Computers

答题卡 1 (Answer Sheet 1)

Part II   Reading Comprehension (Skimming and Scanning)   (15 minutes)

1. [Y] [N] [NG]   2. [Y] [N] [NG]   3. [Y] [N] [NG]   4. [Y] [N] [NG]
5. [Y] [N] [NG]   6. [Y] [N] [NG]   7. [Y] [N] [NG]

8. Proposal includes request statement, proposal paragraphs, mission statement, history of the festival and _____ .

9. Income/expense statement should include _____ of the most recent festival.

10. An overview of the _____ should be included in the budget.

答题卡 2 (Answer Sheet 2)

学校：		
姓名：		
划线要求		

准					考				证					号
[0]	[0]	[0]	[0]	[0]	[0]	[0]	[0]	[0]	[0]	[0]	[0]	[0]	[0]	[0]
[1]	[1]	[1]	[1]	[1]	[1]	[1]	[1]	[1]	[1]	[1]	[1]	[1]	[1]	[1]
[2]	[2]	[2]	[2]	[2]	[2]	[2]	[2]	[2]	[2]	[2]	[2]	[2]	[2]	[2]
[3]	[3]	[3]	[3]	[3]	[3]	[3]	[3]	[3]	[3]	[3]	[3]	[3]	[3]	[3]
[4]	[4]	[4]	[4]	[4]	[4]	[4]	[4]	[4]	[4]	[4]	[4]	[4]	[4]	[4]
[5]	[5]	[5]	[5]	[5]	[5]	[5]	[5]	[5]	[5]	[5]	[5]	[5]	[5]	[5]
[6]	[6]	[6]	[6]	[6]	[6]	[6]	[6]	[6]	[6]	[6]	[6]	[6]	[6]	[6]
[7]	[7]	[7]	[7]	[7]	[7]	[7]	[7]	[7]	[7]	[7]	[7]	[7]	[7]	[7]
[8]	[8]	[8]	[8]	[8]	[8]	[8]	[8]	[8]	[8]	[8]	[8]	[8]	[8]	[8]
[9]	[9]	[9]	[9]	[9]	[9]	[9]	[9]	[9]	[9]	[9]	[9]	[9]	[9]	[9]

Part III Section A   Section B

11. [A] [B] [C] [D] 16. [A] [B] [C] [D] 21. [A] [B] [C] [D] 26. [A] [B] [C] [D] 31. [A] [B] [C] [D]
12. [A] [B] [C] [D] 17. [A] [B] [C] [D] 22. [A] [B] [C] [D] 27. [A] [B] [C] [D] 32. [A] [B] [C] [D]
13. [A] [B] [C] [D] 18. [A] [B] [C] [D] 23. [A] [B] [C] [D] 28. [A] [B] [C] [D] 33. [A] [B] [C] [D]
14. [A] [B] [C] [D] 19. [A] [B] [C] [D] 24. [A] [B] [C] [D] 29. [A] [B] [C] [D] 34. [A] [B] [C] [D]
15. [A] [B] [C] [D] 20. [A] [B] [C] [D] 25. [A] [B] [C] [D] 30. [A] [B] [C] [D] 35. [A] [B] [C] [D]

Part III Section C

Almost 20,000 whales have been slaughtered since a (36) _____ on commercial whaling was introduced in 1986 and the death (37) _____ is rising each year. Norway and Japan killed over 1,000 whales in 1999 and they plan to kill even more. As the (38) _____ concerns increase, whaling is no longer the issue as it was or (39) _____ to be. With little public awareness of the increasing whale slaughter, there has been no pressure to stop it. (40) _____, the political will confront the whalers and (41) _____ the whaling ban that has (42) _____ away. Commercial whaling has (43) _____ whale population worldwide, (44) _____. There is still great scientific uncertainty about the size and status of remaining whale populations. (45) _____. They need to be protected, not hunted. (46) _____.

答题卡 2 (Answer Sheet 2)

Part IV   Section A

47. [A][B][C][D][E][F][G][H][I][J][K][L][M][N][O]
48. [A][B][C][D][E][F][G][H][I][J][K][L][M][N][O]
49. [A][B][C][D][E][F][G][H][I][J][K][L][M][N][O]
50. [A][B][C][D][E][F][G][H][I][J][K][L][M][N][O]
51. [A][B][C][D][E][F][G][H][I][J][K][L][M][N][O]
52. [A][B][C][D][E][F][G][H][I][J][K][L][M][N][O]
53. [A][B][C][D][E][F][G][H][I][J][K][L][M][N][O]
54. [A][B][C][D][E][F][G][H][I][J][K][L][M][N][O]
55. [A][B][C][D][E][F][G][H][I][J][K][L][M][N][O]
56. [A][B][C][D][E][F][G][H][I][J][K][L][M][N][O]

Section B

57. [A] [B] [C] [D]
58. [A] [B] [C] [D]
59. [A] [B] [C] [D]
60. [A] [B] [C] [D]
61. [A] [B] [C] [D]
62. [A] [B] [C] [D]
63. [A] [B] [C] [D]
64. [A] [B] [C] [D]
65. [A] [B] [C] [D]
66. [A] [B] [C] [D]

Part V   Cloze   (15 minutes)

67. [A] [B] [C] [D]   72. [A] [B] [C] [D]   77. [A] [B] [C] [D]   82. [A] [B] [C] [D]
68. [A] [B] [C] [D]   73. [A] [B] [C] [D]   78. [A] [B] [C] [D]   83. [A] [B] [C] [D]
69. [A] [B] [C] [D]   74. [A] [B] [C] [D]   79. [A] [B] [C] [D]   84. [A] [B] [C] [D]
70. [A] [B] [C] [D]   75. [A] [B] [C] [D]   80. [A] [B] [C] [D]   85. [A] [B] [C] [D]
71. [A] [B] [C] [D]   76. [A] [B] [C] [D]   81. [A] [B] [C] [D]   86. [A] [B] [C] [D]

Part VI   Translation   (5 minutes)

87. _____

88. _____

89. _____

90. _____

91. _____

PRACTICE TEST 5

Part I Writing (30 minutes)

注意：此部分试题在**答题卡**1上。

Part II Reading Comprehension (Skimming and Scanning) (15 minutes)

Directions: *In this part, you will have 15 minutes to go over the passage quickly and answer the questions on **Answer Sheet 1**.*

For questions 1 – 7, mark
Y *(for YES)*   *if the statement agrees with the information given in the passage;*
N *(for NO)*   *if the statement contradicts the information given in the passage;*
NG *(for NOT GIVEN)*   *if the information is not given in the passage.*
For questions 8 – 10, complete the sentences with the information given in the passage.

Six Tips for Success Right Out of College

Job opportunities abound across all sectors（部门）for the graduating class of 2007. According to *Job Outlook 2007*, employers plan to hire 17.4 percent more new college graduates this year than from the class of 2006, the fourth straight year of double-digit growth according to the National Association of Colleges and Employers.

Many of the approximately 3 million students graduating from U.S. colleges this year will enter the workforce for the very first time. They'll have to adapt to new cultures, expectations, and schedules.

And while success will no longer be about getting good grades in class, they shouldn't fool themselves — they'll still be graded every day. In the workplace, however, "grades" are far more subjective and ill-defined than in school.

Advice from the Top

If you're starting a new job fresh from school, Christie Hefner, chairman and CEO of Playboy Enterprises, has some sage (聪明的，贤明的) advice. (Full disclosure: The company I work for, Spencer Stuart, has done client work for Playboy Enterprises.)

"A key to success in your new job is recognizing that it's no longer about your individual achievement, but the success of the team, the organization," says Hefner. "You should start out by listening — a lot. Make the effort to understand the culture and learn the history and strategy of the organization.

"Make an effort to meet people, to make friends, to learn what other people need and value," she continues. "That includes your boss, your department, your colleagues, and the company. If you make them look good, you'll look good."

To build on Hefner's counsel, here are six guidelines to help launch your career with real momentum:

1. Maintain a Positive Attitude

This seems obvious, but attitude is the single most important asset you'll bring to the early days of your job. It's also something over which you have complete control.

Be upbeat and optimistic. Be the kind of person who creates rather than saps energy from other people. Be proactive and take initiative.

Don't wait to be asked how your project is going — make an appointment with your boss or go see the project manager to share your progress and check to see if you're on track. Listen attentively and ask good questions. Above all, don't be a know-it-all.

2. Work Hard

There's no escaping the fact that hard work on a consistent basis is a foundational requirement for success. High-level performance only comes with experience acquired through hard work and practice.

A deep body of evidence supports this contention (论点); the top performers in any field, from business to science to sports to music, work harder than others. So as you start your career, get into the office early and stay late.

The most successful people don't just work harder, though — they also work smarter. It's not just the number of hours you put in at the office that counts, it's what you do with those hours. Don't work hard just to build a reputation. Do it to get a higher caliber (水平，品质) of work done, and to train in and practice the central skills that are required for achievement in your job.

You'll need to make an effort to avoid becoming a one-dimensional workaholic, however. It takes self-discipline to work hard in your job and still find the time to tend to your personal life and family obligations, and keep yourself in good physical shape. But long-term success demands it.

Taking advantage of the technology and mobile communications in your workplace will help. Handle the emails, reading, and writing you don't have time for in the office at home, either early in the morning or at night.

3. Deliver on Your Commitments

Become known as someone who can be counted on to successfully complete projects on time and with high quality. This is just as important for small tasks as it is for major projects.

Don't be disappointed if your first job is narrowly defined, and some of your early assignments seem menial. They aren't — they're opportunities to demonstrate that you can meet your commitments, and when you do, you'll earn trust and confidence.

You'll be surprised at how quickly larger and more significant assignments come your way when you develop a reputation for delivering on commitments.

4. Perform Completed Staff Work

"Completed staff work" is a concept that means going beyond a basic work assignment to understand why something is needed, how it will be used, and what form it will take once it's completed. This helps avoid delaying a project with incomplete, piecemeal solutions.

For instance, if a sales manager asks you for an analysis of a target client, applying the doctrine of completed staff work results in a finished product that can be shared throughout the department, passed along to upper management, or used directly with the client. Set this as the standard for all your work.

5. Focus on the Success of Others

I've written about this principle consistently in my column, but it can't be stated often enough. It's a fail-safe success strategy to make others around you successful, and you'll be successful as a natural result.

Why is this true? The most talented people will want to work with you. You'll become in demand for the most important projects by the most senior people, and you'll build a network of supporters across the organization who'll be invested in your success. Develop this habit from day one of your career.

But how, you might ask, can I help others be successful if I'm brand new in the job myself? Look for ways to be helpful. Be proactive. Be willing to take on extra or unpopular work. Stay focused on the goals of your boss, your team, and your company，and make their goals your goals.

6. Be a Technology Mentor

Today's college graduates have a huge advantage over anyone born before 1980. If you've grown up with digital technology as a normal and integral part of your life，you have the opportunity to bring the tech-phobic senior members of your office into the modern era.

Teach them how to use *Facebook*，how to upload a video to *YouTube*，how to organize digital photos on *Flickr*，how to create a profile on *MySpace*，or even how to watch reruns of "Gilligan's Island" on TV Links. Even relatively standard activities like creating PowerPoint presentations can benefit from your know-how as a member of the class of 2007.

注意：此部分试题请在**答题卡 1** 上作答；8－10 题在**答题卡 1** 上。

1. This passage aims to instruct the new college graduates how to achieve success in the workplace.
2. According to National Association of Colleges and Employers，job opportunities for new college graduates have been increasing in recent four years.
3. Hefner suggests that a key to success in a new job is individualism.
4. Maintaining a negative attitude is very important for the success of a college graduate in the early days of his job.
5. Top performers in any field usually work harder than others.
6. If you helps others around you achieve success，then naturally you will be successful.
7. If a person knows how to create a profile on *MySpace*，he will have more job opportunities than others.

Part III Listening Comprehension   (35 minutes)

Section A

Directions: *In this section, you will hear 8 short conversations and 2 long conversations. At the end of each conversation, one or more questions will be asked about what was said. Both the conversation and the questions will be spoken only once. After each question there will be a pause. During the pause, you must read the four choices marked A), B), C) and D), and decide which is the best answer. Then mark the* *corresponding letter on **Answer Sheet 2** with a single line through the centre.*

注意：此部分试题请在**答题卡**2上作答。

11. A) She agrees with him entirely.
    B) She does not agree with him.
    C) She advises him to be careful.
    D) She suggests that the teacher be strict with the students.

12. A) In a street.   C) At home.
    B) At the doctor's.   D) At the office.

13. A) The rooms are better but not the meals.
    B) The meals are better but not the rooms.
    C) They are even worse.
    D) Both meals and rooms are better.

14. A) A newspaper story.   C) A job vacancy.
    B) A situational dialog.   D) The Internet service.

15. A) Washington.   C) Chicago.
    B) New York.   D) Los Angeles.

16. A) Swimming.   C) Tennis.
    B) Skiing.   D) Watching TV.

17. A) High pay can keep a clean government.
    B) She doubts that high pay alone can maintain a clean government.
    C) There is less bribery in developed countries.
    D) Human desire will decide the existence of bribery.

18. A) 8:00.   C) 7:30.
    B) 7:45.   D) 7:00.

Questions 19 to 22 are based on the conversation you have just heard.

19. A) They are talking about their fathers.
    B) They are talking about their friendship.
    C) They are talking about baseball.
    D) They are talking about drinking beer.

20. A) Four years ago.   C) One year ago.
    B) One month ago.   D) Four months ago.

21. A) To drink beer.
    B) To join the Navy.
    C) To make friends with other people.
    D) To see the Brooklyn Dodgers.

22. A) Because he was dumb.
    B) Because he was deaf.
    C) Because he was blind.
    D) Because he was crippled.

Questions 23 to 25 are based on the conversation you have just heard.

23. A) To see the horse racing.
    B) To see a film.
    C) To see the car racing.
    D) To have lunch together.

24. A) Because she doesn't want to go.
    B) Because there will be much traffic.
    C) Because Sue will pick her up.
    D) Because it is out of Bill's way.

25. A) Four.
    B) Three.
    C) Two.
    D) Five.

Section B

Directions: *In this section, you will hear 3 short passages. At the end of each passage, you will hear some questions. Both the passage and the questions will be spoken only once. After you hear a question, you must choose the best answer from the four choices marked A), B), C) and D). Then mark the corresponding letter on* **Answer Sheet 2** *with a single line through the centre.*

注意：此部分试题请在**答题卡**2上作答。

Passage One

Questions 26 to 29 are based on the passage you have just heard.

26. A) 17,000.
    B) 1,700.
    C) 24.
    D) 9,000.

27. A) It's located in a college town.
    B) It's composed of a group of old buildings.
    C) Its classrooms are beautifully designed.
    D) Its library is often crowded with students.

28. A) Teachers are well paid at Deep Springs.

B) Students are mainly from New York State.

C) The length of schooling is two years.

D) Teachers needn't pay for their rent and meals.

29. A) Take a walk in the desert.   C) Watch TV programs.

    B) Go to a cinema.   D) Attend a party.

Passage Two

Questions 30 to 32 are based on the passage you have just heard.

30. A) They learn to read by reading word by word.

    B) They learn to read by reading the words out.

    C) They learn to read by sounding out the letters and decoding the words.

    D) They learn to read by practicing more.

31. A) $0.5 - 0.6$ C) 2.5

    B) $3.5 - 4$ D) 3.6

32. A) A child who reads a book with stops.

    B) A child who reads one word at a time.

    C) A child who reads without expression or meaning.

    D) A child who reads with expression and meaning of the sentences.

Passage Three

Questions 33 to 35 are based on the passage you have just heard.

33. A) Because of their carelessness.

    B) Because of their inadequate education.

    C) Because of their detailed introduction.

    D) Because of their names being crossed out.

34. A) Continue to work hard.

    B) Give them up and shift to something else.

    C) Draw another picture.

    D) Make as great improvements as possible.

35. A) Failure is the father of success.

    B) Adjustments are the key to success.

    C) Goals are more important than details.

    D) Details can be ignored in all cases.

Section C

Directions: *In this section, you will hear a passage three times. When the passage is read for the first time, you should listen carefully for its general idea. When the passage is read for the second time, you are required to fill in the blanks numbered from 36 to 43 with the exact words you have just heard. For blanks numbered from 44 to 46 you are required to fill in the missing information. For these blanks, you can either use the exact words you have just heard or write down the main points in your own words. Finally, when the passage is read for the third time, you should check what you have written.*

注意：此部分试题在**答题卡 2** 上；请在**答题卡 2** 上作答。

Part IV Reading Comprehension (Reading in Depth)
(25 minutes)

Section A

Directions: *In this section, there is a passage with ten blanks. You are required to select one word for each blank from a list of choices given in a word bank following the passage. Read the passage through carefully before making your choices. Each choice in the bank is identified by a letter. Please mark the corresponding letter for each item on Answer Sheet 2 with a single line through the centre.* ***You may not use any of the words in the bank more than once.***

A new, lightweight fuel cell that runs on methanol may one day ___47___ your electric car. Sooner still, the new cell may fuel smaller devices such as your lap-top computer or mobile phone.

If they work, methanol fuel cells could be a major ___48___ in energy consumption and conservation. The brave new technology could drastically ___49___ air pollution from auto emissions and other sources.

Whether they are used to run cars and buses or to make electricity for other ___50___, fuel cells operate by ___51___ hydrogen to electricity without combustion. They are akin to continuously-recharging batteries. Hydrogen and oxygen are fed into a stack of plates that create electricity, with harmless water vapor as the by-product.

These silent, zero-emission gadgets have long been used in NASA spacecraft. They represent the great hope of many ___52___ to power the first mass-produced electric car.

While batteries alone haven't ___53___ the performance most drivers want, proponents believe that fuel cells, probably combined with batteries, hold the promise of performance, range and better mileage ___54___ with today's internal combustion engines.

The size and weight of fuel cells have always been problems. New fuel-cell technology promises to solve those issues.

Fuel cells can use various sources of hydrogen, including a simple tank of compressed gas. But methanol, a liquid usually produced from natural gas, is a much more ___55___ way to store hydrogen. This is why the first wave of fuel cells in cars will likely use an indirect methanol fuel cell, in which the methanol passes through a mechanism called a "reformer" which ___56___ the hydrogen.

注意：此部分试题请在**答题卡**2上作答。

A) despair	I) extracts
B) applications	J) supplied
C) external	K) inefficient
D) cut	L) environmentalists
E) converting	M) preserve
F) breakthrough	N) efficient
G) arrogant	O) compared
H) power	

Section B

Directions: *There are 2 passages in this section. Each passage is followed by some questions or unfinished statements. For each of them there are four choices marked A), B), C) and D). You should decide on the best choice and mark the corresponding letter on* **Answer Sheet 2** *with a single line through the centre.*

Passage One

Questions 57 to 61 are based on the following passage.

The practice of making New Year's resolutions is growing rare in France, perhaps because we spread them out from January to December, a demonstration of a delicate balance between good will and willpower. Descendants of the spiritual exercises of the ancients, resolutions are both educational and therapeutic.

In declaring resolutions, if possible before witnesses, we nourish the illusion that changing our lifestyles will change our lives: "This year, I will read Proust." "This year, I will not invade Iraq." "This year, I will be faithful to my wife." "This year, I will reduce unemployment in France."

Westerners are athletes of introspection — we never stop analyzing ourselves. "It is never too late or too early to care for the well-being of the soul," Epicurus said, and so we make our lives a study of ourselves.

If the end of the year brings a flood of resolutions to change, it is because we are faced with an existence that is invaded by the routine, by the rush of demands. We can't bear it. We know that another life exists, more beautiful, more passionate, one that laziness and apathy keeps us from attaining.

I have to break with time to overcome my obstacles, to rediscover myself, to be myself in all innocence. I can change my life, at least in some small way. Making resolutions demonstrates optimism, the desire to make oneself better, a faith, naïve and beautiful at once, that declarations can spontaneously become actions, that saying means doing.

Oh, the glorious day of making a resolution, the belief that starting tomorrow I will be the pilot of my existence, that I will stop being the plaything of external circumstances, that I will govern myself. I'm better than I seem to be — a person obsessed by little irritants, addicted to talking nonsense — and I'm going to prove it to the world. The certainty that soon, thanks to my willpower, I will no longer be someone who is habitually late, a slave to my cell phone, a glutton, a distracted driver ... can galvanize me, prompt me to change, tear away my imperfect personality.

Knowing that you can change your behavior, even by an iota, is essential for holding yourself in esteem. Resolutions are perhaps lies, but they're lies of good faith, necessary illusions. As long as we can make them, we are saved, we can control the chaos of destiny; it doesn't matter that we break them and that others view us with skepticism. Every resolution is good simply because it is declared. It is a comedy, perhaps, but it keeps us sane.

注意：此部分试题请在**答题卡**2上作答。

57. It can be assumed that the paragraph preceding the passage most probably discusses _____.
    A) New Year's celebration
    B) New Year's customs in France
    C) a decision made by a French writer
    D) change in people's lifestyle

58. The word "apathy" in the fourth paragraph most probably means _____.

A) being enthusiastic about something   C) being lazy

B) not being interested in anything   D) being skeptical

59. What does the author mean by saying "Westerners are athletes of introspection"?
   A) They are good at thinking.
   B) They are interested in philosophical thinking.
   C) They tend to think a lot about their own thoughts and feelings.
   D) They like to think about something that happened in the past.

60. What's the author's attitude towards New Year's resolutions?
   A) They are very helpful because they can keep us sensible and reasonable.
   B) They will help people view us with skepticism.
   C) They are lies that can't be carried out.
   D) They can tear people away from their personality.

61. Which of the following can be the most suitable title of the passage?
   A) A Happy Day in the New Year
   B) On Resolution
   C) Changing Your Behaviors in the New Year
   D) Another Last Chance to Change Your Life

Passage Two

Questions 62 to 66 are based on the following passage.

Twenty-eight years ago, when I was twenty-four, I did something that adults often fantasize about doing: I went back to high school, and for four months I pretended to be seventeen again. With the help of my literary agent, who posed as my mother, I enrolled at a large public school about an hour and forty minutes outside New York City. I worried at first that one of my teachers or classmates would pick me out as an obvious impostor, but none of them did.

Well, my memories of my time-reversing escapade are still so vivid that it's hard for me to believe that nearly thirty years have passed. Recently, I had a brainstorm: Why not try to pull it off again? I'm fifty-two now, but I'm still a kid at heart. Yes, I said to myself, I'll do it: I'll try to pass for forty-five.

The first thing I had to do was make myself look seven years younger. Twenty-eight years ago, I did that by swapping my horn-rim I-need-a-job glasses for a pair of wire-rim aviators and buying a Led Zeppelin T-shirt. This time, I required a more drastic makeover. I went to the men's department at JCPenney and, with a couple of quick glances over my shoulder, picked out a pair of Dockers with a thirty-six-inch waist — the size I used to wear back in my mid-forties, before I gave up and started buying pants that almost actually fit. The Dockers felt pretty darn snug when I pulled them on in the dressing room, but, by inhaling deeply and hopping quickly from one foot to the other, I managed to get them buttoned.

As I carried my new pants to the counter, my heart was pounding. Would the cashier spot my deception — and, perhaps, ask if I wouldn't like for her to gift-wrap the pants so that I could give them to someone seven or so years younger? But no. She rang up my purchase and put the pants in a bag. I had passed!

In addition to changing my physical appearance, I had to modify my world view. Rather than thinking like someone born in the mid-nineteen-fifties, that is, I had to train myself to think like someone born in the early sixties. "Do you remember where you were when President Kennedy was assassinated?" I asked a middle-aged stranger. "Because I sure don't." At a party a couple of weeks later, I fell into conversation with some people I didn't know, who appeared to be about fifty or fifty-one, or maybe fifty-three or fifty-four. The subject of the nineteen-sixties came up, and, instead of joining them in bragging about all the drugs I used to take, I said, "Boy, did I ever miss out! I was still in elementary school, or possibly early junior high school, when all that cool stuff was goin' down!" Some of the people I said that to looked at me with scorn, and others looked at me with pity, but none of them looked at me with suspicion. They believed me! I had passed!

注意：此部分试题请在**答题卡 2** 上作答。

62. From the passage, we can infer that the word "imposter" in the first paragraph means _____.
    A) a newly-enrolled student
    B) a person who pretends to be somebody else
    C) a person who is intended to deceive people
    D) a fake student

63. As used in the passage, the phrase "rang up" in the fourth paragraph suggests _____.
    A) the cashier made a telephone call to the manager
    B) the cashier turned down the author's purchase
    C) the cashier entered the cost of goods the author bought on a cash register
    D) the cashier accepted the author's advice

64. What's the author's attitude towards what he had done 30 years ago?
    A) It was vivid.　　　　　　　　C) It was unpleasant.

B) It was an exciting adventure. D) It was absurd.

65. From the passage, it can be inferred that _____.
 A) the author's mother agreed to send him back to high school
 B) the cashier in the shop was asked to gift-wrap the pants
 C) the author's thinking matches his appearance
 D) the author had taken drugs once

66. Which of the following best reflects the main idea of the passage?
 A) The author likes to be young in appearance.
 B) The author is still young at heart.
 C) The author looks younger than his age.
 D) The author is skillful in deceiving people.

Part V Cloze   (15 minutes)

Directions: *There are 20 blanks in the following passage. For each blank there are four choices marked A), B), C) and D) on the right side of the paper. You should choose the ONE that best fits into the passage. Then mark the corresponding letter on **Answer Sheet 2** with a single line through the centre.*

注意：此部分试题请在**答题卡** 2 上作答。

Geography is the study of the relationship between people and the land. Geographers compare and contrast __67__ places on the earth. But they also __68__ beyond the individual places and consider the earth as a __69__. The word *geography* __70__ from two Greek words, *ge*, the Greek word for "earth" and *graphein*, __71__ means "to write." The English word *geography* means "to describe the earth." __72__ geography

67. A) similar C) various
 B) distant D) famous

68. A) pass   C) reach
 B) go   D) get

69. A) whole C) part
 B) unit   D) total

70. A) falls   C) removes
 B) results D) comes

71. A) what   C) that
 B) which D) it

72. A) Some C) Many
 B) Most D) Few

books __73__ on a small area like a town or city. Others deal with a state, a region, a nation, or an __74__ continent. Many geography books deal with the whole earth.

Another __75__ to divide the study of

__76__ is to distinguish between physical geography and __77__ geography . The former

focuses on the natural world; the __78__

starts with human beings and studies __79__ human beings and their environment act __80__ each other. __81__ when geography is

considered as a single subject, __82__ branch can neglect the other.

A geographer might be described __83__ one who observes, records, and explains the __84__ between places. If places were alike, there would be little need for geographers.

We know, __85__ , that no two places

are exactly the same. Geography, __86__ , is a point of view, a special way of looking at places.

73. A) rely   C) reckon
    B) rest   D) focus
74. A) extensive   C) entire
    B) overall   D) enormous
75. A) way   C) habit
    B) mean   D) technique
76. A) word   C) geography
    B) earth   D) globe
77. A) mental   C) economic
    B) military   D) cultural
78. A) second   C) later
    B) next   D) latter
79. A) when   C) where
    B) what   D) how
80. A) upon   C) for
    B) as   D) to
81. A) And   C) Therefore
    B) But   D) For
82. A) neither   C) either
    B) one   D) each
83. A) for   C) to
    B) as   D) by
84. A) exceptions   C) differences
    B) sameness   D) famous
85. A) moreover   C) however
    B) meanwhile   D) or else
86. A) still   C) never
    B) then   D) moreover

Part VI   Translation   (5 minutes)

Directions: *Complete the sentences on **Answer Sheet** 2 by translating into English the Chinese given in brackets.*

注意：此部分试题请在**答题卡 2** 上作答。

87. If you can come back on time，we'll catch the train. But _____ _____（如果你天黑之前回不了家怎么办）?

88. It is something _____（没有先例的）in our department that you are given a flat after working in our school less than two years.

89. The manager was chatting with the chairman of the board about something that concerned the future of their cooperation and I could tell that he _____ _____（当时措辞相当小心）.

90. Broadly speaking，the congress had _____（起到了主导作用）in the struggle for human rights during that period.

91. Cyberspace is _____（一个你可以随意出入的地方），that is，if you don't love it，leave it.

答题卡 1 (Answer Sheet 1)

学校:						准			考			证			号	

| | 准 | 考 | 证 | 号 | |

[0]	[0]	[0]	[0]	[0]	[0]	[0]	[0]	[0]	[0]	[0]	[0]	[0]	[0]	[0]
[1]	[1]	[1]	[1]	[1]	[1]	[1]	[1]	[1]	[1]	[1]	[1]	[1]	[1]	[1]
[2]	[2]	[2]	[2]	[2]	[2]	[2]	[2]	[2]	[2]	[2]	[2]	[2]	[2]	[2]
[3]	[3]	[3]	[3]	[3]	[3]	[3]	[3]	[3]	[3]	[3]	[3]	[3]	[3]	[3]
[4]	[4]	[4]	[4]	[4]	[4]	[4]	[4]	[4]	[4]	[4]	[4]	[4]	[4]	[4]
[5]	[5]	[5]	[5]	[5]	[5]	[5]	[5]	[5]	[5]	[5]	[5]	[5]	[5]	[5]
[6]	[6]	[6]	[6]	[6]	[6]	[6]	[6]	[6]	[6]	[6]	[6]	[6]	[6]	[6]
[7]	[7]	[7]	[7]	[7]	[7]	[7]	[7]	[7]	[7]	[7]	[7]	[7]	[7]	[7]
[8]	[8]	[8]	[8]	[8]	[8]	[8]	[8]	[8]	[8]	[8]	[8]	[8]	[8]	[8]
[9]	[9]	[9]	[9]	[9]	[9]	[9]	[9]	[9]	[9]	[9]	[9]	[9]	[9]	[9]

Part I   **Writing**   **(30 minutes)**

Directions: *For this part, you are allowed 30 minutes to write an application letter based on the following condition.*

假如你叫李明,是一所大学的大四学生。你从当地一家报纸上了解到本地一所高中要招聘一位英语老师,想应聘这一职位。请写一封申请信,字数不少于120字。

答题卡 1 (Answer Sheet 1)

Part II   Reading Comprehension (Skimming and Scanning)   (15 minutes)

1. [Y] [N] [NG]   2. [Y] [N] [NG]   3. [Y] [N] [NG]   4. [Y] [N] [NG]
5. [Y] [N] [NG]   6. [Y] [N] [NG]   7. [Y] [N] [NG]

8. Long term success demands _____ to work hard in your job and still find the time to tend to your personal life.

9. You will earn _____ if you meet your commitments even though your early assignment seems menial.

10. The concept of "_____" means going beyond a basic work assignment to understand why something is needed, how it will be used, and what form it will take once it's completed.

答题卡 2 (Answer Sheet 2)

| 学校: |
| 姓名: |
| 划线要求 |

准 考 证 号														
[0]	[0]	[0]	[0]	[0]	[0]	[0]	[0]	[0]	[0]	[0]	[0]	[0]	[0]	[0]
[1]	[1]	[1]	[1]	[1]	[1]	[1]	[1]	[1]	[1]	[1]	[1]	[1]	[1]	[1]
[2]	[2]	[2]	[2]	[2]	[2]	[2]	[2]	[2]	[2]	[2]	[2]	[2]	[2]	[2]
[3]	[3]	[3]	[3]	[3]	[3]	[3]	[3]	[3]	[3]	[3]	[3]	[3]	[3]	[3]
[4]	[4]	[4]	[4]	[4]	[4]	[4]	[4]	[4]	[4]	[4]	[4]	[4]	[4]	[4]
[5]	[5]	[5]	[5]	[5]	[5]	[5]	[5]	[5]	[5]	[5]	[5]	[5]	[5]	[5]
[6]	[6]	[6]	[6]	[6]	[6]	[6]	[6]	[6]	[6]	[6]	[6]	[6]	[6]	[6]
[7]	[7]	[7]	[7]	[7]	[7]	[7]	[7]	[7]	[7]	[7]	[7]	[7]	[7]	[7]
[8]	[8]	[8]	[8]	[8]	[8]	[8]	[8]	[8]	[8]	[8]	[8]	[8]	[8]	[8]
[9]	[9]	[9]	[9]	[9]	[9]	[9]	[9]	[9]	[9]	[9]	[9]	[9]	[9]	[9]

Part III   Section A   Section B

11. [A] [B] [C] [D]   16. [A] [B] [C] [D]   21. [A] [B] [C] [D]   26. [A] [B] [C] [D]   31. [A] [B] [C] [D]
12. [A] [B] [C] [D]   17. [A] [B] [C] [D]   22. [A] [B] [C] [D]   27. [A] [B] [C] [D]   32. [A] [B] [C] [D]
13. [A] [B] [C] [D]   18. [A] [B] [C] [D]   23. [A] [B] [C] [D]   28. [A] [B] [C] [D]   33. [A] [B] [C] [D]
14. [A] [B] [C] [D]   19. [A] [B] [C] [D]   24. [A] [B] [C] [D]   29. [A] [B] [C] [D]   34. [A] [B] [C] [D]
15. [A] [B] [C] [D]   20. [A] [B] [C] [D]   25. [A] [B] [C] [D]   30. [A] [B] [C] [D]   35. [A] [B] [C] [D]

Part III   Section C

French Defense Minister Michele Alliot-Marie says her government is (36) _____ to help train Iraq's police and military but rules out sending French (37) _____ there. The French official made her (38) _____ Friday in Washington, where she is (39) _____ to smooth relations that soured over France's opposition to the US-led war in Iraq.

Ms. Alliot-Marie told a (40) _____ at the Center for (41) _____ and International Studies in Washington that France would be (42) _____ to help train Iraq's future military and police forces, (43) _____ to what France and Germany are doing in Afghanistan.

Ms. Alliot-Marie, a close political ally of President Chirac, (44) _____ _____, which soured over French opposition to the US-led war in Iraq. (45) "_____ _____," said Michele Alliot-Marie. "We simply want to promote our vision of things as we respect that of others. (46) _____ _____."

答题卡 2 (Answer Sheet 2)

Part IV Section A

47. [A][B][C][D][E][F][G][H][I][J][K][L][M][N][O]
48. [A][B][C][D][E][F][G][H][I][J][K][L][M][N][O]
49. [A][B][C][D][E][F][G][H][I][J][K][L][M][N][O]
50. [A][B][C][D][E][F][G][H][I][J][K][L][M][N][O]
51. [A][B][C][D][E][F][G][H][I][J][K][L][M][N][O]
52. [A][B][C][D][E][F][G][H][I][J][K][L][M][N][O]
53. [A][B][C][D][E][F][G][H][I][J][K][L][M][N][O]
54. [A][B][C][D][E][F][G][H][I][J][K][L][M][N][O]
55. [A][B][C][D][E][F][G][H][I][J][K][L][M][N][O]
56. [A][B][C][D][E][F][G][H][I][J][K][L][M][N][O]

Section B

57. [A] [B] [C] [D]
58. [A] [B] [C] [D]
59. [A] [B] [C] [D]
60. [A] [B] [C] [D]
61. [A] [B] [C] [D]
62. [A] [B] [C] [D]
63. [A] [B] [C] [D]
64. [A] [B] [C] [D]
65. [A] [B] [C] [D]
66. [A] [B] [C] [D]

Part V   Cloze   (15 minutes)

67. [A] [B] [C] [D]   72. [A] [B] [C] [D]   77. [A] [B] [C] [D]   82. [A] [B] [C] [D]
68. [A] [B] [C] [D]   73. [A] [B] [C] [D]   78. [A] [B] [C] [D]   83. [A] [B] [C] [D]
69. [A] [B] [C] [D]   74. [A] [B] [C] [D]   79. [A] [B] [C] [D]   84. [A] [B] [C] [D]
70. [A] [B] [C] [D]   75. [A] [B] [C] [D]   80. [A] [B] [C] [D]   85. [A] [B] [C] [D]
71. [A] [B] [C] [D]   76. [A] [B] [C] [D]   81. [A] [B] [C] [D]   86. [A] [B] [C] [D]

Part VI   Translation   (5 minutes)

87. _____

88. _____

89. _____

90. _____

91. _____

PRACTICE TEST 6

Part I Writing   (30 minutes)

注意：此部分试题在**答题卡**1上。

Part II Reading Comprehension (Skimming and Scanning)
(15 minutes)

Directions: *In this part, you will have 15 minutes to go over the passage quickly and answer the questions on **Answer Sheet 1**.*

For questions 1 – 4, mark
Y *(for YES)*   *if the statement agrees with the information given in the passage;*
N *(for NO)*   *if the statement contradicts the information given in the passage;*
NG *(for NOT GIVEN)*   *if the information is not given in the passage.*

For questions 5 – 10, complete the sentences with the information given in the passage.

Buying Your First Home

Finding the right first home starts with a price range and a short list of desirable neighborhoods. But there are many other factors you'll need to consider before investing in what may be your biggest asset.

1. Buying Your First Home

Home ownership is the cornerstone of the American Dream. But before you start looking, there are a number of things you need to consider. First, you should determine what your needs are and whether owning your own home will meet those needs. Do you picture yourself mowing the lawn on Saturday, or leaving your urban condo for the beach? The best advice is to look at buying a home as a lifestyle investment, and only secondly as a financial investment.

Even if housing prices don't continue to increase at the torrid pace seen in recent years in many areas, buying a home can be a good financial investment. Making mortgage payments forces you to save, and after 15 to 30 years you will own a substantial asset that can be converted into cash to help fund retirement or a child's education. There are also tax benefits.

Like many other investments, however, real estate prices can fluctuate considerably. If you aren't ready to settle down in one spot for a few years, you probably should defer buying a home until you are. If you are ready to take the plunge, you'll need to determine how much you can spend and where you want to live.

2. How Much Mortgage Can You Afford?

Many mortgages today are being resold in the secondary markets. The Federal National Mortgage Association (Fannie Mae) is a government-sponsored organization that purchases mortgages from lenders and sells them to investors. Mortgages that conform to Fannie Mae's standards may carry lower interest rates or smaller down payments. To qualify, the mortgage borrower needs to meet two ratio requirements that are industry standards.

The housing expense ratio compares basic monthly housing costs to the buyer's gross (before taxes and other deductions) monthly income. Basic costs include monthly mortgage, insurance, and property taxes. Income includes any steady cash flow, including salary, self-employment income, pensions, child support, or alimony payments. For a conventional loan, your monthly housing cost should not exceed 28% of your monthly gross income.

The total obligations to income ratio is the percentage of all income required to service your total monthly payments. Monthly payments on student loans, installment loans, and credit card balances older than 10 months are added to basic housing costs and then divided by gross income. Your total monthly debt payments, including basic housing costs, should not exceed 36%.

Many home buyers choose to arrange financing before shopping for a home and most lenders will "prequalify" you for a certain amount. Prequalification helps you focus on homes you can afford. It also makes you a more attractive buyer and can help you negotiate a lower purchase price. Nothing is more disheartening for buyers or sellers than a deal that falls through due to a lack of financing.

In addition to qualifying for a mortgage, you will probably need a down payment. The 28% to 36% debt ratios assume a 10% down payment. In practice, down payment requirements vary from more than 20% to as low as 0% for some Veterans Administration (VA) loans. Down payments greater than 20% generally buy a better rate. Lowering the down payment increases leverage (the opportunity to make a profit using borrowed money) but also increases monthly payments.

3. Costs of Buying a Home

Many home buyers are surprised (shocked might be a better word) to find that a down payment is not the only cash requirement. A home inspection can cost $200 or more. Closing costs may include loan origination fees, up-front "points" (prepaid interest), application fees, appraisal fee, survey, title search and title insurance, first month's homeowners insurance, recording fees and attorney's fees. In many locales, transfer taxes are assessed. Finally, adjustments for heating oil or property taxes already paid by the sellers will be included in your final costs. All this will probably add up to be between 3% and 8% of your purchase price.

4. Ongoing Costs

In addition to mortgage payments, there are other costs associated with home ownership. Utilities, heat, property taxes, repairs, insurance, services such as trash or snow removal, landscaping, assessments, and replacement of appliances are the major costs incurred. Make sure you understand how much you are willing and able to spend on such items.

Condominiums may not have the same costs as a house, but they do have association fees. Older homes are often less expensive to buy, but repairs may be greater than those in a newer home. When looking for a home, be sure to check the actual expenses of the previous owners, or expenses for a comparable home in the neighborhood.

5. Choosing a Neighborhood

Before you start looking at homes, look at neighborhoods. Schools and other services play a large part in making a neighborhood attractive. Even if you don't have children, your future buyer may. Crime rates, taxes, transportation, and town services are other things to look at. Finally, learn the local zoning laws. A new pizza shop next door might alter your property's future value. On the other hand, you may want to run a business out of your home.

Look for a neighborhood where prices are increasing. As the prices of the better homes increase, values of the lesser homes may rise as well. If you find a less expensive home in a good neighborhood, make sure you factor in the cost of repairs or upgrades that such a house may need.

6. Finding a Broker

If you are a first-time home buyer, you will probably want to work with a broker. Brokers know the market and can be a valuable source of information concerning the home buying process. Ask lots of questions, but remember that most brokers are working for the seller, and in the end, their primary obligation is to the seller and not to you. An alternative is a so-called buyer's broker. This individual does work for you, and therefore is paid by you. Seller's brokers are paid by the seller.

Make sure that the broker has access to the Multiple Listing Service (MLS). This service lists all the properties for sale by most major brokers across the country. Brokerage commissions average 5% to 7% and are split between the listing broker and the broker that eventually sells the home. Don't be surprised if your broker is eager to sell you their own listing since they would then earn the entire commission.

Home Buying Costs	
Down Payment	0% − 20% of purchase price
Home Inspection	$200 − $500
Points	$1,000 and up for 1% − 3%
Adjustments	3% − 8% of purchase price

Once you've determined a price range and location, you're ready to look at individual homes. Remember that much of a home's value is derived from the values of those surrounding it. Since the average residency in a house is seven years, consider the qualities that will be attractive to future buyers as well as those attractive to you.

Although it can be difficult, try to remember that you will probably want to sell this home someday. The more research you do today, the better your decision will look in the years to come.

注意：此部分试题请在**答题卡**1上作答。

1. Buying a home can mean building significant value through the years.
2. Prequalifying with your lender is a good way to determine how much mortgage you can afford.
3. There will be no ongoing costs besides your mortgage payments when buying a home.
4. Most Americans prefer houses to condos because condos have more association fees.
5. The first step in finding the right first home is to determine _____ and a location.
6. Possessing a home is the cornerstone of _____.

7. The housing expense ratio compares _____ to the buyer's gross monthly income.

8. Many home buyers are shocked to find that a down payment is not the only _____.

9. _____ are important considerations when selecting a neighborhood.

10. Brokers usually represent the seller, but they can be a _____ for buyers as well, concerning the home buying process.

Part III Listening Comprehension   (35 minutes)

Section A

Directions: *In this section, you will hear 8 short conversations and 2 long conversations. At the end of each conversation, one or more questions will be asked about what was said. Both the conversation and the questions will be spoken only once. After each question there will be a pause. During the pause, you must read the four choices marked A), B), C) and D), and decide which is the best answer. Then mark the corresponding letter on **Answer Sheet 2** with a single line through the centre.*

注意：此部分试题请在**答题卡**2上作答。

11. A) It's smaller than the old one.   C) It's quieter than the old one.
    B) It's larger than the old one.   D) It's worse than the old one.

12. A) He is unable to complete his plan.
    B) The woman does not agree with him.
    C) The approval of his plan has been delayed.
    D) He has to restart his work from the very beginning.

13. A) It is not difficult to pass the test.   C) The test is impossible to pass.
    B) The professor is considerate.   D) The professor is very strict.

14. A) The man drank the orange juice up.
    B) The man doesn't like orange juice.
    C) The man was in a car crash this morning.
    D) The man broke the container of juice.

15. A) At home.   C) On the counter.
    B) In the car.   D) In the auditorium.

16. A) At the Front Desk. C) At the Coffee Shop.
    B) At the office. D) At the Business Center.

17. A) One's last education entry should be listed last.
    B) One's work experience should be listed in chronological order.
    C) A long resume tends to impress the employer.
    D) A resume should not be too long.

18. A) Setting some time to work every day.
    B) Setting some time every day to imagine success.
    C) Dreaming with passion.
    D) Dreaming every day.

Questions 19 to 21 are based on the conversation you have just heard.

19. A) Because she is beautiful.
    B) Because she has a sweet voice.
    C) Because she won the singing competition.
    D) Because she is perfect.

20. A) The dress fits her very well.
    B) The dress is very expensive.
    C) She made the dress herself.
    D) She won the competition in the dress.

21. A) Because she has a date with her boyfriend.
    B) Because she will have dinner with her boss.
    C) Because she has to go home.
    D) Because she has to take part in the singing competition.

Questions 22 to 25 are based on the conversation you have just heard.

22. A) The humid weather. C) The warmer climate.
    B) The colder climate. D) The rain.

23. A) Carbon monoxide. C) Oxygen.
    B) Carbon dioxide. D) Hydrogen.

24. A) Don't burn any more wood or coal.
    B) Don't use aerosol hair sprays.
    C) Depend more on air-conditioners.
    D) Depend less on refrigerators.

25. A) The climate will become warmer and warmer.
    B) The earth will become a greenhouse.
    C) The polar icecaps will dissolve.
    D) The sea level will go down.

Section B

Directions: *In this section, you will hear 3 short passages. At the end of each passage, you will hear some questions. Both the passage and the questions will be spoken only once. After you hear a question, you must choose the best answer from the four choices marked A), B), C) and D). Then mark the corresponding letter on **Answer Sheet 2** with a single line through the centre.*

注意：此部分试题请在**答题卡 2** 上作答。

Passage One

Questions 26 to 28 are based on the passage you have just heard.

26. A) They enjoy more freedom and rights.
    B) They can spend their money as they like.
    C) Their relatives help them with childcare.
    D) They have all the power of the family.

27. A) Women are unwilling to get outside help.
    B) Older women often have to live alone.
    C) Family structure is more patriarchal.
    D) Their husbands don't help them as usual.

28. A) Because they have to stay home.
    B) Because they don't have enough money.
    C) Because they are too busy to have free time.
    D) Because they have to look after their children.

Passage Two

Questions 29 to 31 are based on the passage you have just heard.

29. A) Russia.   C) The Middle East.
    B) Africa.   D) Canada.

30. A) A few years after 1932.   C) In 1932.

     B) A few years after 1908.   D) In recent years.

31. A) This region produces most of the world's oil supplies.

     B) This region produces 1/3 of the world's oil supplies.

     C) This region produces 2/3 of the world's oil supplies.

     D) This region produces less oil than any other regions.

Passage Three

Questions 32 to 35 are based on the passage you have just heard.

32. A) A plan to turn Mars into a little earth.

     B) The necessity of changing Mars.

     C) Mars supporting life.

     D) Finding water in the Mars.

33. A) The project would wipe out all the native life forms on the Mars.

     B) The project will cost too much money and work.

     C) We would ruin Mars.

     D) We are destroying our own world at an unbelievable speed.

34. A) Water is a crucial factor for life.

     B) The project will have little effect on the native life forms supposed to live on the Mars.

     C) Monica Grady is in favor of carrying out the little earth project.

     D) The idea turning Mars into a little earth is nothing but a science fiction.

35. A) Scientists found liquid water in the Mars.

     B) Scientists found signs of methane in the Martian atmosphere.

     C) Scientists found a lot of good soil on the Mars.

     D) Scientists found some creatures living on the Mars.

Section C

Directions: *In this section, you will hear a passage three times. When the passage is read for the first time, you should listen carefully for its general idea. When the passage is read for the second time, you are required to fill in the blanks numbered from 36 to 43 with the exact words you have just heard. For blanks numbered from 44 to 46 you are required to fill in the missing information. For these blanks, you can either use the exact words you have just heard or write down the main points in your own* *words. Finally, when the passage is read for the third time, you should check what you have written.*

注意：此部分试题在**答题卡**2上；请在**答题卡**2上作答。

Part IV   Reading Comprehension (Reading in Depth)

(25 minutes)

Section A

Directions： *In this section, there is a short passage with 5 questions or incomplete statements. Read the passage carefully. Then answer the questions or complete the statements in the fewest possible words on* **Answer Sheet 2.**

Questions 47 to 51 are based on the following passage.

One of England's biggest celebrations is Guy Fawkes Night，which commemorates the defeat of an anti-government plot on November 5，1605. English Catholics led by Guy Fawkes were caught before they could blow up the House of Parliament. Today，on November 5，children make stuffed figures of Guy Fawkes and ask their neighbors for "a penny for the guy." The money is used to buy fireworks and the guy is tossed into a bonfire.

The nearest Sunday to November 11，Remembrance Day，honors Britain's war dead. People wear red paper poppies that symbolize the flowers in World War I burial grounds. They attend services at churches and war memorials and observe two minutes of silence.

During the Christmas season，choirs sing carols in churches and people may go out in the evenings to sing carols in front of their neighbors' houses. On Christmas Eve，people place presents under a decorated Christmas tree and children hang stockings or pillowcases at the foot of their beds. They are hoping for gifts from Father Christmas (the English name for Santa Claus). Many families attend morning church services and listen to the Queen's Christmas message on the radio or television. At midday or in the evening，families sit down to a hearty meal，with roast turkey，goose or beef，and a rich Christmas pudding made with dried fruit and nuts and crowned with flaming brandy. Children usually have two weeks' holiday at Easter time. Many families mark Easter Sunday by attending church services，decorating eggs and preparing a special family meal.

For centuries，England did not celebrate a special national holiday. Recently， however，St. George's Day，April 23，has been celebrated as England's national day. Some people display flags bearing the red and white cross of St. George，the country's patron saint，and exchange greeting cards.

注意：此部分试题请在**答题卡** 2 上作答。

47. The passage is mainly about _____.

48. Stuffed figures are tossed into a bonfire in the celebration of _____.

49. When do people observe two minutes of silence?

50. Where are carols sung during the Christmas season?

51. What does the Queen do on Christmas?

Section B

Directions: *There are 2 passages in this section. Each passage is followed by some questions or unfinished statements. For each of them there are four choices marked A)，B)，C) and D). You should decide on the best choice and mark the corresponding letter on **Answer Sheet 2** with a single line through the centre.*

Passage One

Questions 52 to 56 are based on the following passage.

In 1985，a precursor to the Internet was devised by two men in San Francisco. One was Larry Brilliant，a maverick public health physician who now heads the Google Foundation. The other was Stewart Brand，a journalist and entrepreneur who had the knack of being present at revolutions in culture and technology.

Their invention was the Well，an electronic network intended to be a "virtual community" similar to the communes founded in the hills of northern California，Colorado and New Mexico. The Well let members debate topics from technology to The Grateful Dead via a form of instant messaging.

It is easy to spot what the Well of 1985 became：Web 2.0. The virtual community has been replicated in social networks such as Myspace and user-generated content such as YouTube. Go back a further 20 years and you can see another root of the Internet：the counter-culture revolution of the 1960s.

Mr. Brand was also an instrumental figure in 1967. His seminal act was to publish the Whole Earth Catalog，a kind of Sears catalogue for hippies from which the Well got its name (Whole Earth 'Lectronic Link). The catalogue featured everything from tents to calculators.

The Internet has a similarly utopian quality: the co-founders of Google have "Don't be evil" as their informal motto. Ventures such as Wikipedia, the online volunteer-compiled encyclopedia, are based on the belief that communities of volunteers can do things as well as, or better than, individuals in hierarchical organizations.

The story of how the communes of the 1960s gave birth to the technology entrepreneurs of the past three decades is intriguing. One version has been told by John Markoff in *What the Dormouse Said: How the 60s Counterculture Shaped the Personal Computer*. This one is recounted by Fred Turner, a Stanford academic, in greater detail and with a tendency to categorize things into submission.

Turner focuses on one irony of the personal computer and Internet revolution: it grew from government-funded military research in the postwar period. The military-industrial complex required innovation that was dreamed up in cross-disciplinary laboratories such as Los Alamos and Oak Ridge. These became the early models for the approach to innovation at Silicon Valley companies.

The 1960s revolutionaries raged against the power of the corporation and oppressive technology in the form of the mainframe computer. By taking to the hills, they wanted to return to a pre-technological state of nature. Yet the children of the 1960s went on to invent the personal computer, sold by Steve Jobs at Apple Computer as a weapon against dull conformity. Technology had been reclaimed for the purposes of liberation.

注意：此部分试题请在**答题卡**2上作答。

52. From the passage, we can infer that the word "precursor" in the opening sentence means _____.

   A) a thing that comes before something else

   B) a thing that is quite old in history

   C) a thing that comes before something similar and influences its development

   D) a thing that comes before something different

53. Why was Mr. Brand an "instrumental figure" in 1967?

   A) Because he was powerful in his business.

   B) Because he was better at revolutions.

   C) Because he played an important role in the founding of the Well.

   D) Because he published an important catalogue for hippies.

54. What is "Sears" according to the passage?

A) It is a book for hippies.

B) It is a book including everything from tents to calculators.

C) It is a complete list of items of things that everyone should know.

D) It is a book showing goods for sale that people can buy.

55. All of the following are the origins of Web 2.0 EXCEPT _____.

A) the Well

B) the counter-culture revolution

C) the Whole Earth 'Lectronic Link

D) Myspace and YouTube

56. It is implied in the passage that _____.

A) Wikipedia is a revolutionary organization

B) the story of the origin of the technology entrepreneurs of the past three decades is very interesting

C) innovation had been worked out in some very strict laboratories

D) Steve Jobs sold personal computer as a weapon against the chaos he did not like in the society

Passage Two

Questions 57 to 61 are based on the following passage.

This time of the year, the windows of America are beginning to be dotted with carefully carved jack-o'-lanterns, but in a week or so, the streets will be splotched with pumpkin guts. Orange gourds will fly from car windows, fall from apartment balconies, career like cannon fire from the arms of pranksters craving the odd satisfaction of the dull thud.

There are, to be sure, more productive ways to deploy a Halloween pumpkin. Λ pumpkin grower in Wisconsin once turned a 500-pound Atlantic Giant into a boat.

But what we Americans almost certainly won't do is eat it. First cultivated more than 10,000 years ago in Mexico, cucurbitaceae were mainstays of the Native American diet. If for no other reason than its status as one of America's oldest cultivated crops, an honest pumpkin deserves our reverence.

The current batches that will soon litter the pavement, however, are for the most part cheap replicas inflated for the carving knife. Food in name only, they're a culinary trick without the treat.

During the colonial era, the pumpkin was just one squash among dozens, a vine-ripening vegetable unmarked by a distinctive color, size or shape. Native Americans grew it to be boiled, roasted and baked.

They routinely prepared pumpkin pancakes, pumpkin porridge, pumpkin stew and even pumpkin jerky.

Europeans readily incorporated the pumpkin into their own diet. Peter Kalm, a Swede visiting colonial America, wrote approvingly about "pumpkins of several kinds, oblong, round, flat or compressed, crook-necked, small, etc." He noted in his journal — on, coincidentally, Oct. 31, 1749 — how Europeans living in America cut them through the middle, take out the seeds, put the halves together again, and roast them in an oven, adding that "some butter is put in while they are warm."

Sound tasty. But one would be ill advised to follow Kalm's recipe with the pumpkins now grown on America's commercial farms. The most popular pumpkins today are grown to be porch décor rather than pie filling.

Fortunately, the edible pumpkin is not completely lost. By growing heirloom pumpkins, Americans can have their jack-o'-lantern and eat it too. Or they can search out heirloom pumpkins at some farmers' markets.

Next year, let's replace a fake pumpkin with a real one. It might cost a bit more, but there will finally be a credible reason not to smash the thing at the end of the evening. And most important, as Peter Kalm observed back in 1749, we could once again split it open, roast it, add butter and remind ourselves that some traditions — like cultivating vegetables to eat — should never be destroyed.

注意：此部分试题请在**答题卡 2** 上作答。

57. The word "pranksters" in the first paragraph probably refers to _____.
    A) people who like to do something interesting
    B) people who like to play tricks on somebody else
    C) people who are in the bad habit of scattering rubbish
    D) people who are satisfied with what they have done

58. What does the author mean by saying "If for no other reason than its status as one of America's oldest cultivated crops, an honest pumpkin deserves our reverence"?
    A) Because of its origin, we should pay more attention to an honest pumpkin.
    B) Because the pumpkin is the oldest crop in America, we should respect it.
    C) Because the native Americans depend mostly on pumpkins, we should protect the crop.
    D) Because of its position in history, we should have a feeling of admiration for real pumpkins.

59. How about the pumpkins grown on America's commercial farms?
    A) They can be filled into pies.

B) They are very delicious to eat.

C) They are expected to decorate Americans' houses.

D) They can be cooked following Kalm's recipe.

60. From the passage, it can be inferred that _____.

A) people can't eat pumpkins completely nowadays

B) Europeans did not enjoy eating pumpkins

C) native Americans depended mainly on pumpkins in their diet

D) pumpkin was first cultivated by Europeans

61. Which of the following can be the most suitable title for the passage?

A) Edible Pumpkins in America

B) Smash the Fake Pumpkins

C) The History of Pumpkins of Halloween

D) Meanwhile: A Halloween Pumpkin You Can Eat, Too

Part V   Error Correction   (15 minutes)

Directions: *This part consists of a short passage. In this passage, there are altogether 10 mistakes, one in each numbered line. You may have to change a word, add a word or delete a word. Mark out the mistakes and put the corrections in the blanks provided. If you change a word, cross it out and write the correct word in the corresponding blank. If you add a word, put an insertion mark (∧) in the right place and write the missing word in the blank. If you delete a word, cross it out and put a slash (/) in the blank.*

注意：此部分试题在**答题卡**2上；请在**答题卡**2上作答。

Part VI   Translation   (5 minutes)

Directions: *Complete the following sentences on **Answer Sheet 2** by translating into English the Chinese given in brackets.*

注意：此部分试题请在**答题卡**2上作答。

72. _____（谈到计算机和因特网），students all become

excited，eager to say something about their experience.

73. They _____（中断了生意来往）with that company as it suffered huge losses in the last financial year and went bankrupt.

74. Excessive exercise _____（对身体健康弊多利少）. Therefore we must control the amount of exercise we do.

75. It is a traditional Chinese virtue for the young on buses to yield their seats to _____（老弱病残）.

76. I should do this job _____（不管他们同意与否）.

答题卡 1 (Answer Sheet 1)

Part I   **Writing**   **(30 minutes)**

Directions: *For this part, you are allowed 30 minutes to write a composition on the topic* **Women in the Modern World**. *You should write at least* **120** *words following the outline given below in Chinese:*

1. 在当今社会中,妇女所起的作用日益增强
2. 随着妇女社会地位的改变,她们在家庭中的地位也得到了提高
3. 妇女的地位虽然有了一定改善,但是妇女的解放还没有完全实现

Women in the Modern World

答题卡1 (Answer Sheet 1)

_____
_____
_____
_____
_____
_____
_____
_____
_____
_____
_____
_____
_____
_____
_____
_____
_____
_____
_____
_____
_____
_____

Part II   Reading Comprehension (Skimming and Scanning) (15 minutes)

1. [Y] [N] [NG]   5. _____   8. _____
2. [Y] [N] [NG]
                       6. _____   9. _____
3. [Y] [N] [NG]
4. [Y] [N] [NG]   7. _____   10. _____

答题卡 2 (Answer Sheet 2)

Part III   Section A   **Section B**

11. [A] [B] [C] [D]   16. [A] [B] [C] [D]   21. [A] [B] [C] [D]   26. [A] [B] [C] [D]   31. [A] [B] [C] [D]
12. [A] [B] [C] [D]   17. [A] [B] [C] [D]   22. [A] [B] [C] [D]   27. [A] [B] [C] [D]   32. [A] [B] [C] [D]
13. [A] [B] [C] [D]   18. [A] [B] [C] [D]   23. [A] [B] [C] [D]   28. [A] [B] [C] [D]   33. [A] [B] [C] [D]
14. [A] [B] [C] [D]   19. [A] [B] [C] [D]   24. [A] [B] [C] [D]   29. [A] [B] [C] [D]   34. [A] [B] [C] [D]
15. [A] [B] [C] [D]   20. [A] [B] [C] [D]   25. [A] [B] [C] [D]   30. [A] [B] [C] [D]   35. [A] [B] [C] [D]

Part III   Section C

The automobile has many advantages. Above all, it (36) _____ people freedom to go where they want when they want to. To most people, cars are also personal (37) _____ machines that serve as (38) _____ of power, success, speed, excitement, and (39) _____. In (40) _____, much of the world's economy is built on producing vehicles and supplying roads, services, and repairs of vehicles. Half of the world's paychecks are (41) _____.

In spite of their advantages, motor vehicles have many harmful effects on human lives and on air, water, land and wildlife resources. Though we (42) _____ to deny it, (43) _____ in cars is one of the most dangerous things we do in our daily lives.

Every year, (44) _____, and they injure or permanently disable ten million more. (45) _____

_____.

Motor vehicles are the largest sources of air pollution, producing a haze of smog over the world's cities. (46) _____.

答题卡 2 (Answer Sheet 2)

Part IV   Section A   Part V   Error Correction   (15 minutes)

47. _____

_____

48. _____

_____

49. _____

_____

50. _____

_____

51. _____

_____

Changes in the way people live bring about changes in the jobs that they do. More and more people live in towns and cities instead on farms and in villages. Cities and states have to provide service city people want, such like more police protection, more hospitals, and more schools. This means that more policemen, more nurses and technicians, and more teachers must be hired. Advances in technology has also changed people's lives. Dishwashers and washing machines do jobs that were once done by the hand. The widespread use of such electrical appliances means that there is a need for servicemen to keep it running properly.

62. _____

63. _____

64. _____

65. _____

66. _____

Part IV   Section B

52. [A][B][C][D]
53. [A][B][C][D]
54. [A][B][C][D]
55. [A][B][C][D]
56. [A][B][C][D]
57. [A][B][C][D]
58. [A][B][C][D]
59. [A][B][C][D]
60. [A][B][C][D]
61. [A][B][C][D]

People are earning higher wages and salaries. This leads changes in the way of life. As income goes down, people may not want more food to eat or more clothes to wear. But they may want more and better care from doctors, dentists and hospitals. They are likely to travel more and to want more education. Nevertheless, many more jobs are available in these services.

The government also affects the kind of works people do. The governments of most countries spend huge sums of money on international defense. They hire thousands of engineers, scientists, clerks, typists and secretaries to work on the many different aspects of defense.

67. _____

68. _____

69. _____

70. _____

71. _____

Part VI   Translation   (5 minutes)

72. _____

73. _____

74. _____

75. _____

76. _____

PRACTICE TEST 7

Part I Writing   (30 minutes)

注意：此部分试题在**答题卡**1上。

Part II Reading Comprehension (Skimming and Scanning)
(15 minutes)

Directions: *In this part, you will have 15 minutes to go over the passage quickly and answer the questions on **Answer Sheet 1**.*

For questions 1 – 4, mark
Y *(for YES)*   *if the statement agrees with the information given in the passage;*
N *(for NO)*   *if the statement contradicts the information given in the passage;*
NG *(for NOT GIVEN)*   *if the information is not given in the passage.*
For questions 5 – 10, complete the sentences with the information given in the passage.

History of the Royal Observatory, Greenwich

The Royal Observatory, home of Greenwich Mean Time and the Prime Meridian line, is one of the most important historic scientific sites in the world. It was founded by Charles II in 1675 and is, by international decree, the official starting point for each new day, year and millennium (at the stroke of midnight GMT as measured from the Prime Meridian).

The Royal Observatory is entering one of the most exciting periods in its history. The Time and Space Project is a £15 million redevelopment of the site which includes a new, state-of-the-art planetarium, new galleries and an education centre.

The first milestone of the redevelopment was the opening of the Time galleries in February 2006. Fundraising was completed in November 2005 — over a year before the planetarium and Space galleries open.

The Observatory, part of the National Maritime Museum, is one of the most famous features of Maritime Greenwich — since 1997 a UNESCO World Heritage Site. Visitors to the Observatory can stand in both the eastern and western hemispheres simultaneously by placing their feet either side of the Prime Meridian — the centre of world time and space. The Observatory galleries unravel the extraordinary phenomena of time, space and astronomy; the Planetarium lets visitors explore the wonders of the heavens; and Flamsteed House, Sir Christopher Wren's original building, also has London's only public camera obscura.

Charles II appointed John Flamsteed as his first Astronomer Royal in March 1675. The Observatory was built to improve navigation at sea and "find the so-much desired longitude of places" — one's exact position east and west — while at sea and out of sight of land, by astronomical means. This was inseparable from the accurate measurement of time, for which the Observatory became generally famous in the 19th century.

A disaster at sea in 1707 killed over 2,000 men and prompted greater calls for more reliable means of navigation. In 1714, Parliament established a panel of experts, the Board of Longitude, and offered a massive £20,000 reward (equivalent of about £2 million today) to anyone who could solve the problem of finding longitude at sea. It took nearly 60 years for the prize to be claimed. In the end it went not to a famous astronomer, scientist or mathematician, but to a little-known Yorkshire carpenter turned clockmaker, John Harrison.

Harrison's H4 was to change navigation forever. All four of his ground-breaking timekeepers are kept in full working order on display in the Harrison gallery — the highlight of a visit to the Observatory. Find out more about John Harrison and his 50-year quest to solve the longitude problem in our online feature.

The Royal Observatory is also the source of the Prime Meridian of the world, Longitude 0°0'0". Every place on the Earth is measured in terms of its distance east or west from this line. The line itself divides the eastern and western hemispheres of the Earth — just as the Equator divides the northern and southern hemispheres.

The Prime Meridian is defined by the position of the large "Transit Circle" telescope in the Observatory's Meridian Building. This was built by Sir George Biddell Airy, the 7th Astronomer Royal, in 1850. The cross-hairs in the eyepiece of the Transit Circle precisely define Longitude 0° for the world.

Since the late 19th century, the Prime Meridian at Greenwich has served as the co-ordinate base for the calculation of Greenwich Mean Time. Before this, almost every town in the world kept its own local time. There were no national or international conventions to set how time should be measured, or when the day would begin and end, or what the length of an hour might be. However, with the vast expansion of the railway and communication networks during the 1850s and 1860s, the worldwide need for an international time standard became imperative.

The Greenwich Meridian was chosen to be the Prime Meridian of the World in 1884. Forty-one delegates from 25 nations met in Washington, D.C. for the International Meridian Conference. By the end of the conference, Greenwich had won the prize of Longitude 0° by a vote of 22 in favour to 1 against (San Domingo), with two abstentions (France and Brazil). There were two main reasons for the victory:

- the USA had already chosen Greenwich as the basis for its own national time-zone system;
- at the time, 72% of the world's commerce depended on sea-charts which used Greenwich as the Prime Meridian.

The decision, essentially, was based on the argument that by naming Greenwich as Longitude 0°, it would inconvenience the least number of people. Therefore, the Prime Meridian at Greenwich became the centre of world time, and the starting point of each new day, year and millennium.

In 1960, shortly after the transfer of the Royal Greenwich Observatory (RGO) to Herstmonceux (and later Cambridge), Flamsteed House was transferred to the National Maritime Museum's care and over the next seven years the remaining buildings on the site were also transferred and restored for Museum use. Here the collections of scientific, especially astronomical instruments has continued to grow. Following the closure of the RGO at Cambridge in October 1998, the site is now again known as the Royal Observatory, Greenwich.

注意：此部分试题请在**答题卡 1** 上作答。

1. The passage introduces the history of the Royal Observatory, one of the most important historic scientific sites in Great Britain.
2. The Royal Observatory attracts millions of tourists every year.
3. The Royal Observatory has been famous all over the world since it was founded in 1675.
4. The Royal Observatory is the official starting point for each new day, year and millennium.
5. The opening of the Time galleries in February 2006 is _____ of the redevelopment of the Royal Observatory.
6. People can stand in both _____ at the same time by placing their feet either side of the Prime Meridian.
7. A disaster at sea in 1707 showed that people need more _____.
8. Since the late 19th century, the Prime Meridian at Greenwich has served as the

coordinate base for _____.

9. In the year _____, Greenwich had won the prize of Longitude 0° by a vote of 22 in favour to 1 against, with two abstentions.

10. People argued that it would inconvenience _____ by naming Greenwich as Longitude 0°.

Part III Listening Comprehension (35 minutes)

Section A

Directions: *In this section, you will hear 8 short conversations and 2 long conversations. At the end of each conversation, one or more questions will be asked about what was said. Both the conversation and the questions will be spoken only once. After each question there will be a pause. During the pause, you must read the four choices marked A), B), C) and D), and decide which is the best answer. Then mark the corresponding letter on **Answer Sheet 2** with a single line through the centre.*

注意：此部分试题请在**答题卡 2** 上作答。

11. A) Understanding and respect.
    B) Good price.
    C) Famous institutions.
    D) Employees' graduation certificates.

12. A) None.   B) One.   C) Two.   D) Three.

13. A) Making his speech interesting.
    B) Making the concepts easier to understand.
    C) Making the students interested in engineering.
    D) Having no idea how to simplify the procedure.

14. A) It's going to rain.
    B) It's very dark.
    C) The man's watch stopped three hours ago.
    D) It's ten o'clock at night.

15. A) At 10:00.   B) At 9:00.   C) At 8:45.   D) At 9:15.

16. A) He's not going to ask for his professor's colleagues for help.
    B) He's going to rely on his professor's colleagues for help.

C) He's going to accept any assistance he can find.

D) He's not going to depend on his own connections.

17. A) The speech was too long.

B) He had a late class.

C) He doesn't like the president.

D) The rain didn't let up until after the speech.

18. A) Archaeologist.   B) Philosopher.   C) Sociologist.   D) Architect.

Questions 19 to 21 are based on the conversation you have just heard.

19. A) England.   B) Spain.   C) Germany.   D) Italy.

20. A) Bright red.   B) Dark red.   C) Brown.   D) Blue.

21. A) The address of where the traveler is staying in England.

B) The address of the traveler's home.

C) The address of the traveler's office.

D) The address of the traveler's friend.

Questions 22 to 25 are based on the conversation you have just heard.

22. A) Because he thinks people can always make money by investing in the stock market.

B) Because he thinks it has been a bear market for more than four years, and now it's time for it to pick up.

C) Because he has a lot of money to lose.

D) Because he is an expert in investing in the stock market.

23. A) She thinks negatively about the market.

B) She agrees with the man.

C) She encourages the man to invest in the stock market.

D) She thinks there is no risk in investing in the stock market.

24. A) About four years.   C) About ten years.

B) About five years.   D) About seven years.

25. A) He decides to invest his money in the stock market.

B) He decides to spend all his money.

C) He decides to lend his money to the woman to invest in the stock market.

D) He decides to put his money in the bank.

Section B

Directions: *In this section, you will hear 3 short passages. At the end of each passage, you will hear some questions. Both the passage and the questions will be spoken only once. After you hear a question, you must choose the best answer from the four choices marked A), B), C) and D). Then mark the corresponding letter on **Answer Sheet 2** with a single line through the centre.*

注意：此部分试题请在**答题卡 2** 上作答。

Passage One

Questions 26 to 28 are based on the passage you have just heard.

26. A) More than 10,000 men and women have lost their lives on the slopes.
    B) The first men reached the top were both from New Zealand.
    C) To conquer Qomolangma is an honor for every mountaineer.
    D) Chinese team got to the top of Qomolangma on May 23.

27. a. extremely cold   b. no plants there   c. wild animals   d. falling ice
    e. too many people   f. lack of oxygen   g. no money   h. avalanches

    A) a, d, e, f   C) b, d, g, h
    B) a, d, f, h   D) c, f, g, h

28. A) It's boring.   C) It's terrible.
    B) It's meaningless.   D) It's exciting.

Passage Two

Questions 29 to 31 are based on the passage you have just heard.

29. A) Unmarried man.   C) Unmarried women.
    B) Spouseless families.   D) Young children.

30. A) She had to look after her baby.
    B) She got married.
    C) Her family could not support her any longer.
    D) She hated school.

31. A) Nobody wants to help them.
    B) There is not enough housing.
    C) They have no money to rent a house.

D) They live an undisciplined life.

Passage Three

Questions 32 to 35 are based on the passage you have just heard.

32. A) Light darkens silver salt.
    B) Light darkens natural salt.
    C) Light darkens silver.
    D) Light darkens self-developing film.

33. A) By making use of special paper.　　C) By making the temporary image.
    B) By adding common salt to silver.　　D) By using a special piece of metal.

34. A) 1727.　　　　B) 1826.　　　　C) 1839.　　　　D) 1860.

35. A) He was a brave soldier.　　　C) He painted portraits.
    B) He took war photographs.　　D) He designed a portable camera.

Section C

Directions: *In this section, you will hear a passage three times. When the passage is read for the first time, you should listen carefully for its general idea. When the passage is read for the second time, you are required to fill in the blanks numbered from 36 to 43 with the exact words you have just heard. For blanks numbered from 44 to 46 you are required to fill in the missing information. For these blanks, you can either use the exact words you have just heard or write down the main points in your own words. Finally, when the passage is read for the third time, you should check what you have written.*

注意：此部分试题在**答题卡 2** 上；请在**答题卡 2** 上作答。

Part IV　Reading Comprehension (Reading in Depth)
(25 minutes)

Section A

Directions: *In this section, there is a short passage with 5 questions or incomplete statements. Read the passage carefully. Then answer the questions or complete the statements in the fewest possible words on **Answer Sheet 2**.*

Questions 47 to 51 are based on the following passage.

Sex prejudices are based on and justified by the ideology that biology is destiny. According to the ideology, basic biological and psychological differences exist between the sexes. These differences require each sex to play a separate role in social life. Women are the weaker sex — both physically and emotionally. Thus, they are naturally suited, much more so than men, to the performance of domestic duties. A woman's place, under normal circumstances, is within the protective environment of the home. Nature has determined that women play care-taker roles, such as wife and mother and homemaker. On the other hand men are best suited to go out into the competitive world of work and politics, where serious responsibilities must be taken on. Men are to be the providers; women and children are "dependents."

The idea also holds that women who wish to work outside the household should naturally fill these jobs that are in line with the special capabilities of their sex. It is thus appropriate for women, not men, to be employed as nurses, social workers, elementary school teachers, household helpers, and clerks and secretaries. These positions are simply an extension of women's domestic role. Informal distinctions between "women's work" and "men's work" in the labor force, according to the ideology, are simply a functional reflection of the basic differences between the sexes.

Finally, the ideology suggests that nature has worked her will in another significant way. For the human species to survive over time, its members must regularly reproduce. Thus, women must, whether at home or in the labor force, make the most of their physical appearance.

So goes the ideology. It is, of course, not true that basic biological and psychological differences between the sexes require each to play sex-defined roles in social life. There is much evidence that sex roles vary from society to society, and those role differences that do exist are largely learned. But to the degree people actually believe that biology is destiny and that nature intended for men and women to make different contributions to society, sex-defined roles will be seen as totally acceptable.

注意：此部分试题请在**答题卡**2上作答。

47. There are _____ between the sexes according to the ideology that biology is destiny.

48. According to this ideology, who are supposed to take more serious responsibilities, men or women?

49. Why are jobs such as nursing and teaching considered suitable for women?

50. This passage is mainly about _____.

51. What is the author's opinion about "sex-defined roles"?

Section B

Directions: *There are 2 passages in this section. Each passage is followed by some questions or unfinished statements. For each of them there are four choices marked A), B), C) and D). You should decide on the best choice and mark the corresponding letter on* **Answer Sheet 2** *with a single line through the centre.*

Passage One

Questions 52 to 56 are based on the following passage.

Still no word on whether a stitch in time really does save nine, but a UC Irvine professor has uncovered evidence to support another famous proverb, "Good fences make good neighbors."

In a study of 15,000 Americans, economist Jan Brueckner found that suburban living is better for people's social life than city dwelling. The less crowded a neighborhood is, the friendlier its residents become, the report says.

For every 10% drop in population density, the likelihood of people talking to their neighbors once a week goes up 10%, regardless of race, income, education, marital status or age. Involvement in hobby-oriented clubs also soars as population density falls, the study found.

Such behavior contradicts a wide-spread criticism that suburban sprawl causes social isolation and anonymity.

"Our findings suggest the old proverb may be true: 'Good fences make good neighbors,'" Brueckner said.

The professor, who co-wrote the study with Ann Largey of Dublin City University in Ireland, offered several theories on why city slickers don't mingle as much as their suburban counterparts.

In crowded environments, "people are in your face all the time and you kind of want some privacy." Fear of crime can exacerbate wariness, he said.

Another possible factor: the abundance of museums, theaters and other entertainment options in urban areas means "you don't have to reach out to others to entertain yourself," he said.

The idea that generous amounts of personal space and boundaries help people get along has been under assault for years.

In 1914，poet Robert Frost took a swipe at the "good fences, good neighbors" theory in "Mending Wall":

"Before I built a wall I'd ask to know

What I was walling in or walling out ..."

注意：此部分试题请在**答题卡**2上作答。

52. The following are the possible results of the fall of the population density EXCEPT that _____.
    A) people will become friendlier with their neighbors
    B) people will take an active part in clubs
    C) people will live in anonymity
    D) people are likely to talk with their neighbors

53. What does the word "anonymity" mean in the fourth paragraph?
    A) Social isolation.　　　　　　C) Familiarity.
    B) Hostile condition.　　　　　D) Good relationship.

54. Which of the following is NOT correct according to the passage?
    A) It is once believed that with the spreading of suburbs, people tend to become strangers.
    B) Jan Brueckner proved in his research that the old famous proverb "Good fences make good neighbors" was correct.
    C) People living in the suburbs enjoy a better social life.
    D) City slickers have few options to entertain themselves.

55. An inference which may be made from the passage is that _____.
    A) the author must be living in the suburb
    B) city slickers take an active part in social events
    C) people have long believed that enough personal space and boundaries will help people get along well
    D) fear of crime may separate city dwellers from each other

56. What's the attitude of the poet Robert Frost towards the theory "good fences, good neighbors"?
    A) He thought highly of the theory.
    B) He believed that there should be a wall between people.
    C) He agreed to mend a wall.
    D) He criticized the theory.

Passage Two

Questions 57 to 61 are based on the following passage.

To produce the upheaval in the United States that changed and modernized the domain of higher education from the mid-1880's, three primary causes interacted. The emergence of a half dozen leaders in education provided the personal force that was needed. Moreover, an outcry for a fresher, more practical, and more advanced kind of instruction arose among the alumni and friends of nearly all of the old colleges and grew into a movement that overrode all conservative opposition. The aggressive "Young Yale" movement appeared, demanding partial alumni control, a more liberal spirit, and a broader course of study. The graduates of Harvard College simultaneously rallied to relieve the college's poverty and demand new enterprise. Education was pushing toward higher standards in the East by throwing off church leadership everywhere, and in the West by finding a wider range of studies and a new sense of public duty.

The old style classical education received most crushing blow in the citadel of Harvard College, where Dr. Charles Eliot, a young captain of thirty-five, son of a former treasurer of Harvard, led the progressive forces. Five revolutionary advances were made during the first years of Dr. Eliot's administration. They were the elevation and amplification of entrance requirements, the enlargement of the curriculum and the development of the elective system, the recognition of graduate study in the liberal arts, the raising of professional training in law, medicine, and engineering to a postgraduate level, and the fostering of greater maturity in student life. Standards of admission were sharply advanced in 1872 − 1873 and 1876 − 1877. By the appointment of a dean to take charge of student affairs, and a wise handling of discipline, the undergraduates were led to regard themselves more as young gentlemen and less as young animals. One new course of study after another was opened up — science, music, the history of the fine arts, advanced Spanish political economy, physics, classical philosophy, and international law.

注意：此部分试题请在**答题卡 2** 上作答。

57. What's the meaning of "upheaval" in the opening sentence?
    A) Emergence.
    B) Turbulence.
    C) Outcry.
    D) Opposition.

58. According to the passage, the changes in higher education during the later 1800's were the result of _____.

A) rallies held by westerners expecting to compete with eastern schools

B) the demands of social organizations

C) efforts of interested individuals to redefine the educational system

D) plans developed by conservatives

59. Which of the following can be inferred about Harvard College before progressive changes occurred?

A) Classes ended earlier.　　　　　　C) Courses were more practical.

B) Students were younger.　　　　　　D) Admission standards were lower.

60. It can be concluded that a characteristic of the classical course of study was _____.

A) courses were so difficult that most student failed

B) most students majored in education

C) students were limited in their choice of courses

D) students have to pass five levels of study

61. Which of the following is the author's main purpose in the passage?

A) To explain the history of Harvard College.

B) To compare Harvard with Yale before the turn of the century.

C) To criticize the conditions of the United States' universities in the nineteenth century.

D) To describe innovations in the United States' higher education in the later 1800's.

Part V　Error Correction　　　　　　　　　(15 minutes)

Directions: *This part consists of a short passage. In this passage, there are altogether 10 mistakes, one in each numbered line. You may have to change a word, add a word or delete a word. Mark out the mistakes and put the corrections in the blanks provided. If you change a word, cross it out and write the correct word in the corresponding blank. If you add a word, put an insertion mark (∧) in the right place and write the missing word in the blank. If you delete a word, cross it out and put a slash (/) in the blank.*

注意：此部分试题在**答题卡 2** 上；请在**答题卡 2** 上作答。

Part VI   Translation   (5 minutes)

Directions: *Complete the following sentences on Answer Sheet 2 by translating into English the Chinese given in brackets.*

注意：此部分试题请在**答题卡**2上作答。

72. _____. （从长远看，我们应该学习更多的科技知识。） Besides our major subjects, knowledge of computers, English and driving is necessary for our work.

73. _____ （他们也许可以选择其他任何人做这工作），but they picked me.

74. In spite of the fact that _____ （移动电话的资费通常是固定线路电话资费的两倍），they are still very popular, especially among the young people.

75. A change in the money supply brings _____ （支出的相应变化）.

76. Whenever conflicts arose between her and her husband, she _____ （占上风），for she alone controlled the bulk of the family fortune.

答题卡 1 (Answer Sheet 1)

学校:	准 考 证 号

学校:

姓名:

划线要求

准 考 证 号

[0] [0] [0] [0] [0] [0] [0] [0] [0] [0] [0] [0] [0] [0] [0]
[1] [1] [1] [1] [1] [1] [1] [1] [1] [1] [1] [1] [1] [1] [1]
[2] [2] [2] [2] [2] [2] [2] [2] [2] [2] [2] [2] [2] [2] [2]
[3] [3] [3] [3] [3] [3] [3] [3] [3] [3] [3] [3] [3] [3] [3]
[4] [4] [4] [4] [4] [4] [4] [4] [4] [4] [4] [4] [4] [4] [4]
[5] [5] [5] [5] [5] [5] [5] [5] [5] [5] [5] [5] [5] [5] [5]
[6] [6] [6] [6] [6] [6] [6] [6] [6] [6] [6] [6] [6] [6] [6]
[7] [7] [7] [7] [7] [7] [7] [7] [7] [7] [7] [7] [7] [7] [7]
[8] [8] [8] [8] [8] [8] [8] [8] [8] [8] [8] [8] [8] [8] [8]
[9] [9] [9] [9] [9] [9] [9] [9] [9] [9] [9] [9] [9] [9] [9]

Part I　　　　　　　　　**Writing**　　　　　　　　**(30 minutes)**

Directions: *For this part, you are allowed 30 minutes to write a composition on the topic* ***The Relationship Between Teaching and Learning****. You should write at least 120 words following the outline given below in Chinese:*

1. "教"与"学"的关系有积极与消极之分
2. 怎样建立积极的"教""学"关系
3. 积极的"教""学"关系的效果

The Relationship Between Teaching and Learning

答题卡 1 (Answer Sheet 1)

Part II   Reading Comprehension (Skimming and Scanning) (15 minutes)

1. [Y] [N] [NG]   5. _____   8. _____

2. [Y] [N] [NG]

3. [Y] [N] [NG]   6. _____   9. _____

4. [Y] [N] [NG]

7. _____   10. _____

答题卡 2 (Answer Sheet 2)

学校:

姓名:

划线要求

准 考 证 号

[0]	[0]	[0]	[0]	[0]	[0]	[0]	[0]	[0]	[0]	[0]	[0]	[0]	[0]	[0]
[1]	[1]	[1]	[1]	[1]	[1]	[1]	[1]	[1]	[1]	[1]	[1]	[1]	[1]	[1]
[2]	[2]	[2]	[2]	[2]	[2]	[2]	[2]	[2]	[2]	[2]	[2]	[2]	[2]	[2]
[3]	[3]	[3]	[3]	[3]	[3]	[3]	[3]	[3]	[3]	[3]	[3]	[3]	[3]	[3]
[4]	[4]	[4]	[4]	[4]	[4]	[4]	[4]	[4]	[4]	[4]	[4]	[4]	[4]	[4]
[5]	[5]	[5]	[5]	[5]	[5]	[5]	[5]	[5]	[5]	[5]	[5]	[5]	[5]	[5]
[6]	[6]	[6]	[6]	[6]	[6]	[6]	[6]	[6]	[6]	[6]	[6]	[6]	[6]	[6]
[7]	[7]	[7]	[7]	[7]	[7]	[7]	[7]	[7]	[7]	[7]	[7]	[7]	[7]	[7]
[8]	[8]	[8]	[8]	[8]	[8]	[8]	[8]	[8]	[8]	[8]	[8]	[8]	[8]	[8]
[9]	[9]	[9]	[9]	[9]	[9]	[9]	[9]	[9]	[9]	[9]	[9]	[9]	[9]	[9]

Part III   Section A

Section B

11. [A] [B] [C] [D]   16. [A] [B] [C] [D]   21. [A] [B] [C] [D]   26. [A] [B] [C] [D]   31. [A] [B] [C] [D]
12. [A] [B] [C] [D]   17. [A] [B] [C] [D]   22. [A] [B] [C] [D]   27. [A] [B] [C] [D]   32. [A] [B] [C] [D]
13. [A] [B] [C] [D]   18. [A] [B] [C] [D]   23. [A] [B] [C] [D]   28. [A] [B] [C] [D]   33. [A] [B] [C] [D]
14. [A] [B] [C] [D]   19. [A] [B] [C] [D]   24. [A] [B] [C] [D]   29. [A] [B] [C] [D]   34. [A] [B] [C] [D]
15. [A] [B] [C] [D]   20. [A] [B] [C] [D]   25. [A] [B] [C] [D]   30. [A] [B] [C] [D]   35. [A] [B] [C] [D]

Part III   Section C

There are many (36) _____ about the beginning of drama in ancient Greece. The one most widely accepted today is based on the assumption that drama (37) _____ from ritual. The argument for this view goes as follows. In the beginning, human beings viewed the natural forces of the world, even the seasonal changes, as (38) _____, and they (39) _____, through various means, to control these unknown and (40) _____ powers. Those measures which appeared to bring the (41) _____ results were then retained and repeated until they (42) _____ into fixed rituals. Eventually stories (43) _____ which explained or veiled the mysteries of the rites. (44) _____

_____.

(45) _____.

According to this view, tales are gradually elaborated, at first through the use of impersonation, action and dialogue by a narrator and then through the assumption of each of the roles by a different person. (46) _____

_____.

答题卡 2 (Answer Sheet 2)

Part IV   Section A   Part V   Error Correction   (15 minutes)

47. _____

48. _____

49. _____

50. _____

51. _____

A rock painting in a Spanish cave, dating from prehistoric time, shows a man raising a honeybee hive. The honeybee has been a friend to man for untold centuries.

62. _____

The honeybee we know, Apis Mellifera, introduced into New England early in the seventeenth century. Our familiar saying, "as busy as a bee," refers into this industrious creature. Central to the life of the honeybee hive is the queen, a bee that is fed on royal jelly with the worker bees and thus becomes a queen. The only function of the males (drones) is to provide few possible mates for the queen. Once mated, the queen can continue to lay fertile eggs for several years. At times she may lay a thousand or two a day, but even more. The busy worker bees, all females, must care for these eggs, and for the emerging young, as just one of its duties in helping to continue the honeybee species. The drones, who do no work, are tolerated until the supply of nectar decreases. Then these males are forcibly removed from the hive and are refused to reenter by the guards at entrance. A disabled worker will be removed just as promptly. Only productive workers are tolerated. Thus we see in the hive three parts: the queen, the productive worker bees and the males, or drones. The bees that you and I commonly observe in a summer day in the country are all workers. We may see them on the alert, guarding the hive entrance or flying about busily gathering food for the hive. At the very height of its development, a hive may hold as much as 70,000 bees.

63. _____

64. _____

65. _____

66. _____

67. _____

68. _____

69. _____

70. _____

71. _____

Part IV   Section B

52. [A][B][C][D]

53. [A][B][C][D]

54. [A][B][C][D]

55. [A][B][C][D]

56. [A][B][C][D]

57. [A][B][C][D]

58. [A][B][C][D]

59. [A][B][C][D]

60. [A][B][C][D]

61. [A][B][C][D]

Part VI   Translation   (5 minutes)

72. _____

73. _____

74. _____

75. _____

76. _____

PRACTICE TEST 8

Part I Writing (30 minutes)

注意：此部分试题在**答题卡**1上。

Part II Reading Comprehension (Skimming and Scanning) (15 minutes)

Directions: *In this part, you will have 15 minutes to go over the passage quickly and answer the questions on **Answer Sheet 1**.*

For questions 1 – 4, mark

Y *(for YES)*　　　　　*if the statement agrees with the information given in the passage;*

N *(for NO)*　　　　　*if the statement contradicts the information given in the passage;*

NG *(for NOT GIVEN)*　*if the information is not given in the passage.*

For questions 5 – 10, complete the sentences with the information given in the passage.

Tuition Fees

Tuition fees are charged on the basis of an academic session of three terms. For certain lecture courses special fees may be charged. All tuition fees and payment terms are subject to annual revision. Information on up-to-date fee rates will be sent to all applicants in the March before the October start of session. Up-to-date fees information is available at the Student Finance website.

Home and European Union Students

The fees for home and EU undergraduate courses for 2008 entry have yet to be confirmed. However, in 2007 the College will charge the maximum tuition fee level, £3,070, allowed under government legislation. The figure for 2008 is subject to an annual increase in line with inflation and will be finalised nearer the time.

Overseas Students

Tuition fees for 2008 – 09 have yet to be finalised. Fees for 2007 – 08 are detailed below as a guide.

Faculty of Engineering (except the Department of Bioengineering)	£18,500
Department of Bioengineering	£17,350
Faculty of Natural Sciences (except Department of Chemistry, Department of Mathematics, BSci and MSci in Biomedical Science)	£17,350
Department of Chemistry	£18,400
Department of Mathematics	£14,400
BSci/MSci in Biomedical Science	£18,350
Faculty of Medicine (Pre-clinical)	£22,650
Faculty of Medicine (Clinical)	£33,800

Students completing the MBBS course without qualifying may extend their course by payment of a proportion of the appropriate annual fee. Extension fees are payable even if arrangements are made for revision to take place away from the College.

Students spending a full year away from the College on an approved SOCRATES-ERASMUS exchange are exempt from fees for that academic year.

Payment of Tuition Fees

While home and EU undergraduate students can elect to pay their fees directly to the College at the time of registration, they will also be eligible to take out a tuition fee loan from the Student Loans Company. Students who take this option will start to repay the loan only after graduation and when they are earning above a specified salary. For further information regarding tuition fee loans students from England and Wales should contact their Local Authority (LA); students from Scotland should contact the Student Support Agency for Scotland (SSAS); students from Northern Ireland should contact their Education and Library Board (ELB).

Students who already hold an Honours degree from a publicly funded UK higher education institution are not entitled to any student support unless they are studying Medicine. Students studying for the MBBS are eligible to apply for a student loan for maintenance for the length of their course and will be eligible for NHS funding in their final two years of study. The support available to students who already have a degree without Honours or who have previously studied in higher education depends on the duration of their previous studies. This information is correct at the time of going to press. Students are strongly advised to contact their Local Education Authority for further information.

Self-supported students whose tuition fees exceed £2,000 may pay fees on the basis of two instalments. A facility charge is payable on these fees if paid by instalments.

Students who fail to pay the full fee or any instalment amount by the due date will be required to pay a late payment surcharge, in addition to any facility charge, where applicable.

The preferred method of payment is by debit card via the Imperial College epayments website. Remittances from overseas (including Eire) should be in the form of a sterling banker's draft drawn on a UK clearing bank. Payment of tuition fees with a credit or debit card can be made via the secure website. Please note that in order to make payment in this way you will require your CID number — the security code printed on the card.

Students who receive their invoices after the start of session are required to settle their account within 28 days. Tuition fee invoices issued prior to the commencement of session must be settled by the end of the first week of session.

Any students whose tuition fees or residence charges have not been paid in full will not be allowed to proceed to the next year of their course and will be required to withdraw from the College. If any fees or charges are still unpaid at the time when a student enters for the last examination necessary to qualify for the award of a degree/diploma, the award will not be conferred, and no certificate in respect of the award will be issued, until the debt has been paid in full.

Enquiries concerning tuition fees should be addressed to the Assistant Registrar (Student Finance). The fees and payment terms detailed above are subject to alteration.

Overseas Students

To ensure students are able to complete their studies without financial difficulties undergraduate overseas students will be expected to have a **minimum of £13,000** for a 12-month period in addition to fees, and to provide a formal declaration that they have the necessary funds to cover the period of their course.

Married students will require a further £8,000 per annum, with an additional £4,000 (minimum) for each dependent child. Possession of these financial resources is essential for each full calendar year a student spends in London. The College will be unable to finance students if for any reason their funds from overseas are restricted before the end of their course or research.

Overseas Students Fee Liability

Whether a student is regarded as "home" or "overseas" for fee-paying purposes is determined in accordance with the UK Education (Fees and Awards) Regulations 1997.

Guidelines prepared by the College can be found online at www3. imperial. ac. uk/registry/admission/classifyingstudents and a printed copy is available on request. Further information can be found on the websites of UKCOSA, and of the Department for Education and Skills. Please note that whilst it is possible to provide general advice, the College will not give individual assessment of fee status prior to the receipt of an application.

The fee status of an applicant is initially assessed by means of the information supplied on the UCAS application. Where further clarification is required, an applicant will be asked to complete a supplementary questionnaire and to supply appropriate documentary evidence before an assessment is made. Applicants who are classified as overseas for fee-paying purposes have the right of appeal against this decision only if they are able to provide material evidence to show why the classification is incorrect. Details of the appeals process are available at www3. imperial. ac. uk/registry/admission/classifyingstudents.

Students from European Union countries who satisfy various residence requirements are eligible to have their tuition fees paid by HM Government. Further details are available from the Assistant Registrar (Student Finance).

Any student in doubt as to his or her position should send full details with supporting documentation/evidence to the Assistant Registrar (Undergraduate Admissions).

注意：此部分试题请在**答题卡**1上作答。

1. This passage gives an introduction to the tuition fees at a British college for undergraduates.
2. Overseas students enjoy the same tuition fees policy as home and European Union students.
3. Tuition fees at Imperial College are the lowest among the colleges in UK.
4. The fees for home and EU undergraduate courses for 2008 entry are subject to an annual increase in line with inflation.
5. Fees for 2007－08 are _____ if a Chinese student studies at the Department of Bioengineering in this college.
6. Students spending a full year away from the College on an approved SOCRATES-ERASMUS exchange are _____ for that academic year.

7. Home and EU undergraduate students will be eligible to _____ from the Student Loans Company.

8. Overseas students will be expected to _____ that they have the necessary funds to cover the period of their course.

9. If for any reason funds of the students from overseas are restricted before the end of their course or research, the College will be _____.

10. Whether a student is regarded as "home" or "overseas" for fee-paying purposes is determined in accordance with _____.

Part III   Listening Comprehension   (35 minutes)

Section A

Directions: *In this section, you will hear 8 short conversations and 2 long conversations. At the end of each conversation, one or more questions will be asked about what was said. Both the conversation and the questions will be spoken only once. After each question there will be a pause. During the pause, you must read the four choices marked A), B), C) and D), and decide which is the best answer. Then mark the corresponding letter on **Answer Sheet 2** with a single line through the centre.*

注意：此部分试题请在**答题卡 2** 上作答。

11. A) He is going to take the field trip, rain or shine.
    B) He is going to investigate quite a few regions on this field trip.
    C) He is not sure whether his team members are ready for the trip.
    D) He is quite sure the weather will be fine for the next few days.

12. A) Families with cars.
    B) Americans' heavy dependence on cars.
    C) Roads and highways.
    D) Traffic problems in America.

13. A) Disconnect his telephone.
    B) Blow a whistle into the receiver.
    C) Just write down the time of annoyance calls.
    D) He should contact the police.

14. A) 95.   C) 94.
    B) 93.   D) None of the above.

15. A) Because it was freezing cold.   C) Because the restaurant was closed.
    B) Because the food was very bad.   D) Because the weather was not good.

16. A) Inform Mrs. Jones.
    B) Dial the international code number first.
    C) Pay in advance.
    D) Use his own phone.

17. A) He didn't want to answer.   C) The girl died in the war.
    B) He didn't know.   D) The girl married her sweetheart.

18. A) Disney cartoons are very popular.
    B) Disney cartoons are something funny.
    C) Disney cartoons aren't serious.
    D) Disney cartoons make people laugh.

Questions 19 to 21 are based on the conversation you have just heard.

19. A) At a bus station.   C) At an airport.
    B) At a train station.   D) At a port.

20. A) Alex's brother.   C) A cat.
    B) Alex's sister.   D) A dog.

21. A) To eat properly.
    B) To dress warmly when it's cold.
    C) To stay up late.
    D) To write to her as soon as he gets there.

Questions 22 to 25 are based on the conversation you have just heard.

22. A) Next week.   C) Three months later.
    B) Next month.   D) A few days ago.

23. A) The garment department.
    B) The produce section.
    C) The toy department.
    D) The electrical appliance department.

24. A) Three years.   C) Three months.
    B) A few months.   D) A few days.

25. A) To announce it through TV.

B) To put an announcement in the newspaper.

C) To telephone the customers.

D) To post an announcement in store windows.

Section B

Directions: *In this section, you will hear 3 short passages. At the end of each passage, you will hear some questions. Both the passage and the questions will be spoken only once. After you hear a question, you must choose the best answer from the four choices marked A), B), C) and D). Then mark the corresponding letter on* **Answer Sheet 2** *with a single line through the centre.*

注意：此部分试题请在**答题卡**2上作答。

Passage One

Questions 26 to 28 are based on the passage you have just heard.

26. A) People feel cool when they are near a lake or an ocean.

    B) Scientists can explain everything we want to know.

    C) Scientists can explain many things，but not everything.

    D) The salt in the ocean comes from rocks.

27. A) Air.   C) Rain.

    B) Rocks.   D) Rivers and lakes.

28. A) Because we know nothing about the world.

    B) Because we know little about the world.

    C) Because there are still many answers we do not have.

    D) Either A) or B).

Passage Two

Questions 29 to 31 are based on the passage you have just heard.

29. A) Because he set as many as sixty-five different records.

    B) Because he led his team to many championships.

    C) Because he still played the game after he retired.

    D) Because he didn't stop playing even when his wrist was broken.

30. A) To build a big house.

B) To break the previous records set by himself.

C) To play for a New York team once again.

D) To win one more championship for his team.

31. A) He was knocked out during one contest.

    B) He lost the final chance to win a championship.

    C) He broke a bone in the wrist during the match.

    D) He was awarded with a luxury house.

Passage Three

Questions 32 to 35 are based on the passage you have just heard.

32. A) For education.   C) To enjoy themselves.

    B) For adventure.   D) To look for a different lifestyle.

33. A) It has a dense population.

    B) It has many towering buildings.

    C) There are 200 vehicles for every kilometer of roadway.

    D) There are many museums and palaces.

34. A) It has many big and beautiful parks.

    B) It is quite crowded.

    C) It possesses many historical sites.

    D) It is an important industrial center.

35. A) It makes our life more interesting.

    B) It enables us to get first-hand knowledge.

    C) It helps develop our personalities.

    D) It brings about changes in our lifestyle.

Section C

Directions: *In this section, you will hear a passage three times. When the passage is read for the first time, you should listen carefully for its general idea. When the passage is read for the second time, you are required to fill in the blanks numbered from 36 to 43 with the exact words you have just heard. For blanks numbered from 44 to 46 you are required to fill in the missing information. For these blanks, you can either use the exact words you have just heard or write down the main points in your own words. Finally, when the passage is read for the third time, you should check what you have written.*

注意：此部分试题在**答题卡** 2 上；请在**答题卡** 2 上作答。

Part IV   Reading Comprehension (Reading in Depth)

(25 minutes)

Section A

Directions: *In this section, there is a short passage with 5 questions or incomplete statements. Read the passage carefully. Then answer the questions or complete the statements in the fewest possible words on* **Answer Sheet 2**.

Questions 47 to 51 are based on the following passage.

The quality of patience goes a long way toward your goal of creating a more peaceful and loving self. The more patient you are, the more accepting you will be of what life is, rather than insisting that life be exactly as you would like it to be. Without patience, life is extremely frustrating. You are easily annoyed, bothered, and irritated. Patience adds a dimension of ease and acceptance to your life. It's essential for inner peace. Becoming more patient involves opening your heart to the present moment, even if you don't like it. If you are stuck in a traffic jam, late for an appointment, being patient would mean keeping yourself from building a mental snowball before your thinking gets out of hand and gently reminding yourself to relax. It might also be a good time to breathe as well as an opportunity to remind yourself that, in the bigger scheme of things, being late is "small stuff."

Patience is a quality of heart that can be greatly enhanced with deliberate practice. An effective way that I have found to deepen my own patience is to create actual practice periods — periods of time that I set up in my mind to practice the art of patience. Life itself becomes a classroom, and the curriculum is patience. You can start with as little as five minutes and build up your capacity for patience over time. What you'll discover is truly amazing. Your intention to be patient, especially if you know it's only for a short while, immediately strengthens your capacity for patience. Patience is one of those special qualities where success feeds on itself. Once you reach a little milestone — five minutes of successful patience — you'll begin to see that you do indeed have the capacity to be patient, even for longer periods of time. Over time, you may even become a patient person.

Being patient will help you to keep your perspective. You'll see even a difficult situation, say your present challenge, isn't "life or death" but simply a minor obstacle that must be dealt with. Without patience, the same scenario can become a major emergency complete with yelling, frustration, hurt feelings, and high blood pressure.

注意：此部分试题请在**答题卡** 2 上作答。

47. What does the expression "goes a long way toward" in the first sentence of the first paragraph mean?

48. _____ is essential for inner peace.

49. What's the main idea of the first paragraph?

50. Patience can be cultivated with _____.

51. People with patience will treat a difficult situation as _____.

Section B

Directions: *There are 2 passages in this section. Each passage is followed by some questions or unfinished statements. For each of them there are four choices marked A), B), C) and D). You should decide on the best choice and mark the corresponding letter on **Answer Sheet 2** with a single line through the centre.*

Passage One

Questions 52 to 56 are based on the following passage.

What could be more revealing than a list of one's search queries? The efficiency of finding what we need on the Web encourages us to quest away — whether we're researching a car purchase, puzzling out some medical symptoms, or wondering what happened to an old friend. "Your search record involves aspirations and dreams," says Marc Rotenberg of the Electronic Privacy Information Center. "It becomes almost a reflection of what's in one's head." And, as we learned recently, when America Online temporarily released the search history of thousands of customers for the use of researchers, those reflections can be retained by search companies — and, ultimately, exposed.

In the AOL case, the records were supposedly anonymous, but since people commonly type in their own names and addresses into search engines, it's often trivial to identify who is searching. Indeed, The *New York Times* was able to deduce the identity of a 62-year-old widow in Georgia who researched Italian vacations, termites and hand tremors.

The intimacy of our searches has led Rotenberg and other privacy experts to urge companies like Google，Yahoo and Microsoft not to retain such logs. But the top researchers in the search field argue that such limits would ultimately be destructive. These wizards believe that the information extracted from studying the way individuals search has been crucial in raising the quality of search to its present level. "Our searches have improved dramatically because we have that data," says Alan Eustace, Google's senior vice president of engineering and research.

In particular，these companies hope to introduce schemes by which one's searching success would be enhanced by previous behavior. For instance，when a fishing buff types in "bass," he or she would get a different result than the same search from a Paul McCartney fan.

As you would expect，search companies like Google and Yahoo say that protecting the information on those search logs is assigned highest priority. (Though I bet if you asked folks at VOL about this before the semipublic release of its users' most intimate data，they would have said the same thing.) Yahoo even has a security group referred to informally as "the paranoids," whose motto is "We worry about these things so you won't have to."

But even if the companies are flawless in protecting that information，there's still reason to worry. The federal government has already expressed interest in such records，and if the data is subpoenaed the companies must turn it over.

It is possible to search without a trail. So-called anonymizing services can mask your identity when you surf. And some smaller search engines do not keep session logs. The big players，though，are betting that you'll stick around — because，they say，access to your dreams makes their searches great.

注意：此部分试题请在**答题卡** 2 上作答。

52. The word "wizards" in the third paragraph refers to _____.
    A) people who are believed to have magic powers
    B) people who are especially good at searching for information
    C) the top researchers in the search field
    D) people who are very powerful in their business

53. Why do people like to surf online according to the passage?
    A) Because they can easily find all the information they need.
    B) Because the efficiency of finding the useful information encourages people to surf.
    C) Because their search records are anonymous.
    D) Because the search companies can keep their privacy.

54. What could be the possible result if a fishing buff types in the word "bass"?
   A) A sea or freshwater fish that is used for food.
   B) The lowest tone or part in music, for instruments or voices.
   C) The bass songs of Paul McCartney.
   D) The information of a fisherman who is very interested in fishing and knows a lot about it.

55. All of the following are true EXCEPT that _____.
   A) with the help of the search record, the quality of search is greatly improved by the search companies
   B) because people usually type in their own names and addresses into search engines, the search companies can find their identity easily
   C) people are quite sure that the search companies are flawless in protecting their personal information
   D) it is possible for people to search online without revealing their identity

56. Which of the following can be the most suitable title of the passage?
   A) Will You Let Them Store Your Dreams?
   B) Do You Want to Surf the Net?
   C) Find Your Dreams Online
   D) Anonymizing Services

Passage Two

Questions 57 to 61 are based on the following passage.

The boy has drawn, in his third-grade class, a global warming timeline that is his equivalent of the mushroom cloud. "That's the Earth now," the 9-year-old says, pointing to a dark shape at the bottom. "And then," he says, tracing the progressively lighter stripes across the page, "it's just starting to fade away."

Alex Handel of Arlington County is talking about the end of life on our beleaguered planet. He taps the final stripe, which is so sparsely dotted that it is almost invisible. "In 20 years," he pronounces, "there's no oxygen." Then, to dramatize the point, he collapses, "dead," to the floor.

For many children and young adults, global warming is the atomic bomb of today. Fears of an environmental crisis are defining their generation in ways that the Depression, World War II, Vietnam and the Cold War's lingering "War Games" etched souls in the 20th century.

Parents say they're searching for "productive" outlets for their 8-year-olds' obsessions with dying polar bears. Teachers say enrollment in high school and college environmental studies classes is doubling year after year. And psychologists say they're seeing an increasing number of young patients preoccupied by a climactic Armageddon. "Our parents had the civil rights and antiwar movement," says Meredith Epstein, 20, a junior at St. Mary's College of Maryland. "But for us, this is what we need to take immediate action on."

Young people might not be turning out at demonstrations against the war in Iraq in numbers rivaling Vietnam War protests. But the environment is becoming their galvanizing force: The topic is more than an issue. It's personal.

It's not as though every student in the United States is turning green. For many, the biggest anxieties are still status, class standing and SATs.

"But there's a pretty significant minority of kids trying to convince their friends: 'This is serious. You or your family is wasting gas, and you're not recycling,'" says Mark Goldstein, a child psychologist and school-system consultant. Goldstein adds: "In my practice, they bring this up. Some of the kids are scared, and it's interesting, because I've seen an evolution — kids used to have fears of war and nuclear annihilation. That's dissipated and been replaced by global warming."

It's not just a U.S. phenomenon: A United Kingdom survey, by the Somerfield supermarket chain, of 1,150 youngsters aged 7 to 11 found that half felt anxious about global warming — and many were losing sleep over it, convinced that animal species will soon die out and that they, themselves, will be victims of global warming.

注意：此部分试题请在**答题卡**2上作答。

57. What's the possible meaning of the word "beleaguered" in the second paragraph?
    A) Experiencing a lot of criticism.
    B) Being surrounded by an enemy.
    C) Being in great difficulties.
    D) Being dangerous.

58. Which statement can be inferred from the passage?
    A) Alex Handel is eager to know everything about global warming.
    B) Alex Handel once drew a picture of a mushroom.
    C) The number of people who protested the war in Iraq is equal to that of people against the Vietnam War.
    D) Many children and young adults are worrying about global warming.

59. What does the author probably mean by saying "It's not as though every student in the United States is turning green"?
    A) Most students are worrying about their achievements at school.

B) Many students are young and lacking experience.

C) Almost every student in the U.S. is worrying about the environment.

D) Not all the students in the U.S. are concerned with protecting the environment.

60. The expression "nuclear annihilation" in the seventh paragraph means _____.

A) nuclear weapons

B) the power of nuclear weapons to destroy mankind completely

C) the great power of nuclear weapons

D) nuclear bombs in the war

61. It can be concluded from the passage that _____.

A) people should take immediate actions in protecting the environment; otherwise, they will be victims of global warming

B) anxiety about global warming causes many American people to lose their sleep

C) an increasing number of young patients are greatly concerned with climatic changes

D) most kids are scared by global warming nowadays

Part V Error Correction   (15 minutes)

Directions: *This part consists of a short passage. In this passage, there are altogether 10 mistakes, one in each numbered line. You may have to change a word, add a word or delete a word. Mark out the mistakes and put the corrections in the blanks provided. If you change a word, cross it out and write the correct word in the corresponding blank. If you add a word, put an insertion mark (∧) in the right place and write the missing word in the blank. If you delete a word, cross it out and put a slash (/) in the blank.*

注意：此部分试题在**答题卡 2** 上；请在**答题卡 2** 上作答。

Part VI Translation   (5 minutes)

Directions: *Complete the following sentences on **Answer Sheet 2** by translating into English the Chinese given in brackets.*

注意：此部分试题请在**答题卡**2上作答。

72. One of the characteristics that _____ （区别雄鸟与雌鸟）is that the male bird has beautiful feathers.

73. Her expression had become vacant，_____ （似乎她的注意力已经飘到别的什么地方去了）.

74. He had to kill the rattlesnake because its presence was _____ （对农场里的人和动物来说都是一个潜在威胁）.

75. _____ （信不信由你），his discovery has created a stir in scientific circles.

76. _____ （正如近二十年来国内生产总值增长率表明的那样），China's reform and open policy is a great success.

答题卡 1 (Answer Sheet 1)

学校:
姓名:
划线要求

准				考				证				号		
[0]	[0]	[0]	[0]	[0]	[0]	[0]	[0]	[0]	[0]	[0]	[0]	[0]	[0]	[0]
[1]	[1]	[1]	[1]	[1]	[1]	[1]	[1]	[1]	[1]	[1]	[1]	[1]	[1]	[1]
[2]	[2]	[2]	[2]	[2]	[2]	[2]	[2]	[2]	[2]	[2]	[2]	[2]	[2]	[2]
[3]	[3]	[3]	[3]	[3]	[3]	[3]	[3]	[3]	[3]	[3]	[3]	[3]	[3]	[3]
[4]	[4]	[4]	[4]	[4]	[4]	[4]	[4]	[4]	[4]	[4]	[4]	[4]	[4]	[4]
[5]	[5]	[5]	[5]	[5]	[5]	[5]	[5]	[5]	[5]	[5]	[5]	[5]	[5]	[5]
[6]	[6]	[6]	[6]	[6]	[6]	[6]	[6]	[6]	[6]	[6]	[6]	[6]	[6]	[6]
[7]	[7]	[7]	[7]	[7]	[7]	[7]	[7]	[7]	[7]	[7]	[7]	[7]	[7]	[7]
[8]	[8]	[8]	[8]	[8]	[8]	[8]	[8]	[8]	[8]	[8]	[8]	[8]	[8]	[8]
[9]	[9]	[9]	[9]	[9]	[9]	[9]	[9]	[9]	[9]	[9]	[9]	[9]	[9]	[9]

Part I   **Writing**   **(30 minutes)**

Directions: *For this part, you are allowed 30 minutes to write a composition on the topic* **How to Achieve Success**. *You should write at least* **120** *words following the outline given below in Chinese:*

1. 人们都渴望成功
2. 成功的秘诀——决心、毅力和勤奋
3. 结论

How to Achieve Success

答题卡 1 (Answer Sheet 1)

_____

_____

_____

_____

_____

_____

_____

_____

_____

_____

_____

_____

_____

_____

_____

_____

_____

_____

_____

_____

_____

_____

_____

_____

_____

_____

Part II   Reading Comprehension (Skimming and Scanning) (15 minutes)

1. [Y] [N] [NG]   5. _____   8. _____
2. [Y] [N] [NG]
3. [Y] [N] [NG]   6. _____   9. _____
4. [Y] [N] [NG]
                         7. _____   10. _____

答题卡 2 (Answer Sheet 2)

Part III   Section A   **Section B**

11. [A] [B] [C] [D] 16. [A] [B] [C] [D] 21. [A] [B] [C] [D] 26. [A] [B] [C] [D] 31. [A] [B] [C] [D]
12. [A] [B] [C] [D] 17. [A] [B] [C] [D] 22. [A] [B] [C] [D] 27. [A] [B] [C] [D] 32. [A] [B] [C] [D]
13. [A] [B] [C] [D] 18. [A] [B] [C] [D] 23. [A] [B] [C] [D] 28. [A] [B] [C] [D] 33. [A] [B] [C] [D]
14. [A] [B] [C] [D] 19. [A] [B] [C] [D] 24. [A] [B] [C] [D] 29. [A] [B] [C] [D] 34. [A] [B] [C] [D]
15. [A] [B] [C] [D] 20. [A] [B] [C] [D] 25. [A] [B] [C] [D] 30. [A] [B] [C] [D] 35. [A] [B] [C] [D]

Part III   Section C

It is common knowledge that music can have a powerful effect on our (36) _____. In fact, since 1930s, music therapists have (37) _____ on music to soothe (38) _____ and help control pain. Now psychologists are (39) _____ that music can also help (40) _____ depression and improve concentration. For instance, in a recent study, 15 surgeons were given some highly (41) _____ math problems to solve. They were (42) _____ into three groups: one worked in silence, and in another, the surgeons listened to music of their choice on headphones; the third listened to (43) _____ music chosen by the researchers. The results of the study may surprise you. (44) _____. One possible explanation is that listening to music you like stimulates the Alfa-wave in the brain, increases the heart rate and expands the breathing. That helps to reduce stress and sharpen concentration. Other research suggests a second relation between the music and the brain: (45) _____, the researchers found that some students showed a large increase in endorphin, a natural pain reliever; (46) _____.

答题卡 2 (Answer Sheet 2)

Part IV   Section A

47. _____

_____

48. _____

_____

49. _____

_____

50. _____

_____

51. _____

_____

Part IV   Section B

52. [A][B][C][D]

53. [A][B][C][D]

54. [A][B][C][D]

55. [A][B][C][D]

56. [A][B][C][D]

57. [A][B][C][D]

58. [A][B][C][D]

59. [A][B][C][D]

60. [A][B][C][D]

61. [A][B][C][D]

Part V   Error Correction   (15 minutes)

Prolonging human life has decreased the dependency load. In all societies people who are disabled or too young or too old to work are dependent on the rest of society to provide them. In hunting and gathering cultures old people who could keep up might be left behind and die. In times of famine infants might be allowed to die unless they could not survive when their parents starved; whereas when their parents survived they could have another child. In most contemporary societies people feel a moral obligation to keep people live whether or not they can work. There are a great many people today who live past the age in which they want to work or are able to work; there are rules requiring people to retire at a certain age. If these people are able to save money for their retirement, somebody else must support them. In the United States many people live on social security checks, which are so considerable that they must live near poverty. Elder people are more liable to be taken ill than young or middle-aged people; unless they are wealthy or providing with private or government insurance, they must often "go on welfare" if they fall seriously ill.

62. _____

63. _____

64. _____

65. _____

66. _____

67. _____

68. _____

69. _____

70. _____

71. _____

Part VI   Translation   (5 minutes)

72. _____

73. _____

74. _____

75. _____

76. _____

PRACTICE TEST 9

Part I   Writing   (30 minutes)

注意：此部分试题在**答题卡** 1 上。

Part II   Reading Comprehension (Skimming and Scanning)
(15 minutes)

Directions: *In this part, you will have 15 minutes to go over the passage quickly and answer the questions on **Answer Sheet 1**.*

For questions 1 – 4, mark

Y *(for YES)*   *if the statement agrees with the information given in the passage;*

N *(for NO)*   *if the statement contradicts the information given in the passage;*

NG *(for NOT GIVEN)*   *if the information is not given in the passage.*

For questions 5 – 10, complete the sentences with the information given in the passage.

GPS

The Global Positioning System is a space-based triangulation system using satellites and computers to measure positions anywhere on earth. It is first and foremost a defense system developed by the United States Department of Defense, and is referred to as the "Navigation Satellite Timing and Ranging Global Positioning System" or NAVSTAR GPS. The uniqueness of this navigational system is that it avoids the limitations of other land-based systems such as limited geographic coverage, lack of continuous 24-hour coverage, and the limited accuracies of other related navigational instruments. The high accuracies obtainable with the Global Positioning System also make it a precision survey instrument.

GPS components: the Space Segment, the Control Segment, and the User Segment.

Space Segment

The Space Segment of the system consists of the GPS satellites. These space vehicles (SVs) send radio signals from space.

The GPS Operational Constellation consists of 24 satellites that orbit the earth in 12 hours. There are often more than 24 operational satellites as new ones are launched to replace older satellites. The satellite orbits repeat almost the same ground track (as the earth turns beneath them) once each day. The orbit altitude is such that the satellites repeat the same track and area over any point approximately each 24 hours (four minutes earlier each day). There are six orbital planes (with four SVs in each), equally spaced (60 degrees apart), and inclined at about 55 degrees with respect to the equatorial plane. This constellation provides the user with between five and eight SVs visible from any point on the earth.

Control Segment

The Control Segment consists of a system of tracking stations located around the world.

The Master Control facility is located at Schriever Air Force Base (formerly Falcon AFB) in Colorado. These monitor stations measure signals from the SVs which are incorporated into orbital models for each satellite. The models compute precise orbital data and SV clock corrections for each satellite. The Master Control station uploads orbital data and clock data to the SVs. The SVs then send subsets of the orbital ephemeris data to GPS receivers over radio signals.

User Segment

The GPS User Segment consists of the GPS receivers and the user community. GPS receivers change SV signals into position, speed, and time estimates. Four satellites are required to compute the four dimensions of X, Y, Z (position) and time. GPS receivers are used for navigation, positioning, time distribution, and other research.

Navigation in three dimensions is the primary function of GPS. Navigation receivers are made for aircraft, ships, ground vehicles, and for hand carrying by individuals.

Precise positioning is possible using GPS receivers at reference locations providing corrections and relative positioning data for remote receivers. Surveying, geodetic control, and plate tectonic studies are examples.

Time and frequency distribution, based on the precise clocks on board the SVs and controlled by the monitor stations, is another use for GPS. Astronomical observatories, telecommunications facilities, and laboratory standards can be set to precise time signals or controlled to accurate frequencies by special purpose GPS receivers.

Research projects have used GPS signals to measure atmospheric parameters.

GPS Accuracy

At present the system consists of 24 satellites at an altitude of about 20,000km having an orbital inclination of 55 degrees. The orbits are almost circular and it takes 12 hours for a satellite to complete a pass around the earth. GPS signals are broadcast from a cluster of 24 or more earth orbiting satellites. Because the GPS signals are derived from the atomic frequency standards on board each satellite, they are widely used as a reference for time synchronization and frequency adjustment. The real time positioning accuracy of a single receiver is normally up to 100 meters horizontally and 150 meters vertically. However, various methods have been developed which enable much higher accuracy (centimeter level).

GPS Receivers

There are a variety of different types of GPS receivers on the market for commercial and public use. Prices range from $500 - $30,000, reflecting the accuracy and capabilities of the instruments. For the general outdoorsman, a good GPS receiver should have eight satellite tracking capability and be capable of receiving the GPS satellite signals through forest covering in northern Ontario shield area; for the professional user, a minimum eight satellite tracking capability, high memory capacity, differential GPS capability, and resistance to signal weakening under forest covering is essential; for the professional surveyor requiring high level precision and accuracy capability, they should assess the project or application for which the technology is to be used with the help of an unbiased consultant, in order to determine the most cost effective and appropriate instrument.

Navigational Units

Small hand-held units at relatively low cost allow boaters and hikers to know their position within a few hundred meters. This accuracy is sufficient for recreational use.

Mapping

There is also the hand-held or similar unit at mid-range price that is linked to a fixed broadcast base station. These units allow utility companies, municipalities and others to locate various items (telephone poles, waterlines, valves) with a positional tolerance of several meters. This is suitable for some Geographical Information System (GIS) mapping purposes.

GPS and Policing

GPS technology offers numerous benefits to law enforcement agencies of all types. For some agencies, the navigational capabilities offered by GPS enhance efficiency and safety. These navigational applications can be used to support a variety of policing and criminal justice functions. Other agencies use GPS positioning technologies to carry out special operations or to provide enhanced personnel safety.

For example, using computerized maps of their rights given by law, cooperated with GPS, aviation personnel can determine location, speed and time.

The positioning capabilities offered by GPS may also contribute to the success of specialized law enforcement operations such as in controlling vehicles. One such program operated in Minneapolis led to a 60% reduction in auto theft after only one month. The automatic vehicle location systems can not only provide efficiency of response and help ensure officer safety, but also provide officers with accurate information concerning the best response route to an incident. What's more, they can provide officers information that allows the closest patrol officers to be dispatched to a particular incident.

Advanced Transportation Management Systems (ATMS) are heavily dependent upon GPS technology to provide data about the road system. GPS allows law enforcement personnel to clear roadway blockage to ensure the safety of motorists.

Most people associate law enforcement with the prevention, reduction, and prosecution of criminal activity. In fact, a large portion of local law enforcement resources are involved in facilitating the movement of people and vehicles in a safe manner.

In conclusion, large-volume commercial applications such as cellular phones, personal communication systems, and in-vehicle navigation systems will fuel continued development of these technologies. What was ultimately the domain of the Department of Defense is rapidly becoming available for business, private, and general government use. Policing and public safety, in general, will benefit from these market forces. It is clear that there are a number of GPS applications for policing.

注意：此部分试题请在**答题卡**1上作答。

1. The passage mainly discusses the components of GPS.
2. GPS satellites are space vehicles which send radio signals from space.
3. The highest positioning accuracy of a receiver can now reach meter level.
4. The more expensive a GPS receiver is, the more accurate it will be.
5. GPS is made up of the Space Segment, the Control Segment and _____.
6. The Control Segment consists of a system of _____ located around the earth.

7. _____ is the primary function of GPS.

8. A hand-held or similar unit at mid-range price is suitable for some GIS _____.

9. Using computerized maps with GPS, aviation personnel can determine _____.

10. A large part of local law enforcement resources are used for _____ in a safe manner.

Part III Listening Comprehension   (35 minutes)

Section A

Directions: *In this section, you will hear 8 short conversations and 2 long conversations. At the end of each conversation, one or more questions will be asked about what was said. Both the conversation and the questions will be spoken only once. After each question there will be a pause. During the pause, you must read the four choices marked A), B), C) and D), and decide which is the best answer. Then mark the corresponding letter on **Answer Sheet 2** with a single line through the centre.*

注意：此部分试题请在**答题卡 2** 上作答。

11. A) He set a difficult essay question.
    B) He found the history exam difficult.
    C) He has a good memory.
    D) His memory is declining.

12. A) Steven works hard, but Suzie does not.
    B) Suzie works hard, but Steven does not.
    C) Both work hard.
    D) Neither works hard.

13. A) Mrs. Jones is fat.   C) The boy never tells lies.
    B) Mrs. Jones is thin.   D) The mother always tells lies.

14. A) A new restaurant.   C) A new hospital.
    B) A new hotel.   D) A new airport.

15. A) Forty-five.   C) Thirty-five.
    B) Twenty-two.   D) Twenty-three.

16. A) In the winter.   C) In September.
    B) In July.   D) In April.

17. A) The man and woman shopped all over town.

    B) The woman went to many different stores.

    C) The woman bought some bookcases on sale.

    D) The man sold the woman some expensive bookcases.

18. A) He thinks his new car came in too late.

    B) He is worried that the dealer is careless.

    C) He is worried that he hasn't got his driver's license.

    D) He is eager to ride in the car himself.

Questions 19 to 21 are based on the conversation you have just heard.

19. A) Because he is busy preparing for the English exam.

    B) Because he is absorbed in the experiment.

    C) Because he is very unhappy and is lost in his own thoughts.

    D) Because he doesn't know the answer.

20. A) Because his girlfriend has just broken up with him.

    B) Because he failed his English exam again.

    C) Because he forgot to go to his girlfriend's mother's home for dinner.

    D) Both A) and B).

21. A) Three times.   C) Twice.

    B) Four times.   D) Only once.

Questions 22 to 25 are based on the conversation you have just heard.

22. A) It was not easy for her to become a doctor in those days.

    B) The job of being a doctor enabled her to be independent.

    C) She was able to travel to many places as a doctor.

    D) She became a doctor because her father wanted her to do so.

23. A) In Malaysia.   C) In Africa.

    B) In Japan.   D) In the Middle East.

24. A) Three.   C) Five.

    B) Four.   D) One.

25. A) She was once a doctor, but now she is a writer.

    B) She likes traveling very much.

    C) Both her father and her husband were doctors.

    D) She got the Nobel Prize for Literature.

Section B

Directions: *In this section, you will hear 3 short passages. At the end of each passage, you will hear some questions. Both the passage and the questions will be spoken only once. After you hear a question, you must choose the best answer from the four choices marked A), B), C) and D). Then mark the corresponding letter on **Answer Sheet 2** with a single line through the centre.*

注意：此部分试题请在**答题卡 2** 上作答。

Passage One

Questions 26 to 28 are based on the passage you have just heard.

26. A) Emotional rest and psychological rest.
    B) Physical rest and emotional rest.
    C) Passive rest and active rest.
    D) Passive sleep and more active sleep.

27. A) Physical rest is more important than emotional rest for our health.
    B) Emotional rest is more important than physical rest for our health.
    C) Dreams occur in passive sleep.
    D) Dreams occur in active sleep.

28. A) Eight hours.   C) One hour and a half.
    B) One hour.   D) A half hour.

Passage Two

Questions 29 to 31 are based on the passage you have just heard.

29. A) A widespread and continuous interest in the language seems unimaginable.
    B) Only a few colleges and large Chinese communities concentrated on the study of Chinese in the past.
    C) The enthusiasm in the Chinese language decreased in 1989.
    D) Spanish and French are traditionally the most popular second languages in North America.

30. A) Nowadays Chinese has ranked 7th among the foreign languages used in the US.
    B) Chinese is becoming popular with Americans at present.

C) More graduate students in US colleges and universities are enrolled in Chinese classes in recent years.

D) Chinese has recently overtaken Spanish in growth rate.

31. A) The Chinese language is bound to be the most popular foreign language in North America.

B) The enthusiasm in the Chinese language had a brief decrease in the 1990s.

C) The Chinese language is likely to surpass German and Japanese someday in North America.

D) The enthusiasm in the Chinese language has been on steady rise in recent years.

Passage Three

Questions 32 to 35 are based on the passage you have just heard.

32. A) It can cause difficulties in speaking.

B) It can make people feel tired for a few weeks.

C) It can be only found in flight attendants.

D) It can be caused by flying over several time zones.

33. A) The conclusion is refuted by many scientists.

B) Scientists fear that this research is not done properly.

C) Every scientific conclusion needs the support from many tests.

D) The women who were examined in the research were not healthy.

34. A) The women who have longer rest at home show better memory.

B) The women who fly at shorter intervals have smaller right temporal lobes.

C) The women who have longer flights failed the memory test.

D) The women who rest more than 14 days produce less hormones.

35. A) The cause of jet lag.

B) A story of a group of flight attendants.

C) The importance of having enough rest after long flights.

D) A research about the effects of jet lag on the brain.

Section C

Directions: *In this section, you will hear a passage three times. When the passage is read for the first time, you should listen carefully for its general idea. When the passage is read for the second time, you are required to fill in the blanks numbered* *from 36 to 43 with the exact words you have just heard. For blanks numbered from 44 to 46 you are required to fill in the missing information. For these blanks, you can either use the exact words you have just heard or write down the main points in your own words. Finally, when the passage is read for the third time, you should check what you have written.*

注意：此部分试题在**答题卡** 2 上；请在**答题卡** 2 上作答。

Part IV   Reading Comprehension (Reading in Depth)

(25 minutes)

Section A

Directions: *In this section, there is a short passage with 5 questions or incomplete statements. Read the passage carefully. Then answer the questions or complete the statements in the fewest possible words on **Answer Sheet 2**.*

Questions 47 to 51 are based on the following passage.

Over 44 million families are online, and over half of their members — about 25 million people — may qualify as compulsive surfers. So, is "Internet Addiction" a new psychological phenomenon? In a study published recently in the *Journal of Affective Disorders*, researchers from the University of Florida (UF) and the University of Cincinnati examined the habits of 20 people who had spent more than 30 nonworking hours a week online for the past three years. The participants described skipping sleep, ignoring family responsibilities, and showing up late for work to fulfill their desire to visit chat rooms and surf the Web. The consequences were severe: Many suffered from marital problems, failed in school or lost a job, and accumulated debt. The evidence points to a psychological disorder, so researchers probed further and found that the participants' habits met the criteria for impulse control disorders, mental illnesses characterized by an uncontrollable desire to perform a behavior that, once executed, is often followed by a huge sense of relief. Most of the participants had a history of additional psychiatric problems like eating disorders and manic depression.

Despite their apparent sufferings, the study's participants were not easily identifiable, says Nathan Shapira, a UF assistant psychiatry professor and co-author of the study. "These people were intelligent, well-respected community members," he says. "They were like your next-door neighbor — who just lost control."

Given the confounding nature of the participants' various symptoms, Shapira believes the essential issue remains: Is "Internet Addiction" a distinct disorder or a symptom of another well-defined disorder? "It's too early to know," he says. "But my sense is that this problem is going to get worse as the size and speed of the Internet increase."

注意：此部分试题请在**答题卡**2 上作答。

47. More than half of the members of over 44 million families online may be regarded as _____.

48. The consequences of "Internet Addiction" include _____, failing in school, losing a job and running into debt.

49. What does the evidence of the study suggest?

50. Impulsive control disorders are characterized by _____ to perform a behavior.

51. Why will "Internet Addiction" become worse?

Section B

Directions: *There are 2 passages in this section. Each passage is followed by some questions or unfinished statements. For each of them there are four choices marked A), B), C) and D). You should decide on the best choice and mark the corresponding letter on Answer Sheet 2 with a single line through the centre.*

Passage One

Questions 52 to 56 are based on the following passage.

Salt-codfish cakes with tapenade and fried oregano may be one of the healthier items on the lunch menu at the United Nations delegates' dining room in New York. But it's also one of the more controversial. The cod, along with tuna, swordfish and other dinner-table favorites, has soared to the top of the UN agenda. A recent World Wildlife Fund report says that if stocks continue to decline at the current rate, cod will be extinct in the Atlantic Ocean in less than 15 years. Last week the European Commission delivered a report to the UN General Assembly calling for an end to "bottom gear" fishing — which employs towed dredges and netting — and requiring states to identify and map vulnerable marine habitats so they can be preserved.

Although scientists have known for years that fish stocks are being depleted, climate change has added new urgency to the issue. Although some ocean regions are governed by international regulatory bodies, many others aren't. As sea temperatures rise, many fish that would have been relatively safe in the Atlantic, say, are moving north into the colder, unregulated Arctic waters, where they're particularly vulnerable to "pirate" boats. "You can't educate fish on where they can and cannot go," says Simon Cripps, director of the WWF's global marine program. Without worldwide controls on fishing, stocks could be depleted, with little chance of recovery. The EC wants the United Nations to set up more regional fisheries-management organizations, in which UN member countries would enforce rules on deep-sea trawling (拖网捕捞).

Some environmentalists have applauded the initiative, but critics say the plan won't work. For one thing, by the time a resolution is debated and passed and enforcement begins, the fish stocks may already be too far gone. And even if the United Nations could act more quickly, enforcement is always difficult on the high seas. Countries like Mongolia and some Central American nations, seen as more lax in their licensing of fishing vessels, will have to be persuaded to tighten their controls. Still, even if stricter regulations prove tough to enforce, creating stronger regional organizations is a step in the right direction, says Mireille Thom, spokeswoman for the EC's fisheries directorate. More UN regulation of the oceans "is not the perfect solution," says Thom, "but it is the most realistic solution, and one that is the most likely to bear fruit." The frutti di mare can only hope that it's not too little, nor too late.

注意：此部分试题请在**答题卡**2 上作答。

52. Which of the following is NOT the method to preserve fish stocks?
    A) Putting an end to "bottom gear" fishing.
    B) Using towed dredges and netting.
    C) Identifying and mapping vulnerable fish.
    D) Strengthening regulations and management.

53. What is the possible meaning of "'pirate' boats" in the second paragraph?
    A) People's own fishing boats.
    B) Boats used by people to attack other ships at sea in order to steal from them.
    C) Illegal boats used to catch fish at sea.
    D) Boats used by people to protect fish at sea.

54. The following are the reasons why some critics say the plan of worldwide controls on fishing won't work EXCEPT that _____.
    A) it will take a long time for the UN to enforce the resolution
    B) it is difficult to enforce the resolution in some countries

C) the efficiency of the UN is rather low

D) some countries are lax in their controls upon fishing boats

55. All of the following statements are correct EXCEPT that _____.

A) without worldwide controls on fishing, fish stocks may become extinct

B) some environmentalists welcome the plan of controls on fishing

C) scientists have known that fish stocks are being depleted for a long time

D) the UN has already set regulatory bodies to regulate Arctic waters

56. What is the possible meaning of "frutti di mare" in the last sentence?

A) Fresh seafood.

B) Countries like Mongolia.

C) Some Central American nations.

D) People who employ "bottom gear" fishing.

Passage Two

Questions 57 to 61 are based on the following passage.

My objective is to analyze certain forms of knowledge, not in terms of repression or law, but in terms of power. But the word power is apt to lead to misunderstandings about the nature, form, and unity of power. By power, I do not mean a group of institutions and mechanisms that ensure the subservience of the citizenry. I do not mean, either, a mode of subjugation that, in contrast to violence, has the form of the rule. Finally, I do not have in mind a general system of domination exerted by one group over another, a system whose effects, through successive derivations, pervade the entire social body. The sovereignty of the state, the form of law or the overall unity of a domination are only the terminal forms power takes.

It seems to me that power must be understood as the multiplicity of force relations that are immanent in the social sphere; as the process that, through ceaseless struggle and confrontation, transforms, strengthens, or reverses them; as the support that these force relations find in one another, or on the contrary, the disjunction and contradictions that isolate them from one another; and lastly, as the strategies in which they take effect, whose general design or institutional crystallization is embodied in the state apparatus, in the formulation of the law, in the various social hegemonies（霸权）.

Thus, the viewpoint that permits one to understand the exercise of power, even in its more "peripheral" effects, and that also makes it possible to use its mechanisms as a structural framework for analyzing the social order, must not be sought in a unique source of sovereignty from which secondary and descendent forms of power emanate （发源）but in the moving substrate（底层）of force relations that, by virtue of their inequality, constantly engender local and unstable states of power. If power seems omnipresent, it is not because it has the privilege of consolidating everything under its invincible unity, but because it is produced from one moment to the next, at every point, or rather in every relation from one point to another. Power is everywhere, not because it embraces everything, but because it comes from everywhere. And if power at times seems to be permanent, repetitious, inert, and self-reproducing, it is simply because the overall effect that emerges from all these mobilities is a concatenation (一系列相关联的事物) that rests on each of them and seeks in turn to arrest their movement. One needs to be nominalistic (唯名论的), no doubt: power is not an institution, and not a structure. Neither is it a certain strength we are endowed with. It is the name that one attributes to a complex strategic situation in a particular society.

注意：此部分试题请在**答题卡2**上作答。

57. The word "subjugation" in the first paragraph means _____.
    A) subservience
    B) subjection
    C) the state of being defeated
    D) the state of gaining control over others

58. What's the author's main purpose of defining power in the passage?
    A) To help people better understand the connotations of power by giving concrete examples.
    B) To prevent confusing uses of the term.
    C) To prevent possible misinterpretations resulting from the more common uses of the term.
    D) To establish a compromise among those who have defined the term in different ways.

59. The statement that best describes the relationship between law and power is _____.
    A) law is the source of power   C) law is the protector of power
    B) law is a product of power   D) law sets limits to power

60. Which of the following statements can be inferred from the passage?
    A) Power originates from the people and their deeds.
    B) Power may be abused by some people.
    C) To love knowledge is to love power.
    D) Knowledge is power.

61. The author's attitude toward the various kinds of compulsion employed by social institutions can be best described as _____.
    A) critical and disturbed　　　　C) concerned and sympathetic
    B) suspicious and doubtful　　　D) scientific and detached

Part V　Error Correction

(15 minutes)

Directions: *This part consists of a short passage. In this passage, there are altogether 10 mistakes, one in each numbered line. You may have to change a word, add a word or delete a word. Mark out the mistakes and put the corrections in the blanks provided. If you change a word, cross it out and write the correct word in the corresponding blank. If you add a word, put an insertion mark (∧) in the right place and write the missing word in the blank. If you delete a word, cross it out and put a slash (／) in the blank.*

注意：此部分试题在**答题卡**2上；请在**答题卡**2上作答。

Part VI　Translation

(5 minutes)

Directions: *Complete the following sentences on **Answer Sheet 2** by translating into English the Chinese given in brackets.*

注意：此部分试题请在**答题卡**2上作答。

72. Nothing is more damaging to a nation than _____（未能教育好孩子）.

73. It would be fatal for the nation to overlook the urgency of the moment and _____（低估黑人的决心）.

74. Stronger adaptability to market changes, lower management costs and higher labor intensity have _____（确保这些公司具有相对优势）and, consequently, competitiveness in the global market.

75. At no time in history has there been _____（大批人口从农村移居到城市）as is happening now.

76. _____（用信用卡在网上购物）are lowering costs and reducing inventories for America's leading companies as the information technology industry mushrooms.

答题卡 1 (Answer Sheet 1)

学校:									准		考		证			号			

[0]	[0]	[0]	[0]	[0]	[0]	[0]	[0]	[0]	[0]	[0]	[0]	[0]	[0]	[0]
[1]	[1]	[1]	[1]	[1]	[1]	[1]	[1]	[1]	[1]	[1]	[1]	[1]	[1]	[1]
[2]	[2]	[2]	[2]	[2]	[2]	[2]	[2]	[2]	[2]	[2]	[2]	[2]	[2]	[2]
[3]	[3]	[3]	[3]	[3]	[3]	[3]	[3]	[3]	[3]	[3]	[3]	[3]	[3]	[3]
[4]	[4]	[4]	[4]	[4]	[4]	[4]	[4]	[4]	[4]	[4]	[4]	[4]	[4]	[4]
[5]	[5]	[5]	[5]	[5]	[5]	[5]	[5]	[5]	[5]	[5]	[5]	[5]	[5]	[5]
[6]	[6]	[6]	[6]	[6]	[6]	[6]	[6]	[6]	[6]	[6]	[6]	[6]	[6]	[6]
[7]	[7]	[7]	[7]	[7]	[7]	[7]	[7]	[7]	[7]	[7]	[7]	[7]	[7]	[7]
[8]	[8]	[8]	[8]	[8]	[8]	[8]	[8]	[8]	[8]	[8]	[8]	[8]	[8]	[8]
[9]	[9]	[9]	[9]	[9]	[9]	[9]	[9]	[9]	[9]	[9]	[9]	[9]	[9]	[9]

姓名:

划线要求

Part I	Writing	(30 minutes)

Directions: *For this part, you are allowed 30 minutes to write a composition on the topic* **Private Cars in Modern China.** *You should write at least* **120** *words following the outline given below in Chinese:*

1. 私家车在现代中国城市里的发展
2. 使用私家车的优缺点
3. 你对于私家车在现代中国的发展前景有什么看法

Private Cars in Modern China

答题卡 1 (Answer Sheet 1)

Part II   Reading Comprehension (Skimming and Scanning) (15 minutes)

1. [Y] [N] [NG]
2. [Y] [N] [NG]
3. [Y] [N] [NG]
4. [Y] [N] [NG]

5. _____

6. _____

7. _____

8. _____

9. _____

10. _____

答题卡 2 (Answer Sheet 2)

学校：

姓名：

划线要求

准 考 证 号

[0] [0] [0] [0] [0] [0] [0] [0] [0] [0] [0] [0] [0] [0] [0]
[1] [1] [1] [1] [1] [1] [1] [1] [1] [1] [1] [1] [1] [1] [1]
[2] [2] [2] [2] [2] [2] [2] [2] [2] [2] [2] [2] [2] [2] [2]
[3] [3] [3] [3] [3] [3] [3] [3] [3] [3] [3] [3] [3] [3] [3]
[4] [4] [4] [4] [4] [4] [4] [4] [4] [4] [4] [4] [4] [4] [4]
[5] [5] [5] [5] [5] [5] [5] [5] [5] [5] [5] [5] [5] [5] [5]
[6] [6] [6] [6] [6] [6] [6] [6] [6] [6] [6] [6] [6] [6] [6]
[7] [7] [7] [7] [7] [7] [7] [7] [7] [7] [7] [7] [7] [7] [7]
[8] [8] [8] [8] [8] [8] [8] [8] [8] [8] [8] [8] [8] [8] [8]
[9] [9] [9] [9] [9] [9] [9] [9] [9] [9] [9] [9] [9] [9] [9]

Part III   Section A   Section B

11. [A] [B] [C] [D]   16. [A] [B] [C] [D]   21. [A] [B] [C] [D]   26. [A] [B] [C] [D]   31. [A] [B] [C] [D]
12. [A] [B] [C] [D]   17. [A] [B] [C] [D]   22. [A] [B] [C] [D]   27. [A] [B] [C] [D]   32. [A] [B] [C] [D]
13. [A] [B] [C] [D]   18. [A] [B] [C] [D]   23. [A] [B] [C] [D]   28. [A] [B] [C] [D]   33. [A] [B] [C] [D]
14. [A] [B] [C] [D]   19. [A] [B] [C] [D]   24. [A] [B] [C] [D]   29. [A] [B] [C] [D]   34. [A] [B] [C] [D]
15. [A] [B] [C] [D]   20. [A] [B] [C] [D]   25. [A] [B] [C] [D]   30. [A] [B] [C] [D]   35. [A] [B] [C] [D]

Part III   Section C

Seals (36) _____ so many needs of the people who live in the Far North. The meat of the seal is a (37) _____ source of food. Oil from the blubber, or fat, becomes (38) _____. Seal oil, when set on a fire, maintains a steady flame. Sealskins are made into boots and other articles of clothing. The bones become (39) _____ or tools. No part of the animal goes to (40) _____.

The number of seals (41) _____ greatly in different parts of the Arctic. Wherever there are strong ocean currents, resulting in broken (42) _____, you will find an (43) _____ of these animals. (44) _____

_____.

Arctic seal hunting has been an active industry since the early part of the nineteenth century. (45) _____.
More than 500,000 animals are killed each year by hunters operating in the main sealing grounds. (46) _____.

答题卡 2 (Answer Sheet 2)

Part IV   Section A   Part V   Error Correction   (15 minutes)

47. _____

    _____

48. _____

    _____

49. _____

    _____

50. _____

    _____

51. _____

    _____

Quite recently researchers have reviewed the
causes of motion sickness and methods with which
it may be suppressed. They concentrated first of all
in motion sickness which develops in children   62. _____
traveling in the back seat of cars.

A lot of children suffer terribly from car sickness.
What's required is to provide the child with the   63. _____
visual field he has when walk. So objects at a   64. _____
distance in the centre of the field remain stationary
while those in the peripheral (周围的) field appear
to move. This can be achieved by positioning the
child in a raised seat in the front of the car, that, of   65. _____
course, isn't very sensible on terms of safety.

Looking at the horizon is always beneficial to
anyone develops sea sickness, because it's the only   66. _____
object which doesn't move. If he is below deck,
closing his eyes is helpful. It's better to have no
visual information but something which results in   67. _____
conflict.

Taking drugs is one way to prevent motion
sickness. In the fact, it's interesting to note that   68. _____
these have been excluded in medical kits (药箱)   69. _____
used in space flights. Astronauts have been known
to develop motion sickness, too. Drugs are fine in
moderation. We human beings, moreover, are not   70. _____
alone in our suffering. Dogs, cats and horses are
also easily effected; even fish in glass containers on   71. _____
ships sometimes become sick.

Part IV   Section B

52. [A][B][C][D]
53. [A][B][C][D]
54. [A][B][C][D]
55. [A][B][C][D]
56. [A][B][C][D]
57. [A][B][C][D]
58. [A][B][C][D]
59. [A][B][C][D]
60. [A][B][C][D]
61. [A][B][C][D]

Part VI   Translation   (5 minutes)

72. _____

73. _____

74. _____

75. _____

76. _____

PRACTICE TEST 10

Part I Writing   (30 minutes)

注意：此部分试题在**答题卡** 1 上。

Part II Reading Comprehension (Skimming and Scanning)
                                                       (15 minutes)

Directions: *In this part, you will have 15 minutes to go over the passage quickly and answer the questions on **Answer Sheet 1**.*

For questions 1 − 4, mark

Y *(for YES)*   *if the statement agrees with the information given in the passage;*

N *(for NO)*   *if the statement contradicts the information given in the passage;*

NG *(for NOT GIVEN)*   *if the information is not given in the passage.*

For questions 5 − 10, complete the sentences with the information given in the passage.

A Fairyland — Pure New Zealand

I had my honeymoon in New Zealand. It was a nine-day-self-driving tour. At first I thought we were crazy to have chosen New Zealand given the price of the whole budget. Besides，I was a bit apprehensive as it was my first time to go to an unfamiliar place without joining a tour package. However，the fear and anxiety were quickly dissolved by the marvelous scenery as well as the kindness and warmth of New Zealanders. When I finally visited the place，I simply fell in love with it.

Heaven on the Earth

New Zealand is a nature lover's paradise. You don't need contrived amusement parks or fenced-off scenic areas. All you have to do is take a stroll and you can breathe，touch and see the beauty of this country. Wondrous scenery, pollution free, good climate, challenging activities ... what more can one ask for?

No skyscraper in cities at all. A four- or five-storied building is a high and huge one in the South Island. Hence there is nothing to block the sight. I like the fact that walking outside and, even on the way to the grocery store, I can see the most breathtaking scenery all around me.

Secluded inlets, rugged snowcapped mountains, wild coasts and picturesque farming plains, all are like something that appears only in fairy tales. The west coast beaches attracted me most. Sitting in the black shimmering sand, listening to the wind singing, watching the fantastic tiding, we were exposed to a wild and pristine picture. It is really "heaven comes true"!

We could not help killing thirteen rolls of films during our stay. These photos allow us to relish our memories of New Zealand even till today.

Visitor Information Center

What else impresses us most is the efficient service system. We rented a car and drove throughout the South Island ourselves. There are several international car rental companies like Herz, Avis and Budget in the island. You can make a reservation through the Internet. It is quite convenient to get and return the car. We started driving in Christchurch and stopped in Dunedin seven days later.

Fortunately we could find local Visitor Information Centers in most areas. In them there are maps, guide books, and brochures of local events and entertainment, information of accommodation and restaurants, bulletins of attractions and activities, gifts, souvenirs, stamps and phone cards. Also friendly staffs with extensive local knowledge are available. They will answer any question you may have with patience, and provide advice regarding local attractions, travel, and accommodation requirements.

Most Visitor Information Centers can make reservations for accommodation, and may also be able to make direct bookings for travel, tours, accommodation and attractions. All the service is free. One lady there once helped us to book the motel in Arrowtown when there was no vacancy in Queenstown. We were charged only NZ $1.50 and that is the long-distance call fee. There was no extra spending at all.

This New Zealand Visitor Information Network (VIN) is an official one. Therefore, the information provided here is reliable. It is easy to recognize. Each center is identified by the distinctive logo and a green letter "i".

In the Dunedin Information Center we found a Souvenir Coin change machine. You can put all the left coins up to NZ $2, then it will give you a two-dollar New Zealand coin as a souvenir. Quite interesting!

Gourmet Food

In the restaurant, the décor and service are bright and spirited and the lack of professionalism among the staff is made up for with friendliness and the welcoming, casual air. The food reflects the unpretentious, generous spirit of the New Zealanders. The waiter suggested that the best dish on the menu that night was kangaroo meat, and he sure was right! Imagine a traditional comfit of kangaroo, bathed in an ultra-fiery curry sauce, all soothed with a fragrant mound of jasmine rice. Equally delicious — and served piping hot from a large ceramic covered dish — was the braised veal knuckle with preserved lemons and lentils, a comforting stew that hit the spot on a chilly spring evening. For a pleasantly modern touch on a great classic, try their Caesar salad, a generous tangle of greens seasoned with Parmesan, anchovies, and a poached egg, all tossed with a garlic mayonnaise. Of course, great food needs to be served with good wine. There you will be treated to the entire panoply of wonderful wines from New Zealand, which includes New Zealand's top Cloudy Bay 1994 Sauvignon blanc and 1992 Chardonnay.

Sense of Environment

Around New Zealand, there is a notice in the bathroom of every hotel, which reads "We care for our environment. We don't want to pollute the water with harmful substance of the detergent. Put the towels on the rack if they are still clean enough to use." In New Zealand, you cannot see rubbish in public places. The country is so clean that you can sit anywhere you like without dirtying the clothes. The bottles are made of glass and the packages are made of paper or other natural materials that can be recycled.

Simple-hearted New Zealanders

New Zealanders call themselves Kiwi. That is a special species existing merely in this island. The characteristic of it is simple and kind. That is just what a New Zealander has.

On the way, the engine suddenly stalled. No matter how we tried, it just refused to work again. There was not even one car passing by. What should we do? Just then two bicycle-riding guys saw the parking car and came to us asking what was wrong. With their help, finally the car could move again.

Another time we lost the car key in Queenstown. When we realized it, we searched the way we walked inch by inch, hoping to find it, but failed. Then we were in panic for some time as all the things were in the car and what's more, the car number tag was on the key. We were a little relieved when we saw the car was still there. Then we just went to the Lost-and-Found to try our luck. The policeman was quite gentle and gave us all keys found within one hour to check. Our key was lying there! We only spent about one hour finding our key, including the time spent in our own searching.

This is New Zealand, a simple but splendid place!

注意：此部分试题请在**答题卡**1上作答。

1. At first the author thought it's not worth the price to travel in New Zealand.
2. There are no contrived amusement parks in New Zealand.
3. The thing the author likes most is walking outside in New Zealand.
4. All Visitor Information Centers can make reservations for accommodation.
5. Herz, Avis and Budget are the names of _____.
6. Since VIN is an official one, the _____ is reliable.
7. As is reflected in their food, New Zealanders have a _____ spirit.
8. In New Zealand, packages tend to be made of _____.
9. The characteristic of New Zealanders is _____.
10. Finally the author found the lost key in _____.

Part III Listening Comprehension (35 minutes)

Section A

Directions: *In this section, you will hear 8 short conversations and 2 long conversations. At the end of each conversation, one or more questions will be asked about what was said. Both the conversation and the questions will be spoken only once. After each question there will be a pause. During the pause, you must read the four choices marked A), B), C) and D), and decide which is the best answer. Then mark the corresponding letter on **Answer Sheet 2** with a single line through the centre.*

注意：此部分试题请在**答题卡**2上作答。

11. A) A driving test. C) A police movie.
    B) A traffic accident. D) The best way to make signals.

12. A) To be well-informed.
    B) To learn how to separate the important from the unimportant.
    C) Because he reads too many books.
    D) Because he always wastes his time.

13. A) Because the man will polish the scratch on the cabinet.

B) Because she received a discount on the cabinet.

C) Because she paid only $50 for the cabinet.

D) Because the regular price of the cabinet was reasonable.

14. A) She will pay $0.45. C) She will pay $1.15.

B) She will pay $1.00. D) She will pay $0.55.

15. A) The happiness of being alone.

B) The art of communication.

C) The freedom of action.

D) The quietness of the home environment.

16. A) The interest in sports.

B) The criticism of sports.

C) The usefulness of sports events.

D) The influence of sports events.

17. A) To grow trees. C) To go to the desert.

B) To close the windows. D) To visit Beijing.

18. A) The Thai Air Counter is on the right side.

B) There is a long queue at the Thai Air Counter.

C) The British Airways Counter is Counter 26.

D) The British Airways Counter is next to Counter 26.

Questions 19 to 21 are based on the conversation you have just heard.

19. A) Christmas and the Spring Festival.

B) Thanksgiving and the Mid-Autumn Festival.

C) Halloween and the Double Ninth Festival.

D) Easter and the Dragon-Boat Festival.

20. A) They are both major holidays.

B) They are both holidays for family reunions.

C) They are both holidays to celebrate the harvest.

D) They are both holidays for people to make fun of each other.

21. A) Turkey. C) Pumpkin pie.

B) Ham. D) Corn-on-the-cob.

Questions 22 to 25 are based on the conversation you have just heard.

22. A) Because he is sick and wants to ask for leave.

   B) Because he wants to hand in his term paper.

   C) Because he wants to bring his roommate's term paper to her office.

   D) Because he wants to ask her how to write the term paper.

23. A) Because he needs one more humanities course to graduate.

   B) Because he is interested in landscape painters very much.

   C) Because he is an art major.

   D) Because his roommate asks him to do so.

24. A) To take the final exam.

   B) To write a term paper.

   C) To give a major presentation on an individual painter.

   D) To look at the history and politics of the era in which the painters lived.

25. A) Later today.

   B) At 3 o'clock in the afternoon.

   C) Any time in the afternoon.

   D) Any time tomorrow afternoon.

Section B

Directions: *In this section, you will hear 3 short passages. At the end of each passage, you will hear some questions. Both the passage and the questions will be spoken only once. After you hear a question, you must choose the best answer from the four choices marked A), B), C) and D). Then mark the corresponding letter on **Answer Sheet 2** with a single line through the centre.*

注意：此部分试题请在**答题卡 2** 上作答。

Passage One

Questions 26 to 28 are based on the passage you have just heard.

26. A) To take pity on the homesick.

   B) To share his feelings about staying abroad.

   C) To introduce the knowledge of culture shock.

   D) To encourage and cheer up the culture shock sufferers.

27. A) He should stay inside all the time for safety.

   B) He should phone his parents or friends in his home country for comfort.

   C) He should work hard to build a new self-image.

   D) He should get to know the new surroundings and gain experience.

28. A) The successful ones in their community have less difficulty in a foreign environment.
    B) Culture shock doesn't include such factors as customs, one's native language and so on.
    C) Culture shock gives rise to the feeling of being lost.
    D) The specialists going abroad won't experience the stages of culture shock.

Passage Two

Questions 29 to 31 are based on the passage you have just heard.

29. A) You can get help from specialists when choosing a dog.
    B) It is common sense that is the most important when choosing a dog.
    C) You should decide what kind of dog you want.
    D) Size and characteristics of the dogs should be considered too.

30. A) The color of the dog.
    B) The price of the dog.
    C) Whether the dog will fit the environment.
    D) Whether the dog will get along with the other pets in the house.

31. A) It must be trained so that it won't bite.
    B) It demands more food and space.
    C) It needs more love and care.
    D) It must be looked after carefully.

Passage Three

Questions 32 to 35 are based on the passage you have just heard.

32. A) Most of the companies listed on NASDAQ are smaller companies.
    B) Stock brokers are more important when trading takes place.
    C) More technology companies can be found on NASDAQ.
    D) Central location isn't as necessary as that of others.

33. A) Because all the stocks are handed over a counter.
    B) Because no trade takes place in a set place.
    C) Because all the trade is handled directly between brokers and market makers.
    D) Because counters are used in trade.

34. A) NASDAQ Stock Market is the first electronic and truly global stock market.
    B) All the companies on NASDAQ have achieved their desired growth.

C) Companies all over the world prefer to choose NASDAQ Stock Market over any other stock market.

D) NASDAQ Stock Market has made a lot of private companies into public ones.

35. A) NASDAQ Offered Great Help in Business
    B) A Stock Market with No Central Location
    C) NASDAQ, NYSE, or AMEX?
    D) A Different Stock Market

Section C

Directions: *In this section, you will hear a passage three times. When the passage is read for the first time, you should listen carefully for its general idea. When the passage is read for the second time, you are required to fill in the blanks numbered from 36 to 43 with the exact words you have just heard. For blanks numbered from 44 to 46 you are required to fill in the missing information. For these blanks, you can either use the exact words you have just heard or write down the main points in your own words. Finally, when the passage is read for the third time, you should check what you have written.*

注意：此部分试题在**答题卡 2** 上；请在**答题卡 2** 上作答。

Part IV Reading Comprehension (Reading in Depth)

(25 minutes)

Section A

Directions: *In this section, there is a short passage with four questions and one incomplete statement. Read the passage carefully. Then answer the questions and complete the statement in the fewest possible words on Answer Sheet 2.*

Questions 47 to 51 are based on the following passage.

To the casual observer, Robert was living in the American dream. Through hard work and an ability to sense something new, he had moved through the ranks of a Fortune 1,000 company. He and his wife, Jeannie, had just celebrated twenty good years together. They lived in a modest but tasteful home in a leafy suburb of Philadelphia, and in a few short years of mortgage payments the house would be theirs, free and clear. Robert and Jeannie's three children, aged seventeen, fifteen;

and nine, had always been a source of great joy.

But lately for Robert, the dream had faded. His nine-year-old son had struggled in school since the first grade, and he was having real difficulties in learning. His lively and expressive fifteen-year-old daughter had become a stranger who was often rebellious in whatever she did. Robert's job and his marriage had been the two important events in his life, but neither provided the spark it once did. He had devoted fifteen years to his company, but he had not made any progress in the last few years, and the promotional path was no longer clear. With the recent rumors of downsizing, Robert became increasingly anxious about his family's financial future. Three college tuition bills lay ahead, and little money had been invested for retirement. And then there was his marriage. Robert and Jeannie had always been close, but between the demands of work and the kids they rarely got any time alone.

At the age of forty-seven, Robert was ill-prepared to manage the misfortunes in his life, as routine or commonplace as they may seem. Somehow, somewhere, Robert had lost his way. The parts of his life that had once given him such fulfillment now left him feeling empty.

注意：此部分试题请在**答题卡**2上作答。

47. How long had Robert been married to his wife, Jeannie?

48. Robert bought the house through _____.

49. Of Robert's three children, who had difficulties in learning?

50. What does the word "downsizing" in the second paragraph mean?

51. Why did Robert feel uncertain about the future?

Section B

Directions: *There are 2 passages in this section. Each passage is followed by some questions or unfinished statements. For each of them there are four choices marked A), B), C) and D). You should decide on the best choice and mark the corresponding letter on **Answer Sheet 2** with a single line through the centre.*

Passage One

Questions 52 to 56 are based on the following passage.

Most of us tell one or two lies a day, according to scientists who study these things. And we rarely get caught, because the lies we tell are usually little ones: "I got stuck in traffic." "That color looks good on you." "I was just about to call." But even the smallest fib may soon be systematically exposed, at least in the virtual world. Researchers at several universities are developing software that can detect lies in online communications such as instant messages, e-mails and chatrooms. The ability to spot "digital deception," as researchers call it, has never been more crucial. Today, much of our business and social life is conducted online, making us increasingly vulnerable. White-collar criminals, sexual predators, scammers, identity thieves and even terrorists surf the same Web as the rest of us.

Conventional lie detectors look for physiological signs of anxiety — a bead of sweat or a racing pulse — but online systems examine only the liar's words. "When we're looking at language, we're looking at the tool of the lie," says Jeff Hancock, an assistant professor of communication and a member of the faculty of computing and information science at Cornell University.

Hancock, who recently received a $680,000 grant from the National Science Foundation to study digital deception, says there is a growing body of evidence that the language of dishonest messages is different than that of honest ones. For example, one study led by Hancock and due to be published this spring in *Discourse Processes* found that deceptive e-mail messages contained 28 percent more words on average and used a higher percentage of words associated with negative emotions than did truthful messages. Liars also tend to use fewer first-person references (such as the pronoun "I") and more third-person references (such as "he" and "they"). This may be the liar's subconscious way of distancing himself from his lie.

To identify the patterns of deceit, Hancock has developed an instant-messaging system at Cornell that asks users to rate the deceptiveness of each message they send. The system has already collected 10,000 messages, of which about 6 percent qualify as patently deceptive. Eventually the results will be incorporated into software that analyzes incoming messages. For now, the Cornell researchers are working only with the kinds of lies told by students and faculty. It remains to be seen whether such a system can be scaled up to handle "big" lies, such as messages sent by con artists and terrorists.

Fortunately, the research so far suggests that people lie less often in e-mail than face-to-face or on the phone. Perhaps this is because people are reluctant to put their lies in writing, Hancock speculates. "An e-mail generates multiple copies," he says. "It will last longer than something carved in rock." So choose your words carefully. The Internet may soon be rid not only of deceit but also of lame excuses.

注意：此部分试题请在**答题卡 2** 上作答。

52. A kind of software developed by researchers can NOT detect lies in _____.
    A) text messages   C) chatroom messages
    B) e-mails   D) communications

53. Which of the following statements is NOT correct according to the passage?
    A) Since much of our business and social life is conducted online, we may be deceived by evildoers.
    B) People who tell lies tend to be anxious with a racing pulse.
    C) The author reminds people to choose their words carefully in online communication.
    D) The system developed by Hancock can be used to analyze all sorts of lies.

54. The following are the descriptions of dishonest messages EXCEPT that _____.
    A) liars like to use "I" and "we" in their messages
    B) there are more words that will arouse bad feelings in dishonest messages
    C) deceptive messages contain more words referring to the third person
    D) liars tend to use more words in dishonest messages

55. What does the expression "con artists" in the end of the fourth paragraph mean?
    A) Confident artists.   C) Liars and artists.
    B) Conservative artists.   D) Persons who regularly cheat others.

56. What does the last sentence of the passage imply?
    A) There will never be lies and excuses on the Internet.
    B) Lies and weak excuses may disappear from the Internet.
    C) Lies and weak explanations will be easily spotted on the Internet.
    D) Lies and excuses will be eliminated from the Internet.

Passage Two

Questions 57 to 61 are based on the following passage.

When Google introduced Google Earth, free software that marries satellite and aerial images with mapping capabilities, the company emphasized its usefulness as a teaching and navigation tool, while advertising the pure entertainment value of high-resolution flyover images of the Eiffel Tower, Big Ben and the pyramids. But since its debut last summer, Google Earth has received attention of an unexpected sort. Officials of several nations have expressed alarm over its detailed display of government buildings, military installations and other important sites within their borders.

India, whose laws sharply restrict satellite and aerial photography, has been particularly outspoken. "It could severely compromise a country's security," secretary in India's federal Department of Science and Technology said of Google Earth. And India's surveyor general said, "They ought to have asked us." Similar sentiments have surfaced in news reports from other countries. South Korean officials have said they fear that Google Earth lays bare details of military installations. Thai security officials said they intended to ask Google to block images of vulnerable government buildings. And an analyst for the Federal Security Service, the Russian security agency that succeeded the K.G.B., was quoted by Itar-Tass as saying: "Terrorists don't need to reconnoiter their target. Now an American company is working for them."

But there is little they can do, it seems, but protest.

American experts in and outside government generally agree that the focus on Google Earth as a security threat appears misplaced, as the same images that Google acquires from a variety of sources are available directly from the imaging companies, as well as from other sources. Google Earth licenses most of the satellite images, for instance, from Digital Globe, an imaging company in Longmont, Colo.

"Google Earth is not acquiring new imagery," said John Pike, director of Globalsecurity org., which has an online repository of satellite imagery. "They are simply repurposing imagery that somebody else had already acquired. So if there was any harm that was going to be done by the imagery, it would already be done."

注意：此部分试题请在**答题卡 2** 上作答。

57. The most accurate definition of Google Earth may be _____.
   A) it is free software which enables people to find directions
   B) it is free software about directions developed by Google
   C) it is free software used as a teaching and navigation tool
   D) it is free software made up of satellite and aerial images and mapping capabilities

58. What does the word "debut" in the first paragraph refer to?
   A) First public appearance of Google Earth.
   B) A device first developed by Google.
   C) A formal discussion concerning Google Earth.
   D) Public opinions concerning Google Earth.

59. What are the attitudes of American experts towards Google Earth?
   A) It is a security threat to a country.
   B) It should be criticized.
   C) The criticism on it seems not appropriate.

D) They thought it quite useful.

60. Which of the following statements is NOT mentioned in the passage?
    A) Google Earth has displayed some important information of the United States.
    B) Google Earth may bring the security of a country into great danger.
    C) Terrorists don't have to seek for information for military purposes because of the existence of Google Earth.
    D) Google Earth acquired images from many other imaging companies.

61. The most suitable title of the passage may be _____.
    A) The Capable Google Earth
    B) The Powerful Google Earth
    C) Governments Tremble at Google's Bird's-Eye View
    D) High-Resolution Flyover Images of Google Earth

Part V   Error Correction   (15 minutes)

Directions: *This part consists of a short passage. In this passage, there are altogether 10 mistakes, one in each numbered line. You may have to change a word, add a word or delete a word. Mark out the mistakes and put the corrections in the blanks provided. If you change a word, cross it out and write the correct word in the corresponding blank. If you add a word, put an insertion mark (∧) in the right place and write the missing word in the blank. If you delete a word, cross it out and put a slash (/) in the blank.*

注意：此部分试题在**答题卡** 2 上；请在**答题卡** 2 上作答。

Part VI   Translation   (5 minutes)

Directions: *Complete the following sentences on **Answer Sheet 2** by translating into English the Chinese given in brackets.*

注意：此部分试题请在**答题卡** 2 上作答。

72. _____ （经过40多年齐头并进的发展）, the information and life sciences — computing and biology — are fusing into a single,

powerful force that is laying the foundation for the biotech century.

73. He _____ (遭受了一个又一个打击)last year：his company went bankrupt；his wife divorced him.

74. Three section managers wanted to _____ (填补这一空缺) after the president resigned for the sake of his health.

75. The teacher gave a comprehensive analysis of _____ (对中国各行业的正面和负面影响) when China entered WTO.

76. The jury eventually decided that Mary was guilty and she _____ (被判处三年有期徒刑).

答题卡 1 (Answer Sheet 1)

学校:
姓名:
划线要求

准　　考　　证　　号

[0]	[0]	[0]	[0]	[0]	[0]	[0]	[0]	[0]	[0]	[0]	[0]	[0]	[0]	[0]
[1]	[1]	[1]	[1]	[1]	[1]	[1]	[1]	[1]	[1]	[1]	[1]	[1]	[1]	[1]
[2]	[2]	[2]	[2]	[2]	[2]	[2]	[2]	[2]	[2]	[2]	[2]	[2]	[2]	[2]
[3]	[3]	[3]	[3]	[3]	[3]	[3]	[3]	[3]	[3]	[3]	[3]	[3]	[3]	[3]
[4]	[4]	[4]	[4]	[4]	[4]	[4]	[4]	[4]	[4]	[4]	[4]	[4]	[4]	[4]
[5]	[5]	[5]	[5]	[5]	[5]	[5]	[5]	[5]	[5]	[5]	[5]	[5]	[5]	[5]
[6]	[6]	[6]	[6]	[6]	[6]	[6]	[6]	[6]	[6]	[6]	[6]	[6]	[6]	[6]
[7]	[7]	[7]	[7]	[7]	[7]	[7]	[7]	[7]	[7]	[7]	[7]	[7]	[7]	[7]
[8]	[8]	[8]	[8]	[8]	[8]	[8]	[8]	[8]	[8]	[8]	[8]	[8]	[8]	[8]
[9]	[9]	[9]	[9]	[9]	[9]	[9]	[9]	[9]	[9]	[9]	[9]	[9]	[9]	[9]

Part I　　　　　　　　　　**Writing**　　　　　　　　　**(30 minutes)**

Directions: *For this part, you are allowed 30 minutes to write a composition on the topic* **College Students' Way of Spending Summer Vacation.** *You should write at least 120 words following the outline given below in Chinese:*

1. 十年前大学生如何过暑假
2. 近几年大学生过暑假的方式有何变化
3. 发生这种变化的原因是什么

College Students' Way of Spending Summer Vacation

答题卡 1 (Answer Sheet 1)

Part II   Reading Comprehension (Skimming and Scanning) (15 minutes)

1. [Y] [N] [NG]
2. [Y] [N] [NG]
3. [Y] [N] [NG]
4. [Y] [N] [NG]

5. _____
6. _____
7. _____

8. _____
9. _____
10. _____

答题卡 2 (Answer Sheet 2)

学校:

姓名:

划线要求

准 考 证 号

[0]	[0]	[0]	[0]	[0]	[0]	[0]	[0]	[0]	[0]	[0]	[0]	[0]	[0]	[0]
[1]	[1]	[1]	[1]	[1]	[1]	[1]	[1]	[1]	[1]	[1]	[1]	[1]	[1]	[1]
[2]	[2]	[2]	[2]	[2]	[2]	[2]	[2]	[2]	[2]	[2]	[2]	[2]	[2]	[2]
[3]	[3]	[3]	[3]	[3]	[3]	[3]	[3]	[3]	[3]	[3]	[3]	[3]	[3]	[3]
[4]	[4]	[4]	[4]	[4]	[4]	[4]	[4]	[4]	[4]	[4]	[4]	[4]	[4]	[4]
[5]	[5]	[5]	[5]	[5]	[5]	[5]	[5]	[5]	[5]	[5]	[5]	[5]	[5]	[5]
[6]	[6]	[6]	[6]	[6]	[6]	[6]	[6]	[6]	[6]	[6]	[6]	[6]	[6]	[6]
[7]	[7]	[7]	[7]	[7]	[7]	[7]	[7]	[7]	[7]	[7]	[7]	[7]	[7]	[7]
[8]	[8]	[8]	[8]	[8]	[8]	[8]	[8]	[8]	[8]	[8]	[8]	[8]	[8]	[8]
[9]	[9]	[9]	[9]	[9]	[9]	[9]	[9]	[9]	[9]	[9]	[9]	[9]	[9]	[9]

Part III   Section A   Section B

11. [A] [B] [C] [D]   16. [A] [B] [C] [D]   21. [A] [B] [C] [D]   26. [A] [B] [C] [D]   31. [A] [B] [C] [D]
12. [A] [B] [C] [D]   17. [A] [B] [C] [D]   22. [A] [B] [C] [D]   27. [A] [B] [C] [D]   32. [A] [B] [C] [D]
13. [A] [B] [C] [D]   18. [A] [B] [C] [D]   23. [A] [B] [C] [D]   28. [A] [B] [C] [D]   33. [A] [B] [C] [D]
14. [A] [B] [C] [D]   19. [A] [B] [C] [D]   24. [A] [B] [C] [D]   29. [A] [B] [C] [D]   34. [A] [B] [C] [D]
15. [A] [B] [C] [D]   20. [A] [B] [C] [D]   25. [A] [B] [C] [D]   30. [A] [B] [C] [D]   35. [A] [B] [C] [D]

Part III   Section C

Most Americans start school at the age of five when they enter (36) _____. Children do not really study at this time. They only (37) _____ for half the day and learn what school is like. Children attend (38) _____ school for the next six years. They learn to read and write and work with numbers. They also study the world and its people. After six years, children go to (39) _____ high school for three years and senior high school for another three years. This is called secondary education.

In their secondary schooling, children cover more (40) _____ knowledge and begin to concentrate on their special (41) _____. They usually study further in history, geography, government, English and literature. They may (42) _____ to study foreign languages, advanced mathematics or science, such as physics or chemistry.

Higher education takes place in colleges and universities. The (43) _____ course is four years. (44) _____.

After four years, they earn a bachelor's degree. (45) _____
_____.

(46) _____
_____

答题卡 2 (Answer Sheet 2)

Part IV   Section A   Part V   Error Correction   (15 minutes)

47. _____

_____

48. _____

_____

49. _____

_____

50. _____

_____

51. _____

_____

Part IV   Section B

52. [A][B][C][D]

53. [A][B][C][D]

54. [A][B][C][D]

55. [A][B][C][D]

56. [A][B][C][D]

57. [A][B][C][D]

58. [A][B][C][D]

59. [A][B][C][D]

60. [A][B][C][D]

61. [A][B][C][D]

Job interview is a minefield. Your prospective employers have a stack of resumes from talent applicants. Now they want to know what makes you to tick.

To make a better impression, Dee Soder, a New York executive coach, recommends you can prepare by writing an "employment ad" that describes your dream job. This forces you to focus on exactly what you want and what you have to offer even the interviewer doesn't ask you. Interviewers know many people leave jobs because they hate their boss; they have job-hopped with the same reason themselves. But few employers want to hear it. If you are fired because of conflict with a boss, however, you may be better off telling interviewers yourself, rather than have them rely on industry gossip.

If you want to switch careers, you'd better explain how your skills, personality and goals are more suited to the new career, or that you want to "add" something for your experience that will help you achieve a long-term goal.

Employers can't legally ask about such things as age, health and marriage. But if an employer does ask one of them, don't cry foul if you don't want the job. Chances are the interviewer is really asking how much you're willing to travel or work overtime.

When asking to name your weaknesses, be honest, but emphasize the actions you've taken to deal with a weakness. Once you had stated one or two weaknesses and their solutions, stop talking.

62. _____

63. _____

64. _____

65. _____

66. _____

67. _____

68. _____

69. _____

70. _____

71. _____

Part VI   Translation   (5 minutes)

72. _____

73. _____

74. _____

75. _____

76. _____

PART TWO

KEY AND NOTES

Practice Test 1

Part I　Writing

Examination-Oriented or Quality-Oriented Education

(Student's sample)

The current education system is not aimed at students' quality but at their ability in tests. So from primary school to college, all the students are struggling for high scores. But many students often do poorly in practical application of the knowledge and theory they have learned.

China is changing examination-oriented education into quality oriented education. The alternative will pay attention to the students' ability as a whole. It emphasizes students' ability to solve concrete problems independently, and helps the students to adapt themselves to the society when they graduate from schools. The exam results will not be the only way to evaluate a student.

I firmly believe in the magic force of this new policy. I can imagine the students will have more creative minds. Our education will bring up a new generation.

(Improved sample)

From primary school to college, students, teachers and parents — **all** are struggling for high scores. **This is because** the current education system is not aimed at students' quality, but **only** at developing their ability to perform well on the test. **As a result,** many students, **even those** with high scores, often do poorly **when it comes to** the practical application of **what** they've learned.

Therefore, China is **challenging** examination-oriented education **by advocating** quality-oriented education. The alternative will **focus on** the students' ability as a whole. **That is to say,** it emphasizes not only on students' required knowledge but on their ability to solve concrete problems independently. The exam results will **no longer play a key role** in evaluating a student.

Personally，I firmly believe in the magic force of this new policy. **It seems that I have seen in my mind's eye** the more colorful life，the **looser environment**，**yet** the more **creative minds** of the future students. Our education，**so to speak**，will bring up a new generation.

Part II　Reading Comprehension (Skimming and Scanning)

1. N　大多数航空公司要求新招收的职员语言达标，但是现有的员工不必参加任何语言达标培训。

   细节题。根据关键词 new recruit 和 existing staff，可以快速定位至第一部分的 a 和 b 两个条目，解读其意思可知，航空公司不仅要求新招收的职员语言达标，而且对现有职工也加以语言培训以使其达到语言要求。题目的表述和文章内容不符，故此陈述应被判断为错误。

2. Y　语言熟练程度的评价包括"说与听的能力"。

   细节题。根据关键词 speaking and listening ability，可以把本题定位至文章第二部分的第一句。通过比较，这一陈述的表达与文中的意思一致，故应被判为正确。

3. N　语言达标者只需在面对面的情况下准确、清楚地交流。

   细节题。文中第三部分的条目 a 明确规定，语言达标者应该能在 voice-only (telephone/radiotelephone) 和 face-to-face 两种情况下有效交流。题目的表述和文章内容不符，故此陈述应被判断为错误。

4. N　在任何情况下，语言达标者都不允许犯语法错误。

   细节题。根据本题的关键词 errors，可以把本题定位至第四部分的 Structure 标准之下。根据最后一句话的意思，当非正常或突然情况发生时，在不影响意思表达的前提下，允许出现句子结构的错误。题目的表述和文章内容不符，故此陈述应被判断为错误。

5. Y　当语言达标者在某些特殊的情况下缺乏词汇时，他可以用已掌握的词语表达看法而不影响意义。

   细节题。本题的关键词为 lacking vocabulary，据此可以把本题定位至第四部分的 Vocabulary 标准之下，阅读最后一句，可知题目的说法与其一致，故答案应选择 Y。

6. NG　本族语者的测试程序比外国人的少。

   细节题。虽然文章中的第五部分提到了本族语者也要接受语言能力测试，但并没有将本族语者和非本族语者的测试进行比较。因此根据文章的表述，得不出题目的结论，故此题答案应选 NG。

7. N　对外语的测试，航空公司可以决定评价的形式。

   细节题。根据关键词 the format of the formal assessment，可以把本题定位至第六部分的最后一段：The format of the formal assessment will be determined by the State，可知航空公司无权决定评价形式，此题应被判为错误。

8. **not appropriate** 大多数的商业化英语测试不适合用来测试飞行员。

本题的答案可以在原文最后一部分的第二段中找到。该段第一句告诉我们，像托福这样的商业化英语测试不适合用来测试飞行员和航空交通管制员。所以此处应该填 not appropriate。

9. **a context（e.g. business）** 一些现有的口语测试不能令人满意,因为它们通常是为与民用航空没有关系的语境(比如商务语境)设置的。

本题的答案可以在原文最后一部分第二段的最后一句话中找到。题目只是该句子的同义改写。显然空白处应该填 a context（e.g. business）。

10. **the computerized versions** 应用其他测试方式是不合适的,尤其是那些只使用机考的测试。

本题的答案可以在原文最后一句话中找到:其他的测试方法,尤其那些只使用机考的测试方法是不合适的。题目的表述只是原文句型的变换。故此处应填 the computerized versions。

Part III Listening Comprehension (35 minutes)

Section A

11. D   12. C   13. A   14. C   15. A
16. D   17. D   18. B   19. C   20. A
21. B   22. D   23. C   24. B   25. A

Section B

26. C   27. D   28. A   29. B   30. D
31. B   32. C   33. B   34. A   35. A

Section C

36. conclusive   37. counters   38. pavement   39. confirm
40. published   41. Journal   42. aged   43. persistent

44. The team looked through all the factors in lifestyle

45. But they found no evidence to link regular jogging with early death

46. Finally the researchers concluded that a vigorous activity such as jogging is associated with a beneficial effect on mortality

Part IV Reading Comprehension (Reading in Depth)

Section A

47. **K** 从句子结构上看,这里应填入名词。根据下文提到的 food, shelter, clothes,可以判断需要填入的是"生活必需品",初步符合题意的只有 essentials 和 articles 这两个词。essentials 指的是必不可少的东西、必需品,比如 the bare essentials（最基本的用品）;而 article 常常用来指整套物品中的一件,如 articles of clothing（衣物）,toilet articles such as soap, toothpaste and shampoo（诸如肥皂、牙膏、洗发剂之类的盥洗用品）。故此处应选择 essentials 这个词。

48. M 从句子结构看，这里应填入过去分词。再根据这句话的意思（"到目前为止，这些需求被_____是不必要的"）可以判定应选择 regarded 或 looked。当 look 作"把……看作；把……视为"解时，只能用 look on sb. /sth. as sb. /sth. 这个结构，所以只能选择 regarded 这个词。

49. C 从句子结构看，在 in order to 后面只能填动词原形。再根据空格后的 a given standard of living，可以看出这里能用 earn 或 make 构成词组，例如 earn one's living；make a good/decent/meager living（过优裕的/体面的/贫困的生活）。而 cling 虽然有保持、坚持的意思，但只能用 cling to 这个结构。故此处应选择 earn 这个词。

50. H 从上下文看，这里应填入 former 或 latter 两个词，因为空格后为 alternative（可供选择的事物），前文已提到，"要么我们把生活标准再提高一步，使之超越已足够舒适和愉快的档次，要么我们把标准停留在这一档次而把工作时间缩短"，而下文是："人们在他们取酬的职务岗位中的工作时间将愈来愈短"，所以此处应选择 latter 这个词。

51. F 根据下文所说"家庭主妇将指望能完全摆脱日常的家务操作"可以判断，她们能在生活中获得更多的闲暇，所以此处应选择 leisure 这个词。

52. N 根据句子结构，空格前为 without，后面是 her standard of living，因此可判断应填入一动词-ing 形式，lowering 和 lessening 可供选择。lower 意思是在质量、价值方面的减少、缩小、降低，而 lessen 侧重于音量、风险、影响、效果、重要性等的变小、减弱、减轻。故此处应选用 lowering 一词。

53. E 上文中有"随着文明在技术领域不断发展，它会超越满足食、住、衣、暖等所有基本生活要素这一界限"，下文又提到机器人佣工，可以判断家庭佣人将不复存在。cease 就是停止、终止、结束的意思，后面可以加 to + 动词原形的结构，所以应选 ceased 一词。

54. O 根据句意，有了机器人佣工，家庭主妇自然就能摆脱家务；从句子结构看，这里应填入动词原形，relieve 为正确选择，词组 relieve sb. of sth. 意为"帮助……减轻负担"，正符合题意。所以此处应选 relieve 一词。

55. J 从句子结构看，这里应填入名词，只有 emotions 符合题意；再根据句意，机器人佣工是一台机器，它像汽车一样有存储指令的能力，但没有感情，所以此处应选择 emotions 一词。

56. L 根据下文举例，真空吸尘器和洗衣机都属于专门化的机械，而 specialized 一词是形容词，意为"专业的、专门的、专用的"，比如 specialized equipment（专用设备），故 specialized 是正确的选择。

Section B

57. C 主旨题。全文由三段组成。第一段的中心是"有两种主要的假设说明了现代人类的出现"，第二和第三段则分别从化石、头骨和基因研究三方面提出关于人类起源争论的证据。选项 A 总结了第二段的内容,选项 B 给出了支持其中一种理论的证据,而选项 D 只是第三段的一个次要内容,这三个选项都只局限于某个方面,不够全面。只有选项 C 能比较完整地总结全文内容。

58. D　细节题。选项 A“‘源自非洲说’从学者那里得到更多的支持”是第二段中明确提出的一个内容;选项 B“‘多地域说’把人类出现的时间上溯得更远”可以在第一段中找到:“源自非洲说”把人类出现的时间确定在150 000到200 000年前,而“多地域说”则把时间确定在二百万年前,所以这个选项是正确的;选项 C 提到“文章中涉及到三种搜集证据的方法”,从文中可知,可以作为证据的有化石、头骨和DNA 测试,因而这一选项也是正确的;选项 D“DNA 研究为将来提供明确的证据提出了一个更好的方法”并不能从文中推断出来,所以只有这个选项是错误的。故此题的正确答案为 D。

59. A　推理题。从文章的最后一段可知古人类学家对人类起源的争论仍将继续,所以只有选项 A“这场争论不可能平息下来”是可以从中推断出来的;选项 B“这场争论将吸引历史学家加入进来”和选项 C“将来这场争论有可能变得不重要”不能从文中推断出来;选项 D“在不久的将来这场争论有可能结束”正好和文章内容相反。故此题的正确答案为 A。

60. D　归纳题。从文中对两种假说的阐述可以得知:“多地域说”把人类出现的时间确定得比“源自非洲说”更早,两种假说都把非洲定为发源地,基因研究支持两种假说,所以选项 A、B、C 都是正确的。选项 D“两种假说都把(石器时代生活于欧洲的)尼安德特人看作是现代人类的祖先”不能从文中归纳出来,故此题的正确答案为 D。

61. B　细节题。文中第一段已明确指出:支持“多地域说”的学者认为不同地域的人们通过基因和文化交流联系在一起,而其他选项都与文章内容不符。故此题的正确答案为 B。

62. B　主旨题。全文由两段组成。第一段的中心是对一些人提出的“文科教育是无用的奢侈品,应使学生们学到‘有销路的技能’”这种观点进行批驳;第二段从正反两方面论述学校应该培养学生的学习能力,而不只是教给他们“有销路的技能”。从文章内容分析,作者是赞成相对于职业教育、专门技术教育而言的文科教育的。故此题的正确答案是 B。

63. C　词义理解题。从主句 Home construction skills are another example of *varying salability*(建筑技术是另外一个销路变化不定的例子)来看,从句意思应为“劳务市场不断变化”,所以 fluctuate 的意思是“变化、波动”。而选项 A“遵循一个固定的模式”、选项 B“保持稳定”和选项 D“变得越来越糟”都不符合题意。故此题的正确答案是 C。

64. B　细节题。在第二段中,作者指出了学校的职责在于“使学生更好地了解周围的世界,在变化的世界里有更强的适应能力”,所以学校应该关注的是学生适应变化的能力,而不是考虑什么技能是有销路的、在未来的劳务市场上畅销。故此题的正确答案为 B。

65. B 细节题。文章最后一句话 learning to learn is one of the highest liberal skills 明确表明了作者的态度：只有具备自学能力的人才有可能在失业率较高的时候找到工作，因为他们在变化的世界里有更强的适应能力；而建筑工人、汽车修理工只具备一些"有销路"的技能，未必有较强的适应变化的能力，所以找到工作的机会不多。故此题的正确答案为 B。

66. C 推理题。选项 A"许多学生感到他们被教育制度欺骗了"是学校只教给学生"有销路"的技能带来的后果；选项 B"那些教授实践技能的学校在困难时期发展得更好"正好和第二段的内容相反，作者反对学校只教授实践技能；选项 D"课外活动比课堂教学更重要"在文中并未提及；选项 C"文科教育现在受到了挑战"和第一段开头内容吻合，一些人提出的"文科教育是无用的奢侈品，应使学生们学到'有销路的技能'"的观点正是对文科教育的质疑。故此题的正确答案是 C。

Part V Cloze

67. B 本题测试介词的用法。sth. is done by doing sth. 是英语中常用的结构，by 的意思是"通过"。此处 new ones were created by converting old colleges of technology into universities 的意思是"通过把那些老的技术学院转变成大学，新的大学建立起来了"。故此题的正确答案是 B。

68. D 本题测试近义词的辨别。四个词中，只有 number 能用来指人的数量，所以此题的正确答案是 D。

69. A 本题测试对上下文的理解和词组 more than 的用法。在这里"学生的数量翻了一番还要多"，描述了一个人数激增的趋势，故应选择 more than 而不是 less than。所以此题的正确答案是 A。

70. B 本题测试固定搭配 aged from ... to ... 的用法。men aged from eighteen to twenty-one 意思是"年龄在 18 到 21 岁之间的男子"。所以此题的正确答案是 B。

71. C 本题测试形容词的用法。self 指自身，常和物主代词一起构成复合名词，如 itself；kind 意为"种类"；personal 指（人类中）"个人的"；只有 its own 表示"它自己的"，符合上下文的要求。所以此题的正确答案是 C。

72. C 本题测试近义词的辨析。表示"包括"时，常用 including；consist 要和 of 连用，make 和 take 两个词通常没有这样的意义。所以此题的正确答案是 C。

73. D 本题测试短语 as well as 的用法，所以此题的正确答案是 D。

74. A 本题测试对上下文的理解和时间副词的用法。ago 最符合题意；before 一般用于使用过去时或过去完成时的语境中，after 和 ever 在这里不符合上下文的意思。所以此题的正确答案是 A。

75. D 本题测试对上下文的理解。根据 grants 一词，可以推测出该处所填词的意思应为"资金"。所以此题的正确答案是 D。

76. B 本题测试对上下文的理解。根据前一句可知，这里谈论的是学校资金的来源，故此处应为"交学费"（pay the fees），所以此题的正确答案是 B。

77. C 本题测试定语从句引导词的用法。四个选项中只有 where 能引导地点。所以此题的正确答案是 C。

78. C 本题测试对上下文的理解以及搭配。对于学生来讲,除了学费之外,花费最多的当然是住宿和膳食。另外 lodging and food 是一个常用的搭配。所以此题的正确答案是 C。

79. D 本题测试对上下文的理解。本句讲学生上学费用的问题,并没有涉及到家长的品质,故可以排除 B 和 C。根据该句子的意义,学生都可以得到资助,除非其家长很有钱。所以此题的正确答案是 D。

80. B 本题测试对上下文的理解。根据这个段落的内容可知,该句是在讲学生假期打工补贴学费的问题,应该选"学生"(students)。所以此题的正确答案是 B。

81. D 本题测试介词 for 的用法。about six weeks 是一个时间段,故应排除 at 和 since;而 with 通常不引导时间。所以此题的正确答案是 D。

82. B 本题测试对上下文的理解。本句子的前半部分讲大多数学生 take jobs,限制了这个词只能和 jobs 同义,所以应选 work。因此此题的正确答案是 B。

83. A 本题测试固定搭配 take responsibility for,意思是"对某件事情负责"。所以此题的正确答案是 A。

84. C 本题测试对上下文的理解。整个段落都在讲大学(universities)的资金情况。the whole expenditure of the universities 指的是所有大学的花费。所以此题的正确答案是 C。

85. C 本题测试搭配 have an influence on,意思是"对……有影响"。其他几个介词都不能用在 influence 之后。所以此题的正确答案是 C。

86. B 本题测试同义词组的辨析。be composed of 意为"由……构成,组成";be made of 意为"由……制成";consist of 意为"包括",不能用作被动形式;无 be taken of 这样的结构。所以此题的正确答案是 B。

Part VI Translation

87. **Although my grandmother was illiterate**, she had a good stock of myths and legends. (尽管我的祖母不识字,可是她有一箩筐的神话和传奇故事。)
本题测试 illiterate 这个单词。illiterate 意为"目不识丁的,未受教育的";反义词为 literate:"有读写能力的,有文化的";literacy 为名词"读写能力";illiteracy 是 literacy 的反义名词"文盲,无知"。注意 il-是反义前缀。另外,根据上下文,要用过去时。

88. Despite his wealth, Sam Walton still drove around in **an old Ford**. (尽管很有钱,萨姆·沃尔顿仍旧开着一辆福特牌旧汽车。)
本题测试专有名词用作普通名词的用法。当商标用作普通名词时,指代这个商标名下的产品,如:He turned around to look at her, a Budweiser in hand. (他转过身看着她,手里拿着一瓶百威啤酒。)类似的还有用作家、艺术家的名字来指代他们的作品等。

89. In the eyes of some businessmen, consumers' health **comes second to profits**. (在某些商人眼里,消费者的健康不如利润重要。)

本题测试 come second to 这个词组。come second to 意为"不如……重要",如:The interests of individuals come second to those of a country.(国家利益高于个人利益。)当然,用 is less important than profits 也正确。

90. The new president **calls on all the teachers and students of our university to** conduct themselves with honesty and never tell lies.(新任校长要求我们大学内所有的老师和学生诚实行事,永不说谎。)

本题测试 call on/upon sb. to do sth. 这个习惯用语。call on/upon sb. to do sth. 意为"要求/号召/呼吁某人做某事",如:The President called on his people to make sacrifices for the good of their country.(总统号召国人为了国家的利益作出牺牲。)

91. According to the manager, what he wants is **a simple yet effective sales plan**.(对经理而言,他所需要的是一个简单而有效的销售方案。)

本题测试 yet 的用法。yet 的意思很多,其中一个意思是"然而;而;但是",可连接两个有转折意味的形容词,如:As he began sprinting down the runway, something felt wonderfully different, yet familiar.(他沿着跑道开始冲刺,那感觉妙不可言,而又似曾相识。)另外,"销售方案"为 sales plan。

Practice Test 2

Part I   Writing

The Problems of the Only Child in a Family

(Student's sample)

Nowadays parents and teachers often complain that the only child in the family has been spoilt. They are weak in both mind and body. They don't have the strength to accomplish difficult tasks.

Some possible reasons contribute to the problems. First, parents tend to do all for their only child, and don't let their child solve the difficult problems independently. Second, our children have been living too smooth a life since their birth. They can have whatever they want and they never know how hard life can be.

To solve the problem we may take the following measures. First of all, parents should make their child know how to restrain their desires. Secondly, our children should taste the bitterness of hard work in order to cherish the fruits of labor of others. Finally, the child should go out to face the world and brave the storm in order to be able to deal with any difficulties they will meet.

(Improved sample)

Nowadays parents and teachers often complain that the only child in the family has been spoilt. **Feeble and weak in both mind and body,** they don't have the strength to accomplish difficult tasks, **neither do they possess** the courage to face frustrations.

The possible reasons for this phenomenon, I assume, seem as follows. First, parents tend to do all for their only child, **which unconsciously deprives the child of** the opportunity of solving difficult problems by himself/herself. Second, our children have been living too smooth a life since their birth. They can have whatever they want and they never know how hard life can be.

To solve the problems, the following measures should be taken into serious account. First of all, **parents had better practice economy and make their only child aware of** the need to restrain their desires. Secondly, parents should let their only child taste the bitterness of **arduous labor so as to cherish the fruits of labor of others.** Finally, the child should go out to face the world and brave the storm in order to be able to deal with any difficulties they will meet.

Part II   Reading Comprehension (Skimming and Scanning)

1. N   所有的自己动手者都非常喜欢自己动手。

   细节题。根据第一段的内容 For others it has been an unwelcome necessity, driven purely by economic considerations 可知,对一些人来讲,自己动手纯粹出于经济考虑,是生活所迫。这与题目的表述是不一致的。故此陈述被判为错误。

2. Y   自己动手需要体力劳动与技巧。

   细节题。由第一个小标题 DIY as necessity 下的内容 with all of its unfamiliar physical labour and the learning from scratch of new techniques 可以推论出自己动手需要体力劳动与技巧。故此陈述被判为正确。

3. N   对于那些把自己动手看作必需的人来讲,一旦新家收拾好,他们就不再自己动手。

   细节题。在小标题 DIY as necessity 下,可以很快找到 In time, many will migrate to one of the other categories of DIYer, continuing to exercise their new found talents and enthusiasm when no longer forced by financial constraints to do so,据此可知随着时间的推移,许多人将转变成另一种类型的 DIY 者。这与题目的表述是相反的。故该陈述被判为错误。

4. Y   自己动手的动机之一是使他们的房子个性化。

   细节题。在标题 DIY as territorial marking 之下,不难找到 Putting a "personal stamp on the place" was one of the most frequently reported motives for DIY,可知 DIY 的动机之一是在房子上留下个人的印记。这与题目的表述是一致的。所以此陈述被判为正确。

5. Y   自己动手可以帮助年轻人获得信心。

   细节推论题。在第三个小标题 DIY as self-expression 之下的第一段中,可知 DIY 为很多年轻人提供了获得成就感和实现自我价值的机会:opportunities for a sense of achievement and personal fulfillment,其实也就是帮助这些受到挫折的年轻人获得信心。所以此陈述被判为正确。

6. NG   DIY 材料的制造商们教从事 DIY 的人们如何做工作。

   细节题。在第三个小标题 DIY as self-expression 之下的第二段中,虽然提及了 the manufacturers of DIY materials,但并没有提到他们教人们如何自己动手。根据文章的内容无法得出题目的结论。所以此陈述被判为 NG。

7. Y   自己动手者使收尾工作变得不同寻常。

   细节题。由第四个小标题 DIY as perfection-seeking 下的内容 The finishing work, however, was something these people kept for themselves — the final "perfecting" of what otherwise would be just a mediocre result 可以知道,自己动手者一定要把收尾工作留给自己做,否则整个装修效果就会很平淡。这与题目的表述一致。所以此陈述被判为正确。

8. entertainment   DIY 和娱乐类似。

   细节题。在第五个小标题 DIY as leisure activity 下,可以找到 It is not really

work，but something akin to entertainment，该句中 akin to 和 similar to 同义。所以该处填 entertainment。

9.   the dull routines of weekday work   对于自己动手的人来讲，家务活比枯燥的日常工作有意思。

细节题。根据题目提供的信息，该题可以定位至句子 But for these informants home-making was sufficiently different from，and infinitely preferable to，the dull routines of weekday work to constitute a weekend break，可知该处应填写 the dull routines of weekday work。

10.   unwind and rid themselves of tensions and become more sociable   作为一种疗法，DIY 可以帮助人们放松，解除压力，变得更合群。

细节题。根据第六个小标题 DIY as therapy 下的内容 something which allowed them to unwind and rid themselves of tensions，becoming more sociable in the process 可知，DIY 是工作和娱乐之间的一个过渡，它能让人放松，解除压力，变得更合群。所以该处填 unwind and rid themselves of tensions and become more sociable。

Part III   Listening Comprehension (35 minutes)

Section A

11. D	12. C	13. A	14. A	15. A
16. D	17. A	18. B	19. D	20. A
21. A	22. B	23. C	24. B	25. A

Section B

26. D	27. C	28. B	29. D	30. C
31. B	32. D	33. B	34. D	35. B

Section C

36. basis	37. receive	38. minimum	39. insurances
40. retirement	41. obtain	42. tipping	43. purchase

44. Tipping is expected in most restaurants in the United States unless the waiter's service is exceptionally poor

45. If you find a waiter's service to be poor，you must indicate that during the course of your meal

46. Some restaurants also make a practice of automatically including a 15 % tip in the bill for large parties of people eating together

Part IV   Reading Comprehension (Reading in Depth)

Section A

47. H   从句子结构分析，此处应该填入的是宾语成分，多由一个名词充当。而在备选的三个名词 perseverance, cultivation, occasion 中, 从语意上仅有 perseverance 能够与前面的动词 practice 搭配, 表达"培养毅力, 锲而不舍"的含义.

48. J 从句子的结构来看, 所填入的词在 be 动词后作表语, 所以词类上多是形容词, 而且它还是由 or 连接的与 hard 并列的成分, 语义上应该有很强的关联性, 表达"困难、不便"的意思, 据此可以判定选用 inconvenient 一词.

49. C 很显然, 句子空缺的位置应该是谓语动词, 这样才能确保句子结构的正确和完整. 备选词项中共有四个动词, 只有选项 C 能够和后面的宾语从语义上形成自然的搭配, 表达"驱走黑暗, 期待光明"之意.

50. L 从句子结构看, 这里需要填入一个名词作动词短语 pay attention to 的宾语. 在剩余的两个名词当中作出选择, 很显然 cultivation 从语义上比较合适: "如果再回到童年, 我将非常注重培养记忆力".

51. E 结合上句的话语意义, 此处表达"强化、加强"词义的动词非 strengthen 莫属.

52. N 本题考察一个介词短语的固定搭配 on a certain occasion, 表示"在某个特定的场合下", on every possible occasion 自然就是"利用各种场合"的意思了.

53. I 从句子结构考虑, 此处缺失的应该是状语成分, 通常由副词充当. 备选词项中共有四个副词, 而符合语意的只有 accurately, 用来表明记忆的效果.

54. G 首先从句子的结构判定空缺项是一个并列分句的谓语动词; 连接词 but 是表达转折意义的, 该动词的意义应与前面的动词相对. 既然前面说的是"微笑着面对生活", 后面表达的自然便是在生活面前"愁眉不展"的含义了.

55. D 仅剩的一个动词别无选择地要放在这个位置了, 它在此处表示"要求"的意思, 依然是及物动词的用法, 宾语为 more courtesy.

56. K 该空缺既然位于比较级之前, 应该很快使我们联想到 much, still, even 等几个常用的副词. 而备选词项 more 本身就是比较级的形式, 所以不能选用.

Section B

57. B 主旨题. 全文由两段组成. 第一段的段首句即总结了全文的内容: "跟声音有关的一些因素能够反映出说话者的性格". 接着从两个方面说明: 交流的广泛范围, 包括用语言传达信息、和众人或者个人交流、通过表演进行的特殊交流; 其次, 声音能够提供一个人的自我形象、对别人的认识和情感状况等心理线索. 选项 A "交流风格"不是文中的内容, 选项 C "言语能力的产生"在文中也没有涉及到, 而选项 D "声音在表演中的作用"只是第一段的内容之一, 只有选项 B 完整地总结了全文的内容.

58. C 语义理解题. 根据下文的内容"说话者的语气可以自觉或不自觉地反映出直觉的同情或反感、不关心或感兴趣、疲惫、焦虑、热情或兴奋"可知, 说话的口气可以传达出言外之意, 因而只有选项 C 可表达这句话的意思, 而其他选项都不符合.

59. C 细节题. 第一段分别介绍了交流的三种范围, 其中第三种具体说明了公开表演这种高度专业化的交流方式, 而艺术、政治和教育正是这种通过表演进行的特殊交流的例证. 选项 A 把演唱和这三种方式对立起来, 是不对的; 选项 B "介绍表演的特殊性"和题干内容不符;选项 D 把三者当作交流的基本风格也是不正确的。故此题的正确答案为 C。

60. B　词义理解题。第一段中有"说话者的语气可以自觉或不自觉地反映出直觉的同情或反感、不关心或感兴趣、疲惫、焦虑、热情或兴奋,而这些通常都能被敏锐的听者觉察出来",只要理解 acute 一词的意思,就得到了正确的答案。故此题的正确答案为 B。

61. C　细节题。文中第二段介绍了声音能够提供一个人的自我形象、对别人的认识和情感状况等心理线索,最后一句话就指出高兴、愤怒和沮丧时声音所传达出的情感状况。四个选项中与之符合的只有 C 项。

62. C　主旨题。全文由两段组成。第一段的主要内容是介绍圣安德烈亚斯断层的形成、地理位置、构成的地貌及运动变化情况。第二段说明由于断层的不断运动,断层周围的城镇处于地震的威胁之下。选项 A 只说到沿着断层发生的地震,选项 B"不同种类的断层"不是文中的内容,选项 D"断层的位置"仅仅是第一段的内容之一,只有选项 C 能比较完整地总结全文内容。

63. D　细节题。文中第一段提到"断层的有些部分很长时间一点都不运动",所以选项 A 是错误的;选项 B"在不久的将来会有一场灾难性的地震"和第二段的最后一句话"地震发生的可能性在增大"不符;选项 C 指出"人们已经确定了断层的精确长度",这也和第一段中内容不符,因为人们只能推测它的长度。只有选项 D"许多重要城市都处在断层附近"和第二段开头内容吻合。

64. D　细节题。根据第二段最后一句话"沿断层发生的地震是经常性的",只有选项 D"常事"符合题意。

65. B　细节题。断层所处的地理位置在第一段中就已说明,它源于离加利福尼亚湾 600 英里的地方,然后向北到旧金山,又继续向北直达海洋;只有选项 B 符合题意。

66. D　细节题。文章的第一句话已给出了断层的定义,它是"地壳上两个主要板块叠合部分的一条裂缝"。选项 A 认为断层由"强大的压力积聚"而成,颠倒了因果关系;选项 B"偶尔出现的地震"也是断层运动的结果;选项 C 认为断层是"位于北美大陆之下的板块",也不符合文章内容。故此题的正确答案为 D。

Part V　Cloze

67. B　本题测试名词性从句的用法。本句大意为"时间所表达的意义对我们与他人的交往至关重要"。故此题的正确答案是 B。

68. C　本题测试短语搭配。短语 take sth. seriously 意思是"认真对待某事",本句中,sth. 即 their promises to meet deadlines and keep appointments 太长,所以放在了 seriously 之后。故此题的正确答案是 C。

69. A　本题测试短语搭配。短语 impose penalty 的意思是"强制性地给予惩罚";pay the penalty 意为"遭受惩罚",本句中 they 指所有的人,并不是不守时、该受惩罚的人;sponsor(赞助)和 issue(颁布)不符合文意。故此题的正确答案是 A。

70. B　语境题。该题应该选 required(要求的);其他的词 needed(所需要的)、necessary

（必要的）、essential（基本的、本质的）不符合此处的语境。所以此题的正确答案是 B。

71. A 词义识别题。suspension 意为"暂停"，此处指停学；suspend 意为"悬挂"，suspense 意为"悬念"。这几个词中只有 suspension 符合题意，故此题的正确答案是 A。

72. A 本题测试短语搭配。本句的大意是"晚交论文可能会导致最多 10% 的降分，甚至不及格"。result in 意思是"导致，造成……结果"；result from 意思是"起因，由于"；add to 意思是"加上"。故此题的正确答案是 A。

73. A 本题测试词语意义的识别。本句的大意是"文化中最关键的方面可能是时间的使用"。四个选项 critical（关键的，决定性的）、serious（严肃的）、basic（基本的）、elementary（初步的）中，只有 critical 符合题意。故此题的正确答案是 A。

74. D 语境题。本句的大意是"在德国文化中，守时是尊重和礼貌的标志"。在四个选项 symbol（象征）、significance（意义）、remark（评论）、sign（迹象，标记）中，只有 sign 最符合语境。故此题的正确答案是 D。

75. C 本题测试短语搭配。词组 on time 意思是"准时"；in time 意思是"及时，按时"；against time 意思是"争分夺秒地，尽快地"。根据后半句中的 neither too early nor too late，此处应选择 on。故此题的正确答案是 C。

76. A 语境题。本句的大意是"对印度尼西亚人来说，时间是用之不竭的，为什么还要有压力和匆忙呢？"在四个选项中 pressured 的意思是"有压力的，感受到压力的"；urged（受催促的，受力劝的）、depressed（压抑的）、spurred（受刺激的，受激励的）均不合题意。故此题的正确答案是 A。

77. A 本题测试短语搭配。词组 take sth. for granted（认为某事理所当然，认为某事不成问题）是一个固定搭配。故此题的正确答案是 A。

78. D 语境题。根据前文的 take their own time system for granted 和后文中的 misunderstandings，我们可以断定此处应该选 same，意思是"认为其他文化也按照此时间体系运作"。故此题的正确答案是 D。

79. A 本题测试连词的用法。连词 thus 表示因果关系，moreover 表示递进关系，furthermore 也表示递进关系，additionally 表示附加关系。本句与上一句之间是因果关系，所以选 thus。故此题的正确答案是 A。

80. B 词义识别题。四个词语中，available 意为"能够得到的"，inevitable 意为"不可避免的"，inaccessible 意为"不可进入的"，impossible 意为"不可能的"。此处用 inevitable 最恰当，意思是"误解是不可避免的"。故此题的正确答案是 B。

81. A 词语辨析题。to sb. 表示"对某人而言，在某人看来"；as to 和 as for 都表示"至于"。所以此题的正确答案是 A。

82. C 语境和词义识别题。根据上下文，由于时间珍贵，可以节省，所以 promptness（准时）是基本的要求。节省时间并不意味着要匆忙（hurry），而 frankness（坦诚）和 responsibility（责任）显然不符合题意。

83. A 本题考察定语从句的用法。由于该从句的先行词是 one，指代人，且引导词在从句中作主语,所以只能选 who。故此题的正确答案是 A。

84. B　本题测试短语搭配。本题提供的选项中,只有 commit 能和 offense 搭配,词组 commit a grave offense 意思是"严重冒犯"。所以此题的正确答案是 B。

85. A　本题测试短语搭配。词组 come before 意思是"比……重要",come after 意为 "继……而来",come between 意为"介入,妨碍",come into 意为"进入,被卷入"。此处 come before 最恰当,意思是"人们同时做很多事情,人际关系比计划更重要"。所以此题的正确答案是 A。

86. B　本题测试连词的用法。while 意为"与此同时",表示对比。所以此题的正确答案是 B。

Part VI　Translation

87. Obviously, our company couldn't have developed into such a large modern venture **without technological innovations and inventions**.（很显然,如果没有技术上的革新和发明,我们公司就不可能发展成这样一个现代化的大企业。）

本题测试 innovation 和 invention 这两个单词。innovation 意为"革新;创新;改革",invention 意为"发明,创造"。

88. The World Bank **has urged China to reform its retirement insurance system** to overcome the social and economic pressure expected to result from the rising life expectancy rate.（世界银行敦促中国改革养老保险制度,从而克服人口预期寿命比不断提高造成的社会、经济压力。）

本题测试 urge sb. to do sth. 这个结构。urge sb. to do sth. 意为"敦促/恳求某人干某事",如:He always urges his students to guard against conceit.（他总是敦促他的学生们防止骄傲自满。）"养老保险制度"可译为 retirement insurance system。

89. If you do have financial difficulties, you can **apply for a student loan**.（如果确实在经济上有困难,你可以申请学生贷款。）

本题测试 apply for 这个词组。apply for 意为"申请",如:apply for a job/post/passport/visa（申请工作/职位/护照/签证）。"贷款"为 loan,因此"学生贷款"可译为 a student loan。

90. When **some objective questions are used along with some subjective questions**, however, a fairly clear picture of the students' knowledge can usually be obtained.（但是如果客观题和主观题并用,就能较清楚地了解学生掌握知识的情况。）

本题测试 objective 和 subjective 这两个反义词。objective 作形容词,意为"客观的,无偏见的",如:A jury's decision in a court case must be absolutely objective.（陪审团裁定案件必须绝无偏见。）而 subjective 意为"（思想,感情等）主观的",如:a subjective impression（主观印象）。因此,"客观题和主观题"可译为 objective questions and subjective questions。

91. The rise of volcanic activity will **have a catastrophic effect on the Earth's climate**, and millions could die from respiratory ailments as ash and greenhouse gases fill

the air.（火山活动的增加将给地球气候带来灾难性影响，当空气中充满火山灰和温室气体的时候，数以百万计的人们将可能死于呼吸道疾病。）

本题测试 have an effect on sb. /sth. 这个习惯用法。have an effect on sb. /sth. 意为"对……有影响"。如：The book had quite an effect on her.（这本书对她影响极大。）catastrophe 意为"突如其来的大灾难"，它的形容词形式为 catastrophic，因此"带来灾难性影响"可译为 have a catastrophic effect on。

Practice Test 3

Part I　Writing

Keeping Healthy

(Student's sample)

Good health is very important to people's lives. With good health one can live comfortably and effectively. Without it a person will eventually turn out to be a wreckage of modern life.

But how can we be healthy? The first thing we should do is to eat proper food to provide our body with enough nutrition. The second thing which is also important is that we must sleep enough so that we can keep our body and mind strong and alert. The last but not the least thing is that we must do physical exercises to keep our body in good shape.

As far as I am concerned, I always eat the right food, get plenty of sleep and exercise regularly. In this way, I am healthy and can complete my task effectively.

(Improved sample)

Good health is the most valuable possession a person can have. **It is essential to** a happy life as well as a successful one. **Only in good shape can** you expect to live comfortably or work effectively. **In contrast**, without good health, ambitious and promising as a person may be, he will eventually turn out to be a wreckage of modern life.

How to stay healthy, **then? First**, to take in proper nutrition is important for good health. **Second**, we should get proper amount of sleep to make our body and mind strong and refreshed. **Finally**, be sure to set aside enough time to do physical exercises to keep our body in good shape.

As for me, I have always been taking care to eat the right food, get plenty of sleep and exercise regularly. **So**, **I can** keep healthy and pursue my career with high efficiency.

Part II　Reading Comprehension (Skimming and Scanning)

1. Y　这篇文章对 GRE 一般考试作了一个总的描述。
   主旨题。全文介绍了 GRE 一般考试的受试人群、考试的作用、考试的内容和结构等等。题干的表述和原文的内容相符合,故此陈述应被判为正确。

2. Y　GRE 一般考试测试不和任何具体研究领域相关的能力和技巧。
   细节题。本题实际上是文章第一句的缩写,题目表述和原文的内容相符合,故此陈述应被判为正确。

3. N 大学生在毕业前都要参加 GRE 一般考试。

细节题。在第二个小标题 Who Takes It and Why? 下，我们可知，参加 GRE 一般考试的应该是申请研究生学习的人。题目的表达与原文意思不符，所以该陈述应被判为错误。

4. N 只有美国和加拿大提供 GRE 机考。

细节题。在小标题 Where Do People Take It? 下可以找到相关的内容：美国、加拿大和其他许多国家的机考中心都提供 GRE 机考。题目的表达与原文意思不符，所以该陈述应被判为错误。

5. Y 一些学校可以要求或建议申请人参加 GRE 一般考试和 GRE 专业学科考试。

细节题。在小标题 Who Accepts It? 下，我们可以找到相关内容，任何一个研究生招生单位都可以要求或建议它的申请者参加 GRE 一般考试或 GRE 专业学科考试，或者两个都参加。题干的表述和原文的内容相符合，故此陈述应被判为正确。

6. N GRE 机考的时间总共是三个小时，包括调查研究部分。

细节题。在小标题 Computer-Based General Test Content and Structure 下，我们可以找到相关的内容：Total testing time is up to three hours, *not* including the research section。题目的表达与原文意思不符，所以该陈述应被判为错误。

7. NG GRE 机考的费用比纸考的费用要高。

细节题。本文虽然谈及了 GRE 的机考和纸考，但并没有谈及它们的费用。因此根据原文无法判断机考费用是否比纸考高。故本题应被判为 NG。

8. One unidentified pretest 分析写作部分之后的任何一个位置，可能出现一个 unidentified pretest 部分，对此部分的回答不计入最后的总分。

细节题。在小标题 Computer-Based General Test Content and Structure 下的第二段可以找到与这一句对应的内容。故此处填 One unidentified pretest。

9. less apparent 你参加的考试中可能会出现语言和数量测试问题的修改版本，这种修改可以是明显的，也可能不太明显。

根据本题的关键词，我们可以将此句内容快速定位至最后一个小标题 Modified Versions of Verbal and Quantitative Questions 下。在该部分第一段，我们可以找到句子 Some modifications are substantial; others are less apparent。故此处填 less apparent。

10. the feasibility of reusing questions GRE 测试组现在正在调查重新使用那些在已出版的模拟材料中使用过的问题的可能性。

该句内容可以在最后一段的第一句找到。题目是原文句子的简单改写，故此处填 the feasibility of reusing questions。

Part III Listening Comprehension (35 minutes)

Section A

11. C   12. C   13. B   14. C   15. C

16. B   17. D   18. D   19. D   20. B

21. A   22. C   23. B   24. C   25. D

Section B

26. A   27. B   28. C   29. D   30. C

31. B   32. A   33. B   34. D   35. B

Section C

36. urban   37. non-publicly   38. excluded   39. scheme

40. thriftier   41. previously   42. shouldered   43. staff's

44. Of that total, thirty percent will go to employees' personal accounts

45. The rest will be set aside as "overall medical funds"

46. Employees will have to pay two percent of their monthly salaries into their personal medical insurance accounts

Part IV Reading Comprehension (Reading in Depth)

Section A

47. E 从结构上看,此处应该用动词原形。选项 A、C、E、J、K、N 皆为动词,而能够和后面介词 from 搭配的动词却只有 discern,意为"辨别",句意为"品茶不仅能辨别茶的优劣"。

48. L 从结构分析,此处应该填入一个名词,选项 I、L、O 都符合该条件。从语义上讲,take delight in 是一个动词短语,意为"从……中得到快乐",符合题意。

49. J 从结构上分析,该空缺项处应该填入一个动词,因为它显然是与前面出现的另外两个动词 banish 和 improve 形成并列关系。从语义角度来看,用 inspire 联系后面的介词短语 with enthusiasm 真是再合适不过了。该动词短语的意思为"使某人精神振奋"。

50. N 从结构上看,该处应填入一个能和后面副词 up 搭配的动词。根据句意"喝茶细呷慢饮可以使精神境界……到高尚的艺术境地",可知 soar 符合文意,在此意为"高涨,昂扬"。

51. B 从句子构成看,该处应该是一个形容词,和后面其他三个形容词连用修饰名词主语 locale。尽管备选词项中有 B、D、F、G、M 五个形容词,但综合考虑三个并列形容词 refreshing, comfortable, neat,表意为"安静"的 tranquil 最为合适。

52. D 结合上题的选项,知道此句话想要表达的意思是"饮茶环境要求安静、清新、舒适、干净",由此形容词 desirable(合意的、想要的)符合语意。

53. G 本空缺项所在的句子包含了一个 too ... to 结构,因而中间要填入的肯定是一个形容词;再根据 count 一词表示"计数"的意义,确定选 numerous,意为"不可胜数"。

54. A 此句是说茶室的作用,所填的应该是和前面的 rest 并列且语义密切关联的一个动词,故选 recreate 比较符合句意,该词的意思是"使娱乐、消遣"。

55. O 此处应填入一个能和 time-honored 语意相搭配的名词,civilization 恰好符合,表明中国文化源远流长。

56. K 从句子结构上看,该句包含有两个并列的不定式,因而空缺处应该填入一个动词原形;此外从该选项所在的句子所表达的意思——茶点时间来点小食品、糖果和其他食品能够使茶显得更加味道香醇,同时还能解饿——来考虑,complement 表达的正是"补充"之意,故选 K。

Section B

57. C 词义理解题。layman 指的是"非专业人员,门外汉,外行"。句子意思是"在外行看来……";只有选项 C"不像生物学家那样受过专门培训的人"才符合该词在句中的意思。

58. D 细节题。根据第二段前两句话的内容可知:由于人们认为人种学家是业余动物观察者,肯定不是科学家,所以他们在使人们认可其科学家身份方面存在着问题。选项 A"在野外工作的人种学家受到阻碍"、选项 B"人种学家在野外工作时被人轻视"和选项 C"人种学家在野外工作时遇到很多困难"都不符合这句话的意思。故此题的正确答案为 D。

59. B 细节题。hard-and-fast 本义指硬性的、不容更改的。根据文中对试验的科学规则的说明可知,科学研究必须严格遵守试验程序,以免出现虚假、不严谨或者不确切的结果。选项 A"必须严格而又快速地执行"、选项 C"很难但很快执行"和选项 D"对科学家来说很难遵循而又不合理"都不符合题意。故此题的正确答案为 B。

60. D 归纳题。文章在第一段开始处就说明,在外行看来,人种学也许是生物科学中最有趣的。最后一段第一句话又讲到 ethnology 一词源于希腊语 *ethos*,意义是区别一个物种的特点或特征,即某一特定人群的特征,或者从生物学上讲,某一种类的动物的特征。所以选项 A"一门古老的希腊学科"、选项 B"业余爱好者的科学"和选项 C"一门伪科学"都不是人种学的定义,只有选项 D"生物学的一个新的分支"是正确的。

61. C 推理题。根据第二段中的内容"动物生活中的许多情形在实验室里是不可能预计和控制的,比如远距离迁徙的动物返回原地",可以推断出划线部分指的是难以预先计划或控制的动物的家庭行为。而选项 A"行为像一个天然家庭的动物",选项 B"天然的家庭关系"和选项 D"很快出现的家庭关系"显然不符合题意。故此题的正确答案为 C。

62. B 语义理解题。根据该句的意思"在一个几乎完全依靠电能运转的社会,电能够致癌的说法好像很荒谬",只有选项 B 比较符合题意。选项 A"因为人们的生活主要依靠电,所以他们不可能得癌症"这一命题不能成立;选项 C"在一个主要依靠电来发展的社会里,人们很容易得癌症"和选项 D"人们认为在一个主要依靠电来发展的社会里会很容易得癌症"都错误地理解了句义。

63. A 细节题。根据第一段最后一句话的意思,可知作者对科学家的研究结论是不赞成的,因为证据不确定并且相互矛盾。只有选项 A 符合题意,其他选项都不是作者的态度。

64. B 细节题。选项 A"已经证实 60 赫兹的电场是致癌的一个因素"和第二段最后一句话相矛盾;选项 C"关于电磁场导致某些种类的癌症这一点,白宫和 EPA 之间没有争议"和第三段内容不符;选项 D"随后的研究不能证明住在电线附近的人们容易得癌症"和第五段最后一句话相矛盾,因为 buttress 一词是"支持"的意思;只有选项 B"人们对最近的 EPA 报告很关注"符合第三段的意思。

65. C 词义理解题。fall short of 在句中的意思是"未达到标准,不符合人们的要求",只有选项 C 是正确的选择。

66. A 推理题。根据第五段内容,1979 年关于癌症患病几率的研究指出:生活在电线附近的人们患癌症的几率比其他人高出两到三倍,"二者之间好像不大可能存在这样的联系",电力公司也显然难以接受这个结果,所以"出钱重复原先的研究"。只有选项 A 是合理的推断,其他选项都不是电力公司重复原先研究的目的。

Part V Cloze

67. B 语境题。前一句中的 either ... or ... 表明此处讲的是二者之间的关系,应该用 between。

68. A 本题考查动词 hang 的用法。在 have + sth. 之后,可以接 do,doing 或 done 来作宾语的补足语,故可排除选项 C 和 D;而 have ... hanged 常表示"把……绞死,把……吊起来";have ... hanging 表示"把……挂起来"。

69. C 本题考查连接词的用法。该空前面为分号,结合上下文,where 最符合文意。where 在这里引导一个状语从句,意思是"我走到哪里,我的每一个脚印就会出现在哪里"。

70. A 语境题。这里只有 show 最恰当,意思是"我走到哪里,我的每一个脚印就会出现在哪里"。

71. B 词语搭配题。living way 或 the way sb. lives 指生活方式。

72. D 词语搭配和语境选择题。后一句中的 standard 提示此处应该是 standard of morality and ethics,指道德标准。

73. A 词语搭配题。be relative to 是一个固定的搭配,意思是"和……相关联"。

74. C 语境题。这里的四个选项都可以和 behavior 搭配,但由于语境的限制,用 judging 最恰当,意思是"诚实是判断你行为的内在标准"。

75. B 词语搭配题。in short supply 意思是"处于短缺状态"。

76. A 本题考查句子之间的衔接。根据段落的整体意思,此处表达转折关系,意思是:"遗憾的是,如今诚实处于短缺状态——甚至越来越稀罕。**然而**,它却是社会各个领域真正的思想底线。"

77. D　词语搭配题。"社会各个领域"应该是 every area of society。

78. A　本题考查反身代词的用法。由于前面是 we,所以此处应选择 ourselves。

79. C　本题考查引导词的用法。此处选择 what,引导一个名词性从句,作宾语。意思是"检验这种价值的一个有效方法是看看我称为'诚实三原则'的标准"。

80. B　本题考查词语间的辨析。consists of 意为"包括,由……构成";其余三项虽然也都是"组成,构成"之意,但 A 项和 D 项的被动态才适合题意,C 项不和 of 连用。

81. B　词语搭配题。经常和 stand 搭配的是 firm。本句意思是"在个人压力面前,要坚定信念"。

82. B　语境题。上个句子讲到"要坚定信念",所以此处应该是不能"屈服",选择 give in。

83. B　语境题。下文讲到"不要害怕那些可能有更好主意的或者可能比你更聪明的人",所以本题应选择 credit(肯定),意思是"对那些值得赞扬的人要常常给予肯定"。

84. D　词语搭配题。take in 意思是"摄入,吸入",不符合句子的意思;B 项和 C 项不能和 in 搭配;engage in (doing) sth. 意思是"从事,致力于做某事"。此处选择 engage in,意思是"不要设法掩盖你生活中令人不快的方方面面"。

85. C　语境题。根据上句中的 Be yourself 和下文中的 When it's tough, do it tough 可确定此处选择 unpleasant。

86. A　语境题。根据前文对 integrity 的描述,此处应该选 conscience(良心)。句子的意思是"自尊和问心无愧是构成诚实的强有力的成分,是丰富你与他人关系的基础"。

Part VI　Translation

87. The size of the furniture should be **in proportion to the size of the room**.（家具的大小应与房间的大小相称。）

本题测试 in proportion to 这个词组。in proportion to 意为"相对于某事物来说;与某事物成比例",如:Payment will be in proportion to the work done, not to the time spent doing it.（报酬将与工作量成比例,而不是与花费的时间成比例。）

88. Not until many years later **did the whole truth become known**.（直到许多年后整个事件的真相才为世人知晓。）

本题测试 not ... until 的倒装用法。not ... until 意为"直到……才",如果 not until 用在句首,后面的句子要部分倒装,如:Not until the evening did I see Papa.（我直到晚上才见到爸爸。）

89. **Whichever way you look at it**, nuclear power will reduce the problem of an energy shortage.（不管你从哪个角度看,核能都将缓解能源短缺的问题。）

本题测试 whichever 的用法。whichever 等同于 no matter which,意为"无论哪一个,随便哪一个"。作为表示强调的关系代词,whichever 可引导名词性从句,如:Take whichever seat you like.（你坐哪个座位都行。）还可引导让步状语从句,如:

Whichever one of these books you choose, you'll have a good one. (这些书无论你挑哪一本,都准会是本好书。)

90. Though we had put forward a proposal to reduce cost, the board members **didn't appear to take it seriously**. (尽管我们提出了降低成本的建议,董事会的成员们似乎没有认真考虑。)

本题主要测试 take sb./sth. seriously 这个习惯用语。take sb./sth. seriously 意为"认真对待某人/某事物",如: Don't take her promises seriously: she never keeps her word. (她答应的事不必当真,她说话从来不算数。) 另外,时态上应与前面保持一致,用过去时。

91. He **had a narrow escape for many times** during the war but stood loyal to his country even though he underwent many ordeals. (在战争时期,他经历了诸多磨难,多次死里逃生,但对祖国的忠诚始终不渝。)

本题测试 have a narrow escape 这个习惯用语。have a narrow escape 意为"死里逃生;九死一生;险些没逃出"。如: He had a very narrow escape from being caught. (他差点被抓住。)

Practice Test 4

Part I Writing

The Advantages and Disadvantages of Computers

(Student's sample)

With the development of high technology, computers have played a very important role in modern society. They are widely used in science and technology, and bring about great changes in these fields. They are also used in the daily lives. People can use computers to get useful information, do research work, and play games. The usage of computers seems to be limitless.

However, the computer also has its disadvantages. Computers are unemotional. If a person spends too much time in front of the computer terminal, he might become inhuman. What's more, some students are getting so addicted to the computer games and the imaginary world that they waste their time and neglect their studies.

So we should make good use of the advantages of computers and try to avoid its disadvantages.

(Improved sample)

With the development of high technology, computers have **come to** play a very important role in modern society. They are widely used in science and technology, **bringing about fantastic things in these fields**. They are also used in the daily lives. **Ordinary people use them to obtain valuable information, professors use them to** do research works, **and children use them to** play games. **There seems to be no limit to** the work that computers can do.

But each coin has two sides. The computer also has its disadvantages. **First of all**, computers are unemotional. A person, too, might become inhuman if he spends too much time in front of the computer terminal. **Besides**, some students are getting so addicted to the computer games and the imaginary world that they waste their time and neglect their studies.

In conclusion, computers really **benefit us a lot in spite of the disadvantages**. We should use computers properly and try to **avoid the negative effects**.

Part II Reading Comprehension (Skimming and Scanning)
1. Y   这篇文章指导读者如何申请 2007 年电影节资助基金。

主旨题。本文由三部分构成,即申请资格、申请指南和申请模式,旨在告诉读者如何申请资助基金。所以此陈述被判为正确。

2. N　以加拿大为基地的电影节也有资格申请。

细节题。在申请资格部分的第三个段落中可以找到 Only festivals based in the United States ... are eligible to apply,可知题目的表达与原文不符,故此陈述被判为错误。

3. Y　近年来,学院电影基金委员会经常批准预算少于指定金额的申请项目。

细节题。在申请资格部分的最后一个段落可找到 the Academy's Festival Grants Committee may approve grants for less than the amount requested. In recent years, this has been the case more often than not,表述与题目中的陈述一致,所以,此陈述被判为正确。

4. Y　2007年6月29日后的申请将不会得到资助。

细节题。从 Guidelines and Instructions 部分的第一段可知,申请必须在2007年6月29日前提交,任何情况下延期的申请都不会得到资助。所以,此陈述被判为正确。

5. N　资助基金可以被用来支持电影的发展、出品和完成。

细节题。在 Guidelines and Instructions 部分的第五段,列举了许多资助基金不能被使用的地方,the development, production or completion of motion pictures 就在其中。题目的表达与原文相反,故此陈述被判为错误。

6. Y　申请报告里描述的电影节组成元素是最终决定资助与否的最重要因素。

细节题。从 Guidelines and Instructions 部分的倒数第三段可知 the festival elements described in the proposal carry the most weight ... in making the final determinations,该表述与题目一致。所以,此陈述被判为正确。

7. NG　申请表可以在 http://www.oscars.org 网址下载。

细节题。从 Application Template(申请模式)部分的第(1)小部分 Application form 中可知申请表是一个可下载并可填写的 PDF 文件,但文章并未提供下载的网址。所以该陈述无法判断正误。

8.　description of the parent organization　申请报告包括 request statement, proposal paragraphs, mission statement, history of the festival 和 description of the parent organization 五个部分。

主旨题。在申请模式的(2) Proposal 部分,可以找到申请报告的五个部分。该题所填的是第五个部分。

9.　a broad financial overview　收入、花费陈述应包括最近一次电影节的整体财务概况。

细节题。该题可以在申请模式的(4) Income/expense statement 部分下直接找到答案。

10.　entire projected festival budget　预算部分应包括申请资助的电影节的整体预算情况。

细节题。该题可以在申请模式的(5) Budget 部分下直接找到答案。

Part III Listening Comprehension (35 minutes)

Section A

11. D	12. B	13. A	14. B	15. D
16. C	17. A	18. B	19. B	20. A
21. C	22. D	23. A	24. B	25. A

Section B

26. B	27. D	28. C	29. D	30. D
31. C	32. A	33. C	34. D	35. A

Section C

36. ban   37. toll   38. environmental   39. deserves

40. Consequently   41. enforce   42. slipped   43. devastated

44. pushing the entire species to the brink of extinction

45. Whales are facing increasing threats to their survival including increasing pollution, massive over-fishing, boat collisions and climate change

46. Commercial whaling is cruel and unnecessary. It is morally indefensible

Part IV Reading Comprehension (Reading in Depth)

Section A

47. M 从结构上看,该选项包含在 one of the … 的短语结构里,这就要求所填入的应该是可数名词的复数形式,备选项 L、M、O 符合此要求,结合上下文的语意及第二段首句的提示,选 achievements。

48. J 本题空缺项应为后面名词 foods 的修饰语,通常情况下应填入形容词。本组备选词中形容词较多,C、D、H、J 和 F、I、K 三个分词形式都可以作为备选项,但根据上下文的修饰关系,选用 affluent(丰富的,富裕的)恰好符合题意。

49. L 从结构上可以明显看出来,该词与前面的 foods 并列,应为同样的词类——名词;而且从语义场包括的范围来看,所填入的词外延应该比 foods 更加广泛,指除粮食外其他保障国计民生的必需品,综合考虑,选 necessities 一词。

50. O 从结构上考虑,该选项需要填入一个和上文一样的名词,语意上判断时可参考上一题的思路,选 products。

51. A 本选项所在的句子依然含有非常规范的并列关系,备选项词汇中能与 modernization 相适应的只有 application,故选之。

52. D 从结构上说,显然空缺处应该填入一个形容词来修饰 changes;从语义上考虑只有 revolutionary 能够顾全搭配和语意的连贯,意为"革命性的变革"。

53. F 从所在句子的整体结构考虑,空缺项和它后面的逻辑宾语在句子中充当伴随状语,现在分词形式拥有这样的语法功能;在所给出的三个现在分词中,语意上

replacing 最为连贯,表明大量农业机器替代人力和马劳动的事实。

54. I 从结构上分析,所填入的词既在介词 by 之后,其后又带有自己的逻辑宾语,由此可以推断该项一定是动名词的形式,除去上题中的 replacing 已经使用之外,还有两个词作为备选,显然 programming 在语义上更行得通,说明编写计算机程序就可以监控整个饲料加工过程的事实。

55. C 从结构上分析,该空缺处应该填入一个形容词和名词 disease 搭配,epidemic diseases 正是教材中出现过的固定短语,意为"流行病、传染病"。

56. G 从结构分析,文章最后这句话有三个并列的不定式结构,由此判定空缺项应该填入动词原形;另外考虑和后面词汇 professionals 的语意搭配关系,确定选consult。

Section B

57. D 主旨题。文章首先说明了电子邮箱的重要性,然后说明了它的负面影响,表明了作者对它的不满。选项 A"电子邮箱的重要性"是第一段的内容;选项 B"信息时代历史学家所处的状况"是第七段的内容:"历史学家和名人传记作者的前途恐怕会十分黯淡";选项 C"苏格兰的一些卓越人物的数字智库"是第三段的内容。这三个选项都局限于某个方面,只有选项 D"数字时代电子邮件的负面影响"能比较完整地总结全文内容。

58. B 词义理解题。mine 的本义是"开矿,采矿",在这句话里的引申意义是"发掘出有价值的东西",所以只有选项 B 符合该词在文中的意思。

59. D 语义理解题。这句话的意思是"电子邮件把这种效应放大了亿万倍",再联系下文内容,"这种效应"指的是"名人写下的非正式信件在数十年后仍然会重现世间,电子邮件却决不会再次出现",所以只有选项 D"电子邮件不能复制那些宝藏"是正确选项。

60. C 推理题。作者举出自己继承的一封来自一位勇敢女性远亲的信件这样一个例子不是为了表示欣赏她的勇敢,也不是表达对她的感谢,而是为了表达自己对电子邮件的不满。选项 D"表达对当今社会的不满"不是本文的内容。故此题的正确答案为 C。

61. D 归纳题。作者对电子邮件持不赞成态度,并不认为它是"日常生活最重要的方面",所以选项 A 不正确;选项 B"电子邮件可以从档案中收集重要信息"和第五段的内容意思相反;选项 C 和选项 A 意思相近;只有选项 D"人们应该珍视记录历史的一些古老方式,这个任务仅仅依靠电子邮件是难以完成的"才是作者对数字时代电子邮件的态度。

62. D 归纳题。第一段中提到越来越多的英国人抛弃了能使人平静的睡眠,日夜不停地追求享乐主义,他们去俱乐部,到超市购物,看影碟,在网上冲浪等;所以只有选项 D"他们的生活方式"是许多英国人缺乏睡眠的原因,其他选项都不符合题意。

63. D 细节题。根据第五段内容,Dr. Claudio Stampi 的研究结论是一天只睡四个小时是可以生存下去的,所以只有选项 D 符合题意。

64. A 词义理解题。restorative 一词意思为"有助于恢复健康的事物,滋补品",只有选项 A 是该词的正确解释。

65. B 推理题。第一段开头一句话就表明了作家们的态度,首先要知道 hail 一词的意思是"赞扬,称颂",其次通过和主句的对比,就可以推断出作家们对睡眠是表示欢迎的,所以只有选项 B 符合题意。

66. C 主旨题。文章主要介绍一种现象:许多英国人缺乏睡眠,然后指出原因,最后介绍科学家提出的解决办法。选项 A"科学家关于小睡的发现"只是 Dr. Claudio Stampi 的研究结论,选项 B"英国人睡眠时间减少"是前两段的内容,选项 D"睡眠缺失带来的负面影响"是第四段的内容,这三个选项都局限于某个方面,不够全面;只有选项 C 比较完整地总结了全文内容。

Part V　Cloze

67. C 短语辨析题。leave sth. to sb. 意思是"把……留给……",整句话的意思是"但是回收再利用的工作不会被留给消费者"。give to 意思是"给予";leave for 意思是"前往……"。

68. B 本题考查关联词语的用法。根据上下文,此处应选择 instead(相反,反而)。

69. D 词语辨析题。在这四个词中,disposition 意为"性情",discharge 意为"排放,释放",displacement 意为"取代,移植",disposal 意为"处理"。只有 disposal 符合句子的意义,即"这些装置被送回原厂进行适当的处理"。

70. A 短语搭配题。pose a challenge 意思是"提出一个挑战"。

71. A 短语搭配题。with an eye to/towards 意思是"着眼于,为……打算"。

72. B 短语搭配题。combine with 意为"和……结合起来",integrate with/into 意为"与……成为一体",connect with 意为"把……连接起来",synchronize 意为"使同步"。这几个词中,只有 integrate 可以和 into 搭配。本句大意是"他们也把易于回收的材料制成新的产品"。

73. D 语境题。pose an obstacle 意思是"造成障碍"。pose a question(提出问题)不符合题意。

74. B 本题考查介词的用法。with age 意思是"随着年份的增长"。as 表示"随着……",是连词,后应该接句子。

75. A 语境题。even if (即使)符合题意,后面接了一个省略的从句;now that (既然)不合题意;despite(尽管)后面应该接名词;if only(只要,要是……就好了)不符合题意。

76. A 本题考查定语从句的用法。that 不能和介词连用;此处的 which 指代 sandwich,而介词 for 不合题意。

77. B 短语搭配题。in cooperation with 意思是"与……合作"。corporation 意思为"公司,企业"。

78. A 词义辨析题。retain 意思是"保持,保留"。其他三个词 maintain(维修,主张),

conserve（保守，守衡），reserve（储备，预约）都不符合文意。本句中，engineers claim 是插入成分，which 指的是 a new plastic。整个句子的意思是：公司与树脂制造商 Sumitomo Dow 合作，已经开发出一种新型塑料，工程师们称这种塑料在反复回收利用后仍可保持机械特性。

79. D 本题考查非限定性定语从句的用法。作为插入成分的定语从句只能用 which 来引导。

80. A 本题考察段落间的衔接。根据前后两个段落的意义，只有 meanwhile（与此同时）符合文意。

81. A 短语辨析题。in favor of 可以表示"以……来代替，决定要……"。本句大意是"同时，松下品牌的制造商 Matsushita 电器公司回避塑料，决定用镁来代替"。

82. B 短语搭配题。be ideal for 意思是"对……是理想的"。

83. D 本题考查介词的用法。through 表示"通过，经过"。

84. A 词义识别题。unfortunately 意为"不幸地"，misfortunately 意为"灾难地"，accidentally 意为"偶然地"，incidentally 意为"顺便提及"。选 A 最恰当。

85. B 语境题。综合该句和上一句，可以发现它们之间是转折关系，故用 however。

86. B 短语搭配题。bring down price 表示"降价"。

Part VI Translation

87. Operating a vehicle while intoxicated is a serious offence，but few cases **hit/make the headlines** unless they involve serious injury.（醉酒开车是项严重过错，但除非发生重大伤亡，这种事很少能成为报纸头条新闻。）

本题测试 hit/make the headlines 这个习惯用语。hit/make the headlines 意为"成为报纸头条新闻；成为重要新闻；被大肆宣扬"，如：He again made the headlines, scoring three goals in last night's game.（他在昨晚的比赛中进了三个球，又一次成了报纸头条新闻。）

88. The competition **is not important in itself**. What counts is your participation.（比赛本身并不重要，重要的是你的参与。）

本题测试 in itself 这个词组。in itself 意为"就其本身而言"，如：The celebration was a waste of time and money in itself.（这个庆祝就其本身而言是对时间和金钱的浪费。）

89. Looking at him，it's hard to imagine he once **had a promising future** as a smart young New York book editor.（望着他，难以相信他曾经是一位前途无量、年轻聪颖的纽约书籍编辑。）

本题测试 promising 这个单词。promising 意为"有希望的；有前途的"，如："How's your new venture going?" "It's looking quite promising."（"你的新生意进展如何？""看来很有希望。"）另外，根据 once 这个词断定用过去时。

90. **True/It is true there has been a considerable increase in our living costs**, but the quality of our life has improved significantly because our wages have doubled over the

same period.（我们的生活费用确实有很大增长，但是我们的生活质量也大幅度提高，因为与此同时我们的工资也翻了一番。）

本题测试 True/It is true … but … 这个句型。True/It is true … but … 意为"……确实如此，但是……"，根据所给汉语中的"确实"一词，以及后半句中 but 一词的提示，可以确定用此句型。再如：True, the sentence is grammatically correct，but it does not read naturally.（这个句子语法上确实没错，但是读起来很不自然。）

91. **The feedback from the customers** who have tried the new soap is very positive.（从试用这种新肥皂的顾客那里得到的反馈信息是令人乐观的。）

本题测试 feedback 这个单词的用法。feedback 意为"反馈信息"，是不可数名词。如：The company welcomes feedback from people who use its goods.（该公司欢迎用户提供对其产品的反馈信息。）

Practice Test 5

Part I Writing

(Student's sample)

Dear Sir/Madame,

My name is Li Ming and I am writing to you to apply for the teaching position you have advertised in the local newspaper yesterday.

I am a senior student of Henan university, and I'm learning English language and literature. I've done excellent in all my courses and won scholarship in first three academic years, as you can see from the resume attached to this letter. I can speak fluent English and have won the first prize in the English speech contest held in our department last year. I also practice English teaching during the summer vacations and did quite well.

To tell you the truth, I'm very interested in English teaching and I am eager to become a teacher at your school. I hope you give me this opportunity. I'm waiting for your reply.

Sincerely yours,
Li Ming

(Improved sample)

Dear Sir/Madame,

My name is Li Ming and **I am writing to you at this time to inquire about** teaching opportunity in English as a second language. **Your advertisement in the newspaper attracted me** because I know I have the qualification you are seeking.

I am a senior student **working toward a bachelor's degree** in English language and literature. I **have mastered the basic knowledge of these subjects and received special training in English teaching**. I can speak fluent English and have won the first prize in the English speech contest held in our department last year. **Besides,** I worked as a part-time English teacher during summer vacations.

I am particularly interested in teaching. I feel that **I have sufficient education and experiences to fulfill the qualification for your position.**

Enclosed herewith is a copy of my resume for your reference. I **eagerly anticipate** your response.

Sincerely yours,
Li Ming

Part II Reading Comprehension (Skimming and Scanning)

1. Y 这篇文章意在指导刚毕业的大学生如何在职场取得成功。

主旨题。通过略读全文,可知本文就大学生如何在职场取得成功给出了六条建议。题目概括了原文的内容,所以被判为正确。

2. Y 根据 National Association of Colleges and Employers,毕业大学生的就业机会最近四年连年增加。

细节题。根据 National Association of Colleges and Employers,读者可以快速定位至第一段的最后一句。题目是原文的同义改写,所以被判为正确。

3. N Hefner 指出在一份新工作中成功的关键因素是个人的成就。

细节题。根据人名 Hefner,读者可以快速定位至小标题 Advice from the Top 下。根据第二段的第一句,这个关键因素不是个人的成就,而是集体的成功。所以该题目被判为错误。

4. N 持一种消极的态度对大学毕业生早期工作的成功很重要。

细节题。根据 attitude,可以快速定位至小标题 Maintain a Positive Attitude 下,这一部分讲到积极的态度对一个人工作的成功很重要。题目表述与原文相反,所以,该陈述被判为错误。

5. Y 任何领域中的拔尖人物通常比其他人更努力。

细节题。根据 work harder,读者可以定位至小标题 Work Hard 之下的第二段的第一句。该陈述对原文作了简化处理,但意思没有改变,故被判为正确。

6. Y 如果你帮助你周围的人取得成功,你自己自然会成功。

细节题。该题可以定位至小标题 Focus on the Success of Others 下第一段的第二句。原文中讲到帮助别人成功是避免自己失败的好策略,自己自然会取得成功。题目的表述与原文一致,所以被判为正确。

7. NG 如果一个人知道如何在 *MySpace* 网站创建自己的简历,他会比别人拥有更多的就业机会。

细节题。原文在最后一段中提到了在 *MySpace* 网站创建自己的简历,但只是为了说明今天大学毕业生的技术优势,并没有和就业机会联系在一起。所以根据原文无法对该陈述进行判断。

8. self-discipline 要想取得长期的成功,就要具有既努力工作又能找时间照料自己个人生活的自我约束能力。

细节题。本题的内容可以在小标题 Work Hard 之下的第四段中找到。该段最后一句中的 it 指的就是上句中的 self-discipline。

9. trust and confidence 即便最初的工作任务很琐碎,但如果你能出色完成,你也会赢得信任和信心。

细节题。该句的内容可以在小标题 Deliver on Your Commitments 下的第二段中找到。题目实际上是该段的概括。所填写的内容可以在最后一句中直接找到。

10. Y completed staff work "全局观工作"的概念意味着超越基本的工作任务去理

解为什么需要(做)某事,人们会怎样运用它,以及一旦完成,它会以什么样的
形式出现。

细节题。该句的内容可以在小标题 Perform Completed Staff Work 下的第一
段找到。根据该段第一句,可知此处该填 completed staff work。

Part III Listening Comprehension (35 minutes)

Section A

11. B	12. D	13. D	14. C	15. A
16. C	17. B	18. A	19. A	20. C
21. B	22. D	23. C	24. D	25. A

Section B

26. C	27. B	28. D	29. A	30. C
31. B	32. D	33. A	34. B	35. C

Section C

36. willing	37. troops	38. remarks	39. seeking
40. conference	41. Strategic	42. available	43. similar

44. talks frankly about the need to repair French-US relations

45. France definitely does not seek systematically to counter the US in the world or to diminish its influence

46. So let us discuss how to make the most of today's globalized world while preserving the earth's diversity, which is an asset to all

Part IV Reading Comprehension (Reading in Depth)

Section A

47. H 本篇文章讲述的是未来的一种新型燃料,具体到该空缺项,由于其在情态动词 may 的后面,毋庸置疑应该填入一个原形动词。所给备选词项中只有 D、M 符合这一条件,而它们放在该空缺项位置时意思上却说不过去,所以我们需要回头再来看备选项,这时才发现原来其中还有一个我们习惯上多理解为名词的词 power,它在这里用作动词,表示"为……提供能量"。由此题可见,我们在处理类似问题时需要格外注意词类活用。

48. F 从结构上看,此空缺项被前面的冠词和形容词修饰,可确定此处应填入一单数名词,符合该项条件的选项只有 A、F 两项,但显然 A 项与此处文意不符,故只能选 F 项(breakthrough)。填入该词之后,此句的文意是"一旦投入使用,甲醇燃料电池可能是在能源消耗和能源储存方面的一项重大突破"。

49. D 从结构上考虑,同前文第一个空缺项类似,此句中的空缺词位于情态动词 could 之后,应为一个原形动词。将 D、M 作为备选词项后,再结合语意考虑,cut 符合文意,意为"削减",整个句子的意思是"这种美好的新技术能极大地减少汽车尾

气和其他原因造成的空气污染"。

50. B 从句子结构上看,该处应填入一个名词,A、B、L 皆符合要求。但根据词意,applications 有"应用、用途"的意思,放在文中最符合上下文意义:"燃料电池无论是用来驱动小轿车和公共汽车,还是用作其他用途的电源……"。

51. E 从句子结构上看,依据空缺位置前面的介词 by 可以确定该处应填入一个名词或相当于名词的动名词。根据语义,介词 by 表示借助于某种方式,因而选唯一的动名词 converting 最为合适。

52. L 从句子结构考虑,该空缺词由 many 修饰,肯定是一个可数名词的复数形式,备选项中仅有 B、L 两项符合要求,B 项已经选过,基本可以确定用 environmentalists 一词了。再结合句子语义考虑一下,前文提到这种燃料"低噪声、无排放物",据此可以推测这肯定是环保学家们(environmentalists)所寄予的厚望了。

53. J 从句子结构来看,该空缺处前有助动词 haven't,因而应该填入动词的过去分词形式,备选项中有 supplied 和 compared 两个分词,结构上都适合。再从语义上进一步区分,该句的含义是"尽管仅靠蓄电池不能满足大多数驾驶员对车子工作性能的需要,但倡导者们认为……",显然用 supplied 才说得通。

54. O that 引导宾语从句,它表明新型燃料的倡导者有一个信念:"燃料电池,必要时再加上蓄电池,在性能、行驶路程、耗油量等方面有望胜过现在使用的内燃机"。这里显然是要将 fuel cells 与 internal combustion engines 作比较,因此答案选 compared 就不言而喻了。

55. N 从句子结构上分析,该空缺项前面有 much more 作修饰语,可以明确知道此处应该填入一个多音节形容词或副词的原形,C、G、K、N 四个选项进入我们的视野。然后从语义上加以排除,上下文的含义为"燃料电池能使用各种来源的氢气,包括一种简单的压缩气储罐。但通常从天然气中产生的一种液体——甲醇——能更……地储存氢",efficient(高效的)放在此处语意最适合。

56. I 从句子结构上分析,空缺项位于 which 引导的定语从句的谓语中心位置,根据语法常识,动词在人称和数上应该与先行词保持一致,由于先行词指代的是单数意义,因而定语从句谓语动词也应用第三人称单数形式,备选词项中只有 extracts 符合,意为"提取出、提炼出"。结合上下文也可以看出,选用该词较为适当,语意关联性强。上下文连贯起来的意思大致是:从天然气中产生的液体——甲醇——能更有效地储存氢,因而在小轿车中首批使用的很可能是一种间接的甲醇燃料电池。在该类型电池中,甲醇里的氢通过一个叫做"改进器"的机械装置被提取出来。

Section B

57. C 推理题。题干要求推断出文章前一段的内容。从文章的体裁及内容可以断定,作者的目的是鼓励人们立下新志,再根据第一段第一句话"在法国,新年立新志越来越罕见了"可以知道,前面一段和法国有关系,选项 B 和选项 C 可能是正确的,但前者"法国的新年风俗"和文章的主要内容关系不密切,后者"一位法国作家的决定"则具有开启下文的作用。故此题的正确答案为 C。

58. B　词义理解题。apathy 一词的意思是"冷漠，冷淡，无动于衷"，只有选项 B 和该词意思一致。

59. C　语意理解题。西方人是"内省运动员"也就是说他们经常反思自己的思想和情感，时常分析自己，只有选项 C 符合句子的意思。

60. A　主旨题。作者对待新年立新志的态度在最后一段中已明确提到："新志或许是谎言，但却是善意的谎言……只要能立新志，我们就有救……它让我们保持明智。"只有选项 A 能表明作者的态度。

61. D　归纳题。文章的主要内容是说明立新志的好处，鼓励人们立下新志。选项 A"新年里幸福的一天"和选项 C"在新年改变你的行为举止"与文章内容不符；选项 B"论立志"作为题目则太过宽泛；只有选项 D"又一个改变生活的最后机会"归纳出了文章的主要内容，点明了立新志的重要作用。

62. D　词义理解题。imposter 一词的意思是"冒名顶替者；行骗者"，而在句中的意思是冒牌货、假冒的学生。故此题的正确答案为 D。

63. C　词义理解题。rang up 在此并非打电话之意，而是指收银员将款额输入现金出纳机，只有选项 C 符合短语的意思。

64. B　词义理解题。第二段第一句话就指出了作者对自己 30 年前所作所为的态度，只要理解 escapade 一词的意思，就能作出正确的选择。该词指大胆顽皮的冒险行为、恶作剧，只有选项 B 和该词意思一致。

65. D　细节题。从第一段内容可知，作者的写作经纪人装扮成他的妈妈，帮他进入一所公立中学，所以选项 A 不正确；在第四段中，作者担心收银员会识破他，甚至可能会问他是否要她把裤子作为礼品包装起来，选项 B 的意思正好相反；选项 C"作者的思想和他的外表相配"并非是事实，而是作者竭力要做的，这在最后一段开头已有交代；作者和一帮不认识的人聊天时，没有和他们一起吹嘘自己当年用过哪些毒品，从中可以推断出他以前曾经吸毒。故此题的正确答案为 D。

66. B　主旨题。文章的结构很清晰，作者首先介绍自己年轻时的恶作剧，然后又说明一个新的计划：试图假装自己 45 岁，为此他改变了外貌，还竭力调整自己的世界观。选项 A"作者希望在外表上更年轻"只局限于外表，没有涉及到他的思想，这和文章的内容不符；选项 C"作者看起来比他的年龄要小"并非文章内容；选项 D"作者善于欺骗别人"也没有在文章中提到；只有选项 B"作者内心深处依然年轻"表达了全文的主题。

Part V　Cloze

67. C　语义搭配题。various 意为"各种各样，不同的"。句子大意："地理学家比较地球上各种不同的地域的异同"。

68. B　短语搭配题。go beyond 意思是"超越，超过"。

69. A　本题测试语义搭配。as a whole 意思是"作为整体"，常跟在名词后面。本句大意：地理学家不但研究各个具体地域，而且把地球作为整体来考虑。

70. D　本题测试语义搭配。come from 意思是"来自，来源于"。

71. B　本题测试定语从句的用法。which 引导非限制性定语从句，修饰 *graphein*。

72. A　语境题。这里应从语篇的角度去考虑。在后一句中有 others，可知此处使用的是句型 some … others …。

73. D　本题测试语义搭配。四个选项中的动词都可以和 on 搭配构成词组。rely on 意为"依靠"；rest on 意为"基于"；reckon on 意为"指望，依靠"；focus on 意为"集中讨论研究"。该处选择 focus，与后句中的 deal with 照应。

74. C　语境题。entire 意思是"整个的"。该句大意：另一些地理书则研究州、区域、国家或整个大洲。

75. A　本题测试语义搭配。此处 Another way 的意思是"另一种方法"。

76. C　语境题。因为后文中讲到 physical geography，所以此处的叙述对象是 geography。

77. D　语境题。根据后文对该学科分支的描述"从人类着手，研究人类和其周围环境……"可知该处指人文地理或文化地理，故选 cultural。

78. D　本题测试语义搭配。该处应用了句型 the former … the latter …。

79. D　本题测试连接词的意义。句子意思为"后者从人类着手，研究人类和其周围环境如何相互影响"，故选 how。

80. A　本题测试短语搭配。act upon/on 意思是"对……有影响，对……起作用"。

81. B　本题测试上下文的逻辑关系。从上下文看，此句表示语气转折，故选择 But。

82. A　语境题。上文讲到地理学包括自然地理和文化地理，本句大意为"当地理学被看作一门学科时，其中任何一个分支都不能忽视另外一个"，因此该题选择 neither。

83. B　本题测试短语搭配。be described as 意思是"被说成是"。

84. C　语境题。后一句讲到如果地域间完全相同，就几乎不需要地理学家，可见地理学家研究的是地域间的差异，故此题选 differences。

85. C　本题测试逻辑搭配。however 表示语气的转折。

86. B　本题测试逻辑搭配。then 在这里的意思是"这样说来"。

Part VI　Translation

87. If you can come back on time, we'll catch the train. But **what if you can't get home before dark**?（如果你能按时回来，我们还可以赶上火车。但是如果你天黑之前回不了家怎么办？）

    本题测试 what if … 这个句型。what if … 相当于 what would happen if … ，是后者的缩略形式，意为"要是……怎么办？如果……怎么办？"，如：What if the bank does not grant us the loan?（要是银行不贷款给我们怎么办？）

88. It is something **without precedent** in our department that you are given a flat after working in our school less than two years.（你在我们学校工作不到两年就分到了一套住房，这在我们系是没有先例的。）

本题测试 without precedent 这个习惯用法。precedent 是名词,意为"先例;惯例",without precedent 意为"没有先例的;史无前例的",如:The appointment of a female commander of a navy warship is without precedent.（任命一个女海军军舰司令是史无前例的。）

89. The manager was chatting with the chairman of the board about something that concerned the future of their cooperation and I could tell that he **was being careful with his words**.（经理正在同董事长谈论涉及到他们将来合作的事情,我可以断定他当时措辞相当小心。）

本题测试 be 动词的进行时用法。be 动词的进行时表示某人一时的表现,而不是一贯的表现。如:Tom didn't really like the food, but he was being polite and ate quite a bit.（汤姆并不真正喜欢那种食物,但是出于礼貌他还是吃了很多。）

90. Broadly speaking, the congress had **played a leading role** in the struggle for human rights during that period.（大体上讲,议会在那一时期争取人权的斗争中起到了主导作用。）

本题测试 play a role 这个词组。play a role 意为"扮演一个角色;起到一定作用",role 前经常跟一些修饰语。如:The headmaster plays an important role in the good running of a school.（校长对一个学校的正常运作起到重要作用。）本题中的"起到主导作用"可译为 play a leading role。

91. Cyberspace is **a place where you may come and go at will**, that is, if you don't love it, leave it.（虚拟空间是一个你可以随意出入的地方,也就是说,如果你不喜欢,就可以退出。）

本题测试 at will 这个词组。at will 意为"随意;任意"。如:The animals are allowed to wander at will in the park.（这些动物可以在公园里随意走动。）此外,要用 where 引导的从句来修饰 a place。

Practice Test 6

Part I   Writing

Women in the Modern World

(Student's sample)

Women are playing an increasingly important part in society today. They do not only stay at home and attend to their families but go out to do the same work as men and get the same pay. They're doing quite well in some of the working fields. For instance, there are many stateswomen, female diplomats in the modern world.

With the changes in their social role, women's position in the family has been improved as well. They make family decision together with their husbands; they also do the housework together, look after their baby and educate their children together. Of course, their husbands may not do as much as them.

In spite of these changes, the liberation of women has not been completely realized. Women's social status is not as high as men's. They can't share total equality in education and employment. There are still some women who are content to be "a good wife and mother." So the complete liberation of women is still a goal of them.

(Improved sample)

Women are playing an increasingly important part in society today. They no longer merely attend to their families but **have more opportunities** to do the same work as men and get the same pay. And they're doing much better **than they used to do** in some of the working fields. For instance, there are many stateswomen, female diplomats in the modern world. **In addition, women now take part in almost all social activities.**

With the changes in their social role, women's position in the family has been improved as well. They **share equal rights** in family decision; **they as well as their husbands** do the household chores, look after their baby and educate their children. **Though** the latter may not do as much as their wives, **the situation goes better.**

In spite of these changes, the liberation of women has not been completely realized. Women's social status is not as high as men's. They can't share total equality in education and employment. **Furthermore,** some women are still content to be "a good wife and mother." So **there is still a long way to go for the liberation of women.**

Part II   Reading Comprehension (Skimming and Scanning)

1. **Y** 买一套房子可以说是通过许多年积累起一笔可观的财富。

   细节题。本句的内容可以在第一个小标题 Buying Your First Home 下的第二段中找到。该段第一句最后说 buying a home can be a good financial investment，结合后一句当中的"15 到 30 年"，可知题目的表述和原文一致。故该陈述被判为正确。

2. **Y** 放贷人对借款人预先的资格认证是确定你能负担多大按揭款项的好方法。

   细节题。该句的内容可以在第二个小标题 How Much Mortgage Can You Afford 下的第四段找到。该段的第二句 Prequalification helps you focus on homes you can afford 与本题目的意思相同。故该陈述被判为正确。

3. **N** 买房时，除了支付按揭贷款外没有其他后续的费用。

   细节题。根据 ongoing costs，读者可以快速定位至第四个小标题 Ongoing Costs 下。该部分第一段的第一句就讲明除了贷款外还有其他和产权有关的费用。题目的表述与原文相反，故该陈述被判为错误。

4. **NG** 大多数美国人喜欢别墅式住宅（house），不喜欢公寓式住宅（condo），因为公寓式住宅有更多的相关费用。

   细节题。虽然在第四个小标题 Ongoing Costs 下的第二段提到公寓式住宅要花费更多的相关费用，但全文并没有提到美国人更喜欢哪一类住宅，故该陈述判为 NG。

5. **a price range**   寻找合适的第一处住宅的第一步是确定价位和地段。

   细节题。本题的内容可以在原文的第一句中找到。题目是该句子的改写。

6. **the American Dream**   拥有一处住宅是实现美国梦的基础。

   细节题。本题的内容可以在原文第一个小标题下的第一句中找到。题目是该句子的改写。

7. **basic monthly housing costs**   购房费率是购房月供与购房者的月毛收入之比。

   细节题。本题的内容可以在原文第二个小标题下第二段的第一句中找到。题目与原文几乎完全一致。

8. **cash requirement**   许多购房者发现按揭首付款不是唯一的要求用现金支付的款项，这令他们感到震惊。

   细节题。本题的内容可以在原文第三个小标题下的第一句中找到。

9. **Schools and other services**   学校和其他的服务是选择住房地段的重要考虑因素。

   细节题。根据 neighborhood，读者可以快速定位至原文第五个小标题下。在该部分第一段的第二句中可找到答案。

10. **valuable source of information**   房屋经纪人通常代表地产商的利益，但是考虑到买房过程，他们也可以是购房者宝贵的信息来源。

   细节题。根据 Brokers，读者可以快速定位至原文第六个小标题下。在该部分第一段的第二句中可找到答案。

Part III Listening Comprehension (35 minutes)

Section A

11. B   12. C   13. A   14. D   15. C
16. A   17. D   18. B   19. C   20. B
21. A   22. C   23. B   24. C   25. D

Section B

26. A   27. B   28. C   29. C   30. A
31. B   32. A   33. B   34. A   35. B

Section C

36. offers   37. fantasy   38. symbols   39. adventure
40. addition   41. auto-related   42. tend   43. riding

44. cars and trucks worldwide kill an average of 250,000 people

45. Half of the world's people will be involved in an auto accident at sometime in their lives

46. In some countries, they produce at least 50% of the countries' air pollution

Part IV Reading Comprehension (Reading in Depth)

Section A

47. holidays in England 这篇文章主要是关于英国的节日的。
    本题是概括总结题。文章中谈论到了很多节日：Guy Fawkes Night（盖伊·福克斯之夜）；Remembrance Day（荣军纪念日）；Christmas（圣诞节）；Easter（复活节）和 St. George's Day（圣乔治节）。其间，关于英国的词语不断出现，如：England, English, Britain, the Queen 等。由此可见，整篇文章谈论的是英国的节日。

48. Guy Fawkes Night 人像被投进篝火是为了庆祝盖伊·福克斯之夜。
    本题答案可以在第一段中找到。第一段向我们讲述了盖伊·福克斯之夜的来历及庆祝方法。这个节日是为了庆祝挫败盖伊·福克斯领导的叛乱。在 11 月 5 日这一天，人们——特别是孩子——燃放烟火，把做成盖伊·福克斯形状的人像扔进火堆中来进行庆祝。

49. On the nearest Sunday to November 11, Remembrance Day. 在距离 11 月 11 日最近的那个星期天，也就是荣军纪念日，人们要致哀静默两分钟。
    本题答案可在介绍荣军纪念日的第二段中找到。荣军纪念日是为了纪念阵亡将士的。在那一天，人们要参加在教堂或战争纪念馆举行的仪式，并默哀两分钟。

50. In churches and in front of neighbors' houses. 在圣诞节期间，人们在教堂和邻居家门前演唱圣诞节颂歌。
    本题答案可在第三段的第一句中找到：During the Christmas season, choirs sing

carols in churches and people may go out in the evenings to sing carols in front of their neighbors' houses. 在圣诞节期间,唱诗班在教堂演唱圣诞节颂歌,人们也会在晚上到邻居家门前演唱。

51. She delivers a Christmas message on the radio or television. 在圣诞节当天,女王会通过收音机或电视发表讲话。

本题答案可在第三段第四句中找到:Many families attend morning church services and listen to the Queen's Christmas message on the radio or television. 许多人家会参加教会的早礼拜仪式,并通过收音机或电视聆听女王的圣诞节讲话。

Section B

52. C 词义理解题。precursor 意思是"先锋,先导,前身",只有选项 C 最符合该词之意。故此题的正确答案为 C。

53. D 细节题。在第四段开头已经明确指出,布兰德在 1967 年也是一个"推波助澜"的人物,他的创举是出版了《全球目录》,只有选项 D 能够回答这一问题。

54. D 推理题。在第四段提到,《全球目录》是一种类似西尔斯目录的检索册,由此可以推断出西尔斯也是一种用于获取信息的目录册,只有选项 D 最符合这一意思。其实 Sears 的本义是西尔斯百货公司的商品目录。

55. D 细节题。文章第三段指出,Web 2.0 起源于 Well 网站和 20 世纪 60 年代的反正统文化运动,而 Well 这一网络名称是"全球目录电子连接"(Whole Earth 'Lectronic Link)几个词的首字母组合,所以排除了选项 D。

56. B 细节题。选项 A "维基百科全书是一个革命组织"和第五段内容不符,它是由网民志愿编撰的网络百科全书;选项 C "创新常常出现在一些非常严格的实验室里"和第七段"军工机构需要跨学科实验室里酝酿出来的创新思路"不符;选项 D "史蒂夫·乔布斯销售个人电脑来作为对抗他不喜欢的社会混乱局面的武器"和最后一段内容不符,他是为了对抗乏味的整齐划一而销售个人电脑的;只有选项 B 符合第六段的内容。

57. B 词义理解题。pranksters 意思是"喜欢恶作剧的人,喜欢捉弄别人的人",只有选项 B 符合词义。

58. D 语义理解题。文章第三段指出"不为其他原因,就因为它是美洲最古老的农作物之一,一只货真价实的南瓜也应该得到我们的尊重",只有选项 D 确切地表达出了这个意思。

59. C 细节题。文章第八段提到美国商业农场种植的南瓜时指出"如今最常见的南瓜都是为了装饰门廊而不是为了做饼馅而种植的",只有选项 C 表达了这个意思。

60. C 细节题。选项 A "现在人们已完全不能吃南瓜了"和内容不符,因为不能吃的是 fake pumpkins,它们是"名义上的食物,用来玩,不用来吃";选项 B "欧洲人不喜欢吃南瓜"和第七段开头"欧洲人迅速将南瓜纳入他们的食谱"并不一致;选项 C "南瓜是印第安人的主食"是第三段的内容;选项 D "欧洲人首先种植南瓜"和第三段内容不符,因为"葫芦科植物最早在墨西哥种植"。故此题的正确答案为 C。

61. D 归纳题。文章介绍了南瓜的历史和现状：从食用南瓜发展到雕刻成杰克灯的装饰南瓜。选项 A"食用南瓜"、选项 B"砸碎假南瓜"和选项 C"万圣节南瓜的历史"都局限于文章内容的一个方面，只有选项 D"也可以吃的万圣节南瓜"较全面地反映了文章内容，也体现了作者的写作意图。

Part V Error Correction (15 minutes)

62. instead 后加上 of。instead of 为一介词短语，意思是"代替；而不是……"，其后可以跟名词、代词、动名词作宾语；instead 无此用法。

63. like 改为 as。such as 是固定搭配，意思是"诸如"，用来举例说明，其中的 as 不能用 like 替换。

64. has 改为 have。此处属于主语和谓语在数上搭配不当。主语是复数，因此谓语部分的助动词必须用表示复数的 have，不能用表示单数的 has。

65. 删除 by the hand 中的 the。by hand 是固定搭配，意思是"手工做的"，这一短语中间不能加 the。

66. it 改为 them。此处属于指代关系错误。them 指代的是复数名词 appliances，it 只能用来指代单数名词，因此这里只能用 them。

67. leads 后加上 to。lead 在本句中意思是"导致某种结果"，其后跟宾语时必须加上介词 to。

68. down 改为 up。go up 意思是"上升，增长"，go down 意思是"下降，减少"；句子的意思是随着收入的增长，人们的需求会随之改变，因此要用 go up。

69. Nevertheless 改为 Therefore。此处为一逻辑错误。therefore 意思是"因此"，nevertheless 意思是"然而"；根据本段的意思，最后一句是总结句，表示前面所述情况带来的结果，不是表示意思的转折，因此要用 therefore。

70. works 改为 work/job(s)。work 用作名词，此处意思是"工作"，是不可数名词，因此后面不能加 s。

71. international 改为 national。本段指的是国家的防御，不是国际间的防御，根据句意用 national 合适。

Part VI Translation

72. **When it comes to computers and Internet**，students all become excited，eager to say something about their experience.（谈到计算机和因特网，学生们都很兴奋，急切地想说出自己的体会。）

   本题测试 when it comes to ... 这个结构。when it comes to ... 意为"当谈到……；当说到……；当涉及到……"，如：When it comes to art，I am an absolute outsider.（谈到艺术，我完全是个外行。）

73. They **broke off the business relations** with that company as it suffered huge losses in the last financial year and went bankrupt.（他们与那家公司中断了生意来往，因为该公司上一个财政年度损失惨重，已经破产了。）

本题测试 break off 这个词组。break off 意为"中止；中断"，如：Britain threatened to break off diplomatic relations. （英国威胁要中断两国的外交关系。）

74. Excessive exercise **does more harm than good to one's health**. Therefore we must control the amount of exercise we do. （过量的运动对身体健康弊多利少，所以我们必须控制运动量。）

本题测试 do more harm than good 这个习惯用法。do more harm than good 意为"弊大于利；弊多利少"，如：If we interfere, it may do more harm than good. （如果我们进行干预，可能反而弊多利少。）若要加上宾语，表示"对……来说弊多利少"，需在 do more harm than good 后加上介词 to。

75. It is a traditional Chinese virtue for the young on buses to yield their seats to **the old，the weak，the sick and the disabled**. （在公共汽车上年轻人给老弱病残者让座是中国人的传统美德。）

本题测试形容词前加 the 表一类人的用法；类似的还有 the rich（富人）、the poor（穷人）等。其实，该句前面还有一个这样的例子：the young（年轻人）。

76. I should do this job **whether they agree or not**. （不管他们同意与否，我都要做这项工作。）

本题测试 whether ... or not 或 whether or not ... 这个结构。whether ... or not 或 whether or not ... 用以引导出两种非此即彼的可能性。如：Whether it rains or not/Whether or not it rains，we'll play football on Sunday. （无论下不下雨，我们星期天都要踢足球。）

Practice Test 7

Part I Writing

The Relationship Between Teaching and Learning

(Student's sample)

The relationship between teaching and learning can be positive or negative. If a student learns his lessons in an enjoyable and interesting way and the teacher will consider his job worthwhile. This kind of relationship is the positive relationship. But in the negative relationship the student is always discouraged from learning and the teacher will regard his job as an unpleasant task.

In order to build a positive relationship between teaching and learning the teacher and the student should respect each other. The teacher should know how to encourage the student to learn so as to help him to develop a good positive attitude towards his study. On the other hand the student should be eager to learn and willing to work hard. He should listen carefully and be attentive in class. If the student does not do these things, he will not acquire as much knowledge as possible from his teacher's assistance.

In one word, a positive relationship between teaching and learning can be beneficial both to the student and to the teacher. The student gains knowledge eagerly and enjoyably, and the teacher gains satisfaction from his job.

(Improved sample)

The relationship between teaching and learning can be **either** positive or negative. A positive relationship **will make** learning enjoyable and interesting for the student **and will make the teacher's job worthwhile**. A negative relationship, **however**, can discourage the student from learning and make teaching an unpleasant task.

In order to build a positive relationship between teaching and learning, **it is important that** the teacher and the student respect each other. **The teacher needs patience, understanding and good teaching art.** He should know how to encourage the student **without pushing or forcing him**. So the student will develop a good positive attitude towards his study. On the other hand, the student should be eager to learn and willing to work hard. **It is also important** to listen carefully and be attentive in class. If the student does not do these things, he will not **be able to profit fully from his teacher's knowledge and assistance**.

In conclusion，a positive relationship between teaching and learning can be **mutually beneficial**. The student gains knowledge eagerly and enjoyably，and the teacher gains satisfaction from his job.

Part II　Reading Comprehension (Skimming and Scanning)

1. Y　这篇文章介绍了皇家天文台的历史,它是英国最重要的历史和科学遗址之一。
主旨题。通过略读全文,可知该陈述概括了本文的大意,是正确的。

2. NG　皇家天文台每年都吸引成千上万的游客。
细节题。本题描述的内容在原文中并没有提及,故判为 NG。

3. N　从 1675 年建立时起,皇家天文台就举世闻名。
细节题。从原文的第一段中,可知皇家天文台是在 1675 年建立的,但在第五段中有 the Observatory became generally famous in the 19th century,可知它到了 19 世纪才到处出名。所以该陈述与原文不符,是错误的。

4. Y　皇家天文台是国际公认的每一天、每一年和每一个千年的起点。
细节题。本题的内容可以在第一段中找到。题目是该段最后一句的简写,所以该陈述被判为正确。

5. the first milestone　2006 年 2 月落成的时间展馆是皇家天文台再次发展的第一个重要里程碑。
细节题。根据 February 2006,读者可以快速定位至原文的第三段。依据该段的第一句,可以填写出相关的内容。

6. the eastern and western hemispheres　通过把两只脚放在本初子午线的两侧,人们可以同时站在东西两个半球上。
细节题。本题的内容可以在第四段中找到。题目是该段第二句的改写。

7. reliable means of navigation　1707 年的一次海难显示,人们需要更为可靠的领航方式。
细节题。根据 A disaster at sea in 1707,读者可以快速定位至原文的第六段。题目是该段第一句的同义改写。

8. the calculation of Greenwich Mean Time　从 19 世纪后期,格林尼治的本初子午线成为计算格林尼治标准时间的共同基础。
细节题。该题的内容可以在第十段的第一句找到。

9. 1884　在 1884 年,格林尼治以 22 票赞成、1 票反对、2 票弃权赢得了 0 度经线的殊荣。
细节题。该题的内容可以在第十一段找到。

10. the least number of people　人们说,命名格林尼治为 0 度经线,影响的人数最少。

细节题。该题的内容可以在倒数第二段找到。

Part III Listening Comprehension (35 minutes)
Section A
11. A　　12. C　　13. B　　14. C　　15. D
16. A　　17. D　　18. A　　19. B　　20. B
21. A　　22. B　　23. A　　24. C　　25. D

Section B
26. C　　27. B　　28. D　　29. B　　30. A
31. D　　32. A　　33. D　　34. C　　35. B

Section C
36. theories　　　37. evolved　　　38. unpredictable　　39. sought
40. feared　　　　41. desired　　　　42. hardened　　　43. arose

44. As time passed some rituals were abandoned，but the stories persisted and provided material for art and drama

45. Another theory traces the drama's origin from the human interest in storytelling

46. A closely related theory traces drama to those dances that are imitations of animal movements and sounds

Part IV Reading Comprehension (Reading in Depth)
Section A
47. basic biological and psychological differences　根据"生理决定命运"这种思想意识，两性之间有根本的生理上和心理上的差别。
本题答案可在第一段的前两句中找到。第一句告诉我们："性别偏见基于一种认为生理决定命运的思想意识，而这种意识也证明性别偏见是正确的。"第二句中又说："根据这种思想意识，两性之间在生理上和心理上存在着根本差别。"因此，本题答案是 basic biological and psychological differences。

48. Men.　男人应该承担更大的责任。
本题答案可以从第一段中推断出。第一段告诉我们，根据"生理决定命运"的思想意识，男性和女性要在社会中扮演不同的角色：女性更适合承担家庭内的责任，而男性更适宜走出去。男性是养家的人，女性和孩子是被赡养的人。特别是倒数第二句（On the other hand men are best suited to go out into the competitive world of work and politics，where serious responsibilities must be taken on.）明确告诉了我们答案，即男人应该承担更大的责任。

49. Because such jobs grow out of their duties at home./Because these jobs are an extension of their domestic role.　女性适合看护和教育的工作是因为这些工作是她们家庭角色的延伸。

本题答案可在第二段第二、三句中找到。第二句告诉我们女性比男性更适宜于受雇为护士、社会工作者、小学教师、佣人、职员和秘书。第三句告诉我们其原因是这些职位是女性所扮演的家庭角色的延伸。

50. **sex roles** 这篇文章主要谈论了性别角色问题。

本题考查概括总结能力。通读全文可知,本文探讨了男女两种不同性别的不同社会角色。另外,在最后一段中也出现了 sex roles 和 sex-defined roles 等总结性的词语。

51. **Partial acceptance.** 作者对"性别决定角色"观点的态度是部分接受。

本题答案可在最后一段中总结出。最后一段告诉我们 sex-defined roles 这种观点不尽正确,但作者又在某种程度上赞同这种说法,所以作者既不完全赞同,也不完全反对,其态度是 partial acceptance。

Section B

52. **C** 归纳题。根据文中经济学家简·布吕克纳的调查结果,所住地段人口密度越小,居民们彼此越友好,人们对兴趣俱乐部的参与也明显增加,人口密度每下降 10%,人们每周与邻居交谈一次的可能性就增加 10%,所以选项 A、B 和 D 都归纳出了人口密度下降带来的结果,只有选项 C"人们会形同陌路"和他的研究结果正相反。故此题的正确答案为 C。

53. **A** 词义理解题。anonymity 在文中指社会上人与人彼此孤立、互不相识的现象,只有选项 A 符合该词之意。

54. **D** 细节题。选项 A"人们曾认为,郊区的蔓延导致人与人彼此孤立"是第四段的内容;选项 B"简·布吕克纳在他的研究中证实那句谚语——篱笆筑得牢,邻里处得好——是正确的"是第五段的内容;文章第二段提到"住在郊区比住在市区更有益于社交生活",所以选项 C 也是正确的。文中提到"城市有足够的博物馆、剧院和其他娱乐设施供人们选择",和选项 D 正相反。因此正确答案为 D。

55. **D** 细节题。选项 A"作者肯定住在郊区"不是文中内容;选项 B"时髦的城市人能享受丰富的社交生活"和选项 C"人们赞成大量的个人空间和种种界限有助于融洽相处"都不符合文章内容;文中提到"对犯罪的恐惧有时会让人们更为戒备",即会让人们相互疏远,所以选项 D 是正确的。

56. **D** 细节题。最后一部分提到,诗人罗伯特·弗罗斯特在《修墙》中尖锐地批评了"篱笆筑得牢,邻里处得好"的说法,所以只有选项 D 符合此意。

57. **B** 词义理解题。upheaval 意为"动乱,动荡",只有选项 B 符合词义。

58. **C** 细节题。文中第一段提到几个教育界的领导人、老牌大学的校友和朋友、耶鲁大学的年轻人、哈佛大学的毕业生,他们相互作用,从 19 世纪 60 年代到 80 年代中期改变了美国高等教育领域。因此,19 世纪下半叶美国高等教育的变化是感兴趣的个人为了改进教育制度而作出努力的结果。故此题的正确答案为 C。

59. **D** 推理题。文中第二段提到五项改革,其中第一项就是提高和加强入学标准,并且 1872 年到 1873 年和 1876 年到 1877 年间的入学水平大大提高。由此推断,革新以前入学标准偏低。故此题的正确答案为 D。

60. C 推理题。文章在谈到课程量时曾提到"课程的扩展和选择体系的发展",这就说明了原来学习课程的特点是学生被限制在一定的选择范围之内。故此题的正确答案为 C。

61. D 归纳题。文章目的在于说明 19 世纪下半叶美国高等教育革新情况。第一段主要阐述 19 世纪下半叶整个美国教育的改革,第二段说明哈佛大学的教育改革情况,只有选项 D 归纳出了作者的意图。

Part V Error Correction (15 minutes)

62. time 改为 times。本句中的 prehistoric times 意思是"史前时期",time 后加 s 表示"历史时期,时代"。

63. introduced 前加上 was。本句是被动语态,因此 introduced 前必须加系动词 was。

64. into 改为 to。refer to 为固定搭配,意思是"谈到,说到;与……有关",其中的 to 不能替换为 into。

65. with 改为 by。在本句中,the worker bees 是 feed 这一动作的执行者,在被动语态中应由 by 来引导,不能用 with。

66. few 改为 many。从上下文得知,雄蜂(drones)的作用是给蜂王提供尽可能多的交配机会,以便蜂王产卵,根据句意应把 few 改为 many。

67. but 改为 or。这里表示的是一种选择关系,不是转折关系,因此要把 but 改为 or。

68. its 改为 their。此处的代词代替的是 the worker bees,因此必须用指代复数名词的代词 their,不能用指代单数名词的代词 its。

69. entrance 前加上 the。这里的 entrance 是特指蜂窝的 entrance,不是泛指,因此要用定冠词 the。

70. in 改为 on。在本句中,day 前边有修饰语 summer,是特指夏天的某一天,因此要用介词 on,不能用 in。

71. much 改为 many。bee 是可数名词,因此在 as ... as 的结构中,要用修饰可数名词的 many,而不能用修饰不可数名词的 much。

Part VI Translation

72. **In the long run, we should learn more about science and technology.** Besides our major subjects, knowledge of computers, English and driving is necessary for our work. (从长远看,我们应该学习更多的科技知识。除了掌握主修的专业之外,懂得计算机、英语和驾驶是我们工作中必不可少的。)
本题测试 in the long run 这个词组。in the long run 意为"长远来说;最后",如:My mother always told me that in the long run I would be glad I didn't give up the piano. (我妈妈总是对我说我最后将会很高兴自己没有放弃钢琴。)

73. **They might have chosen anyone else for the job**, but they picked me. (他们也许可以选择其他任何人做这工作,可是他们选择了我。)
本题测试虚拟语气 might have done sth. 的用法。might have done sth. 表示推测过

去某动作可能发生,而实际上未发生。如:The plan might easily have gone wrong, but in fact it was a great success.(这计划可能很容易失败,可是事实上大获成功。)

74. In spite of the fact that **the fee for cell phones is typically twice as much as for calls made over fixed lines**, they are still very popular, especially among the young people.(尽管移动电话的资费通常是固定线路电话资费的两倍,它们仍然深受欢迎,特别是在年轻人中间。)

本题测试倍数的翻译方法。倍数的翻译方法很多,此题用到 n times as ... as ... 结构。这里的"两倍"翻译为 twice as much as 来代替 two times as much as。再如:The output of cars this year is about three times as great as that of last year.(今年的汽车产量大约是去年的三倍。)此外,"移动电话"或"手机"可译为 cell phone 或 mobile phone。

75. A change in the money supply brings **a corresponding change in expenditure**.(货币供应量的变化带来了支出的相应变化。)

本题测试 corresponding 这个形容词。corresponding 意为"相应的;相当的;相符的",如:All rights carry with them corresponding responsibilities.(所有的权力都带有相应的义务。)"支出"可译为 expenditure。

76. Whenever conflicts arose between her and her husband, she **had the upper hand**, for she alone controlled the bulk of the family fortune.(无论何时她与丈夫发生冲突,她总是占上风,因为惟有她控制着家庭的大部分财产。)

本题测试 have/get/gain the upper hand 这个习惯用法。have/get/gain the upper hand 意为"处于有利地位;占上风",如:Our team gained the upper hand in the second half.(我们队在下半场占了上风。)

Practice Test 8

Part I Writing

How to Achieve Success

(Student's sample)

Everybody wants to be successful in his life. But how can a person achieve the goal? Here are the keys to success.

Determination, perseverance and diligence are the three important factors that will help you to achieve success. Once you make up your mind to do something you must be firmly determined to fulfill your task. If you are not firmly determined it would be impossible for you to realize your goal. Even if you have determination, you will also remember there is no smooth way to success. You may encounter a lot of difficulties on your way to success. So you must possess the spirit of perseverance, then you will make your dream of success come true. If you hold on to the end the final victory will belong to you. But you cannot attain your goal suddenly. Without hard work you won't become successful in your life.

Therefore, these three fine qualities are very important to success. We must try our best to cultivate these qualities to win success.

(Improved sample)

Success is the goal everybody wants to achieve in his life. But how can a person **attain the goal**? Here are some of the **stepping stones that may help you to gain success**.

Determination, perseverance and diligence are the three important factors **going hand in hand** on the way to success. Once you make up your mind **to be successful** you must be strongly determined to fulfill your task. It is impossible to realize your goal **without firm determination. Yet**, there is no smooth way to success. You may encounter a lot of difficulties **on the ladder to final victory**. With the quality of perseverance you will **persist in making great efforts** to make your dream of success come true. If you hold on to the end the final victory will **undoubtedly** belong to you. Still, you cannot **attain your height through a sudden flight**. Without hard work you won't become successful in your life.

To sum up, these three fine qualities are **essential to** success. We must **arm ourselves with them** and try our best to win **the ultimate** success.

Part II　Reading Comprehension (Skimming and Scanning)

1. Y　这篇文章介绍了英国一所大学针对本科生的学费。

　　主旨题。通过略读全文可知,该篇文章就是在讲英国一所大学针对本科生的学费。该陈述被判为正确。

2. N　海外学生与英国本国和欧盟的学生享有相同的学费政策。

　　主旨题。通过比较可以发现,该校针对海外学生的收费要比本国学生和欧盟学生高得多,另外本国学生还享有助学贷款等优惠,所以该陈述是错误的。

3. NG　帝国大学的学费在全英国大学中是最低的。

　　细节题。该文中并没有提及其他大学的学费,也没有比较不同学校的学费,所以该陈述无法判断。

4. Y　对于 2008 年入学的本国和欧盟的学生来讲,他们的学费要依照通货膨胀有一定程度的年度增长。

　　细节题。本题的内容可以在小标题 Home and European Union Students 下找到。该陈述与原文相符合,应判为正确。

5. 　　£17,350　如果一个中国学生在该大学的生物工程系就读,他 2007–2008 年度的学费是 17 350 英镑。

　　细节题。中国学生当然属于海外学生,所以照此标准,我们不难在第一个 Overseas Students 小标题下的表格里找到生物工程系的收费标准。

6. 　　exempt from fees　学生由于参加已获批准的 SOCRATES-ERASMUS 学生交换项目而离校一学年,可以免交该学年的学费。

　　细节题。根据 SOCRATES-ERASMUS 可快速定位至第一个 Overseas Students 小标题下的最后一段。

7. 　　take out a tuition fee loan　本国和欧盟学生有资格从 Student Loans Company 申请学费贷款。

　　细节题。根据 Student Loans Company 可以快速定位至 Payment of Tuition Fees 小标题下第一段第一句。题目是该句的简写。

8. 　　provide a formal declaration　海外学生需要提供一个有足够资金完成学业的正式声明。

　　细节题。该题目的内容可以在第二个 Overseas Students 小标题下的第一段中找到。

9. 　　unable to finance them　不管因为何种原因,如果海外学生的海外资金来源在他们完成学业或研究前受到限制,学校不能为他们提供资助。

　　细节题。该题目的内容可以在第二个 Overseas Students 小标题下的第二段中找到。此处为避免重复,应用 them 代替 students。

10. 　　the UK Education (Fees and Awards) Regulations 1997　学生在支付学费方面"本国"还是"海外"身份确定要根据 1997 年颁布的《英国教育条例》。

　　细节题。该题目的内容可以在 Overseas Students Fee Liability 小标题下的第一段中找到。括号内的内容可以省掉。

Part III　Listening Comprehension (35 minutes)

Section A

11. D　　12. B　　13. C　　14. B　　15. D
16. A　　17. B　　18. A　　19. B　　20. D
21. C　　22. A　　23. B　　24. C　　25. D

Section B

26. C　　27. B　　28. C　　29. A　　30. D
31. C　　32. A　　33. D　　34. B　　35. B

Section C

36. emotions　　37. relied　　38. patients　　39. confirming
40. relieve　　41. stressed　　42. divided　　43. classical

44. The doctors who got to choose their music experienced less stress and scored better than the others

45. by examining the students' blood after the listening to a variety of classical music collections

46. this supports what music therapists have known for years：music can help refresh or soothe the patient

Part IV　Reading Comprehension (Reading in Depth)

Section A

47. Helps greatly in.　对……大有帮助

本题测试短语 go a long way toward 的含义。go a long way toward 意为 help greatly in，如 Their promises don't go a long way toward solving our present problems.（他们的承诺对解决我们当前的问题没多大帮助。）另外，下文也对理解该短语有所帮助，它是对第一句的进一步解释。下文告诉我们："愈有耐心，就愈能接受现实的生活，而不是强要生活如己所愿。如果没有耐心，生活是极其令人沮丧的。你会很容易感到烦扰和恼火。耐心使你的生活更轻松、更易接受。"因此，第一句的意思是"耐心作为一种素质对塑造更为平和与富有爱心的自我大有裨益"。

48. Patience　耐心对达到内心的平和是必不可少的。

本题答案可以在第一段中间找到。第一段中间有一句是 It's essential for inner peace，通过上下文，可知 it 指的是 patience。

49. The importance of patience.　第一段主要论述耐心的重要性。

本题是概括归纳题。通过对第一段的理解，我们知道它主要论述了耐心在我们生活中的重要性。

50. deliberate practice 耐心可以通过刻意的训练培养。

本题答案可在第二段第一句中找到：Patience is a quality of heart that can be greatly enhanced with deliberate practice.（耐心是一种内心的素养，可以通过刻意的训

练得到显著提高。）

51. a minor thing/a minor obstacle 富有耐心的人把困难视为一件小事／一个小小的障碍。

本题答案可在第三段第二句中找到。该句告诉我们："你会发现即使困难的局面——譬如眼前的挑战——也并非生死攸关，而只不过是一个必须清除的小小的障碍罢了。"因此，答案为 a minor thing 或 a minor obstacle。

Section B

52. C 词义理解题。wizards 原意为"巫师，神汉"，也指"行家，能手"，在文中指那些研究领域里的顶尖学者，所以只有选项 C 符合词义。

53. B 细节题。文章开头已经点明："在网上查找所需的东西很有效率，这促使我们随心所欲地搜索……"，所以只有选项 B 是确切的答案。

54. A 词义理解题。bass 意为"鲈鱼"，也有"低音电吉他，男低音歌手"的意思。第四段中指出：一个钓鱼爱好者输入这个词，得到的信息就和保罗·麦卡特尼的歌迷输入同一个词后得到的查询结果有所不同，所以选项 A 是正确的选择。

55. C 细节题。选项 A、B 和 D 都和文章的内容一致，只有选项 C"人们确信搜索公司在保护上网搜索者的隐私方面做得滴水不漏"和第五、六段的内容不符。故此题的正确答案为 C。

56. A 归纳题。选项 B、C 和 D 作为文章的标题比较片面，只有选项 A"你会让他们保存你的梦想吗？"体现了文章主题。

57. C 词义理解题。beleaguered 在文中指"处于困境中的"，所以只有选项 C 符合词义。

58. D 细节题。选项 A 和文章开头内容不符，因为这个 9 岁的孩子谈论的话题是生命即将在我们这颗麻烦重重的行星上消亡；选项 B 和文章内容不一致，他画的是一个全球变暖年表，对他来说，这就相当于蘑菇云；选项 C 和第五段内容不符；选项 D"许多儿童和年轻人在为环境问题担忧"正是文章的主要内容。

59. D 语义理解题。此句意为"并不是所有美国学生都在'变绿'"，"变绿"的意思是关注并保护环境，只有选项 D 符合此意。

60. B 词义理解题。nuclear annihilation 意为"核灭绝"，只有选项 B 符合此意。

61. A 归纳题。选项 B 和 D 与文章内容不一致，选项 C 只是文中的一个细节，只有选项 A 是文章要表达的主旨。

Part V Error Correction

62. decreased 改为 increased。decrease 意思是"减少"，increase 意思是"增加"；根据本句要表达的意思："人类寿命的延长增加了社会的养老负担"，应该选用 increase。

63. provide 后加上 for。provide 作"抚养，赡养"解时是不及物动词，后面接宾语时必须加上介词 for。

64. could 后加上 not。本句要表达的意思是："在以采集和狩猎为生的文化群落中，跟不上队伍的老人就被留在原地等死"，据此，应该在 could 后加上 not。

65. unless 改为 because。根据上下文意思，这里表示的应是原因而不是条件，因此要用 because，不能用 unless。

66. live 改为 alive。alive 是形容词，意思是"活着的"，在句中作宾语补足语；而 live 无此用法。

67. in 改为 at。本句考查的内容是介词加定语从句的用法。介词和关系代词的选择要根据先行词和从句中谓语动词的关系来确定，本句中先行词是 age，从句的谓语动词是 work，它们之间的关系应该是 work at the age，因此要把介词 in 改为 at。

68. If 改为 Unless。本句要表达的意思是："除非他们能积攒足够的钱来过退休以后的生活，否则其他人就得供养他们。"据此意思，必须把 If 改为 Unless。

69. considerable 改为 little。considerable 意思是"大量的"，little 意思是"很少的"，根据该句要表达的意思应该用 little。

70. Elder 改为 Older。elder 意思是"年龄较大的"，older 意思是"年老的"。本句指的是老人，因此要用 older。

71. providing 改为 provided。provide 在本句中表示被动的意思，而现在分词不表示被动的含义，因此要改为过去分词。

Part VI Translation

72. One of the characteristics that **distinguish the male bird and/from female bird** is that the male bird has beautiful feathers. （雄鸟与雌鸟相区别的特征之一是雄鸟有一身漂亮的羽毛。）

本题测试 distinguish 这个单词的搭配。distinguish 意为"区别，辨别"，常用搭配为 distinguish（between）A and B 或 distinguish A from B，如：The twins are so alike that no one can distinguish one from the other.（这对孪生儿长得很像，无人能分辨出谁是谁。）另外，"雌"和"雄"分别为 female 和 male。

73. Her expression had become vacant，**as though her attention had drifted elsewhere**.（她变得神情茫然，似乎她的注意力已经飘到别的什么地方去了。）

本题测试 as if/as though 的用法。as if/as though 意为"好像，似乎，仿佛"，一般情况下，后面的从句要用虚拟语气，如：He looked at me as if I had come from another planet.（他看着我，就好像我是从另一个星球上来的。）

74. He had to kill the rattlesnake because its presence was **a potential danger to the people and animals at the farm**.（他不得不杀死那条响尾蛇，因为它的存在对农场里的人和动物来说都是一个潜在威胁。）

本题测试 potential 这个词的用法。potential 既可作名词，也可作形容词，在此句中为形容词，意为"潜在的，可能的"，如：The book is arguably a potential best seller.（该书或可成为一部畅销书。）此外，"对……来说是一种危险"用搭配 be a danger to … ，如：Smoking is a danger to health.（吸烟危害健康。）

75. **Believe it or not**, his discovery has created a stir in scientific circles.（信不信由你，

他的发现在科学界引起了轰动。）

本题测试 believe it or not 这个习惯用语。believe it or not 意为"信不信由你"，如：Believe it or not，we were left waiting in the rain for two hours. （信不信由你，我们一直冒雨等了两个小时。）

76. **As is shown by the growth rate of GDP in the last two decades**, China's reform and open policy is a great success. （正如近二十年来国内生产总值增长率表明的那样，中国的改革开放取得了巨大成功。）

本题测试 as 的一个用法。as 作为关系代词，可用来引导一个定语从句，修饰它前面或后面的整个句子，如：As is predicted by some newspapers, there will be a substantial cut in tax on imported cars in the coming year. （正如一些报纸预言的那样，明年进口汽车的关税将有大幅度的削减。）另外，"国内生产总值"英语为 GDP，"增长率"为 growth rate。

Practice Test 9

Part I Writing

Private Cars in Modern China

(Student's sample)

There are more and more private cars in modern China. People drive cars to their workplace, to schools, to shopping centers and so on. These cars have been playing a very important role in the lives of the city people.

Private cars can bring convenience and mobility to the owners. If more people buy cars, the automobile industry will develop very fast. And it will help the other industries grow rapidly, too. These industries include iron and steel production, energy and technological application, and so on. On the other hand, automobiles have also brought about a series of problems, such as pollution, traffic accidents, and energy consumption.

Although private cars have so many defects they still have a bright future. Because private cars are convenient and comfortable the automobile industry is developing very quickly in our country. Private cars will enter the common households in recent years, and there will be a further increase in the number of private cars in 21st century.

(Improved sample)

Private cars are more and more popular in modern China, **especially in the urban areas**. People drive cars to their workplace, to schools, to shopping centers and so on. Private cars **have been playing an increasingly important part** in the daily activities of the city people.

Private cars can bring convenience and mobility to the owners. If more people buy cars, the automobile industry will develop **dramatically**. **What's more**, the growth of the automobile industry can **trigger the boom of other important industries such as** iron and steel production, energy and technological application. On the other hand, automobiles have also **given rise to** a series of problems: pollution, traffic accidents, and energy consumption, **to name just a few, occur in the wake of automobiles**.

In spite of their weak points, private cars still own a bright future. **Because of the convenience and comfort in private cars and the rapid development of the automobile industry in our country**, private cars will enter the common households in recent years. **And the 21st century will surely witness a rapid increase in the number of private cars.**

Part II   Reading Comprehension (Skimming and Scanning)

1. **N**   这篇文章主要讨论全球定位系统的组成。

   主旨题。从各部分的小标题可以看到，前 3 个小标题介绍了全球定位系统的组成，后面部分介绍了全球定位系统的其他方面。该陈述不能概括全文的主旨，故判为错误。

2. **Y**   GPS 卫星就是从太空发送无线电信号的太空飞行器。

   细节题。该题目可根据 space 定位至小标题 Space Segment 部分的第一段。该段第二句的 The space vehicles 指的就是第一句中的 GPS satellites。

3. **N**   一个接收机最高的定位精确度可以达到米的水平。

   细节题。根据 accuracy 本题可以定位至第四个小标题 GPS Accuracy 下的部分。该段的最后一句表明 GPS 精确度可以达到厘米水平。题目表述与原文不符，故判为错误。

4. **NG**   GPS 接收机越贵就越精确。

   细节题。本题可定位至小标题 GPS Receivers 部分的第一段第二句。Prices range from ＄500－＄30,000，reflecting the accuracy and capabilities of the instruments 表明价格可以反映出接收机的精确度，但并不能因此判定接收机越贵越精确。

5.   **the User Segment**   全球定位系统的组成部分包括空间部分、监控部分和用户部分。

   细节题。该题目可以在原文的第二段直接找到答案。

6.   **tracking stations**   监控部分由分布在全世界的跟踪站系统组成。

   细节题。该题目可以在小标题 Control Segment 部分的第一段直接找到答案。

7.   **Navigation in three dimensions**   三维导航是全球定位系统的主要功能。

   细节题。该题目可以在小标题 User Segment 部分的第二段第一句直接找到答案。

8.   **mapping purposes**   中等价位的手提式或类似的设备很适合一些 GIS 绘图目的。

   细节题。根据 GIS 这一特殊字符串可以把该题目定位至小标题 Mapping 部分的最后一句，在此找到答案。

9.   **location，speed and time**   航空人员使用电子地图和 GPS 就能确定位置、速度和时间。

   细节题。根据 aviation personnel 可以把该题目定位至小标题 GPS and Policing 部分的第二段，在此找到答案。

10.   **facilitating the movement of people and vehicles** 大部分地方执法资源用于以安全的方式使人们和车辆的行动变得畅通。

   细节题。根据 law enforcement resources 可以把该题目定位至小标题 GPS and Policing 部分的第五段。从该段第二句中不难找到答案。

Part III　Listening Comprehension (35 minutes)

Section A

11. C	12. D	13. A	14. C	15. D
16. B	17. B	18. D	19. C	20. D
21. A	22. D	23. B	24. C	25. D

Section B

26. B	27. D	28. C	29. D	30. B
31. D	32. D	33. C	34. A	35. D

Section C

36. fill　　　　37. principal　　　38. fuel　　　　　39. instruments

40. waste　　　41. varies　　　　42. ice　　　　　43. abundance

44. They are scarcest where the ice is thick and unbroken, since these conditions offer few opportunities for the seal to come up to breathe the air he needs

45. Today it still brings in substantial financial returns

46. The furs, hides, blubber and oil of the seal bring in many millions of dollars a year

Part IV　Reading Comprehension (Reading in Depth)

Section A

47. compulsive surfers 超过44 000 000上网家庭中有一半多的人可被称为有网瘾的网民。

　　本题答案可以在第一段第一句中找到。该句告诉我们：有44 000 000多家庭上网，其中超过一半的人——即大约25 000 000人——可算得上是有网瘾的网民。

48. marital problems 网瘾的后果包括婚姻出现问题、学习不好、失去工作以及欠债。

　　本题答案可以在第一段中间一句找到：The consequences were severe：Many suffered from marital problems, failed in school or lost a job, and accumulated debt. 在这些后果当中空缺了"婚姻问题"这一项，所以答案是 marital problems。

49. A psychological disorder. 研究的迹象显示出一种心理失调。

　　本题答案可在第一段中找到。该段倒数第二句的前半部分明确告诉我们：The evidence points to a psychological disorder。

50. an uncontrollable desire 冲动控制失调的特点是无法控制做某件事的欲望。

　　本题答案可在第一段中找到。本段倒数第二句告诉我们在得知网瘾和心理失调有关后，研究人员进一步探查发现这些被调查人员的行为符合冲动控制失调的标准；冲动控制失调是精神疾病，特点是无法控制实施某一行为的欲望，而这一行为一旦实施，强烈的解脱感往往随之而来。所以答案就是 an uncontrollable desire。

51. Because the size and speed of the Internet will increase. 网瘾这种现象会越来越严重是因为因特网的规模和速度会增长。

　　本题答案可在第三段最后一句 Shapira 的话中找到。他说："但是我感觉随着因特网规模和速度的增长,这个问题会恶化。""这个问题"指的就是"网瘾"(Internet Addiction)。

Section B

52. B 归纳题。选项 A、C 和 D 都是文中提到的保护鱼类资源的措施,而选项 B"用拖网捕捞和张网捕捞"正是欧盟委员会报告中呼吁停止的。

53. C 词义理解题。pirate boats 本意为"海盗船",在文中的意思是"从事非法捕捞的船只"。故此题的正确答案为 C。

54. C 归纳题。选项 A、B 和 D 均为批评者认为在全世界范围内控制捕捞的计划不起作用的理由,只有选项 C"联合国的办事效率相当低"并非文章内容。

55. D 细节题。选项 A、B 和 C 都是文章内容,选项 D"联合国在北极水域也设立了管理机构"和第二段中"这些鱼向北迁徙,来到比较寒冷且无人管理的北极水域"相矛盾。故此题的正确答案为 D。

56. A 词义理解题。根据题意"……只能希望这样的管理不要太少,也不要太晚",可以排除选项 B"蒙古之类的国家"、选项 C"一些中美洲国家"和选项 D"进行灭绝性捕捞的人们",只有选项 A"海鲜"符合题意。

57. D 词义理解题。subjugation 意为"征服,使服从",只有选项 D 符合该词意思。

58. C 归纳题。在第一段第二句中,作者提到 power 这个词很容易使人们对它的性质、形式等产生误解;然后说明不应该将其理解成什么,而应该怎样理解,以澄清对这个词的误解。所以作者给 power 下定义是想避免人们产生种种误解。故此题的正确答案为 C。

59. B 推理题。该题涉及法律和权力之间的关系。文中第一段最后一句提到:法律的形成是 power 呈现出的最终形式,也就是说,法律是 power 的产物。故此题的正确答案为 B。

60. A 推理题。在文中第三段中作者提到:决不能仅仅从国家统治权方面和它所衍生的辅助权力方面来理解 power,而应该从动态的社会底层力量关系方面来理解,也就是说它产生于人民及社会力量关系的斗争中。故此题的正确答案为 A。

61. D 归纳题。在文章中,作者以客观的态度分析了 power 的性质、形式等,并澄清了对它的误解。在分析过程中,作者没有使用带有责备、怀疑、同情等感情色彩的词语。故此题的正确答案为 D。

Part V Error Correction (15 minutes)

62. 此行第一个 in 改为 on。concentrate on 为固定搭配,意思是"专注于",其中的 on 不能替换为 in。

63. child 前的 the 改为 a。本句中 child 一词是泛指,因此要用表示泛指某类人或事物的不定冠词 a,不能用表示特指的定冠词 the。

64. walk 改为 walking。本句中 walk 用作非谓语动词,when walking 在句子中作时间状语,因此要用 walk 的现在分词形式,不能用原形。

65. that 改为 which。此处的 which 用作关系代词,引导非限制性定语从句,that 只能引导限制性定语从句。

66. anyone develops 之间加 who,或将 develops 改为 developing。develop 一词在本句中不是谓语动词,而是和后面的两个词一起修饰其前面的中心词,因此应置于定语从句中或用现在分词形式。

67. but 改为 than。此处是一比较结构,比较的内容是 to have no visual information 和 (to have) something which results in conflict,而 but 表示意思的转折,因此要用连词 than。

68. 删除 fact 前的 the。in fact 是固定搭配,意思是"事实上,实际上",中间不能加 the。

69. excluded 改为 included。exclude 意思是"不包括",include 意思是"包括"。根据上下文意思,宇航员也会有"晕动病",因此能治疗这种病的药应该被包括在为航天所准备的药箱中,而不是被排除在外。

70. moreover 改为 however。moreover 意为"而且",表示意思的递进;however 意为"然而",表示意思的转折。此处表示句意的转折,因此要用 however。

71. effected 改为 affected。effect 是名词,意思是"结果,效果";affect 是动词,意思是"影响",在句子中是被动态。

Part VI Translation

72. Nothing is more damaging to a nation than **failure to properly educate its children**.(对一个国家来说,没有什么比未能教育好孩子危害更大。)

本题测试抽象名词后用不定式来加以解释的语法现象。本题中抽象名词 failure 和前面的 nothing 相对应,后用不定式加以解释。再如:This only strengthens his determination to realize his dream.(这更增强了他实现自己梦想的决心。)

73. It would be fatal for the nation to overlook the urgency of the moment and **to underestimate the determination of the Blacks**.(忽视当前形势的紧急、低估黑人的决心对国家来说是致命的。)

本题测试 underestimate 这个单词。estimate 意为"估计",underestimate 意为"低估",反义词 overestimate 意为"高估"。此外,该部分和前面的不定式是并列的,也要采用不定式形式。

74. Stronger adaptability to market changes, lower management costs and higher labor intensity have **ensured these companies comparative advantages** and, consequently, competitiveness in the global market.(对市场变化较强的适应能力、较低的管理成本以及较高的劳动密集度确保这些公司具有相对优势,因此它们在全球市场上有竞争力。)

本题测试 ensure 的用法。ensure 意为"确保,保证,担保",后面可跟双宾语,如:These pills should ensure you a good night's sleep.(服下这些药丸可保你睡一宿好觉。)此外,"相对优势"可译为 comparative advantages。

75. At no time in history has there been **such a mass migration of people from country-**

side to city as is happening now.（历史上从没有像今天这样有大批人口从农村移居到城市。）

本题测试 migration 这个单词。migration 意为"移居，迁徙"，表示从一个地方迁移到另一个地方，不一定非要从一国到另一国；通常还用来指鸟类等的迁徙，如：He studies the migration of birds.（他研究鸟类的迁徙。）

76. **Credit-card purchases via the Internet** are lowering costs and reducing inventories for America's leading companies as the information technology industry mushrooms.（在信息技术业蓬勃发展的形势下，用信用卡在网上购物有助于美国各大公司降低成本、减少库存。）

本题测试 via 的用法。via 意为"经由；通过"，如：I can send him a note via the internal mail system.（我可以通过内部通讯系统给他发个通知。）

Practice Test 10

Part I Writing

College Students' Way of Spending Summer Vacation

(Student's sample)

College students usually stayed at home in summer vacation ten years ago. Some of them studied their lessons or helped their parents with housework. Others only idled the time away.

But things have changed greatly in recent years. There are more students who go traveling and do social investigation during summer vacation and fewer students who stay at home.

The reasons for the changes are as follows: first, with the development of economy, many people have become rich. Students can get financial support from their parents for traveling. Second, tourism has greatly developed in recent years and many new scenic spots have been built. Third, our country is paying more attention to the quality education and the government is encouraging the college students to do social investigations. Thanks to these improved situations college students have greatly enriched their ways of spending summer vacation.

(Improved sample)

College students usually stayed at home in their summer vacations ten years ago. Studying their lessons, helping their parents with housework, or even idling their time away, **they generally spent their summer vacation in a rather tedious way**.

But in recent years college students **have greatly changed their ways of** spending summer vacation. Some of them go traveling or do social investigations. Others **occupy themselves with part-time jobs** during summer vacation.

There are several reasons for the changes. Firstly, many families become rich with the economic progress, **which makes it financially possible for college students to go traveling. Secondly**, since tourism has greatly developed, many new scenic spots have been built in our country. **This booming tourism has provided college students with good chances to enjoy the beautiful scenery. In addition**, the government of our country **has been paying** more attention to quality-oriented education and encouraging college students to do investigations **on the rapid development in both urban and rural areas.** Thanks to these improved situations college students have greatly enriched their ways of spending summer vacation.

Part II Reading Comprehension (Skimming and Scanning)

1. **Y** 最初,作者认为到新西兰旅游不值所出的价钱。

   细节题。从第一段的第二句可知,当作者考虑到整个预算时,觉得选择新西兰作为旅游目的地有点 crazy,这与题目的表述是一致的。故此题被判为正确。

2. **NG** 在新西兰没有人工游乐场。

   细节题。从小标题 Heaven on the Earth 下第一段第二句 You don't need contrived amusement parks or fenced-off scenic areas 可知,文章只提到了作者的观点,至于新西兰是否有人工游乐场,根据原文无法判断。

3. **N** 作者在新西兰最喜欢做的事情是外出散步。

   细节题。在小标题 Heaven on the Earth 下的第二段中作者确实提及喜欢 walking outside,但在下一段中又说 The west coast beaches attracted me most,可知题目表述与原文不符,故判为错误。

4. **N** 所有的游客信息中心都能预订住宿。

   细节题。从小标题 Visitor Information Center 下的第三段可知 Most Visitor Information Centers can make reservations for accommodation,题目中的 all 与原文的 most 不符,所以该陈述是错误的。

5. **international car rental companies** Herz、Avis 和 Budget 是国际汽车租赁公司的名字。

   细节题。根据 Herz、Avis 和 Budget 本题可快速定位至小标题 Visitor Information Center 下的第一段。根据原文不难填出答案。

6. **information provided here** 由于 VIN 是一个官方机构,这里提供的信息是可靠的。

   细节题。根据 VIN 本题可快速定位至小标题 Visitor Information Center 下的第四段。可以从该段第二句中找到答案。

7. **unpretentious and generous** 饮食反映出新西兰人有一种谦虚慷慨的精神。

   细节题。本题可快速定位至小标题 Gourmet Food 下。该部分的第二句 The food reflects the unpretentious, generous spirit of the New Zealanders 为该题目提供了答案。

8. **natural materials that can be recycled** 在新西兰包装通常是由可循环利用的天然材料制成的。

   细节题。本题的答案可在小标题 Sense of Environment 下的段落中的最后一句里找到。

9. **simple and kind** 新西兰人的性格特点是简单且友善。

   细节题。题目的内容可在小标题 Simple-hearted New Zealanders 下第一段中找到。

10. **the Lost-and-Found** 最后,作者在失物认领处找到了丢失的钥匙。

细节题。本题可在文章倒数第二段中找到相关内容。

Part III   Listening Comprehension (35 minutes)

Section A

11. B	12. A	13. B	14. C	15. A
16. D	17. A	18. C	19. B	20. D
21. C	22. C	23. A	24. C	25. D

Section B

| 26. C | 27. D | 28. C | 29. B | 30. C |
| 31. C | 32. B | 33. C | 34. A | 35. D |

Section C

36. kindergarten   37. attend   38. elementary   39. junior
40. advanced   41. interests   42. choose   43. average

44. Students choose a major subject and take many courses in this subject

45. Then the students may go on to graduate school and，with a year or two of further study，they can get a master's degree

46. Usually after another four or five years of study and research，they may get a still higher degree such as doctor of philosophy

Part IV   Reading Comprehension (Reading in Depth)

Section A

47. Twenty years.   罗伯特和他的妻子珍妮已经结婚 20 年了。
本题答案可在第一段中找到。该段第三句告诉我们罗伯特和他的妻子珍妮刚刚庆祝过 20 年的甜蜜婚姻生活，因此可知他们已经结婚 20 年了。

48. mortgage payments   罗伯特是通过抵押贷款购买房子的。
本题答案可在第一段中找到。该段第四句告诉我们罗伯特一家住在费城一个绿树成荫的郊区，房子虽不太大但很有品味，再偿还短短几年的抵押贷款，房子就完完全全归他们所有了。因此可知罗伯特是通过抵押贷款购买房子的。

49. His nine-year-old son.   在罗伯特的 3 个孩子当中，9 岁的儿子在学习上有困难。
本题答案可在第二段中找到。第一段的结尾告诉我们罗伯特和珍妮有 3 个孩子，分别为 17 岁、15 岁和 9 岁，都曾是他们的欢乐之源。但是最近一段时间孩子们出现了问题。第二段第二句明确告诉我们罗伯特 9 岁的儿子从一年级开始学习就很吃力，在学习上确实有困难。

50. Reducing the number of employees in a company.   downsizing 意为"缩小规模"，即裁员。
downsizing 一词出现在第二段倒数第四句。它由 down 加上 size 组成，另外，根据它所出现的句子以及上下文，即"最近出现了 downsizing 的传言，罗伯特越来越担心家庭未来的财力,3 份上大学的费用还在等着,以前也没有为将来的退休存钱"等,可猜测出 downsizing 的意思为"裁员",罗伯特担心因此而失业。

51. **Because he was not prepared for the misfortunes.** 罗伯特对将来感到茫然是因为他没有料到会有这么多挫折,有点措手不及。

本题答案可在第三段中找到。第二段具体说明了罗伯特面临的各种各样的困难,第三段明确告诉我们:在 47 岁时,罗伯特没有准备好应对生活中看似平常的不幸,他感到迷失了自己,以前曾给他带来满足感的生活现在让他感到空虚。

Section B

52. **D** 细节题。选项 A、B 和 C 都符合文中第一段的内容:这一软件能侦破短信、电子邮件和聊天室等网上通讯中的谎言;选项 D"通讯交流"内容太宽泛。故此题的正确答案为 D。

53. **D** 细节题。选项 A、B 和 C 与文章的内容一致,而选项 D 和第四段内容不符,因为研究人员目前只研究学生和教职工的谎话,这套系统是否能分析"大"谎还是未知数。故此题的正确答案为 D。

54. **A** 细节题。第三段比较了欺骗信息和诚实信息的不同,只有选项 A 与文章内容不符,因为说谎者多用第三人称,较少用第一人称。故此题的正确答案为 A。

55. **D** 词义理解题。con artist 意为"行骗老手,骗术专家",只有选项 D 符合这一词义。

56. **B** 语义理解题。文章最后一句话意为"因特网很快就要摆脱的或许不仅是谎言,还有蹩脚的借口",只有选项 B 符合这句话的意思。

57. **D** 细节题。Google Earth 的定义在第一段开头就已给出,它是"集卫星图像、航拍图像和地图搜索功能于一身的免费软件",所以选项 D 较完整地概括了它的作用。

58. **A** 词义理解题。debut 本义为"演员、运动员首次亮相或初次登台",文中指 Google Earth 第一次公开亮相。故此题的正确答案为 A。

59. **C** 归纳题。文中第四段提到美国安全专家对 Google Earth 的态度:把它视为对安全的威胁看来是不对的,因为 Google 提供的这些图像都可以直接从图像公司及其他途径获得。故此题的正确答案为 C。

60. **A** 细节题。选项 B、C 和 D 与文章的内容一致,而选项 A"Google Earth 显示了美国的一些重要情报"并非文章内容。故此题的正确答案为 A。

61. **C** 归纳题。文章首先简要介绍了 Google Earth 的功能,然后较为详细地说明了它自首推以来受到的关注:一些国家的官员认为它可能会威胁一个国家的安全。只有选项 C 形象地归纳出了文章的主要内容。

Part V Error Correction (15 minutes)

62. 删除 to。作 make 宾语补足语的动词不定式不带 to。

63. 删除 can,或将 can 改为 should。recommend 后面的宾语从句用虚拟语气,其动词应为动词原形或 should 加动词原形。

64. even 后加 if。even if 的意思是"即使",even 的意思是"甚至"。本句意思是"即使面试者不问你……",因此要用 even if。

65. with 改为 for。for the reason 意思是"因为某种原因",是固定搭配,介词不能换成 with。

66. are 改为 were。根据句意,本条件句应为虚拟语气,而不是真实条件句。

67. have 改为 having。have 和 tell 是平行成分,在形式上应保持一致,因此 have 应改为 having。

68. for 改为 to。add sth. to sth. 是固定搭配,介词不能随便更改。

69. if 改为 unless。本句意思是:"不要责备对方,除非你不想要这份工作"。如果用 if,意思正好相反。

70. asking 改为 asked。这里表示被动含义,因此要用 ask 的被动形式。

71. had 改为 have。根据全文的时态脉络,这里应该用现在完成时,而不是过去完成时。

Part VI   Translation

72. **After more than 40 years of parallel development**, the information and life sciences — computing and biology — are fusing into a single, powerful force that is laying the foundation for the biotech century.(经过 40 多年齐头并进的发展,信息技术与生命科学——即计算机科学与生物学——正在融合为一股强大的力量,为生物技术世纪奠定基础。)

本题测试 parallel 这个单词。parallel 既可作形容词,也可作名词和动词。在此句中 parallel 为形容词,意为"平行的,并列的",如:The road and the railway are parallel to each other.(这条公路与铁路平行。)

73. He **suffered a succession of blows** last year: his company went bankrupt; his wife divorced him.(去年他遭受了一个又一个打击:公司破产,妻子与他离婚。)

本题测试 suffer 和 succession 两个单词的用法。suffer 意为"经历或遭受(不愉快之事)"时,是及物动词,直接跟宾语,如:They suffered huge losses in the financial crisis.(他们在金融危机中损失惨重。)succession 意为"一连串,接二连三,一系列",如:Last week we had a succession of victories in the football matches.(上个星期我们在足球赛中频频获胜。)

74. Three section managers wanted to **fill the vacant position** after the president resigned for the sake of his health.(在总裁为调养身体辞职后,三个部门经理都想填补这一空缺。)

本题测试 vacant 这个单词的用法。vacant 为形容词,意为"空的,没人占用的,(职位)空缺的",如:Is that room of yours still vacant?(你的那间房仍然空着吗?)He applied for a vacant post in the company.(他申请该公司的一个空缺职位。)此外,vacant 的名词形式为 vacancy,意为"空缺,空职",如 We have a vacancy for a typist.(我们缺一个打字员。)"填补空缺"也可直接译为 fill the vacancy。

75. The teacher gave a comprehensive analysis of **the positive and negative influences on**

Chinese industries when China entered WTO.（老师全面分析了加入世贸组织对中国各行业的正面和负面影响。）

本题测试 positive 和 negative 这两个反义词。positive 作形容词时，其中一种意思为"正面的，积极的，有益的，建设性的"，如：They put forward some positive suggestions.（他们提出一些建设性的意见。）此时，negative 为 positive 的反义词，意为"负面的，消极的，无益的"，如：He has a very negative attitude to his work.（他的工作态度很消极。）

76. The jury eventually decided that Mary was guilty and she **was sentenced to three years' imprisonment**.（最后陪审团裁定玛丽有罪，她被判处三年有期徒刑。）

本题测试 be sentenced to ... years' imprisonment 这个表达法，它的意思是"被判处……年有期徒刑"。若是"终身监禁"，可译为 be sentenced to life imprisonment。

PART THREE

TAPESCRIPT

Practice Test 1

Directions: *In this section, you will hear 8 short conversations and 2 long conversations. At the end of each conversation, one or more questions will be asked about what was said. Both the conversation and the questions will be spoken only once. After each question there will be a pause. During the pause, you must read the four choices marked A), B), C) and D), and decide which is the best answer. Then mark the corresponding letter on* **Answer Sheet 2** *with a single line through the centre.*

11. W：In this city there are many kinds of transportation available. Which do you use，Bob?

    M：The buses are so crowded，especially during the rush hours，so I usually take the subway. It's faster and there's less chance of a traffic jam.

    Q：Why does Bob prefer to take the subway?

12. W：Is there any machine translation software that can make our job easier?

    M：Well，we've got several. But I don't think they can turn out any translation that is up to our standard. In fact，I prefer doing it all by myself to revising machine translated texts.

    Q：What does the man mean?

13. W：Tom，how did your football team do in June and July?

    M：We won four times in June and twice in July，lost six times altogether，and tied three times in June and five times in July.

    Q：How many times did they tie altogether?

14. W：Dr. Harrington，as a sociologist what do you think the government should do to help strengthen the marriage bond and reduce divorce rates?

    M：I don't think government policy has caused divorce，and I don't think government policy can make a good marriage. But the climate of a society affects both.

    Q：What does Dr. Harrington mean?

15. W：I'm afraid Dr. Cahill won't be able to see you. His appointment book is filled for the next week.

M: Oh, but I don't have to see him. I'll just leave my teeth in his office and he can look at them when he has time. They are false!

Q: What is Dr. Cahill?

16. W: Why do we always have to argue about money? I would rather go out and spend it all so that we wouldn't have to argue about it.

M: Of course, you'd like to go spending all the money; you don't spend five days a week in a factory. Besides, if it wasn't money, you'd argue about something else; I think you enjoy arguments.

Q: According to the man, which statement best describes the woman?

17. W: I am sorry I did not ask for your preferences before ordering the meal. If you have any dietary restrictions, please tell me and I will change the menu.

M: I suppose no change will be called for. None of us here is a vegetarian, and only one has a dislike for poultry. So practically any kind of food arrangement will be fine for us as a team, as long as there is plenty for us to eat and drink.

Q: What do we learn from the conversation?

18. W: And after that program, we'll have Saturday's Feature Film and then the 10 o'clock news.

M: Good evening, everybody. Tonight we start with the story about the Old Roman Village.

Q: What is this?

Now you'll hear two long conversations.
Conversation One

M: I suppose you speak Japanese?

W: No, I'm Chinese.

M: Yeah, but you look Japanese! Do you speak Korean? You look Korean too.

W: (Sigh) Well, do you speak German?

M: No, I'm Italian. What does Italy have to do with Germany? They are culturally and philosophically different. Besides, we don't look alike at all!

W: To me you do. I've lived here long enough to know, but my mother wouldn't be able to tell you and David apart.

M: That's ridiculous. David's got light brown hair and I've got jet-black hair. And he has brown eyes and mine are green.

W: Yes, but those are not features we look for. We all have black hair and dark brown eyes, so we aren't used to using hair and eye color to distinguish people. We speak about skin-tone and the size of people's eyes. So, you are all pale and have big eyes, so you all look the same.

M: That's amazing! And we think all Asians look alike. So you don't look alike to each other? I wonder if Africans use different features to distinguish each other.

W: For sure they do. As our own societies are special to ourselves, so are others to themselves. It's pure ignorance to think that other races, societies and nations are less intelligent or refined than our own. Each has developed intelligence for its own environment.

M: Yeah, I heard that Australian aborigines can orient themselves in the desert by the sun and stars alone and tell where underground yams are growing. I can't even go to my aunt's house without getting totally disoriented! But instead of yams I can make a great cheese!

W: That stuff's disgusting! How can you stand the smell of the cheese?

M: Ah! Look who's making culturally ignorant statements here!

Questions 19 to 22 are based on the conversation you have just heard.

19. What are the two speakers discussing?
20. Where is the woman from?
21. How can Australian aborigines orient themselves in the desert?
22. Why does the woman dislike cheese?

Conversation Two

W: Mike! Look at the floor!

M: What's wrong with it?

W: What's wrong with it? It's filthy!

M: Oh ...

W: It's filthy because you never wipe your shoes.

M: Sorry, love.

W: What are you looking for now?

M: My cigarettes.

W: Well, they are not here. They are in the dustbin.

M: In the dustbin! Why?

W: Because there's cigarette ash on every carpet in the house. Anyway, cigarettes are a waste of money.

M: Maybe they are, but I earn the money! It doesn't grow on trees, you know. I work eight hours a day, remember?

W: Well, what about my money then?

M: What do you mean "your money"? You don't go out to work, do you?

W: No, I don't go out to work. I work fifteen hours a day ... here!

M：Well，housework is different ...

W：Oh，I see ... so housework is different，is it? Housework doesn't matter. Well，you do it then.

M：Hey，wait a minute，Pat，Pat ...

Questions 23 to 25 are based on the conversation you have just heard.

23．What's the relationship between the two speakers?

24．Where are the man's cigarettes?

25．What is the man's attitude towards housework?

Section B

Directions: *In this section，you will hear 3 short passages. At the end of each passage, you will hear some questions. Both the passage and the questions will be spoken only once. After you hear a question，you must choose the best answer from the four choices marked A)，B)，C) and D). Then mark the corresponding letter on* **Answer Sheet 2** *with a single line through the centre.*

Passage One

In order to learn a foreign language well，it is necessary to overcome the fear of making mistakes. If the primary goal of language use is communication，then mistakes are secondary considerations that may be dealt with gradually as awareness of those mistakes increases. On the other hand，students should not ignore their mistakes. The language learner may observe how native speakers express themselves，and in what way native expressions differ from the way the learner might say them.

For example，a Spanish speaker who has been saying "I do it" to express willing-ness to do something in the immediate future，could，by interacting with native speak-ers of English，observe that native speakers actually say "I'll do it." The resulting difference can serve as a basis for the student to change his way of using the present tense in English. But a student who is unwilling to interact in the first place would lose this opportunity to learn by trial and error.

Questions 26 to 29 are based on the passage you have just heard.

26．How can language learners reduce the number of their mistakes?

27．According to the passage，which of the following is true as to foreign students who do not interact with native speakers?

28．According to the passage，foreign language students should not worry too much about making mistakes. Why?

29．What is the speaker's conclusion about the function of mistakes in foreign language learning?

Passage Two

You may laugh at the idea of an emotional cow. But, the latest research suggests that animals might have feelings just like ours.

New research suggests that animals have far more complex understanding and social skills than we thought. That's the message from a meeting on animal sentience held in London last week.

A team of British scientists there reported that when sheep were isolated from their flock, they experienced stress. This can be measured by increases in heart rate, stress hormones and bleating. And showing them pictures of familiar sheep faces reduced their stress.

In another research, scientists found that cows, too, could recognize a familiar face. And they often form long-lasting, co-operative partnerships. Other research involved offering pigs a choice of two feeding stalls. They can remember being shut in one for several hours previously, and will avoid it. They will go directly for the one they were released from.

None of these findings proves that animals feel pain, or joy, in the same way that humans do. There is no way of testing their subjective experience.

However, scientists said that all the evidence suggested that their brains were, at the very least, aware of what has happened in the past. They can act on that experience in the future.

That awareness should arouse some respect from humans, some animal welfare scientists have said.

Questions 30 to 32 are based on the passage you have just heard.

30. What do pigs tend to do when given a choice of two feeding stalls?
31. What can we learn from the scientists' research about cows?
32. According to the passage, what can be inferred about animals?

Passage Three

Why do people smoke? One reason is that people become addicted to cigarettes. To be addicted means that your body comes to need them. The addictive substance in cigarettes is nicotine. When people smoke the nicotine goes right into the blood stream and makes people feel relaxed. A smoker's body gets accustomed to the nicotine and if he stops smoking he feels nervous. Many smokers try to stop smoking but because of the addiction to nicotine they feel so uncomfortable that they often find it too difficult to stop.

Another reason is that people simply enjoy smoking and what it symbolizes. Having a cigarette for many people means taking a break. For some people smoking becomes part of certain social custom, for example, the cigarette after dinner. Many people enjoy smoking because it gives them something to do with their hands. Reaching for a cigarette, lighting it, flicking the ashes are especially comforting in situations where a person feels tense.

Many people also like the taste of tar in cigarettes. However, it is the tar that causes cancer. While governments and health experts have tried to get people to give up smoking entirely, cigarette manufacturers have tried to keep selling them by producing cigarettes with less tar. Many people in western countries have welcomed these cigarettes since they find it hard to stop smoking but want to reduce the risk to their health.

Questions 33 to 35 are based on the passage you have just heard.

33. Why do so many people become addicted to cigarettes?
34. Which of the following is NOT what smoking symbolizes?
35. What CAN'T we infer from the passage?

Section C
Directions: *In this section, you will hear a passage three times. When the passage is read for the first time, you should listen carefully for its general idea. When the passage is read for the second time, you are required to fill in the blanks numbered from 36 to 43 with the exact words you have just heard. For blanks numbered from 44 to 46 you are required to fill in the missing information. For these blanks, you can either use the exact words you have just heard or write down the main points in your own words. Finally, when the passage is read for the third time, you should check what you have written.*

Scientists say they have (36) **conclusive** evidence that jogging is good for people. This latest European research (37) **counters** headline-making stories about people who die of a heart attack while running on the (38) **pavement**. Danish researchers (39)**confirm** that those who jog regularly are far less likely to die prematurely than those who do not. Their work, (40) **published** in last Saturday's issue of the *British Medical* (41) *Journal*, sifted through data from a Copenhagen heart study. The study covered more than 4,500 men (42)**aged** 20 to 79 with no history of cardiac problems. The group was followed from mid-1970s until November 1998. It is found that (43)**persistent** joggers were nearly two and a half times less likely to die prematurely than non-joggers. (44) **The team looked through all the factors in lifestyle**, including smoking, drinking, diabetes, education and household income to try to explain this big difference in mortality.

(45) **But they found no evidence to link regular jogging with early death.** (46) **Finally the researchers concluded that a vigorous activity such as jogging is associated with a beneficial effect on mortality.**

Practice Test 2

Section A

Directions: *In this section, you will hear 8 short conversations and 2 long conversations. At the end of each conversation, one or more questions will be asked about what was said. Both the conversation and the questions will be spoken only once. After each question there will be a pause. During the pause, you must read the four choices marked A), B), C) and D), and decide which is the best answer. Then mark the corresponding letter on **Answer Sheet 2** with a single line through the centre.*

11. M: How could you expect someone to step into this bathtub and take a shower when the water tap is out of order?
    W: I'm awfully sorry to hear that, sir. What's the room number, please?
    Q: Why is the man complaining?

12 M: We have to admit everybody has limitations. No one is perfect.
    W: Yes, I quite agree. Some recent brain research shows that our view of the world is limited by our genes and the experiences we've had.
    Q: Why is our view of the world limited according to the conversation?

13 W: What time are meals served?
    M: We serve breakfast from 7 to 10, lunch from 12 to 2:30 and dinner from 5 to 8:30.
    Q: If the woman gets up at nine, will she still be able to catch breakfast?

14. W: This doesn't look at all familiar. We must be lost. We'd better get some directions.
    M: Let's pull in here. While I'm filling the tank, you ask about the directions and get me a soft drink.
    Q: Where will the man and woman go for assistance?

15. W: I'd like to enroll in the free seminar you advertised on your website — the one on applying to a graduate school.
    M: I see. But if you looked carefully, the ad said that you have to be a senior to be eligible to participate. Do you qualify?
    Q: What does the man want to know?

16. M: That new position requires a lot of references. I guess the one that my professor wrote for me last year should be fine. Don't you think so?
    W: It's a little dated though. You might need to submit a more current one.
    Q: What is the woman suggesting the man do?

17. W: Would you rather sit over here, facing the engine? Some people get train sick with their back to the engine.

M: It doesn't make any difference to a seasoned traveler like me. I get seasick sometimes when the sea is very rough, but I'm never train sick.

Q: Where does this conversation most probably take place?

18. W: In the old days, people were proud of their work and built things to last.

M: Nowadays you are lucky if they don't fall apart before you get them back home.

Q: How do the man and woman feel about products made nowadays?

Now you'll hear two long conversations.

Conversation One

M: Hamilton Police Station. Can I help you?

W: Yes. It's about my daughter, Kathy. She went to school this morning but hasn't been back yet and it's 5:30 now.

M: Just a moment, Mrs. ...?

W: Mrs. Strong, Kate Strong, 203 Church Street.

M: Thank you. Now Mrs. Strong, what exactly is the matter?

W: Well, Kathy left home at 8:30 this morning, but just now her teacher phoned me and asked why Kathy didn't go to school.

M: Perhaps she went to a friend's home. Have you asked your neighbors?

W: Yes, I've called all the neighbors and their children were all back home.

M: I see. Now, let's have some details. How old is Kathy?

W: She's 7 years old.

M: And what's she wearing?

W: A brown coat, black shoes, and a yellow skirt. Yes, that's right.

M: We'll do our best to find her, Mrs. Strong. Please try not to worry.

Questions 19 to 22 are based on the conversation you have just heard.

19. Where does this conversation most probably take place?

20. Who phoned Mrs. Strong and told her Kathy didn't go to school?

21. How long has Kathy been away from home?

22. What's the color of Kathy's coat?

Conversation Two

W: Carl, did I tell you I have enough money to study in the United States?

M: That's wonderful. It's an exciting opportunity for you. What kind of courses will you take?

W: Computer science. I'll enroll in a computer school.

M: Which program will you enter?

W: Probably in a school at San Diego. I already have an application.

M: Which state is San Diego in? I can't remember.

W: It's in the southern part of California. San Diego is a nice city.

M: Which kind of housing will you choose?

W: One of my relatives is living near San Diego. I'll probably stay with him.

M: Teresa stayed in San Diego. She's studying there until last December.

W: Who is Teresa?

M: She's an acquaintance of mine. You should get in touch with her.

W: I'd like to get her advice. What number should I call her?

M: I can't remember. I'll bring it to school tomorrow, OK?

W: Great. Oh, the lunch break is finished. Time to go back to class.

Questions 23 to 25 are based on the conversation you have just heard.

23. Where will the woman go to make her further study?

24. What course will the woman take?

25. What is the relationship between the two speakers?

Section B

Directions: *In this section, you will hear 3 short passages. At the end of each passage, you will hear some questions. Both the passage and the questions will be spoken only once. After you hear a question, you must choose the best answer from the four choices marked A), B), C) and D). Then mark the corresponding letter on **Answer Sheet 2** with a single line through the centre.*

Passage One

Hotels today are quite different from those of the past. People who stay in them are generally traveling for business, or they are touring or on vacation. So hotels are designed mainly to meet the needs of one of these two groups of people. Hotels designed for business people are known as commercial, or transient, hotels. Hotels for people on vacation are called vacation, or resort, hotels.

Transient hotels are usually located in the business section of town, while resort hotels may be at the seashore, on a mountain lake, or in the desert.

In addition to these two main types, there is a third type of hotel, called a residential hotel. This is designed to meet the needs of people who want to live in a hotel.

Inns and hotels are located in nearly every population center in the world. In the United States alone there are about thirty thousand. Some hotels have as few as ten rooms, others have several hundred. Among the largest hotels in the world today are the Conrad Hilton in Chicago, Illinois, and the Russia in Moscow, each with about three thousand rooms.

In every hotel, travelers find small single rooms meant for the use of one person; larger double rooms for the use of two people; and arrangements of two or more rooms, called suites, which can be used by a group of persons traveling together.

Questions 26 to 29 are based on the passage you have just heard.

26. Which of the following is NOT one of the usual purposes of people who stay in hotels today?
27. What are the three types of hotels mentioned in the passage?
28. How many hotels are there in the United States?
29. Which of the following about a suite is true?

Passage Two

A study conducted on more than 68,000 middle-aged US women suggests that females who don't get enough sleep may end up adding some extra pounds over years. Researchers followed 68,183 middle-aged women for 16 years and found that those who slept 5 hours or less per night were one third more likely to gain weight than those who slept for 7 hours.

Moreover, researchers found that the weight gain was increasing largely with some women even gaining 33 pounds or more. The associations between sleep duration and weight gain persisted even after controlling for factors such as physical activity and calorie consumption in both groups. The findings, presented earlier this year at a medical conference and published in the *American Journal of Epidemiology*, furthers the evidence that sleep habits affect a person's weight.

The exact reasons for association between sleep duration and weight gain aren't clear but some research suggests that a sleep lack alters hormones involved in appetite control and metabolism. Also it's possible that people who sleep fewer hours either eat more or, because of fatigue, exercise less often. The research was led by Dr. Sanjay R. Patel of Western Case Reserve University in Cleveland.

Questions 30 to 32 are based on the passage you have just heard.

30. Which of the following statements is true according to the passage?
31. What's the main idea of the passage?
32. Which of the following is NOT the reason why females sleeping fewer hours are more likely to gain weight?

Passage Three

For thousands of millions of years the moon has been going round the earth. During this time, the moon has been the only satellite of the earth. Today, however, the earth has many other satellites, all made by man. These man-made satellites are very much smaller than the moon. However, some of them will still be going round the earth thousands of years from now.

Man-made satellites do not fall because they are going too fast to do so. As they speed along, they tend to go straight off into space. The pull of the earth, or its gravity, keeps them from doing this. As a result, they travel in an orbit round the earth.

If a man-made satellite travels at a certain height, it can keep going on and on round the earth, just like the moon. This is because it is above the atmosphere, and there is nothing to slow it down. If it travels lower than that, it will be slowed down so much that it will fall to earth.

Questions 33 to 35 are based on the passage you have just heard.

33. What keeps a man-made satellite from going straight off into space?
34. Why can man-made satellites travel in an orbit round the earth?
35. What will happen if a man-made satellite travels in the atmosphere?

Section C

Directions: *In this section, you will hear a passage three times. When the passage is read for the first time, you should listen carefully for its general idea. When the passage is read for the second time, you are required to fill in the blanks numbered from 36 to 43 with the exact words you have just heard. For blanks numbered from 44 to 46 you are required to fill in the missing information. For these blanks, you can either use the exact words you have just heard or write down the main points in your own words. Finally, when the passage is read for the third time, you should check what you have written.*

Most of the waiters, waitresses, and cooks in restaurants are not employed on a full-time (36) **basis**. If they were full-time employees, they would (37) **receive** at least the (38) **minimum** wage plus benefits such as the cost of health, dental, life (39) **insurances** and a saving plan for (40) **retirement**. But for the many who are part-time employees and (41) **obtain** no additional benefits, (42) **tipping** helps defray the additional costs that the part-time employee faces for the outside (43) **purchase** of such benefits. (44) **Tipping is expected in most restaurants in the United States unless the waiter's service is exceptionally poor.** Usually the amount of tip ranges from 10% to 15% of the consumption. (45) **If you find a waiter's service to be poor, you must indicate that during the**

course of your meal, not when you are paying the bill. （46）**Some restaurants also make a practice of automatically including a 15% tip in the bill for large parties of people eating together.** If this is the case，the menu will read "includes tax and gratuity."

Practice Test 3

Section A

Directions: *In this section, you will hear 8 short conversations and 2 long conversations. At the end of each conversation, one or more questions will be asked about what was said. Both the conversation and the questions will be spoken only once. After each question there will be a pause. During the pause, you must read the four choices marked A), B), C) and D), and decide which is the best answer. Then mark the corresponding letter on **Answer Sheet 2** with a single line through the centre.*

11. M: Students always read poetry in the coffee house in the corner near the college. Would you like to go there with me?

    W: I'd love to, thanks. That's where I've been wanting to go for a long time.

    Q: Where would the woman like to go?

12. W: I'm very angry with Tommy! He kicked a football through the bedroom window. There was broken glass everywhere.

    M: I hope no one was hurt.

    Q: What is the man concerned about?

13 W: It is said that men have always been the slaves of their habits.

    M: Yes, I agree, once you've got a habit, it's hard to break it. However, human beings are capable of breaking old habits and forming new ones. Of course that requires us to keep practicing new skills.

    Q: What can we learn from this conversation?

14. M: How long will I have to stay out of school?

    W: That depends. You still have a fever. Let me take your pulse and blood pressure.

    Q: What is the woman's occupation?

15. M: Which dress do you plan to wear?

    W: I like the black one, and it fits me better, but it's probably too dressy. I suppose I'll wear the red one.

    Q: Why doesn't the woman wear the black dress?

16. W: There are so many children at the school. I wonder how the teacher keeps track of them.

    M: I used to get cold feet at the thought of teaching a class of 100. That's a fact.

    Q: What is the man's attitude toward teaching big classes?

17. M: That night was quite an experience.

    W: You're right. It's lucky my daughter was still awake studying when the fire broke out. Her screaming woke us all up.

Q: What happened that night?

18. M: I'm the manager. What seems to be the trouble, madam?

W: Well, you may come and have a look yourself. The room isn't properly vacuumed. The bathtub is dirty, and the tap is dripping. What do you say to all this?

Q: What is the man doing?

Now you'll hear two long conversations.

Conversation One

M: So how did the interview go?

W: It turned out very well. I thought it was going to be a very formal interview, but as it turned out I just went along and met the television producer and he took me out for lunch.

M: Really? What did he ask you about?

W: Well, he asked me, um — about what I'd done before and the job I'd had before and whether I have a degree and — just about my qualifications and things like that. And ... and then he went on to ask me about the documentaries themselves and whether I'd be interested in doing the kind of research that was involved.

M: So what did you say?

W: Well, I said, yes, obviously I was fairly interested in energy ... um because I'd spent a lot of time last year, in fact, going round places finding out about various different kinds of energy. And I'd been to a center for alternative technology, for example, and I'd spent some time there finding out about wind power and solar power and other things like that.

M: Yeah, what are they about then, these documentaries?

W: Well, they're going to cover all kinds of ... of energy sources and the idea is that in six documentaries they'll look at oil and coal and nuclear energy. Then they'll find out about alternative sources of energy to see whether they'd be practical and economical. And so, you know, my experience last year finding out about wind power and solar power could be quite useful, really.

M: Yeah, I should think it could. Do you think he was impressed?

W: I think he probably was, actually, I mean he seemed quite impressed that I'd actually found out about the subjects before I came along to meet him and I knew what he was wanting to get across in his documentaries — um — and I think, really, by about half way through the meal he'd decided that he was going to give me the job, which was nice because I wasn't really expecting that, um ... But then he went on and he started asking me all sorts of very, very strange questions about my personal life，which I found very surprising.

Questions 19 to 22 are based on the conversation you have just heard.

19. How did the interview go according to the woman?
20. What were the first questions the woman answered in the interview?
21. What are the documentaries about?
22. Why does the woman think she made a good impression in the interview?

Conversation Two

M：Hi，Lisa. Busy?

W：Hi，Meg. Yes，pretty busy. I'm doing a cooking course at the local community college. It's two evenings a week.

M：Really? So，you're interested in cooking，are you?

W：Oh，yes. I'm learning to cook Indian food. We've got an Indian teacher，and she's a real enthusiast.

M：I love Indian food.

W：And do you like cooking?

M：No，not really，but I enjoy eating.

W：Oh，by the way，who was the man in your office yesterday?

M：Which man? What did he look like?

W：Tall，athletic. Very tanned. Grey，straight hair.

M：Oh，that's Jack Craig. He's from Sydney. He's an old friend of Geoffrey's. He's been at sea for six months，on an expedition to the Caribbean.

W：What's his job?

M：He's a jack-of-all-trades.

W：What do you mean?

M：Well，he does everything. He's very versatile. Come and meet him tomorrow.

W：Sure，I'd like to meet a jack-of-all-trades. And I don't know any Australians.

M：Well，this is your chance to meet one.

Questions 23 to 25 are based on the conversation you have just heard.

23. What's the woman busy doing?
24. Where is Jack Craig from?
25. What is Jack Craig's job?

Section B

Directions: *In this section, you will hear 3 short passages. At the end of each passage, you will hear some questions. Both the passage and the questions will be spoken only* *once. After you hear a question, you must choose the best answer from the four choices marked A), B), C) and D). Then mark the corresponding letter on **Answer Sheet 2** with a single line through the centre.*

Passage One

According to a legend, the ancient Olympic Games were founded by Hercules, a son of Zeus. Yet the first Olympic Games for which we still have written records were held in 776 B.C., though it is generally believed that the Games had been going on for many years already. At this Olympic Games, a naked runner, Coroebus, won the sole event — a run of approximately 192 meters. This made Coroebus the very first Olympic champion in history.

The ancient Olympic Games grew and continued to be played every four years for nearly 1,200 years. The games gained in scope and became demonstrations of national pride. Winners were given many special privileges. However, Emperor Theodosius put a stop to them in 394 A.D.

The modern Olympic Games, first held in Athens, Greece in 1896, were the result of efforts by Pierre de Coubertin, a French educator, to promote interest in education and culture, also to contribute to better international understanding through the universal medium of youth's love for athletics. His source of inspiration for the Olympic Games was the ancient Greek Olympic Games.

Pierre de Coubertin enlisted 9 nations to send athletes to the first modern Olympics in 1896; now more than 100 nations compete. The winter Olympic Games were started in 1924.

Questions 26 to 29 are based on the passage you have just heard.

26. When did the first recorded Olympic Games take place?
27. In which city were the modern Olympic Games first held?
28. What was the purpose of the modern Olympic Games?
29. How many nations entered for the first modern Olympic Games?

Passage Two

Americans love pets. Many pet owners treat their pets as part of the family. Sometimes they even play interesting videos for their pets or give them amusing toys. If they have an eye for fashion, pet owners can dress their pets in fashionable clothes. Sometimes they can use animal perfume to make their dogs smell less beastly.

In America, there are more households with pets than those with children. At least 43 percent of US homes have pets of some sort. Animals, such as monkeys, snakes and even wolves, find a home with some Americans. More common pets include tropical fish, mice and birds. But the all-time favorites are cats and dogs, even in the White House. Many stores sell tasty pet foods to owners eager to please their pets. In Houston, Texas, dogs can have their dinner delivered to their homes, just like pizza. Pets can even go on a vacation with their owners. Furry guests at Four Seasons Hotels can enjoy meals served on fine china and sleep in soft beds. Americans believe that pets have a right to be treated well. At least 75 animal welfare organizations exist in America. Veterinarians can give animals medical care for a very high price. To pay for the high-tech health care, people can buy health insurance for their pets.

Researchers have discovered that interacting with animals lowers a person's blood pressure. Dogs can offer protection from thieves and unwelcome visitors. Pets can also encourage social relationships: they give their owners an appearance of friendliness, and they provide a good topic of conversation. Pets are as basic to American culture as hot dogs or apple pies. To Americans, pets are not just animals, but a part of the family.

Questions 30 to 32 are based on the passage you have just heard.

30. How can Americans make the lives of the pets more colorful?
31. Which of the following is NOT true according to the passage?
32. Which of the following is the best title for this passage?

Passage Three

Automobiles, as products of modern civilization, have been playing a vital part in the daily activities of human society. As a common means of transportation, automobiles have brought convenience and high efficiency to people's lives. They have also stimulated the development of many countries' industry, business and trade. In fact, the wide use of automobiles has greatly improved people's standard of living.

But automobiles have also given rise to a series of problems. The amount of fertile land is becoming smaller and smaller due to the extending of highways and parking lots. Other problems, such as air and noise pollution, petroleum shortages, traffic jams and car accidents, are becoming more and more serious. Some of them even threaten our existence.

Therefore, automobiles, like anything else, have more than one face. Our society cannot run without them, but they have also brought us serious problems. Ways have to be found to make full use of their advantages and to reduce their disadvantages.

Questions 33 to 35 are based on the passage you have just heard.

33. What is NOT mentioned as a benefit brought about by automobiles?
34. Which of the following is NOT the problem brought about by automobiles?
35. What is the author's attitude toward automobiles?

Section C

Directions: *In this section, you will hear a passage three times. When the passage is read for the first time, you should listen carefully for its general idea. When the passage is read for the second time, you are required to fill in the blanks numbered from 36 to 43 with the exact words you have just heard. For blanks numbered from 44 to 46 you are required to fill in the missing information. For these blanks, you can either use the exact words you have just heard or write down the main points in your own words. Finally, when the passage is read for the third time, you should check what you have written.*

The new medical insurance system that will see gradual introduction this year will change the life and healthcare for China's 400 million (36)**urban** residents.

Unlike now, employees of (37) **non-publicly** owned enterprises will no longer be (38) **excluded** under the new (39) **scheme**. People who have enjoyed virtually free medical care working for government offices and state-owned businesses will have to learn to be (40) **thriftier** when dealing with health problems. Employees of China's state-owned enterprises and institutions (41) **previously** enjoyed free medical care with expenses (42) **shouldered** by the government and state-owned enterprises. According to the new system, both the employers and the employees will share medical expenses.

Enterprises will contribute six percent of the entire (43) **staff's** salaries to medical care insurance. (44) **Of that total, thirty percent will go to employees' personal accounts**. (45)**The rest will be set aside as "overall medical funds"**. (46) **Employees will have to pay two percent of their monthly salaries into their personal medical insurance accounts**.

Practice Test 4

Section A

Directions: *In this section, you will hear 8 short conversations and 2 long conversations. At the end of each conversation, one or more questions will be asked about what was said. Both the conversation and the questions will be spoken only once. After each question there will be a pause. During the pause, you must read the four choices marked A), B), C) and D), and decide which is the best answer. Then mark the corresponding letter on **Answer Sheet 2** with a single line through the centre.*

11. W: I can't understand why Mary didn't call me.

    M: She did! She said she couldn't come to see us this evening, but hoped to be able to next time she came to town.

    Q: What do we learn about Mary?

12 M: Stop for a minute, Jane. I want to have a look at the display in the window.

    W: There are some books on sale. Why don't we go in and see if we can find something on art?

    Q: Where are the two speakers?

13 M: I used to love giving my mother a present on Mother's Day. It always made her cry, then she'd hug me hard enough to squeeze the breath out of me.

    W: Mothers are really no different from anyone else. They love to be loved, that's all.

    Q: What was the mother's response to her son's gift?

14. W: You can buy this one, which is a demonstration model, or we can order one for you and have it here in six weeks.

    M: I would prefer a new car, even though the demonstration model is less expensive.

    Q: What is a demonstration model?

15. W: Have Todd and Lisa Taylor started a family yet? They've been married for two years now.

    M: Todd indicated to me that they'd postpone having children until he gets his law degree.

    Q: How do the Taylors feel about children?

16. W: Are you glad that you came to Washington?

    M: Yes, indeed. I'd considered going to New York or Boston, but I've never regretted my decision.

    Q: Where does the man live?

17. W: Let's go to the restaurant on the corner.

M: Last time I was there I had to wait in line for almost an hour. I don't want to waste time. I have a test at 3 o'clock.

Q: What are they most probably going to do?

18. M: Could I look at your bus schedule? I don't want to drive to work tomorrow if it's snowing.

W: You'd better call the terminal. It's been a long time since I used my schedule and I'm sure it's out of date.

Q: What does the woman mean?

Now you'll hear two long conversations.

Conversation One

M: I still don't understand what it is that you're talking about. What is feminism anyway? Does it mean you don't want to marry me anymore?

W: I'm not sure I can give you a perfect dictionary definition, but I'll tell you how I feel. I want both of us to share all responsibilities equally. Both of us will contribute to the life that we share.

M: But I earn enough money for the both of us. And what about the home?

W: I want to contribute financially so that we can both pay our own way; both of us will clean the house; both of us will raise the children, and so on. It may not be exactly equal, but we can try.

M: I was raised to treat woman with a certain respect: to stand when they enter a room, to open car doors and front doors for them, to let them sit first and eat first.

W: I think those things are old-fashioned. I'm perfectly able to open doors for myself, and do all sorts of other things. And besides, it makes me feel uncomfortable when you treat me as though I were a china doll. I'm not more special than you: I'm your equal.

M: It sounds as though you think men and women — or in our case, boys and girls — can be friends just like two girls or two boys can.

W: I certainly do. And I think we'll all be better for it.

Questions 19 to 22 are based on the conversation you have just heard.

19. What's the relationship between the two speakers?

20. What can we learn about the woman from the conversation?

21. Which statement is NOT included in the ways the man was raised to respect women?

22. What is the man's attitude towards the woman's opinion?

Conversation Two

W：Anything interesting in the paper today?

M：Let's have a look. Well, yeah, there are a few here that might interest us. Here's one for just under $400. It only has one bedroom but it sounds nice. Near a park. It'd be nice to live near a park.

W：Mm. But you know, $390 seems expensive for just one bedroom.

M：Yes, you're right. Oh, here's one that's a little cheaper, near University Avenue. It's $350.

W：How many bedrooms?

M：Just one again. That's not a very nice area.

W：No, it's pretty noisy. I'd prefer a larger place really.

M：Yeah. Let me see the cheapest two-bedroom apartments. Oh, here's real bargain. It's only $350. But it doesn't have any furniture.

W：No. You know how much it can cost to furnish an apartment?

M：Oh, here's another one for just over 400. This sounds very interesting. It's on Metcalf. That's a nice street.

W：Yes, it's quiet. Did you say two bedrooms?

M：Yes, at $415.

W：Why don't we go and have a look at it?

M：OK. I'll give them a call.

Questions 23 to 25 are based on the conversation you have just heard.

23. What are the two speakers doing?
24. What kind of apartment do they prefer?
25. How much will they pay for the apartment near University Avenue?

Section B

Directions: *In this section, you will hear 3 short passages. At the end of each passage, you will hear some questions. Both the passage and the questions will be spoken only once. After you hear a question, you must choose the best answer from the four choices marked A), B), C) and D). Then mark the corresponding letter on* **Answer Sheet 2** *with a single line through the centre.*

Passage One

The world's first totally automatic railway has been built under the busy streets of London. The railway is called the Victoria Line, and it is part of the complete London subway railway. It was opened in 1969. This new line is much different from others.

The stations on the other lines need a lot of workers to sell tickets, and to check and collect them when people board or leave the trains. Startling enough, the Victoria Line is very different from that old operating system. Here a machine checks and collects the tickets, and there are no workers on the platforms.

There is only one worker on the train of the Victoria Line. The man usually just starts it. The train runs and stops automatically. It is controlled by electrical signals which are sent by the so-called "command spots." Each spot sends a certain signal. The train always moves at the speed that the command spots permit. If the command sends no signals, the train will stop by itself.

Most of the control work is done by computers. The computers fix the trains' speeds, and send the signals to the command spots. If one train stays too long at a station, the other trains will then automatically move slower. So there is no danger of accidents on the line.

Questions 26 to 29 are based on the passage you have just heard.

26. When did the world's first completely automatic railway go into operation?
27. What is the biggest difference between the Victoria Line and the other lines in London?
28. What is the man on the Victoria Line expected to do?
29. Which of the following is NOT true about the Victoria Line?

Passage Two

Many years ago there lived a young couple in India. The young couple had wanted a child very much, and when they finally had a baby, they loved him with all their hearts. However, before the baby was one year old, he became sick and soon died. The young couple almost cried their eyes out. They would not let anyone bury the child and asked everyone to help them find the medicine that would make their son come back to life again.

The people in the village did not know what to do. They thought the young couple had gone crazy over the death of the baby. The villagers were worried that the young couple would not be able to return to their old way of life if they continued to focus on the death of the baby. One day, a wise man from another village came and the villagers asked him for help.

The wise man thought for a while and said, "I have what you are looking for. But the medicine lacks one ingredient."

"What is the ingredient?" asked the couple anxiously, "We will find it anyway!"

"All I need is a handful of mustard seeds," said the wise man slowly, "but it must come from a family where no one had died. That means no child, no spouse, and no parent has died in the family." The young couple were so anxious to bring the baby back to life that they did not think about the wise man's words, and set out to look for the mustard seeds. However, after months and months of searching, they came to realize that the wise man's request was impossible to fulfill.

However, the young couple learned something important during their search for the mustard seeds. They saw that every family they visited had lost someone, a child, a parent, or a spouse. All of these families learned to go on with their lives after the death of their beloved ones. The couple saw that death was a part of life cycle. The families' stories helped the young couple feel better, and they realized they were not alone. But most importantly, they learned that they could continue to live a normal life after the death of their child.

Questions 30 to 32 are based on the passage you have just heard.

30. Why were the young couple unable to find the mustard seeds?
31. What can we learn from the story?
32. What would happen to the young couple afterwards?

Passage Three

Often physical and mental handicap prevents a child from learning. In education today new methods are being used in special schools to help the handicapped learn.

Among the many interesting schools for handicapped persons, there is one which is being established in the southern part of New Jersey. It is called the Bancroft Community. The handicapped young adults will be trained to support themselves to get along in the outside world.

The Bancroft Community is not surrounded by walls of any kind. Its director, John R. Tullis, insists that it be open so that the students may gradually develop normal relations with the rest of Bancroft Community students. They will live in apartments or in a house, cooking their own meals, washing their own clothes, and learning to perform other tasks. Gradually, as they become able, they will buy their own furniture, paying for it out of their own earnings. They will pay for rent and pay for their food, too.

As a step towards the goal of becoming independent, each handicapped person will decide what kind of work he wants to be trained to do. While some of the training will be carried on within the Bancroft Community itself, most of the students will receive job training in nearby towns. They will be trained by town people for whom they will work without pay.

Questions 33 to 35 are based on the passage you have just heard.

33. Why are new teaching methods being used in special schools today?

34. What is the main purpose of the Bancroft Community?
35. What can be learned about the training program in the Bancroft Community?

Section C

Directions: *In this section, you will hear a passage three times. When the passage is read for the first time, you should listen carefully for its general idea. When the passage is read for the second time, you are required to fill in the blanks numbered from 36 to 43 with the exact words you have just heard. For blanks numbered from 44 to 46 you are required to fill in the missing information. For these blanks, you can either use the exact words you have just heard or write down the main points in your own words. Finally, when the passage is read for the third time, you should check what you have written.*

Almost 20,000 whales have been slaughtered since a (36) **ban** on commercial whaling was introduced in 1986 and the death (37) **toll** is rising each year. Norway and Japan killed over 1,000 whales in 1999 and they plan to kill even more. As the (38) **environmental** concerns increase, whaling is no longer the issue as it was or (39) **deserves** to be. With little public awareness of the increasing whale slaughter, there has been no pressure to stop it. (40) **Consequently**, the political will confront the whalers and (41) **enforce** the whaling ban that has (42) **slipped** away. Commercial whaling has (43) **devastated** whale population worldwide, (44) **pushing the entire species to the brink of extinction**. There is still great scientific uncertainty about the size and status of remaining whale populations. (45) **Whales are facing increasing threats to their survival including increasing pollution, massive over-fishing, boat collisions and climate change**. They need to be protected, not hunted. (46) **Commercial whaling is cruel and unnecessary. It is morally indefensible**.

Practice Test 5

Section A

Directions: *In this section, you will hear 8 short conversations and 2 long conversations. At the end of each conversation, one or more questions will be asked about what was said. Both the conversation and the questions will be spoken only once. After each question there will be a pause. During the pause, you must read the four choices marked A), B), C) and D), and decide which is the best answer. Then mark the corresponding letter on* **Answer Sheet 2** *with a single line through the centre.*

11. M: I am worried about my exam. I heard that many students got an "F."
    W: Only a few did actually. Most students have been studying hard for the exam.
    Q: How does the woman react to the man's words?

12 M: Hello, Susan. This is Frank. I'm calling from work. How is your sister?
    W: Thanks, Frank. She is home now, but the doctor said she should stay in bed for a few days.
    Q: Where is Frank now?

13 W: I hear the old Delta Hotel has a new manager. Did you notice any change when you stayed there last week?
    M: The food was better than the meals they used to serve and the rooms were surprisingly clean for the Delta, I thought.
    Q: How is the hotel now?

14. M: Did you pick up the paper for me today? I really want to check the job vacancies.
    W: I know, it's over there. There's not much happening though. I had a look already. Maybe you should look on the Net instead.
    Q: What is the man looking for?

15. W: Washington is the most important city in the United States, isn't it?
    M: Yes, it is, in the political sense, although it cannot compete with cities like New York, Chicago or Los Angeles in size and population.
    Q: Which city are they talking about?

16. W: I haven't had much exercise lately. I only watch TV or go to the movies. What do you do in your spare time?
    M: In summer I'd like to play tennis instead of swimming. My favorite sport in winter is skiing.
    Q: What's the man's favorite sport in summer?

17. M: Some people believe high pay can maintain a clean government. What do you think of this?

W: I don't see eye to eye with them. In developed countries and regions, you know, government workers have high salaries, but bribery and some other problems still exist. So I think there is no limit to human desire.

Q: What does the woman mean?

18. W: What time does your bus leave for the office in the morning?

M: It's on an irregular schedule. On Mondays it leaves at 7:30. On Tuesdays and Wednesdays it leaves fifteen minutes later. And on Thursdays and Fridays it leaves thirty minutes later.

Q: What time does the bus leave on Fridays?

Now you'll hear two long conversations.

Conversation One

W: Hey, John, long time no see!

M: Yeah, Mary, it's been a while, huh? How've you been?

W: Not too bad. Can't complain, you know. How about you?

M: (sounding sad) I've been better. I was just thinking about my father. You know, he died almost exactly one year ago.

W: No, sorry man, I didn't know. But I know how you feel. My father's been gone almost four years now. I miss him too, but you know what? I bet if they were here, they'd be doing precisely what we're doing right now!

M: You mean drinking beer (laughs)? (still sad) Yeah, maybe. It's just that my dad was crippled. I know he always envied me because I could get into the Navy and he couldn't. He was reluctant to show it, but that's all he ever wanted to do.

W: Yeah, I know ... it makes you feel shame inside, doesn't it?

M: Yeah, especially now. You know, he urged me to join the Navy just like he urged me to get out there and play baseball with the other kids when I was growing up. I just always felt so wrong having so much fun.

W: Yeah. It's amazing, huh? We complain about the trifles of life, but other people like your father had to adjust to all kinds of stress.

M: Yeah. But my father did well in life, despite his crippled legs. You know, he even got out and took me to see the Brooklyn Dodgers!

W: Wow. Yeah, John, your father was a great man.

M: Thanks, Mary, cheers!

Questions 19 to 22 are based on the conversation you have just heard.

19. What are the two speakers talking about?
20. When did the man's father die?
21. What was it that the man's father always wanted to do but couldn't do?
22. Why couldn't the man's father do many things like other people?

Conversation Two

W: Hello Bill, Sue here.

M: Hello Sue.

W: Well, I saw Barbara and she asked me to thank you very much for the invitation. She's very happy to go. She likes car racing almost as much as I do.

M: Good. I'm going to leave here about nine. That'll give us plenty of time. I'll pick you up first, then we'll pick up Barbara, if that's OK with you.

W: She doesn't want you to pick her up, Bill. It's out of your way. She said she was going to meet us here.

M: I don't mind, you know. There won't be much traffic.

W: No, no. We can all meet here about a quarter past nine. Barbara insisted.

M: OK ... By the way, I'm going to ask Phil Stone to come too, if you don't mind.

W: I don't mind at all. It will be nice to see him again ... I'm certainly looking forward to the racing.

M: I am too. I'm sure we'll enjoy ourselves. See you Sunday at your place about a quarter past nine then.

W: OK Bill, bye.

Questions 23 to 25 are based on the conversation you have just heard.

23. What are they going to do on Sunday?
24. Why doesn't Barbara want Bill to pick her up?
25. How many people will go together?

Section B

Directions: *In this section, you will hear 3 short passages. At the end of each passage, you will hear some questions. Both the passage and the questions will be spoken only once. After you hear a question, you must choose the best answer from the four choices marked A), B), C) and D). Then mark the corresponding letter on **Answer Sheet 2** with a single line through the centre.*

Passage One

Deep Springs is an American college, it is an unusual college. It is high in the wide mountains of California, not in a college town. The campus is a collection of old buildings with no beautiful classrooms. The only college-like thing about Deep Springs is its library. Students can study from the 17,000 books 24 hours a day. The library is never crowded as there are only 24 well qualified male students at the college. In addition, there are only 5 full-time professors. These teachers believe in the idea of this college. They need to believe in it. They do not get much money. In fact, their salaries are only about 9,000 dollars a year, plus room and meals.

The school gives the young teachers as well as the students something more important than money. "There is no place like Deep Springs," says a second-year student from New York State. "Most colleges today are much the same, but Deep Springs is not afraid to be different." He says that students at his college are in a situation quite unlike any other school. Students are there to learn, and they cannot run away from problems. There is no place to escape to. At most colleges, students can close their books and go to a film. They can go out to restaurants or to parties. Deep Springs' students have completely different alternatives. They can talk to each other, or to their teacher. Another possible activity is to go to the library to study. They might decide to do some work. The student who doesn't want to do any of these activities can go for a walk in the desert. Deep Springs is far from the world of restaurants and cinemas. There is not even a television set on campus.

Questions 26 to 29 are based on the passage you have just heard.

26. What is the total number of students at Deep Springs College?
27. What is true of the campus of Deep Springs College?
28. Which of the following is mentioned in the passage?
29. What can students at Deep Springs do in their spare time?

Passage Two

Reading is the key to school success and, like any skill, it takes practice. A child learns to walk by practicing until he no longer has to think about how to put one foot in front of the other. A great athlete practices until he can play quickly, accurately, without thinking. Educators call it "automaticity."

A child learns to read by sounding out the letters and decoding the words. With practice, he stumbles less and less, reading by the phrase. With automaticity, he doesn't have to think about decoding the words, so he can pay more attention to the meaning of the text.

It can begin as early as in the first grade. In a recent study of children in Illinois schools, Alan Rossman of Northwestern University found automatic readers in the first grade who were reading almost three times as fast as the other children and scoring twice as high on comprehension tests. At fifth grade, the automatic readers were reading twice as fast as the others, and still outscoring them on accuracy, comprehension and vocabulary.

"It's not IQ but the amount of time a child spends reading that is the key to automaticity." According to Rossman, any child who spends at least 3.5 to 4 hours a week reading books, magazines or newspapers will in all likelihood reach the average child who spends 25 hours a week watching television. It can happen by turning off the set just one night reading books.

You can test your child by giving him a paragraph or two to read aloud — something unfamiliar but appropriate to his age. If he reads aloud with expression, with a sense of the meaning of the sentences, he probably is an automatic reader. If he reads haltingly, one word at a time, without expression or meaning, he need more practice.

Questions 30 to 32 are based on the passage you have just heard.

30. How do the children learn to read?
31. How many hours should a child spend in reading books every day?
32. Which of the following is an automatic reader?

Passage Three

Paying attention to details is something everyone can and should do — especially in a tight job market. Bob Crossley, a human resources expert notices this in the job applications that come across his desk every day. "It's amazing how many candidates eliminate themselves," he says.

"Resumes arrive with stains. Some candidates don't bother to spell the company's name correctly. Once I see a mistake, I eliminate the candidate," Crossley concludes. "If they cannot take care of these details, why should we trust them with a job?"

Can we pay too much attention to details? Absolutely. Perfectionists struggle over little things at the cost of something larger they work toward. "To keep from losing the forest for the trees," says Charles Garfield, associate professor at the University of California, "we must constantly ask ourselves how the details we're working on fit into the large picture. If they don't, we should drop them and move to something else."

Garfield compares this process to his work as a computer scientist at NASA. "The Apollo II moon launch was slightly off-course 90 percent of the time," says Garfield. "But a successful landing was still likely because we knew the exact coordinates of our goal. This allowed us to make adjustments as necessary." Knowing where we want to go helps us judge the importance of every task we undertake.

Too often we believe what accounts for others' success is some special secret or a lucky chance. But rarely is success so mysterious. Again and again, we see that by doing little things within our grasp well, large rewards follow.

Questions 33 to 35 are based on the passage you have just heard.

33. Why were some job applicants rejected according to the passage?
34. According to the author, what should we do if the parts are not in harmony with the whole?
35. What does Garfield want to tell us by giving the example of the Apollo II moon launch?

Section C

Directions: *In this section, you will hear a passage three times. When the passage is read for the first time, you should listen carefully for its general idea. When the passage is read for the second time, you are required to fill in the blanks numbered from 36 to 43 with the exact words you have just heard. For blanks numbered from 44 to 46 you are required to fill in the missing information. For these blanks, you can either use the exact words you have just heard or write down the main points in your own words. Finally, when the passage is read for the third time, you should check what you have written.*

French Defense Minister Michele Alliot-Marie says her government is (36) **willing** to help train Iraq's police and military but rules out sending French (37) **troops** there. The French official made her (38) **remarks** Friday in Washington, where she is (39) **seeking** to smooth relations that soured over France's opposition to the US-led war in Iraq.

Ms. Alliot-Marie told a (40)**conference** at the Center for (41) **Strategic** and International Studies in Washington that France would be (42)**available** to help train Iraq's future military and police forces, (43) **similar** to what France and Germany are doing in Afghanistan.

Ms. Alliot-Marie, a close political ally of President Chirac, (44) **talks frankly about the need to repair French-US relations**, which soured over French opposition to the US-led war in Iraq. (45) **"France definitely does not seek systematically to counter the US in the world or to diminish its influence,"** said Michele Alliot-Marie. "We simply want to promote our vision of things as we respect that of others. (46) **So let us discuss how to make the most of today's globalized world while preserving the earth's diversity, which is an asset to all**."

Practice Test 6

Section A

Directions: *In this section, you will hear 8 short conversations and 2 long conversations. At the end of each conversation, one or more questions will be asked about what was said. Both the conversation and the questions will be spoken only once. After each question there will be a pause. During the pause, you must read the four choices marked A), B), C) and D), and decide which is the best answer. Then mark the corresponding letter on **Answer Sheet 2** with a single line through the centre.*

11. W: Do you like your new room?
    M: It's nice to have enough space for all my things, so I'm glad I moved. But I miss my friends and neighbors and that beautiful view. I especially miss living so close to the school.
    Q: How does the man's new room compare with the room he had before?

12 M: I know you'll think I'm impatient, Mrs. Knight, but I'm beginning to get really worried about the delay in getting my plan approved. Is there something I don't know about?
    W: Not that I know of. It's just that the approval procedure takes time.
    Q: Why is the man worried?

13 W: Tomorrow we are having our first test in my history class. I'm really worried about it. You've taken one of Dr. Parker's tests, haven't you? I hear they're impossible to pass.
    M: I don't know whom you've been talking about. My experience was just the opposite.
    Q: What does the man mean?

14. W: I just made up a quart of orange juice this morning, and now I can't find it anywhere. Do you know what happened to it?
    M: Did you hear a crash earlier? That was it. I'm just as clumsy as ever.
    Q: What is the problem?

15. M: Are you sure that you brought your purse with you in the first place?
    W: Yes. I had it when I got in the car. I thought that I might have left it on the car seat, but when I went back it wasn't there. Maybe I put it down on the counter when I checked my coat outside the auditorium.
    Q: Where does the woman believe she has left her purse?

16. M: My name is Stone Johnson. I'm expecting a friend. If he comes, please tell him I'm in the Coffee Shop.

W: I'll make a note of that, sir.

Q: Where do you think the man is?

17. M: Would you help me with my resume? Jane said you're good at these things, and I really need someone to edit it. It's way too long.

W: Sure, no problem, give it to me. A good resume should be no more than one page, you know. And it should list your experience in reverse chronological order. I can see we've got some work to do!

Q: Which of the following is true according to the conversation?

18. W: To be successful, it's important to imagine success.

M: Sure. Every day we need to set some time to dream with passion about what we want to achieve. This can work for a person who wants to be successful.

Q: What can help a person succeed according to the man and the woman?

Now you'll hear two long conversations.

Conversation One

M: Linda, I hear you won the singing competition. Well done! Congratulations! Look, these flowers are for you, oh, queen of my heart!

W: Thanks, Willy. They are beautiful. I love them.

M: Beautiful! In my eyes, you are even more beautiful.

W: No, Willy, you can't be serious.

M: Linda, I mean every word of it. And your voice, it's so sweet to my ears! The winner could be nobody else but you.

W: Well, it was nothing really. I was just lucky.

M: Nothing! Oh, no, you are a fantastic singer and luck alone could never bring such success.

W: Well, that's very kind of you to say so, but I've still got a lot to learn.

M: And by the way, what a stunning dress you are wearing. It fits you so well!

W: Thanks, I made it myself.

M: Really? You are just unbelievable!

W: Thanks. In fact I won the competition in this dress.

M: Perfect! You are just perfect!

W: Nobody is perfect, Willy.

M: But you are. Oh, I admire you. Could I have dinner with you tonight, by any chance?

W: I'm afraid I can't. I have a date with my boyfriend. There he is!

Questions 19 to 21 are based on the conversation you have just heard.

19. Why does the man congratulate the woman?

20. Which statement is NOT true about the woman's dress?

21. Why does the woman refuse to have dinner with the man?

Conversation Two

W: How are you getting along during this unusually hot weather?

M: Not well at all. Over last few weeks the hot, humid weather is killing me. I believe the climate has changed.

W: Yeah, summer is hotter, and winter wetter.

M: Do you know why all this has happened?

W: The greenhouse effects bring global warming and rain.

M: What do you mean by greenhouse effects?

W: The earth is now like a real greenhouse made of glass panels that let light in and trap heat. You know, carbon dioxide from earth is a greenhouse gas.

M: I see. Everybody should know what causes global warming; otherwise we won't stop it.

W: The important thing is that human beings should take steps to reduce global warming.

M: What can we do then? Perhaps we should not burn any more wood or coal.

W: Right. Also we should try to produce less CFCs or freon.

M: How can we achieve that?

W: Don't use aerosol spray on your hair, and depend less on air-conditioners and refrigerators.

M: But it's hard to give up all this.

W: But we must take action before polar icecaps melt and oceans rise.

Questions 22 to 25 are based on the conversation you have just heard.

22. What are the two speakers discussing?

23. Which gas is a greenhouse gas that has resulted in global warming?

24. Which statement is NOT included in the steps human beings should take to reduce global warming?

25. Which statement is NOT true if we do not take action to reduce global warming?

Section B

Directions: *In this section, you will hear 3 short passages. At the end of each passage, you will hear some questions. Both the passage and the questions will be spoken only once. After you hear a question, you must choose the best answer from the four choices marked A), B), C) and D). Then mark the corresponding letter on* **Answer Sheet 2** *with a single line through the centre.*

Passage One

The family is changing. In the past, grandparents, parents, and children used to live together, and they have an extended family. Sometimes two or more brothers with their wives and children were part of this large family group. But family structure is changing throughout the world. The nuclear family consists of only one father, one mother, and children; it is becoming the main family structure everywhere.

The nuclear family offers women some advantages: they have freedom from their relatives, and the husband does not have all the power of the family. Studies show that in nuclear families, men and women usually make an equal number of decisions about family life.

But wives usually have to "pay" for the benefits of freedom and power. When women lived in extended families, sisters, grandparents, and aunts helped one another with house work and childcare. In addition, older women in a large family group had important positions. Wives in nuclear families do not often enjoy this benefit, and they have another disadvantage, too; women generally live longer than their husbands, so older women from nuclear families often have to live alone.

Studies show that women are generally less satisfied with marriage than men are. In the past, men worked outside the home and women worked inside. Housework and childcare were a full-time job, and there was no time for anything else. Now women work outside and have more freedom than they did in the past, but they still have to do most of the housework. The women actually have two full-time jobs, and they have not much free time.

Questions 26 to 28 are based on the passage you have just heard.

26. What advantages does the nuclear family offer women?
27. What is a disadvantage of the nuclear family for women?
28. Why are many women dissatisfied with their marriage and the nuclear family?

Passage Two

There are five chief oil regions in the world. They are — the Middle East; the United States of America and Canada; Latin America and the Caribbean; Africa; and Russia. There are also many smaller oil regions in different countries.

The Middle East countries have the largest amount of oil. They have more oil than all the other regions together.

Oil was first discovered in the Middle East in 1908. The first oilfield was opened in Iran — the famous Masjidi-Sulaiman field. A few years later men found oil in other Middle East countries. But they did not produce much oil at that time because nobody knew the size and value of the oilfields. Then in 1932 oil was discovered on Bahrain

Island. The men who discovered this oil said, "If Bahrain has oil, there may be a lot of oilfields in and around the Arabian Gulf."

Immediately men began to search for oil in the countries around the Gulf. During the next few years oil was found in many places. The Middle East oil industry then grew fast.

Today this region produces a third of the world's oil supplies. The Middle East countries now export more oil than any other region. They do not need all their oil. So they are able to export most of their oil to other countries. Europe is one of their chief markets. They supply all the countries of Western Europe and also some of the countries in Eastern Europe. These European countries import millions of tons from other countries. They import some of their oil from North Africa and Latin America, but they buy most of it from the Middle East.

Questions 29 to 31 are based on the passage you have just heard.

29. Which region has the largest amount of oil?

30. When did the Middle East oil industry begin to grow fast?

31. What is the condition of oil production in the Middle East now?

Passage Three

Turn Mars into a blue world with streams and green fields, and then fill it with creatures from the earth — this idea may sound like something from a science fiction, but it is actually being taken seriously by many researchers.

This suggests that future for the "red planet" will be the main topic for discussion at an international conference hosted by NASA this week. Leading researchers as well as science fiction writers will attend the event. It comes as NASA is preparing a multi-billion-dollar Mars research program. "Turning Mars into a little earth has long been a topic in science fiction," said Dr. Michael Meyer, NASA's senior scientist for astrobiology. "Now, with scientists exploring the reality, we can ask what the real possibilities of changing Mars are."

Most scientists agree that Mars could be turned into a little earth, although much time and money would be needed to achieve this goal.

But many experts are shocked by the idea. "We are destroying our own world at an unbelievable speed and now we are talking about ruining another planet," said Paul Murdin, dean of the Institute of Astronomy, Cambridge, UK.

Over the past months, scientists have become increasingly confident they will find Martian life forms. Europe and America's robot explorers have found proof that water, mixed with soil, exists in large amounts on the planet.

In addition, two different groups of scientists announced on March 28 that they had found signs of methane in the Martian atmosphere. The gas is a waste product of living creatures and could be produced by microbes living in the red planet's soil.

But scientists such as Dr. Lisa Pratt, a biologist at Indiana University, say that these microbes will be put in danger by the little earth project. "Before we have even discovered if there is life on Mars, we are talking about carrying out projects that would destroy all these native life forms, all the strange microbes that we hope to find buried in the soil," said Dr. Pratt. This view is shared by Monica Grady, a planetary scientist at the Natural History Museum, London. "We cannot risk starting a global experiment that would wipe out the precious information we are looking for," she said. "This is just wrong."

Questions 32 to 35 are based on the passage you have just heard.

32. What does the passage mainly talk about?
33. Which of the following is NOT the reason why some scientists are against the plan?
34. What can be inferred from the passage?
35. Which of the following supports the conclusion that there might be microbes living in the Mars's soil?

Section C

Directions: *In this section, you will hear a passage three times. When the passage is read for the first time, you should listen carefully for its general idea. When the passage is read for the second time, you are required to fill in the blanks numbered from 36 to 43 with the exact words you have just heard. For blanks numbered from 44 to 46 you are required to fill in the missing information. For these blanks, you can either use the exact words you have just heard or write down the main points in your own words. Finally, when the passage is read for the third time, you should check what you have written.*

The automobile has many advantages. Above all, it (36) **offers** people freedom to go where they want when they want to. To most people, cars are also personal (37) **fantasy** machines that serve as (38) **symbols** of power, success, speed, excitement, and (39)**adventure**. In (40) **addition**, much of the world's economy is built on producing vehicles and supplying roads, services, and repairs of vehicles. Half of the world's paychecks are (41)**auto-related**.

In spite of their advantages, motor vehicles have many harmful effects on human lives and on air, water, land and wildlife resources. Though we (42)**tend** to deny it, (43)**riding** in cars is one of the most dangerous things we do in our daily lives.

Every year, (44) **cars and trucks worldwide kill an average of 250,000 people**, and they injure or permanently disable ten million more. (45) **Half of the world's people will be involved in an auto accident at sometime in their lives**.

Motor vehicles are the largest sources of air pollution, producing a haze of smog over the world's cities. (46) **In some countries, they produce at least 50% of the countries' air pollution**.

Practice Test 7

Section A

Directions: *In this section, you will hear 8 short conversations and 2 long conversations. At the end of each conversation, one or more questions will be asked about what was said. Both the conversation and the questions will be spoken only once. After each question there will be a pause. During the pause, you must read the four choices marked A), B), C) and D), and decide which is the best answer. Then mark the corresponding letter on* **Answer Sheet 2** *with a single line through the centre.*

11. M: Mrs. Smith, what is the most important thing for you when you enjoy some service?

    W: To me, I don't care if every member of an institution is graduated from Harvard or Yale; what I care about is if I'm understood and treated with respect.

    Q: According to the woman, what's the most important thing when a person enjoys some service?

12. W: Of all the holidays people celebrate, like Christmas, Easter, Mother's Day ... which are the most important to you?

    M: Christmas and Easter, because they mark events in Jesus Christ's life: his birth and his escape from a tomb into heaven. The other festivals, I think, were mainly created to increase sales.

    Q: How many holidays does the man believe to be important?

13. W: What's the problem, Paul? You really look panicked.

    M: I'm speaking to a group of high school students about engineering this afternoon, but I have no idea how I am going to simplify some of the concepts for them.

    Q: What is worrying the man?

14. M: It's awfully dark for 4 o'clock. Do you think it's going to rain?

    W: You'd better do something about that watch of yours. It must have stopped hours ago. Mine says seven.

    Q: What conclusion can we draw from this conversation?

15. M: Hello. This is Tom Davis. I have an appointment with Mr. Smith at 9 o'clock this morning. But I'm afraid I'll have to be 15 minutes late.

    W: That's alright, Mr. Davis. Mr. Smith doesn't have another appointment scheduled until 10 o'clock.

    Q: When will Mr. Davis probably meet with Mr. Smith?

16. W: I understand that the professor has several colleagues at that university. They might be able to assist you in finding adequate housing and employment.

    M: Yes, they might, but I'm a little reluctant to ask for their assistance. I'd rather rely on my own resources, and learn by doing.

    Q: What is the man probably going to do?

17. W: Were you drenched that day?

    M: Yes, I left early, before the speech was over. If my wife had not called me and I had stayed until after the president's speech was over, I would not have been.

    Q: What did the man imply?

18. W: What exactly are you looking for, professor?

    M: I'm looking for any remains, any utensils, bones or buildings that will tell us something about the people who lived here 2,000 years ago.

    Q: What is the man's profession?

Now you'll hear two long conversations.

Conversation One

W: So you've arrived from Spain and you've lost all your luggage.

M: Yes, that's right. I've lost all my things.

W: Now, don't worry. Bags usually turn up quite quickly, you know. You kept your receipts, didn't you?

M: Yes, of course.

W: Good. Right then, could you describe the bags to me, please?

M: Yes, there is a suitcase and a holdall.

W: What's the suitcase like?

M: It's red and it's got a brown leather strap around it.

W: Bright red?

M: No, dark.

W: Anything else you could say to describe it?

M: It's quite large.

W: I see.

M: And it's got the address of where I am staying in England on the label.

W: Good. And the holdall? Is it a bag or case?

M: A bag. And it's dark blue with red handles.

W: Fine.

M: Again. It's quite big. The sort of thing tennis players use. Do you know what I mean?

W: Yes.

M: You will find them, won't you?

W: I'm sure we will. OK, if you'd just like to wait over there for a few minutes, I'll go and have a look to see if your stuff is on the trolley. Keep your fingers crossed.

Questions 19 to 21 are based on the conversation you have just heard.

19. Where has the traveler arrived from?

20. What's the color of the suitcase?

21. What is on the label of the suitcase?

Conversation Two

M: I've saved a lot of money over the past years, and now I'd like to invest it for a profit.

W: What sort of investments do you have in mind?

M: The stock market is looking attractive. It's been a bear market for more than four years now, and I think stock prices are pretty depressed.

W: The falling market has discouraged many investors.

M: But all things work in cycles. A bear market will eventually be followed by a bull market.

W: That's true. When the market does touch its bottom, it'll rebound.

M: I hope investors will soon come back to the market and drive it up.

W: But there're still risks. Wars, weather problems — all these affect buyers' confidence. We're not sure if the market has reached its bottom.

M: The bear market has lasted over four years; I think it's time for it to pick up.

W: It's really hard to say. The Japanese stock market has had a bear run of about ten years.

M: Really?

W: And when NASDAQ fell from 5,000 points to 3,000 points, some people believed it was a golden opportunity to enter the market. Then the market plunged.

M: So the stock market is really risky. I may lose money.

W: And maybe even your shirts.

M: Well, perhaps I'd better put my money in the bank.

Questions 22 to 25 are based on the conversation you have just heard.

22. Why does the man want to invest in the stock market?

23. What's the woman's attitude towards the man's investment in the stock market?

24. How long has the Japanese stock market had a bear run?

25. What does the man finally decide to do?

Section B

Directions: *In this section, you will hear 3 short passages. At the end of each passage, you will hear some questions. Both the passage and the questions will be spoken only once. After you hear a question, you must choose the best answer from the four choices marked A), B), C) and D). Then mark the corresponding letter on* **Answer Sheet 2** *with a single line through the centre.*

Passage One

The year 2003 is the 50th anniversary of the first successful climb to Qomolangma. Do you know why so many people wanted to reach the top of the world?

It was breathtaking. It was wonderful and a bit frightening. It was Qomolangma, the highest mountain in the world. For many years, it has attracted tens of thousands of people who tried to climb its dangerous slopes. During May's 50th anniversary of the first successful climb, nearly 600 people from around the world, including a 5-year-old Italian boy, tried to reach the "roof of the world." China Central Television also sent a team to join the adventure. It broadcasted a special program, called "Standing at the world's third pole in 2003," from May 18 to 24 to cover the Chinese climbing Qomolangma. Over the last century, the 8,844-metre-high peak has proven a great challenge for mountaineers. Those who try to stand on top of the world do so at great risk from extreme cold, avalanches and falling ice. At 8,500 meters, the air contains just one-third of the oxygen at sea level, requiring most climbers to use oxygen tanks. Some of those who climbed the mountain paid the highest price — 175 people have lost their lives on the slopes.

On May 29, 1953, Sir Edmund Hillary from New Zealand and Sherpa Tenzing Norgay from Nepal became the first men ever to reach the top of the mountain. Nearly half a century later, the sons of the two pioneers, Peter Hillary and Jaming Tenzing Norgay, followed in their fathers' footsteps. In 2002, they also successfully reached the roof of the world.

Over the last 50 years, more than 10,000 men and women have tried to climb the mountain and more than 1,200 have succeeded. The first Chinese climbers reached the top of the mountain in 1960.

Despite the dangers, many different people are drawn towards the challenge. But why do they suffer such hardship and take such risks to climb Qomolangma?

"I don't think climbing the mountain is blindly risky. Instead, it is a chance to challenge oneself," said Chen Qi, a reporter of CCTV.com, who was among May's mountaineering team.

"Only when you are surrounded by the mountain can you understand the love of nature and the true meaning of life."

Questions 26 to 28 are based on the passage you have just heard.

26. What can be inferred from the passage?
27. Why is it dangerous to climb Qomolangma?
28. From the passage, what can we know about climbing Qomolangma?

Passage Two

It is widely reported that families are the fastest growing segment of the homeless population. In reality, these "Homeless families are almost never husbands and wives with kids in tow."

A nationwide study by the Urban Institute in Washington, D. C. concluded that homeless families are overwhelmingly unmarried mothers with children, on some form of public assistance. "Homelessness," writes demographer Rossi, "is almost identical with spouselessness."

Cindy, 23, lived in a large, poor family in South Bend, Ind. Never married, she had her first baby at 17 and quit school. After a second child by a different father, she got her own apartment. But Cindy spent her welfare checks on restaurant meals, makeup and clothes. She was quickly evicted for nonpayment of rent and ended up in a shelter with her daughters.

According to the Rev Rollie Grauman and his wife, Bonnie, who run the Nashville Union Mission's shelter for women and children, Cindy is like almost all the others they try to help. "It's their undisciplined life styles that got them in trouble," says Grauman.

Questions 29 to 31 are based on the passage you have just heard.

29. What does the homeless population mainly consist of?
30. Why did Cindy quit school at 17?
31. What is the cause of Cindy as well as many other women's homelessness?

Passage Three

Today, I'll be talking about the invention of the camera and photography. The camera is often thought to be an invention. But as early as 1727, a German physicist discovered that light darkens silver salt, a chemical compound. Using as a camera, a big box with a small hole to let the light in, he made temporary images on the salt. Silver salt is still the base of film today.

Then a French scientist made the first permanent picture by using a special piece of metal sensitized with silver salt. A photograph he made in 1826 still exists. The painter Daguerre improved on the process by placing common salt on the metal. This was in 1839, the official date of the beginning of photography, but the problem was the printing of the photographs, and it wasn't until other scientists developed the kind of paper we now use, that good printing was possible and photography became truly modern.

In 1860's, Matthew Bradey was able to take his famous pictures of the American Civil War. In the 20th century, George Eastman of the United States simplified film developing, and Dr. Edwin Land invented the so called "instant" camera with self-developing film. If we say that taking photography came into existence in 1839, it follows that it has taken more than one hundred years for the camera to reach its present condition of technical refinement.

Questions 32 to 35 are based on the passage you have just heard.

32. What discovery was the basis of photography?
33. How was the first permanent picture made?
34. Which does the speaker regard as the official date of the beginning of photography?
35. According to the speaker, why is Matthew Bradey remembered today?

Section C

Directions: *In this section, you will hear a passage three times. When the passage is read for the first time, you should listen carefully for its general idea. When the passage is read for the second time, you are required to fill in the blanks numbered from 36 to 43 with the exact words you have just heard. For blanks numbered from 44 to 46 you are required to fill in the missing information. For these blanks, you can either use the exact words you have just heard or write down the main points in your own words. Finally, when the passage is read for the third time, you should check what you have written.*

There are many (36) **theories** about the beginning of drama in ancient Greece. The one most widely accepted today is based on the assumption that drama (37) **evolved** from ritual. The argument for this view goes as follows. In the beginning, human beings viewed the natural forces of the world, even the seasonal changes, as (38) **unpredictable**, and they (39) **sought**, through various means, to control these unknown and (40) **feared** powers. Those measures which appeared to bring the (41) **desired** results were then retained and repeated until they (42) **hardened** into fixed rituals. Eventually stories (43) **arose** which explained or veiled the mysteries of the rites. (44) **As time passed some rituals were abandoned, but the stories persisted and provided material for art and drama.**

(45) **Another theory traces the drama's origin from the human interest in storytelling.** According to this view, tales are gradually elaborated, at first through the use of

impersonation, action and dialogue by a narrator and then through the assumption of each of the roles by a different person. (46) **A closely related theory traces drama to those dances that are imitations of animal movements and sounds**.

Practice Test 8

Section A

Directions: *In this section, you will hear 8 short conversations and 2 long conversations. At the end of each conversation, one or more questions will be asked about what was said. Both the conversation and the questions will be spoken only once. After each question there will be a pause. During the pause, you must read the four choices marked A), B), C) and D), and decide which is the best answer. Then mark the corresponding letter on **Answer Sheet 2** with a single line through the centre.*

11. W: It seems you've decided to take the field trip tomorrow. But what if it rains?

    M: That's very unlikely. The weather forecast says that in the next three days we will have sunny weather not only in this part of the country, but in most other regions as well.

    Q: What does the man mean?

12 W: You Americans are funny. It seems as if you were married to your cars.

    M: Yes, I guess that's true. The country is becoming one big highway. I was reading that there are about 4 million miles of roads and highways in this country now.

    Q: What are they talking about?

13 M: I've been having annoyance calls for two weeks. When I answer the phone, the other party hangs up without saying anything. I've tried everything including blowing a whistle into the receiver.

    W: Beginning today, I want you to keep a record of the time each call occurs. From this chart, we can get information to help us trace the calls. If necessary, the telephone company can contact the police.

    Q: What does the woman suggest that the man do?

14. M: I hear that you made the highest grade in the class in the exam. I made only one point less than you, but I was not the highest.

    W: All that I know is that I made 94.

    Q: What did the man make in the exam?

15. W: Why? Was the flight delayed?

    M: Yes, the weather was bad and we waited in the airport for three hours. It was freezing cold and the restaurant was closed.

    Q: Why was the flight delayed?

16. W: The phone bill was $160 this month. Someone must have made several international calls without keeping me informed.

M: I'm sorry, Mrs. Jones. I forgot to tell you that I called my girlfriend in Italy a couple of times.

Q: What's the youth supposed to do when he makes a long distance call?

17. W: Did the movie have a happy ending?

M: It was impossible to tell whether the girl was going to die in the war or come home and marry her childhood sweetheart.

Q: What did the man say about the ending of the movie?

18. M: Have you seen Disney cartoons like *The Three Little Pigs*, *Snow-white and the Seven Dwarves*, or *Plane Crazy*?

W: Are you kidding?

Q: What can we understand from the conversation?

Now you'll hear two long conversations.

Conversation One

M: Oh, mum, I'm going to miss you!

W: Me, too, Alex. Do look after yourself!

M: I will, mum. And take good care of yourself and my little Roosevelt.

W: Don't worry, son. I'll take care of him.

M: Don't forget to buy some milk for him. Give him milk for breakfast and bathe him once a week. He loves to be tidy and clean.

W: Don't worry, dear. I won't forget to do all these things for your puppy. And you, Alex, this is the first time you will be away from home and on your own. It's not going to be the same as it is at home.

M: I know, mum, I know how to look after myself. Don't worry.

W: I'm not sure you do. Don't stay up late as you always do at home. And eat properly! And dress warmly when it's cold! And drop me a line as soon as you get there.

M: OK, mum, I will. I will miss you.

W: Alex, behave yourself at school! Now you'd better get onto the train. It's leaving in five minutes.

M: All right, I must be off. Good-bye, mum!

W: Bye! Take care and behave yourself at school!

Questions 19 to 21 are based on the conversation you have just heard.

19. Where does this conversation probably take place?

20. Who is Roosevelt mentioned in the dialogue?

21. Which is NOT included in the things Alex's mother tells him to do?

Conversation Two

M: Emily, I have an urgent matter to discuss with you.

W: What's wrong, Mr. Mason?

M: Nothing is wrong, Emily. What do you know about the store remodeling?

W: Remodeling? This is a surprise to me.

M: The company has decided to make improvements to the store very soon.

W: When did you learn about this?

M: I just learned about it yesterday.

W: When will the remodeling start?

M: The workers will be here next week.

W: Wow, that's only a few days. What will they do?

M: The produce section will be expanded greatly. There will be major changes every-where, including the meat and fish departments.

W: How long will the store be closed for remodeling?

M: Oh, the store will remain open during the remodeling. In fact, our hours will be the same for the next three months.

W: That's good. How will we inform the customers?

M: I want you to prepare an announcement today. We'll post it in store windows im-mediately.

W: Fine, I'll work on it this afternoon after my lunch break.

M: Thanks.

Questions 22 to 25 are based on the conversation you have just heard.

22. When will the store remodeling start?

23. Which section will be expanded?

24. How long will the remodeling last?

25. How will they inform the customers about the store remodeling?

Section B

Directions: *In this section, you will hear 3 short passages. At the end of each passage, you will hear some questions. Both the passage and the questions will be spoken only once. After you hear a question, you must choose the best answer from the four choices marked A), B), C) and D). Then mark the corresponding letter on* **Answer Sheet 2** *with a single line through the centre.*

Passage One

When the weather is hot, you go to a lake or an ocean. When you are near a lake or an ocean, you feel cool. Why? The sun makes the earth hot, but it cannot make the water very hot. Although the air over the earth becomes hot, the air over the water stays cool. The hot air over the earth goes up. Then the cool air over the water moves in and takes the place of the hot air. When you are near a lake or an ocean, you feel the cool air when it moves in. You feel the wind. And the wind makes you cool.

Of course, scientists cannot answer all of our questions. If we ask, "Why is the ocean full of salt?" Scientists will say that the salt comes from rocks. When a rock gets very hot or very cold, it cracks. Rain falls into the cracks. The rain then carries the salt into the earth and into the rivers. The rivers carry the salt into the ocean. But then we ask, "What happens to the salt in the ocean? The ocean does not get more salty every year." Scientists are not sure about the answer to this question.

We know a lot about our world. But there are still many answers that we do not have, and we are curious.

Questions 26 to 28 are based on the passage you have just heard.

26. What is the main idea of this passage?

27. According to the scientists, where does the salt come from?

28. Why are we always curious about our world?

Passage Two

Wilt Chamberlain is retired now. He used to be a famous basketball player. He has set 65 different records, and still holds many of them. During the final years of his career, he drew a large salary and became very wealthy. He even built himself a 1.5-million-dollar house. Yet, despite his personal success, he led his team to only one championship. His team often won enough games to qualify for the final rounds, but they almost always lost in the finals. As a result, Wilt became determined to win one more championship before he retired.

In 1972, while Wilt was playing against a New York team, he fell down and hit his wrist on the floor. He felt pain immediately and knew he had hurt himself badly. When a doctor examined him, the doctor confirmed his fear. The doctor told Wilt that he had broken a bone in the wrist and that he could not play any longer.

Wilt didn't listen to his doctor's advice. The next night, with his many fans watching in surprise, he not only played the entire game, but he was outstanding. His team won the game and the championship. Wilt had realized his dream — to be a winner one last time.

Questions 29 to 31 are based on the passage you have just heard.

29. Why was Wilt Chamberlain regarded as a famous basketball player?

30. What was Wilt Chamberlain determined to do before he retired?

31. What happened to Wilt Chamberlain during a match in 1972?

Passage Three

People enjoy taking trips. But what are the reasons they leave home? One reason is for education. People travel because they want to broaden their horizons — learn about other people and other places. They are curious about other cultures. When people are tourists, they get a quick look at different ways of living. Even a short look at another kind of lifestyle is an important lesson. On a trip, a person can learn directly by visiting museums and historic spots. What does a tourist who sees the art museums, visits the historical places and other scenic spots in Paris and shops along the River Seine learn? He gets a vivid picture, a real-life one of the French people. He learns about their attitudes, and how they feel about business, beauty and history. What about the tourist who goes to Hong Kong? Does he get the same information that he could get from a book? He might read that Hong Kong is crowded, and that there is less than 200 square meters of space for each person. But seeing and feeling the lack of space will impress him much more. He might read that there are nearly 200 vehicles for every kilometer of roadway. But the sight of so many vehicles parked along the roadside would be a much more vivid lesson. The tourist to Hong Kong will never forget the contrast: the straight lines of tall modern buildings and the moving lines of boats that people live in.

Questions 32 to 35 are based on the passage you have just heard.

32. Why do people leave home to travel according to the passage?
33. What do we learn about Paris from the passage?
34. What impression will a tourist get of Hong Kong?
35. What does the passage tell us about traveling?

Section C

Directions: *In this section, you will hear a passage three times. When the passage is read for the first time, you should listen carefully for its general idea. When the passage is read for the second time, you are required to fill in the blanks numbered from 36 to 43 with the exact words you have just heard. For blanks numbered from 44 to 46 you are required to fill in the missing information. For these blanks, you can either use the exact words you have just heard or write down the main points in your own words. Finally, when the passage is read for the third time, you should check what you have written.*

It is common knowledge that music can have a powerful effect on our (36) **emotions**. In fact, since 1930s, music therapists have (37) **relied** on music to soothe (38)

patients and help control pain. Now psychologists are（39）**confirming** that music can also help（40）**relieve** depression and improve concentration. For instance，in a recent study，15 surgeons were given some highly（41）**stressed** math problems to solve. They were（42）**divided** into three groups：one worked in silence，and in another，the surgeons listened to music of their choice on headphones；the third listened to（43）**classical** music chosen by the researchers. The results of the study may surprise you.（44）**The doctors who got to choose their music experienced less stress and scored better than the others**. One possible explanation is that listening to music you like stimulates the Alfawave in the brain，increases the heart rate and expands the breathing. That helps to reduce stress and sharpen concentration. Other research suggests a second relation between the music and the brain：（45）**by examining the students' blood after the listening to a variety of classical music collections**，the researchers found that some students showed a large increase in endorphin，a natural pain reliever；（46）**this supports what music therapists have known for years：music can help refresh or soothe the patient**.

Practice Test 9

Section A

Directions: *In this section, you will hear 8 short conversations and 2 long conversations. At the end of each conversation, one or more questions will be asked about what was said. Both the conversation and the questions will be spoken only once. After each question there will be a pause. During the pause, you must read the four choices marked A), B), C) and D), and decide which is the best answer. Then mark the corresponding letter on* **Answer Sheet 2** *with a single line through the centre.*

11. W: That history exam was really hard. The essay question was terrible!

    M: I know. I wish I were like David. He has a photographic memory, you know. How useful that would be!

    Q: What is true of David?

12 W: How's your group doing with this statistics presentation? Mine's terrible.

    M: Yeah, mine too. David and Mike are OK, but Steven doesn't pull his weight and Suzie's never around. I don't see how we can pass unless Steven and Suzie realize that this is their last chance.

    Q: What can we learn about Steven and Suzie?

13 M: Mom, you and daddy often tell us to be honest and never tell lies. But I have found that you have just lied to the Joneses.

    W: I suppose you were referring to my remarks about Mrs. Jones. I said she didn't look over-weight, just to make her feel less self-conscious and more comfortable.

    Q: What can be inferred from the conversation?

14. W: They may be proud of their new facility, but frankly I'm disappointed. The nurses are not friendly and everything seems to be running behind schedule.

    M: Not to mention the fact that it's noisy because no one observes visiting hours.

    Q: What are the people in the dialogue discussing?

15. M: There are supposed to be forty-five people registered for this course.

    W: I know. But I think thirteen have cancelled their registrations, and ten others indicated that they could not make the first class.

    Q: According to the woman, how many people will not show up for the first class?

16. W: That famous writer Isaac Asimov's new book is coming out in July.

    M: We probably won't be able to find a library copy until September.

    Q: When will Isaac Asimov's new book be published?

17. M: Did you find what you wanted? You've been gone all afternoon.

W: I looked all over town, but couldn't find any bookcases on sale. They're so expensive. I guess I'll wait a while longer.

Q: What is obvious from the conversation?

18. W: I heard your new car arrived today. When will you get to drive it?

M: Oh, it came in two days ago, but I'm beginning to wonder when I'll get to ride in it myself. The dealer is taking his time getting it ready.

Q: How does the man seem to feel?

Now you'll hear two long conversations.

Conversation One

W: John, how do you spell the word "hemorrhage"? (*pause*) Hey, John, did you hear me? How do you spell the word "hemorrhage"? I need it for my paper. (*sympathetically*) What's wrong, John?

M: Nothing, Paula. Nothing. Sorry, I wasn't paying attention. What did you say?

W: How do you spell it?

M: I don't know.

W: John, why do you look so sad? Come on, pal. There must be something the matter. Tell me. What is it?

M: Oh, Paula, Susan has just broken up with me.

W: Oh, that's too bad. I'm so sorry. She's such a nice girl. What happened?

M: You know I'm always late. I often apologize for that. But last week I completely forgot to go to her mother's home for dinner. I was working in the lab and was absorbed. That was the last straw. She said "No more apologies. I've had enough!" Well, you see, that's the end of it, the end of the world, the end of my life, the end of everything!

W: John, it's not the end of the world. Let bygones be bygones! There are many fish in the sea. Forget about her and go on!

M: I know, I know. But not only that. You know, I have trouble with English and I need it for my degree. But I failed the exam again.

W: Oh, that's terrible. That's the third time you sat for it.

M: Oh, if only I had been better to Susan! If only I had studied more!

Questions 19 to 21 are based on the conversation you have just heard.

19. Why doesn't John reply to Paula's question?

20. Why is John so sad?

21. How many times has John failed the English exam?

Conversation Two

M: Could you tell us a bit about your early life?

W: That's a long time ago! I was born in Scotland. My father was a doctor. He had me and three sons, and he wanted them all to be doctors. In the end, though, none of them were.

M: But you studied medicine, didn't you?

W: I certainly did. And it was very difficult for a woman in those days.

M: Did you ultimately get a doctor certificate?

W: Yes, I did. And I'm glad I became a doctor.

M: Why?

W: The job gave me independence. I was an independent woman. I was able to travel to Africa, the Middle East, and the Far East as a doctor. It would have been very difficult to travel to those places if I hadn't been one. But, as it were, I was useful, so I was welcomed everywhere.

M: When did you write your first novel?

W: After I had my first child. I met my husband in Japan; he was a doctor too, you know. We worked together, moving from Japan to Malaysia. My first child was born there. I stopped working, but I got bored, so one day I started to write. I've always thanked my eldest son for turning me into a writer.

M: You had four more children?

W: Yes. And so I went on writing.

M: And three years ago, you were nominated for the Nobel Prize for Literature.

W: Yes. I didn't get it, but it was an honor to be nominated.

M: What have you enjoyed most about your life?

W: Well, I have done a lot of traveling and that has been wonderful. I have visited some strange places and I've met some amazing people. And these days, people come to visit me!

Questions 22 to 25 are based on the conversation you have just heard.

22. Which statement is NOT true about the woman's becoming a doctor?
23. Where did she meet her husband?
24. How many children does the woman have?
25. Which statement is NOT true about the woman?

Section B

Directions: *In this section, you will hear 3 short passages. At the end of each passage, you will hear some questions. Both the passage and the questions will be spoken only once. After you hear a question, you must choose the best answer from the four* *choices marked A), B), C) and D). Then mark the corresponding letter on **Answer Sheet 2** with a single line through the centre.*

Passage One

It's clear that everyone needs to sleep. Most people rarely think about how and why they sleep, however. We know that if we sleep well, we feel rested. If we don't sleep enough, we often feel tired and irritable. It seems there are two purposes of sleep: physical rest and emotional rest. We need to rest our bodies and our minds. Both are important in order for us to be healthy. Each night we alternate between two kinds of sleep: active sleep and passive sleep. The passive sleep gives our body the rest that's needed to prepare us for active sleep, in which dreaming occurs.

Through the night, people alternate between passive and active sleep. The brain rests, then it becomes active, then dreaming occurs. This cycle is repeated several times through the night. During eight hours of sleep, people dream for a total of one and half hours on the average.

Questions 26 to 28 are based on the passage you have just heard.

26. What are the two purposes of sleep?
27. Which of the following is true?
28. On the average, how many hours do people dream during eight hours of sleep?

Passage Two

While English learning has been popular in China for decades, Chinese as a foreign language is just starting to catch on on the other side of the Pacific Ocean.

The study of Chinese used to be concentrated on a few college campuses and in large Chinese communities on both coasts of North America. But now it is spreading to places where, only a decade ago, such a widespread and continuous interest in the language seemed unimaginable. The enthusiasm in the Chinese language began to take shape in the 1980s. After a brief decrease in 1989, it gradually regained momentum in the early 1990s. In recent years, enrollment growth has been steady.

Although Chinese is clearly enjoying a rise in popularity, it is far from being the most popular foreign language in North America and, according to most people interviewed, probably will never be. Spanish and French have traditionally been the most popular second languages. A large number of Latin American immigrants have made Spanish a useful tool for communication in America. In Canada, French is an official language.

In a 2002 survey of US colleges and universities by the Modern Language Association in New York, 746,267 students entered Spanish classes and 34,153 entered Chinese classes. In fact, Chinese ranked 7th, behind Spanish, French (201,979), German (91,100), Italian (63,899), American Sign Language (60,781) and Japanese (52,238).

But when broken down, the collected facts and information give more: Graduate students who took Chinese kept constant over a decade, but two-year and four-year undergraduates had double-digit growth. French and German, despite their high enrolments, have not waved much in popularity, but Chinese has overtaken Spanish in growth rate.

Questions 29 to 31 are based on the passage you have just heard.

29. According to the passage, what's the reason why Chinese is far from being the most popular foreign language in North America?
30. What's the main idea of the passage?
31. What can be inferred about the Chinese language from this passage?

Passage Three

A new study says one part of the human brain may become smaller as the result of a condition known as jet lag. Jet lag results from flying long distances in an airplane. People with jet lag may feel extremely tired for several days. They may also have problems thinking clearly and remembering.

Recently a researcher at the University of Bristol in Britain reported the findings of his jet lag study, which involved twenty young women who worked for international airlines. They had served passengers on airplanes for five years. These flight attendants flew across many countries and at least seven time zones. In the study, the flight attendants had different amounts of time to recover from jet lag. Half the women spent five days or fewer in their home areas between long flights. The other half spent more than fourteen days in their home areas.

The researcher took some saliva from the women's mouths to measure levels of a hormone that increases during stress. He tested them to see if they could remember where black spots appeared on a computer screen. And he took pictures of their brains to measure the size of the brain's temporal lobes.

It was found that the women who had less time between flights had smaller right temporal lobes. This area of the brain deals with recognizing and remembering what is seen. The same group performed worse and had longer reaction times on the visual memory test. And their saliva samples showed higher levels of stress hormones.

The researcher believes the brain needs at least ten days to recover after a long trip. He says airline workers told him their ability to remember got worse after working on planes for about four years. Other studies have shown that increased feelings of stress can cause a loss of cells in the part of the brain that controls memory.

Scientists say more tests are needed to study the effects of jet lag on the brain. They want to find out if too much jet lag could permanently affect memory.

Questions 32 to 35 are based on the passage you have just heard.

32. What can we learn about jet lag from the text?
33. What can be inferred from the passage?
34. What is made clear by the research?
35. What is the subject discussed in the text?

Section C

Directions: *In this section, you will hear a passage three times. When the passage is read for the first time, you should listen carefully for its general idea. When the passage is read for the second time, you are required to fill in the blanks numbered from 36 to 43 with the exact words you have just heard. For blanks numbered from 44 to 46 you are required to fill in the missing information. For these blanks, you can either use the exact words you have just heard or write down the main points in your own words. Finally, when the passage is read for the third time, you should check what you have written.*

Seals (36) **fill** so many needs of the people who live in the Far North. The meat of the seal is a (37) **principal** source of food. Oil from the blubber, or fat, becomes (38) **fuel**. Seal oil, when set on a fire, maintains a steady flame. Sealskins are made into boots and other articles of clothing. The bones become (39) **instruments** or tools. No part of the animal goes to (40) **waste**.

The number of seals (41) **varies** greatly in different parts of the Arctic. Wherever there are strong ocean currents, resulting in broken (42) **ice**, you will find an (43) **abundance** of these animals. (44) **They are scarcest where the ice is thick and unbroken, since these conditions offer few opportunities for the seal to come up to breathe the air he needs.**

Arctic seal hunting has been an active industry since the early part of the nineteenth century. (45) **Today it still brings in substantial financial returns.** More than 500,000 animals are killed each year by hunters operating in the main sealing grounds. (46) **The furs, hides, blubber and oil of the seal bring in many millions of dollars a year.**

Practice Test 10

Section A

Directions: *In this section, you will hear 8 short conversations and 2 long conversations. At the end of each conversation, one or more questions will be asked about what was said. Both the conversation and the questions will be spoken only once. After each question there will be a pause. During the pause, you must read the four choices marked A), B), C) and D), and decide which is the best answer. Then mark the corresponding letter on **Answer Sheet 2** with a single line through the centre.*

11. M: If you had signaled your intention to turn a little sooner, this wouldn't have happened!

    W: But I signaled in time! Just look at the mess you've made of my car! You were driving carelessly and your speed was above the limit! You're the one who's to blame!

    Q: What are they talking about?

12 W: You spend all of your time reading books. How do you expect to be well-informed if you never read a newspaper?

    M: It's my opinion that reading newspapers is a waste of time. A famous man once said that newspapers separate what is important from what is not important and then print that which is not important.

    Q: Why should the man read newspapers according to the woman?

13 W: Finding this china cabinet was a real stroke of luck. Because of the scratch on the side, the dealer charged me $5 less than the regular price.

    M: You were lucky, and with a little polish the scratch won't even show.

    Q: Why is the woman pleased?

14. W: I'd like to make a person-to-person call. How much will that be?

    M: That's forty-five cents for the first three minutes, and ten cents for each additional minute.

    Q: How much will the woman pay for a ten-minute call?

15. M: What on earth do you think is the pleasure of a solitary life?

    W: For one thing you can do whatever you like without interference, and for another, you needn't be afraid of hurting others or offending people when you don't have the same taste, character or mood as them.

    Q: What is the conversation about?

16. W: In my opinion, international games today are not merely sports events. They can help develop the economy of a country, and even inspire the national spirit.

M: And there are negative sides, too. They can also be connected with violence, bribery, or some other illegal acts.

Q: What are they talking about?

17. W: We lived in Beijing some years ago. It was always difficult to keep the house clean with the wind from the north blowing sand from the desert at us.

M: That's why the Chinese government has been encouraging people to plant trees along the edges of the Gobi Desert. Now those trees act as wind barriers.

Q: What has the government been encouraging people to do?

18. M: Excuse me, where do I check in for British Airways to London? I can't find the right check-in counter.

W: You should go to Counter 26 on the left-hand side, sir. It's just next to Thai Air. You'd better hurry, though. There's a long queue.

Q: What can we know from the conversation?

Now you'll hear two long conversations.

Conversation One

W: Will you be spending the Thanksgiving holiday with us this year?

M: No, I'm flying back to the States to spend the holiday with my mother and brother. I haven't seen my family for over a year. You see, Thanksgiving is a big family holiday.

W: In China the Mid-Autumn Festival is also a holiday for family reunions. Do you happen to know the origin of Thanksgiving?

M: It began as a celebration by the Pilgrims. They were happy just to have survived their harsh winter in the new land in 1621.

W: I'm not quite sure of the origin of the Mid-Autumn Festival, but it is said to have something to do with Lady Chang'e who flew to the moon. On a day of full moon her husband longed for her to return to earth. So this may have something to do with family reunions.

M: Thanksgiving is also an occasion to celebrate the harvest. The Pilgrims' first harsh winter was followed by an abundant harvest. That was a good reason to celebrate.

W: Most cultures have some sort of celebration of the harvest. In fact the Chinese Mid-Autumn Festival is a festival to celebrate the harvest month, since fruits, vegetables and grain have been harvested by this time and food is abundant.

M: To observe Thanksgiving, Americans eat turkey, ham, corn-on-the-cob, yams, peas and carrots, and to top it all off, pumpkin pie.

W: Oh, just thinking about all that food makes my mouth water. We Chinese eat moon cakes to mark the occasion. The round moon cakes symbolize a family reunion.

M: Thanksgiving in the States has developed into a major holiday.

W: The Mid-Autumn Festival is one of the most important festivals in China, too. It's believed to be the second most important holiday, next only to the Spring Festival.

Questions 19 to 21 are based on the conversation you have just heard.

19. What are the two holidays in the United States and in China the speakers are discussing?

20. Which statement is NOT true about the similarities of the two festivals?

21. What dish is the most important one on Thanksgiving Day according to the man?

Conversation Two

W: Elizabeth Martin speaking.

M: Dr. Martin, my name is Mark Johnson. My roommate, Benjamin Jones, is in your Art History class. Uh, hm, Art History 502?

W: Yes.

M: Well, he is sick and won't be in your class today. He asked me to bring his term paper to your office.

W: OK. The paper is due by 3 o'clock.

M: I have a class from 1 to 2. I'll bring it to your office after my class.

W: Well, I have a meeting this afternoon. So you can drop it off with the secretary of the Art History Department. She'll see that I get it.

M: OK. Oh I almost forgot. I'm a biology major. But my advisor told me that I need one more humanities course to graduate. I've noticed that you are teaching a course on landscape painters next semester. Could you tell me a little bit about it?

W: Sure. Well, it's a course for non-art majors. We'll be looking at several different painters and examining their works. We'll also look at the history and politics of the era in which they lived.

M: That sounds interesting. What else is required?

W: There is no final exam. And there is only one required book. But each student has to give a major presentation on an individual painter at the end of the course.

M: Hmm. It sounds good. Will you be in your office later today? I'd like to talk to you more about it.

W: Well, my meeting's scheduled to last all afternoon. Why not stop by tomorrow? Any time in the afternoon. My office is in the fine arts building right next to the library.

M: Thanks. I'll do that.

Questions 22 to 25 are based on the conversation you have just heard.

22. Why does the student call the professor?
23. Why does the student want to know more about the professor's course on landscape painters next semester?
24. What is each student required to do at the end of the course?
25. When can the student find the professor in her office?

Section B

Directions: *In this section, you will hear 3 short passages. At the end of each passage, you will hear some questions. Both the passage and the questions will be spoken only once. After you hear a question, you must choose the best answer from the four choices marked A), B), C) and D). Then mark the corresponding letter on Answer Sheet 2 with a single line through the centre.*

Passage One

Experts say that it is not easy to get used to life in a new culture. "Culture shock" is the term these specialists use when talking about the feelings that people have in a new environment. There are three stages of culture shock, say the specialists. In the first stage, the newcomers like their new environment. Then, when the fresh experience dies, they begin to hate the city, the country, the people, and everything else. In the last stage, the newcomers begin to adjust to their surroundings and, as a result, enjoy their life more.

There are some obvious factors in culture shock. The weather may be unpleasant. The customs may be different. The public service systems — the telephone, post office, or transportation — may be difficult to work out. The simplest things seem to be big problems. The language may be difficult.

Who feels culture shock? Everyone does in this way or that. But culture shock surprises most people. Very often the people having the worst culture shock are those who never had any difficulties in their home countries and were successful in their community. Coming to a new country, these people find they do not have the same established positions. They find themselves without a role, almost without an identity. They have to build a new self-image.

Culture shock gives rise to a feeling of disorientation. This feeling may be homesickness. When homesick, people feel like staying inside all the time. They want to protect themselves from the strange environment, and create and escape inside their room for a sense of security. This escape does solve the problem of culture shock for the short term, but it does nothing to make the person familiar with the culture. Getting to know the new environment and gaining experience are the long-term solutions to the problem of culture shock.

Questions 26 to 28 are based on the passage you have just heard.

26. What is the author's purpose of writing this passage?
27. What should one do if he feels homesick due to culture shock?
28. Which of the following facts about culture shock is true?

Passage Two

Most people have had a dog or wanted one as their companion at some time in their lives. If you are thinking of buying a dog, however, you should first decide what sort of companion you need and whether the dog is likely to be happy in the surroundings you can provide. Specialists' advice is useful to help you choose the most suitable kind of dog. But in part the decision depends on common sense. Different dogs were originally developed to perform specific tasks. So, if you want a dog to protect you or your house, for example, you should choose the one that has the right size and characteristics. You must also be ready to devote a great deal of time to training the dog when it is young and give it the exercise it needs throughout its life, unless you live in the countryside and can let it run freely. Dogs are demanding pets. Cats love the house and so are satisfied with their place where it is secure, but a dog is loyal to its master and consequently wants him to show proof of his affection. The best time to buy a baby dog is when it is between 6 and 8 weeks old so that it can transfer its love from its mother to its master. If baby dogs have not established a relationship with the human being until they are over three months old, their strong relationship will always be with dogs. They are likely to be shy when they are brought out into the world to become good pets.

Questions 29 to 31 are based on the passage you have just heard.

29. Which of the following is NOT true according to the passage?
30. What is mentioned as a consideration in buying a dog?
31. Why does the writer say a dog is a more demanding pet than a cat?

Passage Three

NASDAQ, short for the National Association of Securities Dealers Automated

Quotation system, is one of the largest markets in the world for the trading of stocks. The number of companies listed on NASDAQ is larger than that on any of the other stock exchanges in the United States, including the New York Stock Exchange (NYSE) and the American Stock Exchange (AMEX). The majority of companies listed on NASDAQ are smaller than most of those on the NYSE and AMEX. NASDAQ has become known as the home of new technology companies, particularly computer and computer-related businesses. Trading on NASDAQ is started by stock brokers acting on behalf of their customers. The brokers talk with market makers who concentrate on trading specific stocks to reach a price for the stock.

Unlike other stock exchanges, NASDAQ has no central location where trading takes place. Instead, its market makers are located all over the country and make trades by telephone and Internet. Because brokers and market makers trade stocks directly instead of on the floor of a stock exchange, NASDAQ is called an over-the-counter market. The term "over-the-counter" refers to the direct nature of the trading, as in a store where goods are handed over a counter.

Since its start in 1971, the NASDAQ Stock Market has been the pioneer. As the world's first electronic stock market, NASDAQ long ago set a precedent for technological trading concept. Now being the world's first truly global market, the NASDAQ Stock Market is the market of choice for business industry leaders worldwide. By providing an efficient environment for raising capital, NASDAQ has helped thousands of companies achieve their desired growth and successfully make the leap into public ownership.

Questions 32 to 35 are based on the passage you have just heard.

32. Which of the following is NOT a difference between NASDAQ and other stock exchanges?
33. Why is the term "over-the-counter" considered close to the nature of the trading?
34. Which of the following is true according to the last paragraph?
35. Which is the best title for this passage?

Section C

Directions: *In this section, you will hear a passage three times. When the passage is read for the first time, you should listen carefully for its general idea. When the passage is read for the second time, you are required to fill in the blanks numbered from 36 to 43 with the exact words you have just heard. For blanks numbered from 44 to 46 you are required to fill in the missing information. For these blanks, you can either use the exact words you have just heard or write down the main points in your own words. Finally, when the passage is read for the third time, you should check what you have* *written.*

Most Americans start school at the age of five when they enter (36) **kindergarten**. Children do not really study at this time. They only (37) **attend** for half the day and learn what school is like. Children attend (38) **elementary** school for the next six years. They learn to read and write and work with numbers. They also study the world and its people. After six years, children go to (39)**junior** high school for three years and senior high school for another three years. This is called secondary education.

In their secondary schooling, children cover more (40) **advanced** knowledge and begin to concentrate on their special (41) **interests**. They usually study further in history, geography, government, English and literature. They may (42) **choose** to study foreign languages, advanced mathematics or science, such as physics or chemistry.

Higher education takes place in colleges and universities. The (43) **average** course is four years. (44) **Students choose a major subject and take many courses in this subject.** After four years, they earn a bachelor's degree. (45) **Then the students may go on to graduate school and, with a year or two of further study, they can get a master's degree.** (46) **Usually after another four or five years of study and research, they may get a still higher degree such as doctor of philosophy.**